Seven Rules for Breaking Hearts

Seven Rules for Breaking Hearts

KRISTYN J. MILLER

ST. MARTIN'S GRIFFIN
NEW YORK

First published in the United States by St. Martin's Griffin, an imprint of St. Martin's Publishing Group

SEVEN RULES FOR BREAKING HEARTS. Copyright © 2023 by Kristyn J. Miller. All rights reserved. Printed in the United States of America. For information, address St. Martin's Publishing Group, 120 Broadway, New York, NY 10271.

www.stmartins.com

Designed by Meryl Sussman Levavi

Library of Congress Cataloging-in-Publication Data

Names: Miller, Kristyn J., author.
Title: Seven rules for breaking hearts / Kristyn J. Miller.
Description: First edition. | New York : St. Martin's Griffin, 2023.
Identifiers: LCCN 2022056756 | ISBN 9781250861825 (trade paperback) |
    ISBN 9781250861832 (ebook)
Subjects: LCGFT: Romance fiction. | Novels.
Classification: LCC PS3613.I53986 S48 2023 | DDC 813/.6—dc23/eng/
    20221201
LC record available at https://lccn.loc.gov/2022056756

Our books may be purchased in bulk for promotional, educational, or business use. Please contact your local bookseller or the Macmillan Corporate and Premium Sales Department at 1-800-221-7945, extension 5442, or by email at MacmillanSpecialMarkets@macmillan.com.

First Edition: 2023

10 9 8 7 6 5 4 3 2 1

To my husband, George, for listening to me promise not to put all my eggs in one basket and then continuing to support me when I put most of them in the same basket anyway

Seven Rules for Breaking Hearts

PODCAST

Seven Rules for Breaking Hearts

Margo Anderson, Jo Hernandez

About

With over 200k monthly listeners, Seven Rules *started with a pact between two childhood best friends and quickly grew into a twenty-something's boot camp for hooking up without getting hurt. Funny, feminist, and often downright filthy, Jo and Go's casual chemistry and outlandish stories took the nation by storm and started the #SingleNotSeeking revolution. Season Seven streaming now!*

Tags: Relationship, Comedy, Sex

THE RULES

1. Always keep the ball in your court.
2. If you're too embarrassed to tell your girlfriends about him, think twice.
3. Say no to sleepovers.
4. Never exceed his effort.
5. If they take more than twenty-four hours to respond, move along.
6. Only fool around with people who are easily avoidable.
7. Whatever you do, don't catch feelings.

Season Seven, Episode One—The Beginning of the End
12 min 54 sec

Margo: *Have you ever wondered why the record button is always a big, red circle? They could have made it any other color, but I like to think they knew exactly what they were doing. Red is for warnings. Red flags, red lights, red hazard signs (danger: do not enter). That little record symbol is a big, bright, blinking* *red warning. It's telling you to stop and reconsider. Maybe you don't want to record this. Maybe you don't want to spend every waking moment worrying about what part of your life you're going to broadcast to the world next. Constantly worrying about what other people are going to think.*

Things certainly would have been simpler if I'd listened.

Welcome to Season Seven of Seven Rules for Breaking Hearts. *The final season. That's right—as you may have already heard, the podcast is coming to an end. Hopefully, when we reach the end of this season, you'll understand why.*

It all comes down to this: I broke all my own rules.

CHAPTER

1

THREE MONTHS EARLIER

The Blue Room was teeming with amateur influencers. The clubs in Studio City weren't known for a cozy local vibe on the best of nights, but it was especially bad tonight. I sidestepped some guy trying to vlog in the middle of the dance floor—I mean, really?—and shouldered my way to the bar. The flash from a nearby iPhone mingled with the strobe lights.

I didn't want to be here.

"Excuse me," I said to a group crowding the bar to take artsy pictures of their espresso martinis, but my voice was swallowed up by the music—at the moment, a remix of a Dua Lipa song with enough bass to trigger the Big One. I waved my orange wristband at the bartender. "Buttery nipple shot," I shouted over the music, and several people turned to stare. I scowled. How many complimentary shots would it take to forget why we were here tonight? I was determined to find out.

By the second shot, I'd managed to secure a coveted spot at the counter, and by the third, I watched as the employees swapped shifts to finish out the night, the old bartender tapping in a younger guy with a manicured mustache and really tight pants. The newcomer acted like he couldn't hear me on my first couple attempts at ordering a buttery nipple shot; he bowed his head toward mine, his comb-over silhouetted by the Edison bulbs and the blue-and-purple lights gleaming off the subway tile backsplash. I leaned closer to speak into his ear—aaannndd now he was getting an eyeful of my boobs.

While he bent to grab the butterscotch schnapps from the bottom shelf, I hooked my thumbs under the straps of my corset top and hiked it up for more coverage. I'd dressed for pictures, but already I was regretting it, because I'd sincerely rather there was no evidence of me being here tonight. And preferably no memory, while we were at it. The bartender was sliding me my fourth shot and I was debating ordering something stronger when a delicate hand with immaculate red nails darted in front of me. Jo stamped my buttery nipple shot on the counter before tossing it back, then pretended to retch. "Ugh, that tastes like something my grandma would order."

I shook my head, folding my arms against the counter. The whole bar top was made of scuffed-up resin with vintage *L.A. Times* newspapers sealed inside, headlines about Clark Gable and the moon landing and the 1994 Northridge quake. "If I knew you were going to steal it, I would have ordered a tequila shot."

Jo's red lips parted in a winning smile. That was her signature color: that classic Bordeaux red. "I'm pretty sure my maid of honor is contractually obligated to do a tequila shot with me anyway."

I was inclined to agree, but not because I had anything to celebrate.

I hated weddings. By extension, bridal parties ranked pretty high on my list of things that were best left to corny romantic comedies and trashy reality TV like *Say Yes to the Dress*. Mercifully, it wasn't my engagement we were supposed to be toasting to. But it *was* my best friend's engagement, and she'd asked me to be the maid of honor. Which meant I was pretty central to any and all wedding activities—including tonight's little announcement. I couldn't have been persuaded to grin and bear it for anyone else, but Jo was a special case.

"Two shots of Cazadores," I told the bartender when he finally decided to acknowledge my cleavage again. "With lime. And do you have any saltshakers around here?" He tore his eyes from my boobs and gave me a blank look. "Or margarita salt? I'm not picky."

"What does this look like, a sorority party?" he deadpanned.

"I'm gonna be honest here, not really in the mood to be negged by a guy with Buddy Holly glasses and a handlebar mustache."

"Real original. Haven't heard that one before."

Either the flashing blue-and-purple lights were causing me to hallucinate or there were cartoon mustaches printed all over his shirt—a short-sleeved button-down that, up to this point, I had assumed was covered in black blobs and that maybe he was channeling his inner Cruella de Vil. But no, those were definitely mustaches, and they definitely looked like the one that was already on his face. "Can you actually remember the last time you listened to music that wasn't Tame Impala?"

He pointed at the overhead speakers. "Right now. There is literally music playing right now."

As though to drive the point home, the song changed to "Gasolina" by Daddy Yankee.

"Just pour the drinks and I'll leave a good tip," I said, trying not to sound too exasperated as I held out my wristband for the fifth time in a row. "There should be a comped tab under *Anderson*."

With an eye roll that looked almost painful, he turned his back on us and grabbed a bottle from the middle shelf. A part of me couldn't fault him for his irritation. It had to be annoying, people waltzing into your work every week, brandishing orange VIP bands and demanding everything for free. These clubs were always hosting some promotional event or another, Emo Night or

Nineties Throwbacks or whatever else they could come up with to draw tourists and locals alike. Tonight, aspiring actors and musicians and every other brand of L.A. hopeful were packed into The Blue Room, all under the guise of "Influencer Friday."

But whatever the bartender's distaste for influencers, I wanted to get drunk. I would've happily paid for faster service, but I wasn't sure it would make a difference. It seemed he was determined to give us bad service on principle, so I might as well cash in on the perks of showing up tonight.

Jo scrutinized the way his cuffed chinos hugged his ass, not so much checking him out as making a professional assessment. "I can't tell if you hate him or want to go home with him."

I didn't have the energy to illustrate how hard of a pass that was, but I shot her a look. I was taller than Jo on a normal day, but right now, wearing four-inch-heeled boots to her strappy gladiator sandals, there was almost a foot's difference between us. "None of the above. I just want my drinks."

"Speaking of people you hate," Jo segued, "I'm sure you've already thought about this, but Peter is thinking of asking Declan to be the best man, and I wanted to run it by you to make sure . . ." On noticing my expression, she tapered off, but the damage was done. It probably looked like I'd sucked on a lemon, but the bartender hadn't delivered our Cazadores with lime yet.

"You know, I don't want you to be uncomfortable," she finished lamely.

"It's not that it would make me uncomfortable." Contrary to her assumption, I hadn't already thought about this because I'd always assumed Peter and Declan were one of those friendships that wouldn't survive past high school. If there was one thing bound to make an unpleasant event that much more unbearable, it was having to spend it in the company of people I'd hoped to leave in the past. But they seemed to have a way of cropping back up as of late. "Anyway, what are you going to do, tell Peter that he can't have his best friend at the wedding?"

Jo leaned her back against the bar top, facing the sweaty, undulating crowd. Her red lips curled in a frown. "I'll talk to him, if it comes to that. But it has been like, eight years since you've seen each other, and he's way different than you probably remember. He's living in Pasadena now, and he's got this great job at—"

It was hard enough to hear her over the music, and I didn't care to strain my ears just to hear what Declan Walsh had gotten up to in recent years. I forced a smile and patted her arm in a way that I hoped was reassuring, though it felt more awkward than anything. "Stop worrying. I'm not going to go all Red Wedding on your best man." When she didn't look entirely convinced, I added, "Seriously. It's fine. We're all adults, and it's supposed to be your day. And Peter's. You guys should ask whoever you want."

It wasn't the whole truth, but I didn't want Jo to stress over this. I might've hated weddings, but that didn't mean I wanted to complicate hers any further. Marriage was bound to be complicated enough without my help.

"Two tequilas with lime," the bartender announced, sliding a pair of shot glasses across the counter. They were each garnished with the largest wedge of lime I'd ever seen, tinged a muddled purple-gray color by the strobing lights. "Be sure to hashtag The Blue Room when you post a picture," he added without enthusiasm.

He hadn't bothered pointing us in the direction of the nearest saltshaker, but at this point, I didn't care. "Bottoms up," I said to Jo, balancing my phone in one hand to record a hasty clip of our glasses clinking together before we tossed them back. The tequila was a welcome burn in my throat, a promise of distraction— dancing, toasting, whatever it took to get my mind off the weeks looming before me. I stuffed the lime wedge into my mouth, and then I spat it right back out. I narrowed my eyes at the bartender. "Are you sure this is a lime?"

His smile was half-hidden behind his mustache. "Might be a grapefruit. Hard to tell in this lighting."

"Let me guess. You ran out of salt, too."

"Forget him," Jo interrupted, steering me away from the bar before I could take out my bad mood on the bartender's suspenders or hair. "The DJ's doing our shoutout after the next song."

Her shoutout. This was supposed to be a celebratory night, and I was doing my best to celebrate, but I wasn't really up for all the gawking and unnecessary attention. Especially not after the controversial announcement we'd made on our livestream this afternoon. I wriggled free of her grasp on the outskirts of the dance floor. "I'll be there in a minute. I need to get some air first."

Without waiting for a reply, I slipped into the crowd and out the front door, flashing my wristband at the doorman. A queue had formed beneath the gangling palms lining Ventura Boulevard. "Just stepping outside for a moment."

He gave me a curt nod. A few curious faces tracked my movements as my chunky-heeled boots pounded the pavement, putting some distance between me and the club. I came to rest against the stucco wall, well away from the yellow-gold glow of the nearest streetlight, and breathed in the warm, dry night air.

I extracted my phone from my pleather biker shorts. An uncomfortable clothing choice for Studio City in July, but nights like tonight, I needed to be photo ready. I had about a million Instagram notifications and thirty-six unread DMs, at least one of which was bound to be worth looking at, but I ignored all that in favor of posting a quick story of the tequila shots—#TheBlueRoom— before clicking over to the search bar. I typed in *Declan Walsh* and Instagram presented me with a smorgasbord of men, but none who looked anything like the Declan I'd known. I switched over to

Twitter and found much the same: a deluge of notifications and a number of search results, but no sign of my high school nemesis.

Okay, perhaps I had grown a little dramatic over the years, always spinning my stories into something that would entertain the masses. Declan was never my nemesis. In truth, I wasn't sure he'd ever cared much that I existed. I was fifteen years old, struggling to keep up with my classes and harboring lofty dreams of getting in to the music program at USC, when he'd transferred to Sierra Lakes from some science-y charter school. He was a pale, somewhat awkward kid with red hair and a smattering of freckles, and he managed to worm his way in with the popular kids almost immediately. Not because he played football or had super rich parents or knew where to get weed that was halfway decent. No, Declan was popular because he was *funny*.

It was mostly harmless: weird voices when popcorn-reading passages of *The Catcher in the Rye* and jokes in math class about sixty-nine and four-twenty that always had about a fifty-fifty chance of landing him in detention. For a senior prank, he'd wrapped the vice principal's car in enough bubble wrap to pack up a two-bedroom house, which was terrible for the environment but it was admittedly hilarious watching Mr. Alvarez trying to tear it all off. Point being, Declan was funny in that immature way that only worked in high school, before everybody grew up.

Still, it was high school, so I hadn't minded him for the first couple weeks—right up to the point when he stuffed my tuba with shaving cream and I spewed it all over the woodwind section while playing "The Final Countdown" for our homecoming pep rally. When, about a year later, he stopped me in the cafeteria to offer me a tapioca pudding cup that turned out to be filled with mayonnaise, it was the proverbial icing on the cake.

But I was an adult now. I'd long since moved past all my high school hang-ups. My dream of getting into Thornton had been squashed faster than I could say "music appreciation class," but that was unrelated to the homecoming incident. I didn't have the energy to uphold a decade-old grudge. Even if I *did* sort of blame him for the superlative I landed in our senior yearbook. A dark, vindictive corner of my brain found solace in imagining him as a class clown turned adult burnout, performing bad stand-up comedy or somewhere in Venice Beach doing bubble tricks for people on the boardwalk.

Unfortunately, I couldn't confirm either of those theories, because Declan Walsh had no digital footprint.

"Go?"

I nearly leapt out of my skin, fumbling my phone so bad that it clattered on the sidewalk screen-first. I stooped to retrieve it. Black cutout heels were planted on the concrete in front of me, but I paid them no mind. I turned my phone over in my hand. A lightning-bolt crack split the screen. "Shit," I muttered, typing in my passcode. It seemed to be functional, at least.

"Oh my God, I'm sorry!" the girl standing over me whined. "I didn't mean to startle you. It's just, I'm a fan of the podcast and I saw on Twitter that you guys were going to be here tonight, and I was hoping to maybe get a selfie."

I straightened up. She was about college aged, a few years younger than me, with dark barrel curls and cheeks carved out by heavy contour. A headhunter, probably. At least that was what I called them. Sometimes they were aspiring Instagram models and other times they were small-business owners, but whichever they were, they stalked social media to figure out where the more established influencers were going to be that night, all for the sake of snapping a few blurry club selfies that they would unironically caption like we were #besties.

I checked my own makeup using the front camera of my now-cracked phone. My foundation was a bit oily and my signature Phantom Green hair was washed out in the amber glow of the streetlight. But all in all, good enough. "Sure," I said, locking my phone and stuffing it back into a sweaty pocket. I'd deal with the crack in the screen later. "But please don't use any cringey filters or anything."

Not needing to be told twice, the girl whipped out her phone and started testing out different angles. Clubgoers ogled us as they skirted around us on the sidewalk, probably trying to figure out who the hell I was and why this chick was taking a picture with me. A fair number of people had heard of the podcast, but the vast majority of them wouldn't recognize my face.

Over by the front door, the bartender had stepped out on break, chain-smoking American Spirits while he chatted with the doorman.

The girl took a couple pictures and then checked the results. "So cute. Is Jo with you? I'd love to get a picture with her, too. I've always wondered if you guys are, like, friends in *real* life. Like I know you're friends on the podcast and for social media and everything, but I've always wondered if it was all for show."

The bartender stomped out the remains of his cigarette on the gum-riddled sidewalk, but this time he didn't light another. He mumbled something to a pretty brunette with a pixie cut at the front of the line, who nodded in my direction. I prickled with discomfort. People talking about me online I could handle, but I was always a little uncomfortable when gossip managed to find its way into the real world. It blurred the lines. Made it harder to compartmentalize. "I hope not, considering she asked me to be her maid of honor," I said, distracted.

"She . . . what?"

My attention snapped back to the girl in front of me. She was frowning, plainly confused. "I'm guessing you didn't watch the livestream this afternoon."

She took a minute to parse out what I was implying, and then her mouth dropped open. "No way. You're pulling my leg."

Unfortunately, I was not. The DJ was probably giving a shoutout as we spoke. "Jo's getting married?"

"Well, she's too old for a quinceañera," I said dryly. Though you better believe I was on the court of honor then, too. I'd had fewer qualms about that.

"Isn't that against the whole thing, though? Hashtag Single Not Seeking." She laughed uncertainly. "You can't exactly go around hooking up with strangers when you're married. Or, I mean, I guess you could, but that would be pretty messed up."

I glanced over at the bartender, who had moved away from the front door and was hanging out near the base of a towering palm tree. Lurking. Maybe Jo had sent him to find me. "All the more reason to stay single, right?"

"Right," the girl agreed, though she sounded a little put-out.

The bartender waited until she was gone and then sauntered over. I pushed myself off the wall, the lacy fabric of my corset clinging to the stucco like it didn't want to go back inside, either. But I'd have to show face sooner or later. I was surprised Jo hadn't come looking for me yet.

"So." He stopped a few feet away from me, hands stuffed in his too-tight pockets. A mangled box of American Spirits peered out from the breast pocket of his shirt. "Go and Jo, of *Seven Rules* fame, I'm told. Didn't realize I was serving a couple of celebrities."

I had a hard time believing that, all things considered. He'd certainly noticed my VIP bracelet the first few times I'd waved it at him, and his eyes drifted to it now, dangling at my side, though he made a few pit stops to stare at other parts of me along the way. My skin crawled. "We're not celebrities." Not by Hollywood standards at any rate, and you bet your bottom dollar I was going to correct people around Studio City. "Just a couple of girls with a podcast."

"Who's the hipster now?" he joked.

I held up my hands in surrender. "You caught me." But he'd

lost my interest already, and I was overdue to rejoin Jo. "Unless you've come over here to offer me free drinks for life as apology for the truly appalling service, I need to be getting back to my friend."

I was halfway to the door when he worked up the courage to get to the point.

"I had something else in mind."

I stopped, turned to face him. I wasn't sure what his angle was, but he didn't seem threatening—not under the doorman's watchful eye. "I'm listening."

He hesitated. For a moment, I thought he might drop it with a wave of his hand, a *nah, never mind, it was stupid.* "We close at two," he said instead, sheepish. "But I'll still be here cleaning up for a while if you wanted to stick around for a nightcap. Maybe come back to my place afterward?"

There was a time, not very long ago, when I probably would have said yes. This dude wasn't my type. He was pretentious and sort of rude, and I was a bit too tall for him, and his tight pants were giving me the ick. But that was precisely what made him safe. He ticked all the boxes, fit neatly into all seven of the rules:

1. The ball was in my court.
2. I might've cringed a bit telling Jo about it afterwards, but I could've lived with it.
3. There was no way I was going to sleep over in his hipster man cave, which probably smelled like week-old cereal and hazy IPAs.
4. There was no effort involved on my part.
5. I wouldn't have to worry about text messages because there was no chance in hell I was asking for this guy's number.
6. He bartended in Studio City, which was like a twenty-minute drive from NoHo on a good day. The definition of "easily avoidable."

Which all totaled up to passing Rule Number Seven with flying colors: there was no chance of catching feelings.

But rules aside, hooking up had lost some of its luster for me. It wasn't that I was looking for a happily ever after; I'd sworn off any sort of committed relationship a long time ago. I genuinely believed that, with a few exceptions, the whole idea of love was nothing more than a clever marketing scheme. An empty promise, boxed up and gift wrapped and tied with a pretty bow to be sold in Hallmark stores during the holidays. Once I recognized that, it was hard not to feel disillusioned with the whole dating thing.

It was just that, somewhere along the way, I'd started to feel a bit disillusioned with the rest of it, too. With my own brand of empty promises.

"Sorry," I said, with a half-hearted smile and a shrug. "I'm not interested."

Mar[Go] ✅ @margoanderson · Jul 12
Thank you to everyone who tuned in for yesterday's livestream. Poured one out last night for @JoHo_in_NoHo. R.I.P. to another fallen #SingleNotSeeking sister.
💬 64 🔁 4.3k 🖤 23.4k

Raquel O'Brien @raqyoursaqsoff · Jul 12
Replying to @margoanderson
Girl . . . you next! Jk

John Smith @wouldntuliketoknow · Jul 12
Replying to @margoanderson
at least ur still single, beutiful. never get married they take everything from u and stomp ur heart into the dirt

andycakes @miranda_lovee · Jul 12
Replying to @margoanderson

Ughhh I'm sorry but I'm SO over this podcast. Like I was into it at first but they've been recycling the same content for the past two years and now this? @margoanderson girl you used to be funny but it's getting old now. And @JoHo_in_NoHo, pretty sure you're just fake.

Things that are news to no one: Twitter is fucking brutal.

When we first started the podcast four years ago, I'd been at least peripherally aware that cyberbullying happened. It was one of those things that we heard about, that my mom was super paranoid about after watching too many episodes of *Dr. Phil*, but none of my immediate friend group had actually experienced it. I think we were too irrelevant. It wasn't until the first season of the podcast went viral that I felt the full, brutal brunt of the internet. Mostly, people liked us. But the people who hated us *really* hated us, and that hate drove them to be way more vocal than any of our actual fans. I'd learned pretty fast to ignore them. Over the past few years, I'd formed semi-healthy social media habits—as healthy as they could be, at any rate. Avoid the cesspool that is Tumblr at all costs. Quit obsessively refreshing the feed every time you post on Instagram. Don't get into arguments in the comments section on TikTok. And don't read the replies on Twitter.

But in the wake of yesterday's livestream, I found myself reading the replies on Twitter.

To be fair, I was in the middle of trying to piece together our weekly analytics report from the IKEA desk in our apartment in North Hollywood. I didn't go looking for trouble, but trouble had a way of finding me on the internet. Often in the form of the "trending" section, which this morning included #7R4BH and mentions of Jo Hernandez among a slew of other inspiring topics like #HarryStylesIsCancelledParty and something about Senator Montpelier's son. It was always a good idea to double-check why we were trending, although this time I was fairly certain I knew. Yesterday we went live on Instagram to share Jo's plans to get married, and so our fall from grace had begun.

As much as our listeners had been blindsided by the news, I was little better. I'd known Jo most of my life, but she still had a way of throwing me curveballs. We'd met the first day of kindergarten—an event I remembered more by our incessant retellings of it than by any real, tangible memory. She was crying in the corner because it was her first time away from her mom. I tried to cheer her up by smearing Crayola washable paint all over my face and clothes, an effort that inexplicably earned both of us a time-out (I mean, it *was* washable). At any rate, one fifteen-minute time-out and a lot of scrubbing our hands in the sink later, we were friends.

And we'd been glued at the hip ever since. Except for the minor blip where she jumped into college straight out of high school while I was busy working two jobs to help my mom pay the bills, we'd tackled life side by side. Friends, at least, you could count on to stick around.

Except, apparently, you couldn't. Apparently, friends could be bought, snatched right out from under your nose, and all it took was a—

"'All-expenses-paid destination wedding on Catalina Island, courtesy of Castaway Catalina Events,'" Jo read off her phone, sensual as one of those ASMR girls whispering sweet nothings to their listeners. She looked up for approval, but I only shrugged. "Am I saying it weird? I feel like I'm saying it weird."

"Maybe try for less Marilyn Monroe, and more . . ." I swiveled in my chair away from the computer and steepled my fingers like a Bond movie villain, minus the cat—thanks to an exorbitant pet deposit, I'd been forced to leave Cat Benatar at my mom's. "Katharine Hepburn?"

Jo adopted a flawless mid-Atlantic accent without missing a beat. "'All-expenses-paid destination wedding'—well, that's terrible," she said, clearing her throat like the accent was something physical she had to dislodge.

"I'm sure they'll tell you how they want you to say it." The wedding—and the cushy two-week vacation leading up to it—was being paid for by a sponsor in exchange for name-dropping them on the podcast's social media channels and shooting a few promo materials, a handful of which Jo was headed to the island early to record. Just use code JOANDGO15 at checkout and get fifteen percent off your next major life event! "It's not like it's going to be showing at Sundance."

"You're right." Jo feigned a wistful sigh. "And here I thought this was going to be my breakthrough."

"Chin up, darling, that's Hollywood," I said, trying and failing to do a mid-Atlantic accent of my own.

Jo looked appalled. Hey, some of us were too busy learning the *Hawaii Five-O* theme on the tuba to perfect an accent for a high school production of *The Philadelphia Story*. "Please never do that again." She pocketed her phone and wheeled her suitcase over to the door, flapping her free arm at her side like she wasn't sure what to do with it. "Okay," she exhaled. "I guess I'll see you in two days?"

Time apart had been scarce these past few years, mostly occupied by Jo's weekend trips to see her abuela in Mexicali. We lived together, recorded together, and went to promotional events together. We took girls' trips complete with strategic photos to populate our Instagram feeds. When she'd first started seeing Peter last year, I noticed a shift—nights spent away from the apartment and romantic weekend getaways up to wine country, complete with

Instagram pictures I wasn't tagged in, for once—but I chalked it all up to the excitement of finally snagging the unattainable popular guy she'd had a crush on in high school.

But the wedding was a harbinger of real change, something more permanent. Whatever that meant, I didn't want to hold Jo back from it, if she felt it was the right choice for her future. But I couldn't help feeling I was being left in her past in the process. A keepsake to stick in her pocket as a reminder of who she used to be, but with no practical use anymore.

It was a silly thought. Jo was asking me to stand there beside her while she said her vows and signed her life away, and that had to count for something. We had shared social media accounts and contracts with Spotify and sponsors that extended through Season Seven (which we still needed to plan and record). Jo and I had always been inseparable, and our careers reflected that. In two days, I would join her on Catalina Island and be glued to her hip again, through two weeks of cake tastings and rehearsal dinners and God only knew what else.

As much as I dreaded being left in the past, I might have dreaded the reality of the future more.

"Two days," I confirmed.

* * *

Two days passed way too quickly.

"You have to book it through the website," I said, trying to sound patient as I shuffled up the ramp to the ferry, phone pinned between my ear and my shoulder so that I could steer my luggage in front of me. An attendant scanned my boarding pass and waved me aboard. "There's a code. I forwarded you the email."

On the other end of the phone, my mom clacked around on the computer. "On the ferry's website?"

"No, on Castaway Catalina's website." I deposited my suitcase and tote bag in the luggage room and used my newfound freedom to switch my phone to the other ear. "There's a link to the specific page in the email, and then you enter the code to claim your ticket."

"Technology," Mom sighed, followed by more keyboard noises.

The ferry wasn't glamorous. Nothing like the cruise ship my parents had dragged me on for their fifteenth anniversary. This was more reminiscent of a mid-nineties bowling alley, with plastic chairs and colorful patterned carpet like something out of a mushroom trip. There was even a concession stand, right at the heart of it all.

"Okay, done," Mom announced. "It says they're sending me a confirmation. Where are they sending the confirmation?"

"Probably to your email."

Another series of clicks. "Found it. Are you on the boat yet?"

"Yes, I'm on the boat," I said, standing in one of the aisles as I scanned the surrounding seats for familiar faces. None stuck out. Maybe the other members of the wedding party were scheduled on different ferries. I stepped off to the side to allow a family of five to pass by, leaving the beachy scent of Coppertone in their wake. "And before you ask, it hasn't changed much."

"It's been almost a decade now," Mom said after a brief pause, her voice a familiar melancholy. "But I think I'm looking forward to going back."

We'd visited Catalina almost every summer, when I was growing up. My parents had honeymooned there. I'd even worked as a lifeguard for one of the island's summer camps, the summer before senior year. But that had all stopped when Mom and Dad split. Avalon harbored too many memories, turned bittersweet in the wake of everything that had happened. If Mom was looking forward to visiting, maybe that meant she was ready to face those memories again—to forget everything Dad had done. I wasn't quite on the same page.

But I didn't know how to begin to express that, and I wasn't sure I wanted to, so I changed the subject. "Did you know that the song about 'twenty-six miles across the sea' is talking about the distance from L.A.? Which makes no sense when you think about it. There aren't even ferries out of L.A." I'd paid to park my old pickup in a dingy structure in Long Beach for two weeks—an expense unfortunately *not* included in Castaway Catalina's packages.

"Oh, Margo, it's just a song. Did you think The Beatles were singing about an actual submarine?"

"There's a difference between a metaphor and misinformation," I grumbled. Nonsensical songwriting was one of my biggest pet peeves. If you were gonna make a song about it, at least make it make sense. "Anyway, I need to find a seat. Call you later?"

"You better," she threatened cheerily.

Hanging up, I walked over to the concession stand at the center of the boat and paid for an overpriced can of Sprite, a safeguard against seasickness. From one of the nearby seats, a guy in a green Caltech ball cap and wayfarer sunglasses seemed to be watching me, elbows resting on his knees, a pair of wired earbuds dangling between them. The corner of his full lips quirked in a smile, and he raised a hand in a hesitant wave. A faint dimple appeared in his right cheek.

I snorted. *Not happening, dude.* I wasn't in the mood for dealing with random men, good-looking or otherwise. I mustered up my best unapproachable scowl and climbed the stairs to the upper deck.

Once outside, I claimed a seat toward the back of the boat, right beneath the rippling American flag. It was a gusty oceanside day, the sun warming my skin and the breeze cooling it in turns. The ferry pulled away from the dock with an uncomfortable lurching sensation and began the wide, unwieldy turn to exit the harbor. My stomach churned. I popped the tab on my Sprite and took a few glugs for good measure.

Why had that guy stared at me like that, anyway? I wasn't

looking my best, at the moment. Hair in a sloppy bun, wearing leggings and an oversized CSUSB sweatshirt that I'd borrowed from my college roommate and forgot to give back before graduation. Plenty of guys said things disguised as compliments like *I like a girl who's comfortable with herself* or *you look better without makeup*, but there was almost always an agenda behind it. In my experience, they were often lying through their teeth. Not all of them, but enough of them.

The boat had started to pick up speed. The flag whipped loudly overhead and stray hairs threatened to escape from my bun. I polished off my Sprite right as the ferry entered the open ocean. Already I could spy a sliver of island on the horizon, twenty-odd miles away from home.

Season Five, Episode Three—To Ghost, or Not to Ghost?
42 min 13 sec

Go: *One of our listeners—her name is Raquel, shoutout to Raquel for being a loyal listener, she's been listening since Season One, everybody. Anyway, so, Raquel sent us an email this week asking whether we'd ever been ghosted.*

Jo: *Oh, God, yes. I've been ghosted. Have you been ghosted?*

Go: *I'm trying to remember a time that I have, but I can't think of one. I don't think it's happened to me. I mean, I've done a lot of ghosting.*

Jo: *There you have it, folks. The secret to success. Either be the ghost or get ghosted.*

Go: [laughs] *No, but in all seriousness, I've never trusted someone enough for them to have the chance. The thing is, guys always ghost the girl who's chasing, chasing, chasing. I'm not saying that to hurt anybody's feelings, it's just reality. And then they'll turn around and like, smother the girl who's ignoring*

*them. But as soon as she gives him the time of day, they'll proba-
bly ghost her, too. It's just how they are. They can't make up their
minds.*

Jo: *And that's why you have to make it up for them.*

Go: *Exactly. Head things off at the pass.*

Jo: *So, the next part of Raquel's question is what to do when
someone ghosts you.*

Go: *You don't do anything. Rule Number Four: Never exceed his
effort.*

Jo: *I agree. No, don't look at me like that—you guys can't see
this, but she's totally giving me a look right now.*

Go: *I just think you have this tendency to be, like, overly trusting every time you meet a new guy. Sometimes you keep putting
in the effort even as things are fizzling out.*

Jo: *I like to give people the benefit of the doubt.*

Go: *Yeah, but trust is earned, isn't it? You wouldn't go up to a
stray dog and trust it not to bite you. Same thing with people.
Like, sometimes it's just in their nature. I'm not going to blame
them for it, but I'm not going to trust them by default.*

Jo: *But for our listeners out there, don't you think that's a little
strict?*

Go: *Better safe than sorry.*

3

The boat docked about an hour later. The hilly cliffs of Catalina rose out of the sea, grasses fried a faint gold by the summer heat. Avalon was a medley of colors and architectural styles dotting the hillside. On an outcropping of rock sat a massive Mediterranean building known as the Catalina Casino, but then turn your head and there's a Craftsman-style house straight out of the thirties, or a tawdry ice cream shop complete with *Grease*-level mid-century nostalgia.

It was no Maui—which Jo and I had been lucky enough to visit two summers ago for a photoshoot as part of an Instagram partnership with a swimsuit boutique—but Catalina wasn't terrible. It was an easy escape from the constant buzz of the mainland, an illusion of being miles away from your problems, and perhaps that was the root of its charm. Unlike my family, who'd visited every summer, Jo had only visited twice: once for a field trip in elementary school and once with me and my parents in high school. When Castaway Catalina had reached out for a partnership promoting their new social media campaign—"cast off your cares"—I'd scoffed. Catalina was as much the real world as anywhere else, twenty-six miles across the sea or otherwise.

But Jo, who unbeknownst to me had already been talking to Peter about the possibility of getting married, still held on to a shred of that fantasy. She'd bought into the false promise. Before I knew what hit me, she was flashing me a white-gold ring with a teardrop diamond and telling me that she wanted to email Castaway Catalina back about the deal.

A dry heat beat down on the open deck of the ferry as passengers herded toward the exit. It was the sort of Southern California weather that was God-awful when inland but perfect for a day at the beach. I peered over the side of the boat at the crystalline water, where bright orange flecks darted between seaweed and craggy rocks: garibaldi, our state fish, flocking around the ferry.

Back in the storage room, I slung my tote bag over my shoulder and dragged my suitcase behind me. A queue had formed down the ramp, where a distressed employee tried and failed to stop impatient passengers from shoving their way to the front. From the top of the ramp, I spied Jo and Peter with a colorful hand-drawn sign that read HERNANDEZ-FIGUEROA WEDDING PARTY. I let go of my suitcase to wave, just for a second—which was apparently a second too long. Someone bumped me. My suitcase teetered, but I managed to catch it before it plummeted to the water and I turned, ready to give the stranger an earful.

It was the guy in the Caltech hat. He had a gym bag slung over a broad shoulder and it looked like maybe he'd been pushed into me by a gaggle of high school students jockeying to get ahead. His lips parted like he was about to say something, his expression unreadable behind dark sunglasses, but then one of the workers ushered us down the ramp.

"Hiiiii!" Jo sang, flying across the pavement and wrapping me in a hug as soon as I reached solid ground. She wore a fringed swimsuit cover-up and her damp hair smelled like salt water.

"Passengers only beyond this line," a dock worker snapped. A passenger pileup was happening on the ramp behind us, people with armfuls of luggage grumbling and shooting us scornful looks.

"Sorry." I hurried behind Jo to where Peter was waiting a few yards away. For reasons unknown, the guy in the Caltech hat tagged along. Probably waiting for his opening to apologize for almost knocking my suitcase into the bay.

"Peter, you remember Margo."

I gave Jo's fiancé a close-lipped smile. Despite my awareness of their courtship, Jo had spent the past year and some change sneaking around and avoiding the apartment like a teenager hiding her boyfriend from her strict parents. Which meant I hadn't actually seen Peter since high school. I was sickened to see that he still had a full head of thick, dark hair, and adulthood had hollowed out his cheekbones so that he was even more reminiscent of a Greek god than before.

"Of course. Welcome to the island life," Peter said cheerily. He was wearing a Hawaiian shirt and one of those cheap plastic leis, which gave the impression that he was a little confused about which island he was on. A few thousand miles' worth of confused, by my estimate.

"Where is everybody?" I asked.

"Autumn booked the ferry tomorrow and Liv can't be here until Thursday," Jo was explaining, but I was hardly listening. I watched over her shoulder, mystified, as Peter greeted the hat-wearing stranger, pulling him into a rough bro-hug.

Something in my brain clicked into place. "You must be one of the groomsmen," I said.

He removed his sunglasses, hooking them on the neck of his T-shirt. He looked like California's own take on Jamie Fraser, with his faded black Vans and peach-colored board shorts. He smiled guiltily, which only served to deepen his dimple. "Sorry about bumping into you. You know how it gets. They herd people off these things like cattle."

He was taller than me, which at my height was always a plus. "Margo Anderson." I extended a hand, batting my eyelashes in a way that probably would have been helped by a hint of mascara, but I'd neglected even that today.

"Ah." He didn't bother removing his hand from the pocket of his shorts. "We know each other, or . . ." He exchanged an awkward look with Peter. "Used to."

I racked my brain, but came up short on hot *Outlander* doppelgängers. No, pretty sure I'd remember if I had met any of those. For a few seconds, it felt like my brain was running on dial-up internet, registering—a few seconds too late—the dusting of russet-colored freckles across his nose, and the short red hair tucked beneath the Caltech hat.

"Declan Walsh," he prompted. "From high school?"

My hand hovered between us for a beat, still waiting for him to shake it, before I registered what I was doing and returned it to the handle of my suitcase. "You look . . ." I struggled to find something semi-appropriate to say. "Different." Which was an understatement. Either he'd experienced the glow-up of the century or I was remembering him through the opposite of rose-tinted glasses.

"You look the same," he said, which was obviously meant as a jab, because high school me had been deeply unfortunate-looking. Okay, so he didn't shake my hand, and he was insulting me. So much for a fresh start. He might have looked different on the outside, but safe to assume the inside hadn't changed.

Jo must have picked up on some of the awkwardness. "I figured it would be good for the best man and maid of honor to arrive first," she interjected, "to get a feel for things, you know, go over your duties and answer any questions you guys have. How about we get you guys to the hotel, and then maybe we can all go out for dinner tonight? Get down to business?"

"Sounds good to me," Declan agreed.

He caught me staring at him and gave me a faint smile, oblivious to the resentment I'd harbored for the past decade or so.

I exhaled through my nose. I had promised Jo that I could be fine with this, and I was going to be fine with this. High school was full of all sorts of petty crap because everyone was still figuring out who they were supposed to be. Like that one time Jo wore a pair of fake wolf ears to school and I was too embarrassed to talk to her until the next day. (I immediately apologized; the wolf ears mysteriously disappeared from her wardrobe; we haven't spoken about it since.)

Not far from the docks sat a worn-down golf cart, its paint chipped and upholstery fraying. Peter jangled the keys. "Our ride for the next couple weeks."

It wasn't exactly glamorous, but I'll admit, the grouchy "Seriously?" that escaped my lips was probably a little ungrateful. I was getting a vacation, after all. A free vacation. Declan seemed to be the only one who heard me, because he quirked his head in my direction, like band kids were some sort of rare bird he rarely had the chance to observe in the wild.

But we weren't in high school anymore. I was a grown woman. I'd reinvented myself the moment I set foot in college, three years behind schedule and with my far-fetched dreams of auditioning for the Los Angeles Philharmonic well behind me. I shouldn't have been fazed by the washed-up high school soccer player my best friend was marrying, or by his equally washed-up best man. Though it was a bit unnerving that neither Peter nor Declan were looking very washed up at the moment.

Lost in thought, I hoisted my suitcase to load it into the back of the golf cart and stumbled beneath the weight. A pair of large hands caught me by the backs of my arms and steadied me. I caught a hint of a clean, woodsy cologne—pine and crisp seaside air and maybe a hint of spearmint, like a day hiking the redwoods beside the coast.

"Here, let me." Declan let go of my arms to help with the suitcase.

I relinquished it, but my mouth was less compliant. "I don't need help. I got my stuff this far."

"It's no problem," he said with a disinterested shrug. My cheeks warmed, but I didn't try to explain myself further. He tossed his own bag onto the pile and hopped into the front seat. Peter leaned over and muttered something to him, and Declan laughed. My blood boiled. There was nothing I hated like being the butt of a joke, and while the logical part of my brain was screaming *you don't know what they're laughing at*, an insecure part was convinced they were laughing at me.

* * *

The golf cart might have been a bit clunky, but our sponsor had spared no expense when it came to the hotel. Okay, maybe it was kind of worth selling out. I trailed through the elegant, white-tiled lobby of the Santa Catalina Resort and Spa behind my luggage, which had been loaded onto a rack and was now being pushed by a bellboy in a crisp linen shirt. This wasn't the tacky island resort I'd imagined. There were high ceilings, tastefully upholstered furniture, and glazed ceramic planters filled with frilly palm trees that I was almost certain weren't native to California. The bellboy pressed the button to call the elevator. "You're lucky," he said. "The fourth floor has the best view of the water."

The elevator doors slid open, revealing beveled mirror paneling. My reflection served as an unwelcome reminder that I looked like I didn't belong here. Short, broken hairs had sprung loose from my sloppy bun. I tried to make it sit in the middle of my head, at the very least, but it was intent on slumping to the side. No matter. I could freshen up in the room before dinner.

The elevator doors were closing when a well-muscled arm shot in to stop them. Declan wedged his way inside. His only luggage was the small gym bag slung across his shoulder. Our eyes met in the reflection and I averted my gaze, fidgeting with the beads on my bracelet. Peter and Jo had disappeared to their own rooms to freshen up, which meant it was just me, Declan, and the bellhop. Before either of us conjured up any small talk to fill the uncomfortable silence, the bellhop asked, "What floor?"

Declan looked at the printout from the front desk. "It says here room 403. I don't know what floor that is."

I glanced at my own paperwork. 402. I folded it and tucked it into my back pocket with a twinge of annoyance. The ride was short and suffocatingly quiet, and then the elevator spat us out on the top floor. The bellhop led us to the right, to a pair of doors about fifteen feet apart from each other. "Here we are. 402 and 403." He made as though to unload my luggage for me, but I stopped him with a hand.

"No, no, it's fine," I said, wanting this whole interaction to end as soon as possible. "I've got it, just—" Just what? Leave the empty cart for housekeeping to retrieve later? I hadn't thought this through. Rather than disappear into his room, Declan was watching our exchange with a look of mild bemusement.

"I'll send someone up to get the cart," the bellhop suggested.

I forced a tight-lipped smile and nodded, and with that, we were left alone. Me, Declan, and the luggage rack blocking my door. I reached between the metal bars and waved my keycard around until I heard the robotic chirrup of the door unlocking. Then I jostled the cart, trying to steer it out of the way. Or maybe steer it inside. I hadn't figured that part out yet, but I needed to get myself inside at minimum, to find refuge from the sheer awkwardness.

Declan made no motion to head to his own room, but he wasn't exactly offering to help, either. "So," he said, "neighbors."

I had no idea why he was bothering right now, considering he'd spent most of high school ignoring me—when he wasn't tricking me into eating mayonnaise pudding or stuffing my tuba with shaving cream. But I didn't take either of those occasions as any real acknowledgment of my existence, either, since he pulled those stunts on everyone. Anything for the sake of attention. "Looks like it," I grunted. Steering the luggage rack was kind of like steering an overfilled grocery cart with a wonky wheel. I really had to put my back into it, and even then, it wasn't being very cooperative.

"I can ask them to move me to a different room, if you want," he offered.

I parked the rack off to the side. "What do you mean, 'if I want'?" I jiggled the handle, but in the interim, my door had re-locked itself. I tried to use the card again, but went all butterfin-gers and dropped it, like the protagonist in a horror movie who panics so bad she starts fumbling everything. If my life were a movie, I would 100 percent be yelling at the screen right now.

"I don't know, just a . . ." His eyes darted over my stooped form as I retrieved my card, and he frowned. "Body language thing."

"Glad to know you've been staring at my body." Another chir-rup, and I was finally admitted to my room.

He laughed dryly. "Yeah, the flailing arms and the whole 'someone-pissed-in-my-Cheerios' expression. Real sexy."

I stopped in the doorway and turned to face him. "If I was try-ing to be sexy, believe me, you would know." The words had barely left my mouth and already warmth was flooding my cheeks. What was I even trying to prove here? My best bet was to shut the door. Go hide beneath the Egyptian cotton duvet before I embarrassed myself any further.

Declan shrugged. "If you say so."

"Not that I need to try."

"Right."

"Glad we're on the same page," I said, praying my face wasn't turning as red as it felt.

His brow was knit in concern. Maybe for my well-being. He tossed a thumb over his shoulder. "So, should I be seeing some-one about moving rooms, or—"

"Nope. We're cool. Bye."

Before this painful moment managed to drag on any longer, I retreated into my room and shut the door. With a groan, I slumped against the print wallpaper, all moody jungle and flashes of colorful feathers. If I thought our interactions were cringeworthy in high school, it was nothing compared to now. And did he seriously just imply that I wasn't attractive? Please. One episode of the podcast—the one from back in Season Two about how to give a good blowjob would probably do the trick—and he'd be begging me to jump into bed with him.

It was only after I released a breath and straightened up, banishing the thought from my mind, that I realized I'd left my luggage in the hall.

I waited a solid ten minutes before I worked up the courage to retrieve my suitcase and tote bag from the rack outside. Once I was officially settled in, I stepped out on the balcony to take in the view.

Our resort was perched in the foothills that led up into the highlands of Catalina, so it wasn't quite seaside, but the smell of salt and sand wafted on a light breeze. Below, the streets were dotted with colorful rooftops, tiny golf carts and electric bicycles weaving between them. There were few cars on the island. Beyond Avalon, the deep blue Pacific stretched back toward the mainland. I kept a safe distance from the railing. I was never quite comfortable with heights. But a small cast-iron table and chairs were butted up against the white stucco with a fresh arrangement of white lilies, making for a photogenic nook to enjoy coffee or breakfast.

The only downside was the twin balcony right next to mine, though it was mercifully empty at the moment. I stepped back inside and shut the sliding glass door, shooting Jo a quick text before jumping in the shower.

Margo: Dress code for tonight?

I let the warm water rush over me, easing some of the tension of the last couple days. Maybe my defensiveness toward Declan was misdirected. He was just another reminder of a past I would've preferred to forget—a past it felt I couldn't escape, as of late.

I had scrubbed on my hands and knees to wipe the slate clean after a lackluster high school career. And I'd done a damn good job of it. Our podcast had an average of a couple hundred thousand monthly listeners. I'd done more than reinvent myself; I'd built a foundation for a potential long-term career. A future that was well outside the shortsighted expectations everyone had placed on me. For a while, it felt like I'd made a clean break—from the past, from our hometown, from everything I didn't particularly care to look back on.

But then last spring we got invited to Marketing & Mimosas, a social networking brunch out in Cathedral City, where we ran into the blogger and style consultant behind the popular Instagram page Autumn's Closet. Jo had suggested we do a bit of cross-promotion, and before I knew what was happening, a collaboration had evolved into a friendship. Turned out, Autumn just happened to be Peter Figueroa's younger sister. Someone threw Autumn a twenty-first birthday party at this intimate speakeasy in the Fashion District of Downtown L.A., where Jo bumped into Peter, and the rest was history. She'd picked at a loose thread, tugged a little too hard, and started the slow unraveling of four years' worth of work.

By the time I stepped out of the shower, Jo had texted back.

> **Jo:** Cute, but not too dressy. I'm thinking maybe that floral print dress I wore at the resort in Cabo last year?

Okay, I could work with that. I slathered on some lotion and blow-dried my hair. My roots were showing and the green had started to fade to a strange mossy color, like it had forgotten what color it was supposed to be in the first place. It felt brittle as I worked out the tangles with a comb—probably needed a break from the years of abusive bleaching and coloring, but the green had become one of the more recognizable elements of my online presence, so I'd have to touch it up sooner or later. I selected a cotton dress with a low-cut back and paired it with chunky sandals. Not too dressy, not too casual. Then a dab of cream blush and a flick of mascara, and I was ready to go.

* * *

The Bluewater Grill was a pier-side restaurant with outdoor seating, and the hostess's heeled steps echoed off the wood planks as she led us to a table for four overlooking Avalon Bay. It was murky in the fading sun, the lights of the city dancing on the gentle, lapping waves between the yachts and private sailboats—some of them vacant, others lit a bright yellow from within, their occupants drinking on the stern and kicking their feet in the dark water. Jo sat next to Peter, which placed me on the opposite side of the table, elbow-to-elbow with Declan. Our waiter materialized before we managed to exchange any snide remarks.

Jo ordered a glass of sauvignon blanc and Peter a beer, but I decided to steer clear of alcohol—at least for the first night. I wasn't sure I'd recovered all the brain cells I lost at The Blue Room the other night, and our sponsors were often more than happy to ply us with drinks without my helping matters along. "Just a water, please."

"Same for me," Declan said. I glanced at him sidelong. He'd changed into a navy short-sleeved button-down for dinner and smiled when he caught me looking at him—a small, polite smile that emphasized his dimple. I pretended to read the menu, even though I'd already decided I was going to order the salmon.

There was a lot of small talk about how nice the hotel was and how generous our sponsor had been, during which Jo seemed to be doing most of the talking. Despite my best efforts to be present, I couldn't help feeling a little distracted. *Generous* wasn't the word I would use, because when it came to sponsors, we always owed them something in return—a balancing of the scales. Which more often than not translated into numbers: impressions, engagement, click-throughs, and all of that required content.

Once the drinks had arrived and we'd all ordered our food, Jo steered the conversation toward the wedding. "We have two weeks to get everything organized—"

"—with plenty of time to party it up in between," Peter interrupted, clinking a glass of pilsner with Declan's water and waggling a mischievous eyebrow. I could have gagged.

Jo carried on unaffected. "The rest of the bridal party will arrive tomorrow, and they can help. The venue, florist, and caterer are already set up. We still need to do cake tasting, the bachelor and bachelorette parties, the rehearsal dinner, and the actual wedding."

Already my head was spinning, trying to map out a half-coherent schedule. Jo was a planner at heart. She was the one who wrote out the outlines for each season of the podcast and drafted up our social media calendar each month. I was more improv. Composing Tweets on the fly. That sort of thing. We balanced each other out.

But with the wedding and all its obligations, I thought it might be good for me to pick up some of the slack. "What about social media?" I asked. "The marketing team at Castaway Catalina are asking for a minimum of five Instagram posts, and that's not even touching on their plans for TikTok—"

Jo waved a hand like my concerns about our reputation were smoke she could waft away. "We've got two weeks for all that."

She pointed her straw at Declan. "I wanted to touch on whatever you're planning for the bachelor party real quick . . ."

I dug my phone out of my pocket and opened our collaborative social media calendar beneath the table. Jo had already marked dates for various posts in July, so maybe she was more on top of things than I thought.

"So long as it's not the night before the wedding," she was saying. "I'm planning the rehearsal dinner that night."

"And Pete will need a couple days to recover," Declan added.

"You're one to talk," Peter shot back.

By the time one of the food runners delivered our plates, he was in the middle of regaling us with a very run-of-the-mill story about how Declan passed out on the floor of his bathroom after killing a bottle of Bacardi in high school. I mostly tuned it out, focusing on my dinner: a mouthwatering crispy salmon with asparagus. Declan sawed a knife through his steak, bumping elbows with me in the process. To ensure he didn't mistake it for an intentional elbow graze, I tucked my arms in and tried to pretend he didn't exist.

We'd finished dinner and I was on my third glass of water when Jo produced her three-ring binder from somewhere in her bottomless tote. "I've printed sheets with info about some of our guests, to help you remember who's who," she explained, because of course she had. She popped open the metal rings of the binder and extracted two pages, which she passed across the table like they were copies of the syllabus on the first day of class.

It was a lengthy list of names with brief descriptions, including how they knew the bride and groom. Aside from parents and other immediate family members, it listed off the members of the wedding party: five in all, two groomsmen and three bridesmaids, including me and Declan. I scanned over the list. I'd met both of my fellow bridesmaids in the past, but I lingered on the name of the other groomsman. I knew that name, but not because of any high school bullying. I'd heard it on TV. On the cover of gossip rags at the grocery store checkout. Occasionally trending on local Twitter.

"Lucas Montpelier?" I read off. Under *relation to bride and groom*, the only explanation offered was *groom's childhood friend.* "As in Senator Montpelier's son?"

"Tony used to work with my mom," Peter explained. "Lucas and I went to the same daycare, when we were little."

Carol Montpelier was a U.S. senator from our hometown. On the national level, she was a politician, but locally, she was more of a celebrity. Her husband, Tony, was a well-liked local news anchor, and had recently and very publicly filed for divorce after the senator was caught having an affair; my mom had followed the story obsessively, updating me during our weekly phone calls in meticulous detail.

"Will Tony be at the wedding?" I asked.

Peter nodded. "I think so."

"Backside," Jo said, and I flipped the paper over to see Tony's name toward the top of a list labeled OTHER GUESTS TO KNOW. "Though he hasn't responded to the invitation yet," she added glumly. She'd built one of those fancy wedding websites where people could RSVP online and then proceeded to complain every day about how few of them had RSVPed. I might've understood if she was paying per plate, but the whole grand thing was being covered by Castaway Catalina, so in this instance, I thought her need for control was maybe getting the better of her.

I grabbed my phone off the table to text my mom.

Margo: You're never going to believe who's invited to the wedding

Mom: Who?

Margo: No, you have to GUESS

"Could you pass me the salt?" Declan asked.

I looked up, the wedding party list in one hand and my phone in the other, ready to juggle things as needed to grab the salt-shaker. Only it was sitting squarely in the middle of the table. "This table is like three feet across. I'm pretty sure you can reach with your spider monkey arms."

"My arms are a perfectly normal length," he protested.

"They weren't in high school."

"Everyone's disproportionate in high school."

"Peter wasn't," I pointed out, with a nod across the table.

"That's because I'm genetically blessed," Peter chimed in.

Jo nodded. "It's true, he is."

I shook my head and turned my attention back to my phone. While I waited for Mom to answer, I switched back over to the social media calendar. Jo had left a series of vague comments over the next couple of weeks—things like *kayaking*, which I knew referred to the trip I'd booked out of my own pocket as an early wedding present to Jo because she'd always wanted to go. And there were other options for keeping our socials active. Liv would likely be on board for cross-promoting, as we'd done several times in the past. And we could always ask Autumn, but she tended to make more of a fuss, like it was greatly disruptive to her own scheduled Instagram posts to make room for a post on our behalf.

Declan and Peter were exchanging increasingly creative jabs from opposite sides of the table. "Some of us are late bloomers. Haven't you ever read *The Ugly Duckling*? Oh, I forgot. You don't know how to read."

"I'll have you know that I read at a fourth-grade level," Peter shot back.

"How was the last Animorphs, by the way?"

"Great. I liked the part where he turned into a weasel. Reminded me of you."

In the middle of sipping from my glass, I snorted, and water went straight up my nose. Declan reached over and patted between my shoulder blades. "Now look what you've done," he shot at Peter, voice dripping with feigned worry. "You made Margo choke."

"I bet you—"

Someone kicked beneath the table and the whole thing clattered, drinks sloshing out of their glasses. Peter looked like he was holding back laughter, his brown eyes glittering with amusement. Declan's only reply was a faint shake of his head. I glanced at Jo, who only shrugged, apparently as nonplussed as I was. It was like we were teenagers again, never quite in on the joke.

I cleared my throat. "Sorry. It, um—" Declan's hand was warm on my bare skin, and it lingered a few seconds longer than necessary before sliding back to his water. We hadn't been on the island a day, and already we'd had more physical contact than the entirety of the time we spent in high school. "The water went up my nose," I finished lamely, like anyone actually cared.

After that, the moment passed as though nothing odd had happened, but I couldn't quite shake that feeling that I was an outsider, long-dormant insecurities bubbling to the surface. Dinner lasted a lot longer than planned, but not on my account. I was the first to clear my plate and had since asked the waiter for three refills on my water, just so that I had something to keep my hands occupied. Meanwhile, it only took a few drinks for Peter to start reminiscing about his glory days. We listened to his version of the infamous senior prank (apparently, he drove Declan to the U-Haul store on Foothill Boulevard for bubble wrap because the one on Cherry Avenue ran out) and Jo nodded along to stories about the soccer team that she had probably heard a hundred times already.

I found myself wishing I had ordered a glass of wine after all. I didn't have many funny stories of my own from high school, and the ones I did have, I wasn't interested in sharing. But my tolerance level was only so high, so after a while I set down my water and grabbed my bag from where I'd slung it across the back of my chair, excusing myself to the restroom. Declan scooted his chair into the table to let me by, but I was forced to brush against him anyway to avoid bumping the people seated at the table behind ours.

The restroom was outdoors and around the corner, empty except for a woman who had flipped upside down to stick her damp hair beneath the hand dryer, fluffing it with her fingers. I crossed the damp tile floor to one of the stalls and locked the door behind me, where I stood for a few minutes with my arms folded, not entirely sure what I was doing. There was no reason for me to be feeling this way. On a logical level, I knew that, but I was annoyed anyway. At some point, the hand dryer shut off and I was left alone in the restroom. I was just debating whether I should leave the stall to check my reflection above the sink when the main door creaked open.

"Margo? Are you in here?" Jo's voice echoed off the tiled walls.

"Just finishing up," I lied.

Her shadow shifted in the gap beneath the stall door. "Unless you've recently discovered how to pee standing up, I don't believe you."

I sighed and unlatched the door. Jo slumped a shoulder against the frame of the stall like she couldn't hold herself up any longer. "What's wrong?" she asked.

I shrugged. "Nothing."

"Don't give me that. You've been staring at your phone all night. Is it Declan? I know you said you were okay with it, but—"

"It's not Declan," I said curtly. "And I was on my phone because I'm worried about content. That's all. You know how important it is to keep our engagement up during the off-season."

"We're not supposed to be worrying about that tonight." Her breath smelled like wine and I realized that she was maybe a little drunk. Not that I could blame her. We were on vacation, celebrating her engagement. But for reasons that maybe weren't entirely rational, bitterness rose in my throat. It was her nonchalance that bothered me; here I was stressing about the future and everything changing and what that meant for me and the podcast, all while she didn't seem to have a care in the world—and what came out of my mouth next was about as involuntary as a sneeze. "The internet doesn't come to a screeching halt just because Jo Hernandez decided to get married."

I regretted it the moment the words left my mouth. It was one of those thoughts that was better left bottled up, but for some reason it just flew out, like popping the cork on a bottle of champagne. Jo squinted at me like she was having trouble seeing me straight, but I didn't think it was because of the alcohol. "It's always the podcast with you. Everything else comes second."

I tore my eyes away from hers and bit the inside of my cheek, wondering if I should even bother arguing. But she'd backed me into a corner here. Literally. She was blocking the door to the stall and I couldn't leave until this conversation was finished. "I'm just a little worried about the backlash we're getting. Not sure if you've noticed, but your wedding isn't going to pay the rent." Which I was going to have to figure out a way to pay by myself when she moved in with Peter after the wedding. We'd always managed to scrape by between our Patreon and various sponsorships, but despite putting our most glamorous foot forward on social media, we weren't rolling in absurd amounts of cash. Most sponsors paid us in services and tester products. I wasn't sure I could afford the apartment on my own, and I hadn't figured out where I would go if I couldn't.

"I'll help you find another place," Jo suggested, as though she'd read my thoughts. "Or you could stay with me and Peter for a while, at least until . . ."

She trailed off. I tried to imagine what that might look like: Jo, Peter, and me, the squeaky third wheel they were probably better off without. Worse than being left in the dust was the thought of being dragged along out of pity. "I don't need help." And I had no interest in following in Jo's footsteps. I wasn't some lonely single girl pining for a life she didn't have. I'd chosen my own path, and my choice was just as valid as hers. I only worried whether she saw it that way. "I'm just trying to make sure our careers don't tank in the middle of all this."

"Have you ever considered that maybe the podcast could use a little change? Half our comments are complaining about how we're rehashing the same old thing."

"Do we really have to talk about this right now?" I asked, exasperated. We were spinning in circles. "Your fiancé's waiting back at the table."

She lifted a shoulder. "It's just something to keep in mind. Change isn't always a bad thing." She pushed herself off the frame of the stall.

"All right," I agreed. "But I do actually have to pee."

She left and I finished up in the restroom. After washing my hands, I stopped in front of the mirror and combed my fingers through my hair, disentangling a strand from where it had picked a fight with my tragus piercing. The girl in the mirror was one-half of *Seven Rules*, but at the same time she wasn't, because mirrors didn't have Facetune to fill in the gap in my left eyebrow or touch up my roots. Go was the face I showed the world, the one fretting over how I should caption my photos or which Tweet I should pin to my profile, and sometimes I wasn't sure who Margo was beneath her anymore. Whoever she was, she didn't pay the bills.

Maybe Jo was right. Maybe we were limiting ourselves by

sticking to the same old material. Despite everything my college marketing internship had shoved down my throat, reducing ourselves to a single-faceted brand was undeniably limiting. I grabbed my phone out of my cross-body bag. "Siri," I said aloud, my voice echoing off the tile, "create a reminder for tomorrow morning: brainstorm social media for the month." I hesitated, my phone still listening, then added, "And try to think up some fresh content."

Satisfied, I tucked the phone away and pushed through the door—only the door knocked right into something solid. Someone, headed for the men's room. He caught it with a hand and a surprised "Whoa!" just as I stumbled and fell, scraping my knees on the weathered plank floor.

"Shit," I mumbled, sucking air through my teeth as I repositioned myself to inspect the damage. Matching angry red scrapes stared back at me. The bridesmaid dresses fell just above the knee, and judging by how thoroughly I'd skinned my knees, I doubted the scabs would be healed in two weeks. I tossed up my hands. "Cool. Now it's going to look like I was blowing some dude outside the bathroom."

"Most people would just say 'ow.'" Declan offered a hand, his gaze pointedly averted, and I realized my dress was hiked up my thigh. I tugged it down and he helped me to my feet. After a quick glance to ensure I was decent, he looked me up and down to assess the damage. "That looks like it hurts. I can see if they have any Neosporin—"

Warmth stung my cheeks at the thought of him helping me tend to my scraped-up knees like a kid who'd fallen off her bike. I straightened the straps of my dress, made a show of ensuring everything was in order. "Can we please drop the friendly act?"

"Friendly act," he repeated, raising a brow.

I exhaled through my nose. I wasn't in the mood for this. "Look, to be honest, I'm not really buying it after everything you put me through in high school. But for the sake of our friends, and this wedding—" I broke off, because he was frowning at me, and suddenly I wasn't so sure in my assessment of the situation.

"No, please continue. What about high school?"

"Don't play dumb."

He just stared, shook his head faintly, like I was speaking a different language.

"'Most Gullible,'" I prompted. He continued to look dumbfounded, so I kept going. Everyone wanted to reminisce, then we were going to reminisce, all right. "Sophomore year, in the middle of the homecoming pep rally. You stuffed my tuba with shaving cream. I almost popped a blood vessel trying to blow an F sharp. Never mind frosting Jordan Gardner like a fucking cake."

Understanding dawned on Declan's stupid, freckled face. For the briefest of moments, I thought he might apologize. But then he burst into gleeful, fifteen-year-old-boy laughter, and for the first time he actually resembled the Declan I'd known. Knew he was still in there, somewhere. "I haven't thought about that in forever."

"You might've forgotten, but everyone else remembered just fine," I grumbled. The tuba incident was the first in a string of embarrassing incidents that probably contributed to the nickname. Like every single time someone told me there was a stain on my shirt. Or when my lab partner in chemistry briefly convinced me that makeup brands were lab-testing waterproof lipstick on fish. I was ready to sign a petition and everything. "They voted me the 'Most Gullible' in senior year."

And you know what, maybe they had it right. Maybe I was gullible, because it was that same year that I learned my dad had cheated on my mom for eight whole years. They'd stuck together for the sake of making sure I finished school and I was never the wiser until the day they sat me down on the ugly sectional sofa in our three-bedroom house in Rialto, two days after my eighteenth birthday, and told me they were getting a divorce. I was blindsided, but everyone else just shrugged and went on with their lives, because that was the way the world worked. People lied and cheated and got divorced, and if you didn't learn to recognize that, life would kick you while you were down.

From that day on, I swore that I would wise up. Always stay two steps ahead.

"But that's high school," Declan said. "Superlatives don't matter in the real world."

"Never mind," I grumbled. His amusement had mostly evaporated, but left in its place was something resembling concern, and that bothered me more. I didn't want his pity any more than I wanted Jo's. "Can we please go back to the table?" Wait, why was I asking permission? Maybe I hit my head when I fell. Without waiting for his response, I stalked away. No one asked any questions when Declan returned from the restroom seconds after I did, but I didn't miss the curiosity that passed over Jo's expression, just as soon concealed beneath a heady mixture of wine and excitement for the weeks to come.

CHAPTER

5

My reminder went off at seven in the morning. *Brainstorm social media for the month and try to think up some fresh content.* Yeah, okay. Fat chance of me having a coherent thought before nine, but I yawned and stretched and dragged myself out of bed anyway. Jo wanted to take pictures down at the cabanas sometime around ten, which meant I needed plenty of time to wake up and fix my hair and makeup before leaving the hotel.

The coffee maker gurgled to life and I collapsed into a nearby armchair. I dimmed my phone screen and opened my email inbox. Twitter and Instagram were often inundated with DMs from troll accounts and sometimes from downright creeps, which was a lot to handle first thing in the morning, but emails were somewhat safe. Sure, there was the occasional death threat via our contact form, but for the most part, my inbox was strictly business.

And spam. Lots and lots of spam.

I had 1,837 unread emails, most of which were probably years old and buried pages back, never to see the light of day. Among the most recent, though, were an advertisement for twenty percent off an underwear brand that I had Googled once (delete), a scripted email from someone named Kim about increasing our Instagram engagement (delete), and a reply to an inquiry I'd made to a website designer about refreshing our look for Season Seven (open). As I was scrolling, a new email came in from my alma mater. *Save the Date: Join us for* . . . Curious, I clicked on it, only to discover it was an invitation to an alumni dinner. Likely a bad cover-up story for bullying us all into making a donation to the school. Because we all had thousands of dollars lying around less than a year after graduation, never mind rent and bills and student loans. Aaannndd delete.

Sighing, I locked my phone and got up to pour myself a mug of coffee.

I'd only managed to graduate with my bachelor's last fall—a lackluster culmination to four years at an uninspiring state university, and another reminder that my whole college experience was more than a little off schedule. It seemed like everyone in high school either had acceptance letters or scholarships lined up before we turned eighteen. And then there was me, working two jobs to help my mom afford her own apartment while she was going through the divorce. I didn't have time to apply to colleges, and even if I did manage to apply, I had less time for actually attending. It wasn't until my mom got the alimony and figured out her own job situation that I was able to think about enrolling. By then, I was already years behind schedule.

I wasn't really bitter about it. It meant putting my dreams on hold, but my dreams were already shifting by then anyway—I'd realized somewhere along the way that I didn't enjoy performing music so much as I enjoyed listening to it. Where tuba-playing Margo was confined to jazz and classical and the occasional, pitchy rendition of "Eye of the Tiger," concertgoing Margo was free to experiment. To check out local bands or save up for overpriced tickets to Coachella or spontaneously drive to Vegas at 7 p.m. because someone Tweeted a rumor about a pop-up concert.

Of course, none of that totaled up to any obvious career goals. But without a strong sense of direction, I'd majored in music anyway. And I learned some useful skills along the way. An audio engineering course, a part-time student job in the marketing department, and a whole series of encounters led to Jo and I forming the podcast during my second year of college. In a way, it had set me up for the future anyway, even if I hadn't known at the time what that future was going to look like.

I downed the rest of my mediocre coffee, showered, and then took the elevator to the hotel's elaborate breakfast buffet. I piled a plate with French toast and whipped cream and fresh strawberries, which I then smuggled up to my room so that I could eat out on the balcony with a view, rather than in the crowded breakfast hall.

An ocean breeze stirred my damp hair as I stepped outside and slid the door shut behind me. It was a bright, clear morning and the balcony next door was empty again. I balanced the plate on the wooden railing—swallowing the nervous feeling that rose up in my throat, being so close to the edge—and posed the strawberries before snapping a few pictures of my breakfast with Avalon out of focus below. I retreated to the table before geotagging it and posting to my Instagram story, and then I popped the first bite of heavenly, pillowy French toast into my mouth as reward.

It had become a typical morning routine for me: wake up; check my emails and any texts or missed calls as I sipped at my coffee; switch over to social media as I dug into my breakfast. Admittedly, it wasn't quite so glamorous, most days. The window behind the desk overlooked a busy street—honking cars and tangled telephone wires and wadded up In-N-Out bags collected in the gutters. But everything else about my routine was the same as it always was, even on vacation. I conducted a quick Google search for any new articles about the podcast, checked out analytics, read some of the comments even though I wasn't supposed to. This morning, that included reading an argument in the comments on Twitter between one of our frequent commenters and a girl whose handle I didn't recognize:

Jessica @messy_jessy8273 · Jul 15
Replying to @7R4BHpodcast
this is either a sloppy publicity stunt or the biggest
sellout ive ever seen. jo made all her money selling us the
#singlenotseeking lifestyle only for us to find out shes been
dating this guy the entire time? don't believe everything you
see on social media, kids . . . #fakeaf

Raquel O'Brien @raqyoursaqsoff · Jul 15
Replying to @messy_jessy8273
Maybe learn to mind your business. So what if Jo's getting
married? She still gives solid advice to the girls who want to
stay single.

Jessica @messy_jessy8273 · Jul 15
Replying to @raqyoursaqsoff
okay so were supposed to live by these rules but shes not?
that makes no sense. practice what you preach if you
really believe in it but dont go making a podcast just for
clout

Raquel O'Brien @raqyoursaqsoff · Jul 15
Replying to @messy_jessy8273
The podcast isn't about "clout," it's about empowering
women to stay single IF they want to. The rules are just a
way to avoid getting hurt along the way. No one says you
have to follow them.

Jessica @messy_jessy8273 · Jul 15
Replying to @raqyoursaqsoff
the rules are stupid and youre stupid for following
them. either you want to stay single or you dont. jo was
supposedly following the rules (if you believe that) and look
where it landed her

I'd learned long ago to ignore the troll accounts. Replying would only make us look bad, not them, so usually I'd fume for a couple hours, let our other commenters handle it, maybe come up with a few retorts in my head. But now, I couldn't even do that. I couldn't blame *messy_jessy8273* for the things she was saying; she was just voicing what everyone was thinking.

It was true that we'd come up with the rules with the best intentions. The podcast was our answer to a thousand male-run podcasts that touted misogynistic dating advice. The world was still rife with double standards; it had simply gotten a bit better at hiding them. I met guys in college who studied feminist theory and held signs at protests but then turned around and whispered about how *a lock opened by many keys is a shitty lock* while standing over the keg with their friends. I met women who hashtagged #womensupportwomen while they were shaming other women for the way they dressed or who they slept with. Men convincing women to sleep with them got to feel like Achilles sneaking into Troy with the Trojan horse. Women, well . . . we were expected to feel like whatever idiot opened the gates.

Frankly, it was bullshit. People didn't fit into neat little boxes. Just because someone's life choices didn't look like your choices, that didn't mean they were the wrong choices. They were just different.

But if people didn't fit into boxes, maybe they didn't fit into a neat list of rules, either. Maybe we were putting people into boxes in our own way.

I took another bite of French toast and reread the last comment in the thread. *The rules are stupid and you're stupid for following them. Either you want to stay single or you don't.*

Maybe for *Seven Rules* to move forward, we needed to challenge whether we needed the rules in the first place.

I switched over to my recent calls and scrolled back a week

or so, to my last phone conversation with Jo. I clicked call. She answered on the first ring, her voice breathless. "I'm almost ready. Give me another . . ." Something clattered in the background. A fumbled makeup palette or straightener. "Fifteen minutes or so."

"I'm not calling about that." I still looked like the Creature from the Black Lagoon. My damp green hair was plastered to my neck and there were probably dark circles under my eyes to rival a panda. I'd need at least an hour of my own if I was supposed to be photo ready.

"Okay," Jo said slowly. "So then what's up?"

"I have an idea for some new content."

* * *

"We deliberately break the rules," I explained, my voice low. "Or I do, anyway, seeing as you're . . ."

I inclined my head at Peter, who was busy snapping photos of the two of us from several yards away in an attempt to get the cabana in the picture. We were lounging in the shade, overlooking the imported sand and rented lounge chairs parked in front of the glittering blue water of Descanso Bay.

Jo frowned. "I don't know. Does that really make sense with our brand? And how do you purposely break the rules, anyway? It's not like you can go out like, 'I'm going to find a guy who never texts back, and then I'm going to text him first.'"

"I have a feeling that guy would be easier to find than you think," I pointed out.

Peter frowned at the phone. "It looks too . . ." He wobbled his head back and forth, trying—and failing—to conjure up a word. Any word.

"Cluttered?" Jo offered, reaching across my lap to rearrange the throw pillows on the wicker furniture. "Something with the lighting?"

"Awkward," Declan interrupted, returning from putting in our orders over at the bar—a task he'd been all too happy to volunteer for, like he wanted to put as much distance between himself and this photoshoot as possible. He was wearing a pair of swim trunks that showed just the right amount of lean, well-muscled leg and a gray T-shirt with a little palm tree logo stitched over the chest. He'd stayed uncharacteristically quiet on the golf cart ride from the hotel and the whole time we were taking photos, but now, he plunked into a cushioned wicker armchair and kicked his long legs up on the ottoman. "Jo, you're doing something weird with your face. And Margo looks like Gumby."

"I don't even know what that means," I grumbled.

"You know, the little claymation guy, he's green, stands sort of like—"

"I know who Gumby is." I couldn't tell if he meant my posture or if he was making fun of my hair, but I didn't care to find out. I'd never quite gotten the hang of posing for pictures. I didn't always know what I was supposed to be doing with my legs. Or hands. Or any other part of me, the moment someone picked up a camera. Jo was always more comfortable in her own skin. Maybe it was all the theater she did in school. Hard to feel self-conscious after you'd worn a fake mustache and pantaloons in front of half your graduating class.

We were interrupted by a server with choppy, sun-bleached hair delivering our drinks. She set a pair of photogenic red drinks on the low table in front of Jo and me, and handed bottles of Pacífico to the guys. "Cheers," Declan said to her before tilting the bottle to his lips.

At a simple look from Jo, Peter resumed snapping photos. I'd ordered my drink more for pictures than out of any real desire to catch a buzz, but I picked it up anyway and took a sip through the paper straw—for the sake of doing something with my hands, if nothing else. It was like drinking strawberry syrup straight out of the bottle.

Peter's phone chimed, and he lowered it in the middle of taking a picture to check it. "Autumn's here," he announced, turning to Declan. "Want to hop in the golf cart with me to go pick her up from the landing?"

"Happily." Declan pounded his brand-new beer and set the empty bottle on the table, all too eager to put some distance between himself and what he probably saw as a bunch of narcissistic bullshit. People without social media often saw it that way. Like they were somehow morally superior because they'd voluntarily failed to keep up with the times. Sometimes I wondered if my great-grandparents had felt like they were better than everyone for not watching TV or using the phone.

Peter gave Jo a swift peck on the lips, and then they were off.

"AirDrop me the pictures," she called after them. When Peter didn't seem to hear her, she grabbed his half-finished Pacífico and slumped back into her seat, all pretenses forgotten. "Whatever. Maybe we should ask Autumn. She'd probably give better direction, anyway."

"I'm not sure Autumn has quite the same vision," I said, thinking of her Instagram full of Chanel bags and blurry flash photos of runway models. Autumn was successful at what she did, and I respected that about her, but her style was a lot different from ours.

Jo sipped the beer. I wouldn't have minded something to wash down the sickly sweet drinks we'd ordered for our pictures, but the server was nowhere in sight and Declan had pounded the rest of his bottle. I would've gladly drunk after him and risked whatever cooties if it meant washing this syrupy taste out of my mouth.

"Okay, so maybe I don't go out of my way to break the rules," I said, reverting back to our former conversation now that we could speak more openly. "Maybe I just go two weeks without worrying about the rules and whatever happens, happens. We could frame it as a sort of social experiment."

Jo nodded thoughtfully. "Challenging whether or not they

matter in the first place." She got this pensive, faraway look in her eye as she gazed out at the water. I knew that look. She was already envisioning how we could spin it for social media, start promoting it before Season Seven was due to air in September. "Two weeks without rules."

"Why two weeks?" I asked.

"Two-week vacation, seems like the perfect time to step outside your comfort zone." She shrugged, beer poised at her lips so that her next words echoed inside the bottle. "And it'll make it easier to go back to normal, once the experiment's over. Not like you're ever going to see these people again."

I snorted. "I'm not worried about that." There was no fear of me actually catching feelings because I was almost certain at this point that I was incapable of it, but I wasn't beyond faking it. People were questioning why we needed the rules—I was going to show them. Give them a cautionary tale that would stamp out any lingering doubt once and for all. It would take a dash of truth for believability's sake and probably a little embellishing to make it podcast-worthy. A story juicy enough to overshadow Jo's wedding and reel our listeners back in. I could make that happen.

She unsealed the bottle from her lips with a *pop*. "There's one glaring problem with this whole 'no rules' thing, though." I shot her a curious look and she continued, "You haven't hooked up with a guy in, what, the last year?"

"Ten months and counting," I confirmed, only a touch wistfully. I missed sex, but I didn't miss the way I sometimes felt afterwards: a sort of hookup hangover, like I wasn't happy but couldn't quite put my finger on why. It didn't happen every time, but it happened often enough that I'd stopped sleeping with strangers altogether. It was just sex; I could live without it.

I routinely ignored that nagging thought that maybe *just sex* was the problem.

"It's not going to make for very exciting content if it's just a bunch of stories of you sitting around doing nothing," Jo pointed out.

"I'll worry about that." She didn't need to know the way my stomach bottomed out thinking about it, that I couldn't picture myself enjoying a hookup these days any more than I could imagine myself committing to someone. "You focus on getting married."

I reached over to pinch her cheek and she smacked my hand away, laughing. "Shut up."

With a clear vision for Season Seven forming in my mind, I grabbed my phone.

Ramping up some fresh content for Season Seven

July 15 at 1:34 PM

Hello, all our lovely Patrons,

We've been reading your recent comments and want to say first and foremost that WE HEAR YOU.

You started listening to 7R4BH because we were doing something fresh and interesting, pushing the limits of what girls are "supposed" to talk about. But after six seasons, we recognize that some of those conversations have grown stale. So, we're hitting the pavement in search of new content that challenges our way of thinking. We want to start a whole new dialogue by putting our philosophy to the test, forcing ourselves to confront the question: What really *happens if you don't follow the rules?*

To our long-term listeners, we're so grateful for your continued faith in us. To our new listeners, welcome to the #SingleNotSeeking revolution.

Get ready to shake things up.

Love you all,

Go & Jo

Peter and Declan returned about half an hour later with Autumn in tow, and Lucas Montpelier trailing after them. "They arrived on the same ferry," Peter explained. "We took them to the hotel to change and drop off their things."

While Jo got up to introduce herself to Lucas, Autumn came to join me. She was her usual elegant self in a print sarong swept over a black keyhole one-piece, her ink-black hair slicked into a high ponytail. "Hey, girlie." She moved an oversized pillow out of the way so that she could settle on the wicker lounge beside me. "How you been? How's the podcast?"

"Great," I said, because I couldn't even begin to summarize all the various things I'd been since I last saw her over a year ago, *great* not necessarily among them. "It's the off-season, so, you know . . ."

She cast a glance over to where Jo was shaking hands with Lucas before lowering her voice. "Listen, I'm ecstatic to have Jo for a sister-in-law and everything, but even I can recognize that a wedding doesn't really make for the best content."

"We're not too worried about it," I said in what I hoped was an offhanded way. "I'm actually working on some new stuff, starting today."

"Oh, do tell."

"Under wraps for now. What about you?" I asked, hoping to

change the subject. "Any news on the romantic front?" Outside of her expensive and particular taste in bags and shoes, Autumn was notoriously selective in what she revealed about her dating life. Assuming she even had a dating life, because I was pretty sure she intimidated the *shit* out of any man within a twenty-mile radius.

"Oh, you don't want to hear about that." She smiled coyly. "My dating life is pretty boring compared to yours."

"You'd be surprised." Scaring men off seemed like as reasonable an approach as any to avoiding the pitfalls of modern dating. No need to worry about being ghosted the morning after if there was no night before. "What about your brother's friends?" I nodded in Lucas's direction. He wasn't unattractive—his boyish looks were tempered by premature grays and sharp blue eyes—but he'd always struck me as a little conceited. Winking at paparazzi, posting shirtless gym selfies all over Instagram, the rumors that he slid into a different girl's DMs every day of the week. We all played the game, to some extent, but the Montpelier family was batting in an entirely different league.

"I'm not twelve." Autumn rolled her eyes playfully. "Declan is a sweetheart and I've known him forever, but he's not really my type. And Lucas is . . . well, Lucas." She inclined her head in his direction, where the server was touching his arm and leaning in closer than needed to take his order.

I was more stuck on her comment about Declan—a sweetheart? I watched him take a long drag from his beer, Adam's apple bobbing. But before I could pick Autumn's brain any further, Jo rejoined us on the lounge. The wicker crackled beneath the newfound weight. She passed me a michelada with Tajín. So much for keeping the drinking to a minimum, but this was my first full day on the island, and all things considered, it wouldn't kill me to loosen up.

I took a healthy swig of the michelada, the bright, salty flavor a welcome change. "Where's Liv?" I asked. If my memory of the cheat sheet served, she was the only member of the wedding party still absent.

Jo flapped a hand. "She's stuck at some marijuana convention in Vegas until tomorrow."

Probably promoting her newest hemp-based face cream or something. Liv grew up in Boston and only moved to L.A. a few years ago. She was as transplant as they came—she still called it "Cali" and forgot to put the "the" in front of freeway names, but she'd successfully embraced other aspects of West Coast culture, like starting her own line of vegan, cruelty-free skincare. Last I saw her, she had taken an edible at Aquarium of the Pacific and read my palm before she was escorted out by security for trying to crawl into the tank to free the sea lions.

On the other side of the cabana, the conversation had some-how shifted to Lucas ranting about his experiences with the pa-parazzi.

"They're like vultures." He sat on the very edge of one of the lounge chairs like a nervous bird poised to take flight, a pair of Armani sunglasses perched in his gray-streaked curls. "Half the time they're just making shit up. You know my mom dragged me to London last year for a gala, and they fabricated an entire story about my so-called relationship with the PM's daughter? We were photographed leaving the venue at the same time, but I swear to you, we never exchanged a word."

"The most ridiculous part of that story is the implication he'd have an actual relationship," Autumn muttered, folding her arms. I pretended to laugh, but it came out hollow. I didn't have a ton of relationships under my own belt, so I had no right to laugh at Lucas.

But I wasn't sure he even heard us. "And then there's all the nonsense they claim my dad's been saying, ever since the split." He stirred his straw around a frothy brown drink the server had referred to as Buffalo Milk, though she had to assure him several times there wasn't any milk from an *actual* buffalo in it. "You ever notice how it's never a direct quote? It's always 'a source close to the family' or something like that. They're pulling it out of their asses."

"But your mom did cheat on him, didn't she?" Declan asked. He was slumped back in the other lounge chair, picking at the paper label on a fresh bottle of Pacífico and looking bored with this entire conversation. "There were pictures of her with the pool boy and everything."

Lucas shrugged. "What business is that of the public's?"

"Public figure, public scandal," Declan said. "Sort of comes with the territory."

For once, it seemed Declan and I actually agreed on something. As though he sensed my gaze, his eyes cut to me, and we exchanged a look across the cabana. It wasn't a look of camaraderie, exactly— more that we seemed to have realized, at the exact same moment, that the next two weeks were going to be spent with a hodgepodge of personalities that we probably wouldn't have chosen to hang out with, given the option. Left to my own devices, I certainly wouldn't have *chosen* to be exchanging looks with Declan Walsh, of all people, but here we were.

Still, as quickly as we had looked at each other, we were looking away. Pretending to be interested in other people's conversations.

"We didn't sign any paperwork agreeing to this treatment, if that's what you mean," Lucas said.

"Privacy is a tricky subject, in the age of the internet. You can't outlaw gossip."

It was an issue I was all too familiar with—twofold. Jo and I had dealt with our fair share of gossip since stepping into our roles as internet personalities, but more than that, Lucas's insistence on defending a cheater just rubbed me the wrong way. I had my own experiences with homewrecking parents and had little interest in defending them. My own aversion to commitment was rooted in the belief that, if you were going to commit to someone, you better mean it.

I checked out of the rest of the conversation, burying my face in my drink. When I finished my michelada and got up to go order another drink, sandals kicking up the fine sand as I made my way to the outdoor bar, Declan called after me. "Hey, could you grab me another beer?"

I pretended not to hear him.

The speakers above the bar serenaded guests with "Red Red Wine," but there wasn't an actual wineglass in sight. The countertop was riddled with half-empty tumblers of tropical slush topped off with slices of pineapple and toothpick umbrellas. Tan, naked shoulders were pressed together, people fresh from the water in bikinis and swim trunks and the occasional Speedo. I squeezed into an open space and flagged down the bartender. It was the same girl as before, with the shaggy bleached hair. She was busy mixing drinks, but she nodded in my direction to show she was listening.

"There should be a tab open." The speakers were blaring music loud enough that I had to raise my voice. "Either under 'Anderson' or 'Hernandez.' Possibly both." Or maybe it was under Figueroa, seeing as that would be Jo's last name in the very near future. But I figured it was best not to bombard her with names. She popped the cap on the steel shaker and moved over to the register, where a handful of credit cards was laid out.

Her voice was half-buried beneath the music. "Not seeing it."

"It's not on a card."

She turned and gave me a look. Maybe she didn't hear me.

I leaned into the counter, my arms sticking to the wood. "It's not on a card." A few heads whipped around at my raised voice. This would be so much subtler if I could flash a wristband and call it a day.

"I heard you the first time," the bartender said, pouring a neon blue drink out of the shaker and topping it off with a cherry. She slid the glass across the counter to one of the guests and they slid back a twenty without exchanging so much as eye contact, let alone any actual words. She wiped her hands on her apron as she came over and braced herself against the counter. She had a colorful tattoo of orange California poppies on her forearm. "You're one of Renee's people. The YouTubers or whatever."

I knew that tone all too well. It was the same disparaging tone the guy at The Blue Room had used when he called me a *celebrity*. A special brand of barely concealed disdain that people seemed to fling our way without a second thought, because what did it matter? Influencers weren't normal people. That was the thing about being internet famous—the internet didn't necessarily like us, even as they were stalking our profiles and talking about us on Twitter. Which in turn only fanned the flames of the algorithm, and that made them hate us more. It was a vicious circle.

I scratched my forehead, only mildly uncomfortable. "Podcasters," I clarified. "Like I said, there should be a tab."

The bartender's jaw ticked like she was biting back a retort, but she put on a bland customer service voice. "What can I get for you?"

I hadn't looked at the menu, and I didn't want to take the time to peruse it now. "A margarita," I said, because it was the first drink that popped into my head. "On the rocks. Extra salt around the rim."

She turned and busied herself on the other side of the wraparound bar. No nod, no acknowledging my order, but she grabbed the Grand Marnier and a well tequila and started mixing. I released a sigh.

I'd never signed on for being an influencer with a so-called *brand* and a medley of sponsorships; all I wanted to do was run a silly podcast with my best friend. But I sure as hell had to deal with all the negative side effects that came with it, so sue me if I took advantage of the perks every now and then. I was pressed shoulder-to-shoulder with hot and sweaty strangers, and the bar top was sticky with spilled drinks. But I was also on vacation. A free vacation, I reminded myself, no matter how much this island reminded me of things it was easier not to remember. Imported palm trees waved hypnotically in the breeze and the tune playing over the speakers switched to "Don't Worry, Be Happy." A scene carefully crafted to make people leave their problems behind on the mainland. I had to let the island work its magic.

I had better things to dwell on than rude bartenders. Like how I was going to go about this whole no-rules thing. Breaking the rules required a test subject. I scanned the guys at the bar. I needed someone attractive—both for my own sake and for the sake of maybe sneaking a picture or two onto our social media to generate some interest for the upcoming season—and preferably someone who would stick around for the next couple weeks, to provide a decent foundation for some content. With any luck, he'd be begging to get away by the time this vacation was over, and then boom, I'd have the next great cautionary tale to feed to our listeners.

Unfortunately, pickings at the bar were looking pretty slim at the moment.

"Did you order my beer for me?" a deep voice asked, so close that his breath tickled my ear, and I jumped out of my skin.

"Don't *do* that," I snapped, though I was mostly relieved to find it was Declan standing behind me, and not a stranger. "And no, I did not order your beer. One, I don't play waitress for any man, and two, if I was going to play waitress, it wouldn't be for you."

"Ouch." He shouldered his way up to the counter next to me, so that we were squeezed between strangers, our bare arms pressed together. He raised a finger to get the bartender's attention. "Pacífico, please."

She didn't bother questioning *him* about the tab. With your-wish-is-my-command efficiency, she stooped down to the mini fridge, pulled out a beer, popped the top, and slid it over before she bothered finishing my margarita. I pressed my lips together. The treatment shouldn't have come as a surprise, at this point, but that didn't mean I wasn't a little annoyed by it.

"Who would it be, then?" Declan asked.

"What?" I turned. My face was too close to his—the sort of uncomfortable closeness where you noticed odd details you didn't mean to be noticing. I could have counted his eyelashes. They were a dark blondish color, different from the vibrantly red hair on his head, and they framed curious hazel eyes that skittered over my face before he turned back to the bar. He pressed the bottle to his lips.

"The man you would play waitress for," he said after a minute. "Who is it?"

I wasn't entirely sure what I was going to say, but before I was able to conjure something up, the bartender delivered my margarita. She'd forgotten the salt around the rim and it looked a bit watered down, but it was a convenient excuse to look anywhere but Declan's face. "No one," I said finally.

Lowering his beer bottle and licking his lips, he ventured, "Lucas Montpelier?"

I barked a laugh. "No. The whole fuckboy thing doesn't really do it for me."

"Oh, come on. Like you'd pass up the publicity."

I sucked on my margarita and stared out at the water. There were no waves on this side of the island. Just calm, crystalline water gently lapping the shore. A handful of private boats bobbed beyond the buoys. "What are you implying?" I asked, the paper straw already dissolving in my mouth.

"I'm implying," he said slyly, "that you have a reputation."

I nearly choked on the straw, and turned to glare at him. "Are you slut-shaming me?"

"What? No." He pulled an incredulous frown that suggested slut-shaming was nowhere in his wheelhouse, something I had a hard time believing. "I'm talking about your podcast."

"What about it?"

"Just, you know." He shrugged, which made our shoulders rub together. "I know how you internet types get. Always looking for the next way to promote yourselves."

I snorted. "At least us 'internet types' are technologically literate. You realize jobs will Google you, right? Not having social media is the definition of a red flag."

He gave me a funny look. "You tried to look me up."

I plastered on a smarmy smile, even as I was inwardly screaming at myself for bringing this up. "It's called hate-stalking. You'd know all about that, if you weren't too busy living in the Dark Ages."

He shook his head, the shadow of a smile on his face. "I know enough about technology to get by, I promise. That's not what I was getting at."

"Right. You were explaining how I'll do anything for the 'gram."

"Is that an actual thing that people say?" he asked. "Does anyone really call it the 'gram?"

"No one with a shred of dignity."

"Which you obviously have. In spades."

"I appreciate you recognizing that." Somewhere in this conversation, sincerity had crept into my smile—I wasn't quite forcing it anymore. Maybe that was the alcohol, or maybe the island was working its magic. "So, what's this mystery job where they don't expect you to know what a 'Facebook' is? Let me guess: you're a blacksmith. Wait, no"—I snapped my fingers—"I've got it. You're a wizard."

He narrowed his eyes. "Was that supposed to be a Ron Weas-ley joke?"

I rested my chin on my fist and batted innocent eyes at him, stirring my margarita with the soggy straw. "It's whatever you like."

He broke eye contact, looking down at the bar and laughing under his breath. There was a touch of color in his cheeks that I was almost certain had nothing to do with a sunburn. Were we flirting? I wasn't sure what that would look like. But it was by far the longest conversation we'd ever had, and I was actually enjoy-ing it. That had to count for something.

"I'm a mechanical engineer. I work at JPL."

My eyebrows shot upward. "What, like NASA?" That was what JPL usually referred to: the Jet Propulsion Laboratory tucked into the foothills in La Cañada Flintridge. As in, the people who kept putting rovers on Mars.

He withheld a smile, but his dimple gave him away. "Guess I'm more than just a pretty face."

Oh my God. We *were* flirting.

I pinched my straw between my fingers and took another sip, sizing him up. He wasn't wrong about the pretty face thing—he was easier on the eyes than I remembered. Enough so that I wouldn't mind breaking a rule or two. And just like that, the idea started to fall into place. We'd be spending more than enough time together over the course of the next two weeks. It would be easy to slip him into a few pictures for my socials under the guise of various wedding events. The question that remained, then, was whether he'd go for it.

As though he'd read my thoughts, he gestured vaguely with his beer and asked, "And what about you, what's up with all those rules for breaking up, or whatever?"

"Breaking hearts," I corrected him, plucking the lime from my drink.

He arched a brow as he watched me bring the lime to my lips and suck on it. "Broken many lately?"

"I don't kiss and tell."

"Considering you run a podcast about it, I have a feeling you do tell."

"Touché." My drink was nearly empty. I tossed the lime rind onto a napkin and fidgeted with the stem of the glass, twirling it on its coaster. "I'm on a heart-breaking hiatus." It was an answer, but it wasn't an explanation. There was no reason for him to know any more than that. He didn't need to know about the ten-month dry spell, or the plan to abandon the rules.

But I seemed to have piqued his interest anyway. He folded his arms on the bar. Like he wanted to call attention to how nice the curve of his forearms was. I followed the dusting of golden-red hair and the freckles that trailed to his wrist, where they were abruptly cut off by the worn leather band of an Apple Watch. "Seeing someone?"

"No," I said, maybe too quickly, my eyes cutting up to his face. But I might as well go for it. "Why? Are you interested?"

He breathed a laugh. "I can tell you what I'm not interested in," he said, pushing off the bar and grabbing his beer. He tipped it at me in a wordless *cheers*. "Being another anecdote on that show of yours."

With that, he turned to leave. The shift caught me so off guard that for a moment, I only stared after him, my mouth slightly agape. I didn't understand why, but he was pulling away like a wave pulling back from the shore—too swift and decisive to give me enough time to react, to prevent this conversation getting swept off in the current. "What if I promised you wouldn't be?" I couldn't promise that; it just slipped out, but I'd say whatever it took if it meant getting my story.

He turned and walked backwards, his shoes crunching on

fallen dates from a nearby tree. "I wouldn't believe you." Smiling, he spun back around and headed toward the cabana.

Embarrassment creeping over me, I cast a furtive glance at the people seated around the bar, but they didn't seem to be paying any attention. I didn't understand what had just happened. Maybe I'd done something to put him off. Maybe I had bits of lime in my teeth. I ran my tongue over them, but nothing *felt* out of place. Which meant I must have said something wrong. He didn't *believe* me? Well, fair was fair, considering I'd been lying through my teeth, but I didn't expect him to call me on it.

I pushed my empty margarita glass forward to indicate that I'd finished with it. I could easily redirect my efforts elsewhere. Half an hour ago, Declan wouldn't have so much as crossed my mind as an option—well, that wasn't true, considering the completely involuntary thoughts I'd had yesterday after our exchange in the hall, but that wasn't important. I hadn't even run the idea past Jo yet. Still, I couldn't shake the nagging feeling that something about his reaction was worth investigating further. It wasn't the reaction I was used to, and that made things interesting. Interesting was good.

Shrugging it off, I flagged down the bartender to order a tequila shot.

* * *

From: Miriam Casitas (miriam.casitas@strawberriesintimates
.com)
To: Jo Hernandez (jo@sevenrulespodcast.com)
Date: Jul 16, 8:13 AM
Subject: Our Partnership

Hi Jo,

Congratulations on your recent engagement. On behalf of our
team at S&C, I'd like to wish you success and happiness in this
new adventure. Please keep us in mind for your wedding night
apparel.

News has reached us of yesterday's Patreon post and your
potential rebrand. While S&C respects your decision to take
the podcast in a new direction, it's unclear to us whether our
mission to empower women to embrace their sexuality will
continue to align with your message. With that in mind, we've
decided to put our partnership with Seven Rules on hold for the
time being.

We hope this is not goodbye and that we will find a way to
work together in the near future.

Best,
Miriam Casitas
Social Media Coordinator
Strawberries & Cream Intimate Apparel

CHAPTER

7

I woke the next morning to a throbbing headache and a series of texts from Jo.

> **Jo:** Email from S&C this morning

> **Jo:** They're not happy

Below was a screenshot of an email from the lingerie brand we'd partnered with during Season Six. Their social media coordinator, a cheerful-looking woman named Miriam who I'd only seen in the headshot in her signature (higher resolution viewable on LinkedIn), was always a piece of passive-aggressive work, but this email took the cake. I made myself a mug of dark roast before stepping out onto the balcony. Already the sun had seared through the early-morning haze, promising warm weather. A few sips of coffee later and I was awake enough to text Jo back.

> **Margo:** I like the part where she's trying to sell you bridal lingerie while also firing us

> **Jo:** You're not worried?

I was a little worried. Worried that this was the harbinger of a coming trend—long-held alliances crumbling in the wake of our brand becoming a bit muddled, but I kept those concerns to myself.

> **Margo:** There will always be other sponsors. Preferably ones who aren't interested in policing our Patreon posts.

> **Jo:** You're probably right. Just freaking out I guess

> **Jo:** Wondering if this is my fault

I started to type *It's not your fault,* but thought better of it. It was as much the fault of the wedding as it was the Patreon post, if Miriam's strategically timed congratulations were any indication, and that wasn't a comforting thought. As much as I wanted to support Jo in her pursuit of whatever she thought would make her happy, I couldn't lie and pretend that her engagement hadn't shaken the foundations of everything we had built.

So instead, I typed:

> **Margo:** Don't think too far into it. Miriam's a corporate robot.

> **Margo:** Speaking of the Patreon post

> **Margo:** I have a tentative test subject in mind for Season Seven, but I wanted to run it by you first

> **Jo:** OOOHHH spill

Margo: So I know this is going to sound weird

Margo: But you can't mention anything to Peter.

Jo: Omg just tell me

Margo: I was thinking maybe Declan?

The dots indicated she was typing, then disappeared again. After a few seconds, she started typing again, and I waited with bated breath.

After the exchange with Declan at the bar, I'd downed a couple of tequila shots and gone back to the cabana, but we hadn't spoken for the rest of the afternoon. I'd kept an eye out for other options, but it was tricky—despite serving alcohol, the private beach wasn't a bar in the traditional sense, and it was frequented more by couples and vacationing families than it was single men in their mid-twenties. I considered Lucas as an alternative, but I got the vibe there was more to his history with Autumn than she was letting on, and he wasn't my type anyway. Declan was a comfortable middle ground: attractive enough that I wouldn't mind spending time with him, but I also wouldn't feel guilty about pulling one over on him, when it came down to it.

And I was curious. For reasons I wasn't quite able to articulate, so I hoped Jo wouldn't ask.

While I waited, I slipped back inside to refill my coffee mug. The coffee machine was gurgling and Jo was still typing her reply when my screen was overtaken by an incoming call from Mom. I slid to answer, wedging the phone between my ear and my shoulder so that my hands were free to pour the coffee and stir in some cream and sugar. "Hey."

"There she is," came her familiar, cheery voice. "I've been try-ing to get ahold of you. I left you five voicemails."

Mom knew how to text and frequently used her smartphone to browse cat videos on YouTube or Google her favorite celebri-ties, but for some reason, she failed to understand that I could *see* she had left me voicemails. "I know, I got the notifications. Sorry. We're still settling in. Things have been . . . well, stressful, I guess you could say," I finished half-heartedly, mind still on the email from our sponsor and the podcast and the *dot dot dot* of Jo typing her reply.

"At least you're helping your best friend." Jo and I had been friends so long, my mom had practically adopted her. So natu-rally, Mom was invited to the wedding, but that was still almost two weeks away. "Imagine if she didn't have you. It'd probably be worse."

I didn't need to tell my mom that the stressful stuff has very little to do with the wedding. "It would probably be exactly the same, considering Jo is the most organized person on the planet and I am obviously not."

"You're plenty good at organizing things. You juggled two jobs and were paying half the bills when you were only eighteen. How many of your friends can say that?"

I couldn't speak for all these friends she was imagining I had, but there was a note of sadness in her voice when *she* said it. Like she believed I'd missed out on some fundamental part of life in the process. *You grew up too fast*—that was what she always told me, and it wasn't because of my dating habits, or the way I dressed, or the people I hung around. It was because I'd stepped up when my mom had no one, and she thought that was a bad thing. A shortcoming. That it meant she'd somehow failed as a mother. I preferred to think it meant I'd succeeded as a daughter.

"Speaking of jobs," Mom segued, "how are things with the podcast?"

Jo's text pinged in my ear, and I pulled the phone away to glance at it.

> **Jo:** What are you planning to wear today? I wanna make sure we get some pics for . . .

The message preview cut off there. I frowned at it. Okay, so she was changing the subject. A bit weird, but it could wait. I returned the phone to my ear. "I'm on vacation. Do we have to talk about work before noon?" I asked. I wasn't eager to share the news about our partnership with S&C, all things considered. Mom knew a fair amount of the work that went into running the podcast, and she was always very insistent that there had to be something else out there. Something that placed less pressure on me—this magical, imaginary job that would allow me to just be . . . me. It was a nice thought. The sort of thing a parent wanted for their kid. But I had a decent thing already going, and I couldn't just throw that away on the off chance I might find something better.

"I keep telling you, you have the voice for radio. I think that's why your podcast has done so well. And with your degree in music, there's got to be something else out there."

"And when was the last time you listened to the radio, Mom?"

"Since the invention of Bluetooth and phones with music on them, probably never."

"Need I say more?" I finished dumping sugar into my coffee and returned to the balcony. Below, Avalon was waking up. Golf carts puttered to life and bicycles rang their bells at pedestrians before cutting through intersections. The first ferry of the morning was already parked out on the water, bussing in a fresh load of visitors.

"Not everyone has technologically savvy parents, you know." There was a pregnant pause after the plural *parents*. They were two separate parental entities, and had been for years, but the hurt lingered. "Have you talked to your dad recently?"

"Not since Father's Day."

My mom and I had our weekly calls, but I made it a point to only call *him* on major holidays, ever since he'd moved to Florida with his girlfriend, leaving a whole mess of shit in his wake. Including the old Chevy pickup I was stuck driving for the time being. My own car—the run-down Honda I'd bought myself at seventeen with money from lifeguarding—got smushed like a tin can my first week living in NoHo. The stop-and-go traffic on the 101 interchange was no joke. They stopped, I goed, and suddenly I was sandwiched between a brand-new Challenger and some old lady driving a Kia Soul.

I'd been stashing some money here and there to buy something else, but secretly, I kept hoping we'd get offered some unprecedented sponsorship by Hyundai or Volkswagen or something. So far, no luck.

"Speaking of people who have been wronged by cheaters," I said, eager to change the subject, "you never did guess who's going to be at the wedding."

"Well, now you've got me worried."

"Tony Montpelier. And his son's going to be in the wedding. I met him yesterday."

Mom tried to play it cool, but with a minimal social life of her own this past decade, she'd formed a habit of getting way too wrapped up in celebrity drama. I found myself answering questions about how they knew Peter's family and whether Tony would be coming with a plus-one and speculating on whether or not L. Mont *really* got his suits tailored by the same bespoke clothier that made a custom suit for Timothée Chalamet to wear to the last Oscars.

It wasn't long until the conversation trailed off and we hung up with promises of talking again before the wedding. I took another sip of my coffee before speaking into the Notes app on my phone. "Day two without rules." The words materialized on screen and I mulled over what to say next. Since we started the podcast, I'd developed a habit of talking into my phone. I would've liked to compare them to diary entries—maybe then, they'd have felt less clinical—but they were more like bullet points. It started as a way of reminding myself of stories or particularly brilliant thoughts I wanted to share next episode, but it quickly turned into this weird compartmentalization thing. If I couldn't talk to Jo or my mom about something, I could at least talk to Siri.

But the issue was, I didn't really know what to say at the moment. I wasn't sure how to voice my concerns about Jo's wedding and all the muddled implications for the future, and I didn't have any fun anecdotes or witticisms to jot down for the podcast. Yesterday was technically my first day without the rules, but it hadn't felt much different from any other day—which didn't make for very engaging content. The conversation with Declan at the bar was the only interaction of any interest and I wasn't even sure what had happened there.

I switched over to my browser and started to search *what does it mean when a guy flirts with you but doesn't follow through*, but I stopped in the middle of typing to scoff at myself. What was I doing? I was the one who ran a podcast about dating. I shouldn't need to turn to questionable advice on Reddit for help. "Create a daily reminder for the next two weeks," I said to my phone without really thinking. "Do not let the thing with Declan get under your skin."

As though I'd manifested him—*Betelgeuse, Betelgeuse, Betelgeuse*—the glass door on the neighboring balcony slid open, and in my early-morning brain fog, I was too slow to react.

He seemed to do a double take when he found me on the balcony. "Morning," he said uncertainly, hesitating with one foot in the door like he might turn back inside. "Did I just hear my name?" He was wearing one of the plush hotel robes, but he hadn't bothered to tie it. I caught a glimpse of well-toned stomach and coppery hair that trailed down to black boxer briefs before I managed to collect myself, eyes snapping back to his face. He didn't seem to have noticed.

"I was just voicing my concerns to Siri about your dermatological health in this weather," I said with an airy wave at the wide blue sky. "You know, with your complexion. What sunscreen are you using? SPF 500?"

Like me, it appeared he had stepped outside to enjoy his coffee. Or so the unsuspecting observer might think, but I knew better. First, I was fairly certain that Declan Walsh was incapable of enjoying anything that did not involve the emotional torment of people or perhaps small animals. Second, he had plainly been listening to me before he even opened the door, waiting for the opportune moment to interrupt my morning. I was thankful I hadn't voiced much beyond my surface-level frustrations.

He smiled faintly. "You were thinking about me. How sweet."

"Of course. Too many people vastly underestimate the importance of skin care."

"What if I told you I have a five-step routine?" He gestured over his shoulder with a thumb, back into his room. "I just finished a face mask five minutes ago."

"I wouldn't believe you."

I couldn't tell whether he recognized his own words from yesterday. He tore his eyes away from me and rolled his shoulders under the guise of morning stretches, but the movement opened his robe just a touch wider, drawing my attention to things I had no reason to be looking at, like the way his boxers hugged his thighs. He'd obviously hit the gym a few times since high school. "Excited for today?" he asked. I shot him a questioning look. "You know, the zipline thing."

"Zipline thing," I repeated. "What zipline thing?"

He took his dear, sweet time sipping his coffee before he answered. "Peter said they were planning for us to all go ziplining today. Didn't Jo mention it?"

I didn't love how smug he sounded, but whatever his reason for sounding that way, I didn't particularly care. This new revelation took precedence over whatever Declan was or wasn't trying to do. "Excuse me," I said, jumping to my feet so quick that the cold dregs of my coffee sloshed around the mug, threatening to spill over.

"Did I say something wrong?" he called, but I was already slipping inside and shutting the glass door behind me.

Jocelyn Hernandez ✅ @JoHo_in_NoHo · Jul 16
Super stoked to go ziplining today with @AvalonAdventureCo!! Thank you again to our sponsors @castawaycat for making all this happen. Pics coming soon!
💬 32 ⇄ 17 ❤️ 1.3k

Liv, Laugh, Love ✅ @LivHolistic · Jul 16
Replying to @7R4BHpodcast
So jealous! Hope I'm not missing out on ALL the fun 😄

Raquel O'Brien @raqyoursaqsoff · Jul 16
Replying to @7R4BHpodcast
Omg I could never. I'm terrified of heights. Can't wait to see the pics, though!!

Mar[Go] ✅ @margoanderson · Jul 16
😱

CHAPTER
8

After a short elevator ride and a few frantic knocks at Room 317, Jo opened the door. She was still in her pajamas, no makeup on and her black hair in a frazzled braid. She waved me inside. "Are you hungry? I ordered on Postmates from one of the local places. Wasn't feeling the whole fruit and pastry spread they had going downstairs."

I took a moment to gape at her room as I stepped inside and, she shut the door behind me. The bridal suite was an expansive luxury suite on the third floor. There was a wide modern living room with a cushy-looking sofa, a kitchenette, and—down the hall—a massive four-poster California King bed. French doors opened to a private patio overlooking the landscaped courtyard, which looked like a scene imported straight from a Tuscan village.

At the moment, the whole luxurious suite smelled like hot sauce and eggs. The coffee table hosted a paper bag and a few Styrofoam containers, and a yellow wrapper was unfolded on the glass, revealing a half-eaten breakfast burrito. My stomach churned. Nothing against breakfast burritos, but I was already queasy. "Not particularly," I said, as Jo sank cross-legged onto the couch and resumed her breakfast. "What's this I'm hearing about ziplining?"

"I told you we were ziplining today," she said through a mouthful of thick tortilla.

I remained standing. "No, you didn't."

She furrowed her brow. "I put it in the social media calendar."

"I'm not sure that qualifies as telling me," I pointed out. This was something that frustrated me about running the podcast, at times—the moments when we got so wrapped up in being business partners, we forgot to talk to each other like friends. Sometimes I wondered if Jo asking me to be her maid of honor was just another strategic decision. Would she have chosen someone else if we'd never gotten wrapped up in the podcast together?

That was silly. Of course she would have.

Jo sucked Tapatío off the side of her thumb. "Renee asked whether we'd be willing to do a promo shoot as part of their contract with the outdoorsy . . ." She seemed to forget what the business was supposed to be called and made a vague gesture like I could somehow fill in the blank for her. "The adventure company, or whatever, here on the island. I told her it wouldn't be a problem."

I folded my arms, mounting my defenses. Renee was the marketing director for Castaway Catalina, and she'd preferred to work almost exclusively with Jo through the various emails and phone calls. I'd taken the backseat in this whole arrangement. Which made sense, on one hand, considering it was Jo's wedding and not my own, but on the other hand, I was still an equal partner in the podcast, and I didn't appreciate being sidelined. "Why would you tell her that?"

"Because we're professionals." There was a pregnant pause. The end of Jo's burrito lay forgotten in its wrapper. "But I could see about canceling. If you want."

I chewed the inside of my cheek as I considered this. The email from the lingerie company was still fresh in my mind. Losing one sponsor I could live with, but a second sponsor within the same day? It was a risk I wasn't willing to take. Especially when this particular sponsor was so crucial to our plans for the next two weeks. "I'll go," I bit out. "If you tell me why you ignored my text earlier."

Her chewing slowed. "I didn't ignore it." She swallowed. "I mean, I read it."

"You didn't reply to it," I pointed out. "What, are you worried about Declan's feelings or something?"

"It's not that. It's just . . ." She picked at some melted cheese on the paper wrapper. "I feel a little funny about hiding the truth from Peter."

My eyebrows shot up. "I'm not sure what I'm doing is any of your fiancé's business."

"No," she said, hesitant. Then she nodded. "No, you're right. You have my approval." She twirled a hand like she was bestowing some great gift. "Proceed."

Not that I needed her approval, technically speaking. It wasn't like she was the one who was supposed to be breaking the rules for the sake of a story. The rules didn't really concern her, anymore; she'd as good as stuffed them into a shredder, leaving me to tape up the pieces. I gave her a sarcastic curtsy, adopting something that vaguely resembled an English accent. "Thank you, Your Majesty."

"I swear to God, if you do one of your voices during the maid of honor speech, I'll unalive you with the cake knife."

I cracked a smile, though it felt a bit wan, thinking about the day looming ahead of me. "No promises."

* * *

I had never seen so much as a picture of Renee Dunkirk, but she looked nothing like I was expecting. I'd been imagining a real hardline corporate type—Miriam from S&C on steroids, the sort that browsed Upwork for fun—but instead I was greeted by a cheerful woman with sunburned cheeks and khaki shorts that would've made the Crocodile Hunter jealous.

"Pleasure to finally meet you all in person," she said, tucking a yellow notepad under her arm to offer us each a rough handshake in turn. "You know, I have to admit, when I first reached out about this whole promotional thing, I had something a bit smaller in mind." She laughed heartily as she swept the notepad back into her hand and scribbled something with a pen. "Look where we are now."

I'd had something smaller in mind, too—preferably something that didn't involve soaring six hundred feet over Catalina with nothing but a few hooks and cables to prevent me plummeting to my doom, but here we were. I didn't have a clear view of the zipline itself from the lawn that abutted the arid cliffs in Descanso Bay, but if the sharp incline in the hills was any indication, things weren't looking promising.

"And you must be Peter," Renee continued as she beckoned us over to a sort of training grounds, where a few employees were waiting in orange safety helmets and harnesses to give us the rundown. A photographer stood at the ready. "Lucky man, to have captured such an elusive lady."

"The luckiest in the world," Peter agreed, with a starry-eyed look at Jo. She nestled herself under his arm.

"And you," Renee said, looking up from her notes, "I don't think I caught your name."

Lucas had elected to get a two-hour massage rather than join us for ziplining, and Autumn was busy filming her next vlog, which meant Renee could only be talking to one person. Declan was hovering behind us, like he hoped to put as much distance between himself and the whole sponsored side of things as possible. He was just along for the ride. Quite literally, on this particular occasion.

"Oh." He obviously hadn't expected to be acknowledged, but he stepped forward and gave Renee a firm handshake. "Declan Walsh."

"Boyfriend?" Renee asked, and it took me a second to register that she wasn't talking to Declan anymore. She was looking at me, and I didn't miss the hungry curiosity behind it, as though she was wondering whether I was next on the menu—two steps from being gobbled up by the normalcy of commitment, and all the potential publicity that would come with it.

"No," I said firmly. "Just a—" I wasn't sure *friend* was the right word, so I didn't finish the sentence, glancing at Declan. He raised his eyebrows, but otherwise didn't acknowledge the brief but awkward pause.

"He's the best man," Jo jumped in to clarify. "But we all went to high school together."

Renee gave him a quick, assessing look. Declan was more clothed than I'd seen him earlier, though the thin, breathable fabric of his white T-shirt and the cut of his jeans only did a slightly better job of concealing his physique. "Has anyone ever told you that you look like Prince Harry?"

A giggle burst out of me. It was more out of surprise than anything, and I tried to stifle it behind my hand, but everyone looked at me anyway. "Sorry," I said, but offered no further explanation because I didn't really have one.

Declan ran a hand through his hair, obviously self-conscious. "Among other comparisons."

"You have a good face for ad work," Renee continued, as though my interruption had never happened. "Handsome, but approachable." She clicked her pen absently, then turned to the photographer. "Get him in a few pictures for the website."

Declan's face went slack, but Renee didn't seem to have noticed. I was still biting back a grin—sure to be wiped off my face the second they hauled us to the top of the zipline course, but I was going to enjoy it while it lasted—as Renee introduced us to our tour guides.

"Brandon and Yesenia here are going to get you all geared up and walk you through a quick training course and then they'll be taking you up to the ziplines. Rory will be taking pictures the whole time, so try to keep that in mind as far as what you're doing with your face, posture, et cetera." Rory had a ponytail and a camera around his neck that looked like it might've been too heavy for his tiny head. He waved.

"Any last-minute questions?" Renee asked. When no one said anything, she gave us a curt nod. "Then I'll see you all at the bottom."

* * *

The leg straps of the ziplining harness were chafing my inner thighs by the time we descended the wooden stairs to the first platform. The course was built several hundred feet into the hillside above the bay, which was looking a lot less like a hill and more like a mountain from my current vantage point. I kept as far behind the guides as I could get away with, hoping against hope to delay the inevitable. Good thing I skipped breakfast this morning. My eyes were glued to the stairs, the wood dry and creaky beneath the unforgiving sun. Coffee sloshed around in my stomach with every step.

Declan trailed behind me. "Does that happen often?" he asked.

I turned to look at him, and the world rocked on its axis. It felt like the stairs might tilt right out from under me. My hand tightened on the rough wood banister, splinters be damned. "What?"

"People asking about—" he broke off. There was that reddish color in his cheeks again. "Ah, maybe I'm reading too far into things, but I kind of got the impression that—"

"That Renee thought we were dating?" I finished for him.

He confirmed with a curt incline of his head, orange helmet wobbling with the motion. The helmets didn't do us any favors (and I was pretty sure they wouldn't save us, if the line snapped and we plunged six hundred feet to the trees below), but he somehow managed to look good. Even though it clashed majorly with his hair. "It seems like it would get old, people sticking their nose in your business."

"It didn't happen as much before." Although I probably would've welcomed the attempt at conversation under different circumstances, I was having a hard time focusing right now. Any attempts at flirting would have to wait until I was back on solid ground.

"Before," Declan repeated after a beat, and I realized he was waiting for me to elaborate.

"Before the podcast got big." I was distracted as we arrived at the small platform and jostled around to find our own space. Jo offered to go first. It should have been a relief, but I realized now that it might've been smarter to go first and get it over with. The anticipation was only making me antsy. I leaned to sneak a peek over the railing. Greenish-gold grass sloped down the mountainside, disappearing into the tops of trees that looked like tiny broccoli florets in the gully below. The line was strung between hills—a long cable that sagged beneath the weight of the first guide as he zipped ahead to the platform in the distance, where he would wait to ensure we all had a safe landing.

My stomach did a backflip.

Declan leaned against the wood railing beside me, folding his arms. Lightheaded and dazed in the harsh sun, I found myself staring at the sheen of sunscreen on his forearms, the way the light curved with the muscle. "I guess it was nosy of me to ask," he said, apparently interpreting my silence as somehow directed at him. He cast me a sideways glance, gauging my reaction. "Sorry."

"Don't worry about it." The guide below gave a signal, and Jo eased off the platform. The shutter on the camera clicked rapid-fire, the same sound as shuffling a deck of cards.

Peter followed. As soon as he landed on the platform a thousand yards below, the guide named Yesenia set her sights on us. "Next up."

I made no motion to step forward. Declan swept a hand in front of me. "Ladies first."

What had I thought earlier about getting it over with? I'd forgotten already. "Oh, no, it's fine." I stepped backward, away from the zipline. "I'm not exactly a lady."

"Don't be stupid." One of his hands found the small of my back and eased me toward the launch point. My heart thrashed around in my chest like it was trying to escape. "She'll go first," he told the guide before checking in with me. "Right?"

Unable to get the words out for fear of vomiting, I only nodded.

Yesenia buckled me in and gave me a few last-minute tips that my brain wasn't capable of processing at the moment. My knuckles were milk-white on the handhold. Declan had stepped back to let her work, but it felt like his handprint was branded into my back, red-hot.

"Got it?" Yesenia asked when she'd finished.

"Yes," I lied, blood rushing in my ears. I tugged one of the leg straps down my thigh subconsciously. It felt like a rubber band around a water balloon. Why had I chosen to wear shorts today? It had seemed like an appropriate choice, given the heat, but that was before I had considered the logistics of ziplining.

"Then whenever you're ready."

There was an expectant pause. I was acutely aware of everyone watching me. Declan, Yesenia, Rory the Photographer. Probably judging the sweat that had pooled along my backside, or the way all the color had drained from my face. The camera's shutter winked somewhere in the periphery.

But I wasn't moving.

My feet remained firmly on the platform. If I stood there long enough, maybe they'd grow roots, and then no one could force me to move, ever. Except it was very hot standing still like this, the sun beating down on the wooden platform without the mercy of trees or a canopy to shade us. I removed a shaky hand from the handhold to wipe a bead of sweat from my brow and the movement made the handle go lopsided; I gripped it again, but now my hand felt sweaty. I couldn't decide if I should let go again to wipe it on my shorts.

"Are you . . ." Declan was standing a few feet back, but his forehead creased in a frown as he studied me. "Scared of heights, or something?"

"No," I lied again. "I'm just not a huge fan of trusting"—I gestured vaguely at the contraption overhead, holding my life in its carabiners and pulleys—"all that."

"It looks safe enough." He leaned in to inspect the specifics. He smelled good, but in that simple, everyday sort of way. I didn't think the pine scent was cologne after all, now that I was paying attention—it was more like pine-scented soap mingling with sunscreen and maybe a hint of sweat. "Though the regulations for building these things are pretty sporadic." I shot him a murderous look and he added, "It'll be over before you know it. And accidents are statistically pretty rare. Well, kind of rare. It's slightly less dangerous than skydiving, anyway."

"Appreciate the reassurance," I muttered. Trust a former STEM major to mansplain the dangers of ziplining.

"Sir, I'm going to have to ask you to step back from the launch point until it's your turn," Yesenia interjected.

Declan obliged, watching me closely. "You could still back out, you know."

"I know." Aside from the small measure of embarrassment I would feel chickening out at the last second, it seemed like the easier option. But I wasn't sure I liked the idea of taking the easy way out with everyone watching. So I steeled myself, lowering my weight into the harness. "Wish me luck."

Before anyone had a chance to discourage me, I stepped off the platform. The line bowed ever so slightly and my stomach dipped with it, and for one wild moment I thought I was falling. But then it bounced back, adjusting to the weight, as though to reassure me that it had me. My feet dangled high above the gully. I tightened my grip on the handholds as the pulley eased forward. There was no going back now. A quick glance over my shoulder informed me that I was already a couple yards from the platform, though it was taking a few seconds for me to pick up speed.

My heart was beating, but the adrenaline had taken over and it was no longer the nauseating pounding, but instead a tiny, rhythmic blip—my own personal vitals monitor, reminding me that I was alive, that I hadn't flatlined. The world blurred, but at the same time, the things I focused on were sharpened somehow: the rustle of the leaves on the trees below; the laces on my tennis shoes, hundreds of feet above them. Wind rushed in my ears and my stomach swooped like the wind was somehow in there, too, and I let out a noise that was halfway between a laugh and a squeal. I had taken the plunge—gone all in, enjoying the high despite the risks. And when my feet landed on the solid wood planks of the second platform, I was surprised to discover that I was okay with doing it again.

From: Renee Dunkirk (renee@castawaycatalina.com)
To: Jo Hernandez (jo@sevenrulespodcast.com)
CC: Margo Anderson (go@sevenrulespodcast.com)
Date: Jul 16, 5:16 PM
Subject: Pictures

Good evening,

Sorry to bother you after hours—I'm sure you're eager to celebrate and enjoy your vacation—but I thought you might like to review some of the photos we took today and maybe share to your own social media pages. The images are attached in a zip file for your perusal. Per our friends at Avalon Adventure Co., it *would be nice if you could include a tag in the image, and please refrain from using excessive filters or significantly altering the color. Minor touch-ups are fine.*

Talk soon.

Cheers,
Renee

CHAPTER

9

The pictures were about as unflattering as I had expected: messy and windswept, my facial expressions suggesting that I was unaware that my picture was being taken, and not in a fun, candid way. Rory had captured a couple shots of Declan leaning over me to inspect the pulley system, but they were awkward, and his face was too visible—not the sexy, mysterious sort of pictures I needed to generate a hint of drama for Season Seven. Instead, I downloaded one of just me with my back to the camera and shared it to my Instagram as we marched back to the hotel after a hearty dinner of chips and salsa and shrimp fajitas. *Sometimes you have to step outside of your comfort zone*, I captioned, tagging @AvalonAdventureCo in the bottom left corner of the picture. Renee's email had made it sound like a suggestion, but I knew better. Nothing was ever a suggestion when it came to sponsors; it was a contractual obligation.

Chatter bounced off the polished tile floors in the lobby as our group crossed to the elevators, where a small queue had formed. A flock of visitors had arrived on the last ferry of the evening. We joined the throng, too full from dinner and sleepy from the heat and the day's excitement to climb the stairs.

When I pocketed my phone, my eyes caught on Declan's hazel ones and the corner of his mouth hitched up. Not quite a smile, but an acknowledgment of sorts. He'd seemed friendly enough today, with his attempted pep talk—which had kind of had the opposite effect, but still, the intentions were there. But I still didn't have a good grasp on whether he was interested. As soon as he'd looked at me, he was back to looking at his watch.

What was wrong with me? I was supposed to be good at roping guys in. Maybe ten months without any hookups had left me a bit rusty. The only thing that seemed to get me much of anywhere was talking, so I sucked in a breath with a mind toward making casual conversation, though I hadn't figured out what that conversation was going to be yet.

"Was wondering when you'd get back," a familiar voice interjected.

A pretty girl with olive skin and a nose ring approached us, carrying a Hydro Flask covered in stickers that was almost guaranteed to be filled with cheap alcohol.

"Livyyy!" Jo squealed, flying to hug her. "Oh my God, you're early. When did you get here?"

"A couple hours ago. I've been hanging around the bar. The manager mentioned that most of your party was out for some adventure thing today," Liv explained as she extracted herself from the hug. "I got home a day early, and my things were mostly all still packed, so I figured I'd see if I could catch an earlier ferry and surprise you."

I cast a sideways glance at Declan, curious to see whether he was paying any attention to Liv. Maybe I simply wasn't his type. He'd said that thing a couple days ago down at the docks about me not changing much since high school, and I definitely wasn't his type back then. But no—he wasn't paying attention to Liv either, his attention still glued to his watch. I exhaled through my nose. I had no clue how to read this guy.

"How was the convention?" Jo was asking. "Did you find a new supplier?"

"A few potential candidates. There's this one grower that is promising entirely non-GMO product, but I'm a bit skeptical." After a quick hello to Peter, Liv turned to me. "You're looking good," she said as she pulled me into a sideways hug. "Love the 'fit. Very beachy." She indicated my cutoff shorts, which failed to conceal my thighs, rubbed raw by the ziplining harness. I had scabby knees from the fall outside the restaurant bathroom a couple nights ago and now I had chafed thighs to match; at the rate I was going, might as well work on a sunburn and a couple bruises to really round out the look.

"You, too," I said. Liv always dressed like she'd just crawled out of a thrift store. Her makeup had this effortless, slept-in thing going for it, and she'd bought a new opal nose ring since the aquarium incident.

"We'll have to coordinate a day to sit down and work on some of the bachelorette party deets. I have a few ideas." She shot me a conspiratorial wink. "That is, if you're not totally booked up."

"My schedule is wide open." I was grateful for any input. I had loaded my suitcase with more penis-shaped party favors than I could justify (and was grateful that no one on the ferry bothered to inspect luggage), but my experience on Catalina was mostly limited to kid stuff: arcades and mini-golf. And the one summer I had lifeguarded here, but that was at a camp in Two Harbors on the opposite side of the island. "Except for the day of the wedding, of course."

"And a couple of the promo shoots," Jo reminded me.

"Those, too."

The elevator dinged and the last of the newcomers shuffled inside with their luggage, which left only us waiting in the lobby. It wasn't until we were alone that Liv seemed to register that Declan was part of our group. He seemed to have a way of shrinking into the background. "Which side are you?" she asked. "Bride? Groom? Plus-one?"

He looked up from his watch and introduced himself with a brief explanation of how he knew Peter, a story about helping with math homework that I hadn't heard before. I guess I'd never really wondered how they came to be friends—people like them just *were*, these sort of one-dimensional figures in my head, but it was strange now listening to him introduce himself to people. In high school, we'd never been introduced, strictly speaking. He'd just sort of appeared, and within weeks, his reputation spoke for itself. I remembered a scrawny teenager who was all too eager to be the center of attention, but it was hard to tell whether that guy had ever been real or if he was only a figment of my imagination. But people changed. I had changed plenty, so it stood to reason that he had changed as well.

Liv squinted at him. "By any chance, are you related to anyone named Meredith? Because you guys look super alike. Red hair, owns the little clothing boutique down in Escondido?"

"Ah, no," Declan said, with a long-suffering look. "Contrary to popular belief, I am not related to everyone in the world with red hair."

"That's what you think." She swung her little hemp backpack around to extract her phone and started swiping. "Hold on, I'm going to show you a picture."

I caught his eye and he quirked a brow as he waited for her to pull up the picture. I smiled and shrugged. Liv was one of those people you could almost mistake for passive-aggressive, if she weren't so laid-back about everything. Despite her quirks, I'd always liked her, but a part of me also envied how carefree she was. That ability to stumble through life without ever stopping to worry what anyone else thought. Maybe it was all the weed.

She shoved the phone in his face. "See?" She turned the screen back toward herself and held it up to compare to his face. "It's like someone ran your picture through one of those gender-swap apps."

"She's got red hair, all right," he said without much enthusiasm. His indifference cemented my earlier assessment—he wasn't interested in Liv, but his friendliness didn't necessarily mean he was interested in me, either. I needed to make some sort of move. Show my hand. But I'd need to be careful about it, because I couldn't let him think my own interest had anything to do with the podcast.

The elevator pinged to announce its return right as Liv was in the middle of trying to persuade us all to join her in the hotel bar for a drink.

"I don't know." Jo gave Peter a significant look. "We're pretty exhausted after today. I think maybe it's better if we head to bed for the night."

"It's only one drink. We could—oh." His eyes widened in realization. "Yeah, ziplining totally wiped me out."

After drinking yesterday, I was keen to space things out. And I was hoping to maybe talk to Declan outside our neighboring rooms, which seemed more likely if I went upstairs now as opposed to waiting. "Us, too," I said, without really thinking. Jo arched a brow, silently seeking some sort of confirmation, and I realized what it had sounded like. Embarrassment warmed my face. "Us meaning me. I'm going to bed. I can't speak for anyone else."

The rumors were going to write themselves at this rate, which was all fine and good, but I liked to control the narrative if I could help it. I wished someone would say something to change the subject or at least say good night, but the silence seemed to stretch longer than normal. Peter was still holding the elevator. I was almost scared to look at Declan, but my gaze darted to his without my brain fully complying. I wasn't sure if I should be relieved or embarrassed to find him withholding a laugh. His eyes glittered with amusement. "Margo's right. We should probably be getting to bed."

Right. So he ignored my blatant attempts at flirting, but he was more than happy to play along that we were already sleeping together. Because that made things a hell of a lot easier to figure out.

Whatever confusion my own comments had generated only deepened. I felt everyone's eyes on me, but I was too busy wanting to bury my face in my hands to register their expressions. After exchanging a few quick good nights with Liv, Peter withdrew his foot and the elevator doors slid shut. I didn't particularly want to look at anyone, but looking at my phone seemed like a pretty obvious avoidance tactic, so I pretended to be interested in picking at a loose thread in my shorts. My face was on fire. They could hike me back to the top of that mountain and use me as a lighthouse right about now.

We rode to the third floor where Jo and Peter disappeared down the hall—Jo with a pointed look over her shoulder that demanded I explain myself later—and then Declan and I were alone in the elevator. We were standing on opposite sides: me with my back against the railing, him inspecting the safety certification tucked into the plastic sheath above the buttons.

Okay, so maybe I was a bit rusty. Or maybe I just didn't know how to talk to him, stripped of my usual moves.

"They haven't had this thing inspected in three years," he said, pointing.

"Seems dangerous. People could get stuck in here." The words came out throaty, strangled by embarrassment. I cleared my throat. "Sorry about what I said down there. I was just thinking about the fact that our rooms are right next door, I didn't mean—"

"You're good." He moseyed over and leaned his back against the rail beside me. Closer than we needed to be. His arm brushed against mine, and it sent a jolt through me. Maybe I hadn't completely botched this. "I thought it was pretty funny, actually."

I didn't quite see which part was funny. "How so?"

"Did you see their faces? They looked like you just told them you're selling all your things and moving to Montana to be a cattle rancher." Which didn't sound like a bad idea at the moment. De-clan laughed at his own joke, but he got away with it because he was one of those people whose laughter lit up their whole face—crow's-feet crinkling the corners of eyes that threatened to be swal-lowed up by pure joy. "Especially that new chick. She had no clue what to say."

I couldn't help laughing myself, but more out of relief than anything. The elevator doors sprang open and we exited side by side. "Do you always get a kick out of uncomfortable situations?"

"Only when people insist on reuniting me with my long-lost cousins."

"So it *was* a picture of your cousin."

He tossed me a wry smile. "The world may never know." We ar-rived outside our respective—separate—rooms. "Well, good night," he said, unlocking his room with the keycard.

I hesitated. I had made a habit of *not* putting myself out on a limb because it was far too easy for someone else to leave you hanging there, feet dangling and feeling like a complete idiot. That was what the first rule of the podcast was all about: playing it safe. Holding all the cards and not sticking your neck out if you didn't have to. I hadn't asked a guy to hang out since probably the seventh grade.

But if today had taught me anything, it was that maybe I needed to learn to take a few risks. And if this whole no-rules thing was supposed to result in any actual content, it would help things along if I—you know—actually broke a rule or two. "What are you doing tomorrow?"

He paused with his hand on the door handle, obviously sur-prised. His eyebrows did something funny, but whatever it was, he quickly reined it in. "I was thinking of going for a hike," he said slowly, "but I'm open to suggestions."

It wasn't the sexiest of activities, if you asked me, but maybe that was a good thing. So long as I went along with whatever he already had planned, he couldn't suspect me of using him for the podcast. "I like hiking. Jo and I try to hike the trail in Griffith Park every other weekend. I could join you," I offered. "As long as you don't mind if I bring some sangria." Drinking every other day was acceptable while on vacation, I reasoned, and it was something of a ritual for me and Jo to take sangria on our hikes. Plus the calories and the workout canceled each other out, I was pretty sure. Nutrition was never my strong suit.

"Wouldn't it be better to bring water?" he asked, because nutrition probably *was* his strong suit, along with everything else that fell even a little bit under the STEM umbrella. "Or at least Gatorade, or something?"

"It's not like we're hiking Half Dome. How bad could it be?"

His forehead crinkled. "Whatever you say. Meet you here at . . ." He consulted his smartwatch, and it occurred to me that I had never seen a smartwatch on an actual human before. As glued to my phone as I often was, smartwatches struck me as kind of dorky. But he was hot, so I'd let it slide. "Let's say eight tomorrow?"

Eight a.m. sounded like my own personal hell. If people changed after high school, then maybe he'd turned into one of those fitness junkies who shoveled down a couple tablespoons of powdered pre-workout every morning before sunup. That would explain the physique. But I nodded anyway. "Sounds great."

And just like that, I'd broken Rule Number One.

Season One, Episode One—The First Rule
29 min 58 sec

Go: *Hello, all you lovely #SingleNotSeeking ladies, and welcome to* Seven Rules for Breaking Hearts. *You don't know us yet, but you're going to get to know us—*

Jo: *Perhaps a little too well.*

Go: [laughs] *To give you a quick little intro, my name is Margo, but you're all going to know me better as Go.*

Jo: *And I'm Jo.*

Go: *We're not anybody special, just two single gals who are tired of seeing our friends make the same mistakes over and over. Not everyone wants commitment, but society has so many ways of tricking us women into believing we need it, so we decided to create a few rules that women like us can live by. A sort of how-to guide for avoiding all the common pitfalls of modern dating.*

Jo: *And how you can make sure you're the one breaking his heart, not the other way around.*

Go: *Today, we're going to be jumping in by talking about Rule Number One, which is a rule that I actually wrote.*

Jo: *And it's a big one.*

Go: *Keep the ball in your court. You want to be the one calling the shots, which means no asking him on dates, no texting him first. You want to make sure that you hold all the power because that's going to keep him guessing.*

Jo: *It might sound old-fashioned, but believe us, if he's interested, he's going to make the move.*

Go: *The biggest risk when it comes to making the first move, I think, is that you become too invested in the outcome. As soon as you put yourself out there and text him first, or call him, or whatever, then you end up sitting there, biting your fingernails, waiting for him to text or call you back.*

Jo: *So then you call or text him again.*

Go: *That's always the way it goes, isn't it? Because you want to see a little return on your efforts. But—and this really sucks, but* *it's the truth—that's almost always counterproductive because it scares guys off. You get too invested and suddenly he's no longer interested.*

Jo: *Which is why it's always better to play it safe.*

CHAPTER

10

"I'm not sure this is a hike, technically," I said as we crested another rolling hill. I shielded my eyes from the bright morning sun with a hand. "It's more like a drive that you've chosen to take on foot, for some reason."

Several yards behind, Declan shot me a sweaty, irritable look from beneath the brim of his Caltech cap. When he spoke, it was between panting breaths. "We're walking uphill, so it's a hike."

The so-called hike was obviously more than he bargained for. We started off on asphalt, but that soon gave way to dirt and dry California brush. Open-top Hummers, emblazoned with some tour logo or another, drove past us at regular intervals, rumbling off into the hills, leaving clouds of dust in their wake—the only road-legal vehicles I'd seen since arriving on the island, and an intermittent reminder that we definitely didn't need to hike in order to get wherever we were going. But here we were, hiking anyway.

Walking ahead of him worked in my favor. I'd dressed to impress in a pair of Lycra workout leggings, the sheen of the form-fitting black material highlighting some of my best assets, but Declan didn't seem to be paying much attention. Actually, I was starting to worry that he might pass out. "Haven't you ever been on a real hike?" I took a hearty swig from my Gatorade-that-wasn't-

Gatorade—an easy way of concealing my sangria in public—and walked backwards so that I could keep an eye on him, my plan to get him to check out my ass on hold, for now. "Mt. Baldy? Heart Rock? Big Horn Mine?"

"I was an engineering major. I didn't have time to go on leisure hikes."

I suspected that this was a subtle dig at whatever he imagined my major was. There was no way in hell I was going to tell him it was music. None. "Leisure hikes? As opposed to what? Work hikes? School hikes?"

"We did hike to an observatory for class once, yes."

I rolled my eyes. It was apparent, judging by the sweat stain streaking the front of his T-shirt, that he did not hike often. I was actually surprised that someone in his physical condition wasn't an expert hiker. I turned back toward the trail, focusing on my Nikes pounding into the dirt. The trail wound back and forth, climbing up into the dry, hilly highlands of Catalina. At the highest points, the clear blue Pacific and the red-tile rooftops of Avalon peered through the brush, but for most of the hike, it was just grass and weeds and cactus.

"Having trouble back there?" I called over my shoulder. When he didn't answer, I turned to check on him again. There was no cell service up here, so I couldn't call for help if he passed out. I didn't relish the thought of hauling his unconscious body all the way back to town, but I would do what was necessary. Fortunately, he was still conscious. Just miserable-looking. "Come on, this is a baby hill."

"It's not the hill," he panted. "It's the heat. I'm not built for it." He waved a hand up and down his fair, freckly person.

"Ah, yes. Gotta protect the sensitive scalp, too." I tapped my own head where my hair was pulled into a ponytail, and he adjusted the bill of his hat self-consciously, his cheeks flushed with exertion. "You know, this is kind of fun, hanging out," I continued.

"I have all the time in the world to mess with you. Give you a taste of your own medicine." Given, it was probably easier at the moment because he could hardly string a sentence together, but I was going to enjoy that while it lasted.

"If you're talking about the tuba thing, I didn't mean to mess with you. I mean, not specifically."

"Oh? Do tell. What were your intentions?"

"It just seemed like the obvious target. Not you," he amended, "the tuba. I didn't even realize you'd be the one playing it." He doubled over to catch his breath, and I stopped too, several paces ahead. Between the scraggly foliage on the hillside, the water stretched toward the faint silhouette of the smoggy mainland on the horizon. He straightened up and held his hands in a wide circle in front of his body—the way a non-musician might imagine someone holds a tuba. "They're . . . big, you know. And the tuba player is always seated behind the other people."

"And what had you hoped to achieve, exactly?"

His forehead crinkled. "Making people laugh, I guess."

I could kind of understand that, considering homecoming pranks weren't unheard of. And if he said he didn't mean to target me, then I believed him. "Okay, so the pudding incident. What was that about?"

He winced. "You looked like you were having a bad day. I thought I'd cheer you up. Maybe not the best way to go about it, in retrospect—"

"You tried to cheer me up by giving me mayonnaise instead of pudding," I said flatly, trying and failing to follow his logic. "What if I was allergic to mayonnaise?"

"You're not," he said without missing a beat. I narrowed my eyes. "You used to bring those turkey sandwiches to school."

"Okay, first off, it's weird that you even remember that, and second, explain to me again how mayonnaise was supposed to cheer me up?"

He shrugged. "I mean, it distracted you. Do you remember what you were upset about?"

My silence was answer enough. I couldn't conjure up a single memory of that day outside of the pudding cup. In particular, I remembered feeling completely caught off guard when he had offered it to me—I had assumed he was just passing by my table, but then his Vans had squeaked to a halt on the laminate floor of the cafeteria, and he'd held out a cup of Snack Pack pudding, the foil already pulled back. *Hey, do you want this? I opened it before I realized it was tapioca. I haven't touched it, I swear.*

"I am sorry for that, though," he continued. "I hope you believe me when I say that I have no intentions of involving mayonnaise in any of my attempts to cheer you up in the future. Unless you want me to." He shot me a roguish wink, which shouldn't have worked with all the sweat and talk about mayonnaise, but somehow it kind of did.

"Appreciate the offer, but I'd prefer if you left the mayonnaise out of things."

He inclined his head, looking amused by some joke that I wasn't sure I was in on. "Noted."

Our shoes crunched on the gravel as we resumed the hike and an ocean breeze slithered through the dry grass. I took a few healthy swigs from my Gatorade bottle, unease creeping over me. I still couldn't get a read on him. A big part of feeling in control was already knowing *he* wanted *me*, which I didn't know for sure at the moment. That was the whole reason for Rule Number One, which I'd effectively broken last night when I asked him to hang out, but I hadn't expected the effect to be so immediate. I definitely followed the rules for a reason. A part of me wanted to chicken out now, come up with some other content for Season Seven, but it was only two weeks. I could handle two weeks, even if that meant two weeks of feeling a little off-kilter. This was good. This meant I'd have something to talk about for the podcast.

"Now it's my turn to ask you a question," Declan said after a moment, calling me out of my thoughts. "Why do you go by 'Go' on the podcast?"

I waved a hand. "It's a rhyme thing. Jo and Go. It's catchy." It had been Jo's idea. Actually, I'd always kind of hated the fact that my name was modified to fit with hers and not the other way around. Not that I had any solid suggestions for how the other way around would actually work. But it had always bugged me a little. Like a splinter that had wedged itself into my thumb—a tiny prick of annoyance, not enough to really inconvenience me, so I'd never brought it up.

I took another swig of sangria. Declan was watching me closely, now that we were hiking side by side. "I like 'Margo' better," he said, thoughtful. "It sounds . . ."

"Old lady-ish?" I suggested.

He shook his head. "I was going to say 'French.'"

"So I take it you've Googled me." Looked like I wasn't the only one doing a bit of cyberstalking this past week. There was something I could latch on to—an inkling of interest, and a chance that I could take back the reins, steer this whole interaction in a direction that worked for me.

"I've Googled the podcast, yes, but so has the rest of our graduating class," he said in an offhanded way. "A couple of band geeks get super famous for talking about their sex lives, people are going to be curious."

I arched a brow. "Jo wasn't a band geek, she just hung out with us." I wrestled with an odd mixture of emotions. On one hand, I was proud of everything that Jo and I had built together. But beneath that, in this weird and complicated way, I was embarrassed, knowing how much of my life he'd potentially been privy to. There was a difference between strangers listening to my podcast and people I knew listening to me. Social media allowed people from my past to peer into my life through a stained-glass window—rosy-tinted, a blur of shadows and colors, more of a vague suggestion than a clear picture. But in putting myself out there, I had welcomed the voyeurism nevertheless.

"So?" I prompted. "What did you think?"

"I didn't actually listen to it."

I deflated like the rental bounce house after someone canceled the party. There went that inkling of interest. "Are girly podcasts beneath you or something?"

"No. It just felt weird." He shrugged. "Stalkerish."

From somewhere around the bend ahead came the rumbling of an engine, and we both moved off to the side to make way for another Hummer on a return trip. To my surprise, Declan flagged it down. I thought maybe he was going to ask them for a ride back into town so that he didn't have to walk. A gruff-looking middle-aged woman was in the driver's seat. "How far to see the buffalo?" he asked her.

I looked back and forth between them, certain I'd heard wrong. "I'm sorry, the what?"

She waved over her shoulder, back in the direction the Hummer had come from. "They're a bit farther inland today. You're probably looking at a day's hike, maybe two."

Declan looked crestfallen. "Past the first camp?"

"Oh, yeah. A couple hours past, on foot."

"All right, thanks."

"Stay safe."

With that, the Hummer left us in a cloud of dust and exhaust fumes.

"You're telling me there are buffalo on this island?" I asked.

Declan coughed and attempted to waft the dust away with a hand. "Technically bison, but yes. Someone brought some over to shoot a movie, back in the twenties, and I guess they just left them." He turned back the way we came, apparently having given up his unspoken mission to see the buffalo. "Didn't you do any research before coming here?"

I hurried after him. "I didn't need to do research. My family used to visit all the time. And I lifeguarded at the camp for a summer."

"You're telling me you—" He coughed again. "You're telling me you worked here for a whole summer, and you never knew there were bison on the island?"

I hunched my shoulders. "I guess I was too busy making sure children didn't drown."

Clearing his throat, he pointed at the Gatorade bottle in my hand. "Could I—"

An oddly defensive part of me was more than happy to let him choke, but I relinquished the bottle anyway. To my amusement, he chugged it, and then proceeded to go through a rapid-fire version of all five stages of grief. More coughing. "Oh my God," he said, shoving it back in my arms like he couldn't get away from it fast enough. He wiped his mouth on the back of his hand. "That's horrendous."

"I told you I was bringing sangria."

"You could have told me *that* was the sangria. I was expecting Gatorade. And I didn't expect it to be so—"

"Strong?" I offered. I might have picked the highest percentage premixed sangria I could find. Capriccio, fourteen percent. Trying to get the most bang for my buck without chugging hard liquor.

"Hot," he finished. "Like you microwaved it."

Oh. That. I took another swig myself, and yeah, it was pretty warm from hiking out in the sun. Still got the job done, though.

Despite his complaints, once the initial shock had passed, he eyed the half-empty bottle. "Is that all you brought?"

I held my arms wide, turning on the spot. "Do I look like I have another bottle hidden on my person?"

Now his gaze did flick over my leggings, as well as other potential hiding places, but he seemed to decide it was safer not to answer that particular question.

I fought back a smug smile as I passed the bottle back to him. "So what's the story behind the whole loner vibe? You used to be class clown. What happened, the whole younger, hotter Conan O'Brien thing not working for you lately?"

"I am begging you not to compare me to random redheads. How would you like it if I called you—" He stopped short, staring at the top of my head like he was seeing it for the first time. "What color is your natural hair? I've only ever seen it . . ." He made a vague gesture at my green dye, which had faded to a pale swampy color like I'd spent too long in the pool. "Well, dyed."

"Brown," I said, indicating my roots. "Before I got my hands on box dye in seventh grade." I'd dyed it a wide array of colors ever since. There were a few times I'd thought about going back to brown. I missed it, sometimes. My mom used to tell me that it brought out my eyes. But then Jo and I had started the podcast, and my green hair at the time had accidentally ended up being something people recognized, and afterwards I felt like I couldn't change it back.

And on that note, I needed to touch it up before the wedding. There were no beauty stores on the island, but I should probably see if the Vons—the main grocery store serving Avalon—carried any green hair dye.

Declan gave me an odd look. "Wait a second. Can we rewind to a few sentences ago?"

I tried to remember what I had said a few sentences ago, but I was coming up short. "Yes?"

"Did you just call me hot?"

Technically, I had. But I had a feeling he knew full well that he was attractive, and I also didn't need to hand over all the power in this situation. Though I did take his curiosity as a good sign.

"I said 'younger, hotter Conan O'Brien.' How you interpret that comparison is up to you."

"But do you—"

I waved a hand to shut him up. "No further questions. Not until you answer a few more of mine."

He gave me a surly look. "I thought you wanted to hang out, but I realize now this is actually an interrogation." He took a long swig of sangria. When I just watched him expectantly, he sighed. "Fine."

"You've changed a lot since high school," I said. "I know everybody changes, but it's just that you were so social back then, and now you seem sort of . . ." I tried to conjure up the right word, but I was drawing a blank. What sort of person didn't have social media, in this day and age?

"Antisocial?" he offered. I didn't nod, because it wasn't quite the word I was looking for. "I'm not, really. I just—" He broke off, the silence filled only by our footsteps and the slosh of the Gatorade bottle. "At some point, I realized it's not worth it to make friends just for the sake of it. In high school, I did a lot of stuff for the attention. I spent too much time caring what other people thought." He shrugged. "When I realized that practically none of those people mattered after graduation, I guess I decided to stop caring so much."

I wished I knew how to do that. How to just . . . let go. Stop caring. That had always been my problem. It wasn't possible to please everyone, and yet I kept on trying. Trying to ensure our listeners were happy while also supporting Jo through her wedding, and kissing ass for the sake of sponsorships even when they made no sense for our own brand. But I didn't want to weigh down our conversation with all that. "Yeah," I said instead. "I can relate."

"Not buying it. You always did your own thing back then. I kind of envied it, actually."

He was wrong, of course. I'd always cared what people thought;

I was just never very good at meeting their expectations. "Is that the sangria talking?"

The corner of his mouth hitched in a smile. "No way. I'm Irish. I could probably drink a whole bottle of your little fruit juice"—I tried to protest, but he talked right over me—"and not even catch a buzz."

I rolled my eyes. "Everyone always says they're Irish, but then they go to Ireland and meet people actually born and raised there, and those Irish drink the Irish-Americans under the table."

"I take it you have some experience with this?"

"I did a semester abroad in Limerick, my first year of college."

He seemed taken aback. "Who does a semester abroad their first year?"

"I took a couple years off from school to help my mom, so when I finally enrolled, I felt like it was now or never. I sort of added it on to the rest of my student loans and went." I shrugged. It wasn't my happiest memory. You'd think a semester abroad would be a highlight of your early twenties, but in truth, it was kind of a lonely time. I was alone, in a country I knew practically nothing about (beyond my watered-down and thoroughly Americanized understanding of St. Patrick's Day), all because I wanted to run away from my problems at home. News flash: that didn't work.

"I've never actually been," Declan admitted.

"It was a good experience, but I was glad to come home."

We reached the bottom of the hill, where the dirt road met with asphalt. It was early afternoon, and Avalon had come alive with people on bikes and roller skates and self-guided island tours. Golfers in polo shirts and pastel shorts traipsed around the sun-singed golf course, sipping cans of 805. My phone blasted me with missed notifications now that I had solid reception again—Twitter and Instagram and emails, which I swiped through rapid-fire, double-checking to ensure there was nothing from any of our sponsors, but it looked like we were in the clear.

Declan and I had lapsed back into silence, but it was a comfortable one, the sort you didn't feel compelled to fill. It made me
wonder why we hadn't gotten to know each other sooner. Despite
my initial prejudice against him, I had a feeling we would have
gotten along just fine in high school, if we'd ever bothered to try.
All those years in the cafeteria, passing each other on the concrete
walkways between classrooms, suffering through fifth-period history with Mrs. Sutherland, and we'd never exchanged more than
a few words.

His smartwatch made a pinging noise, but he ignored it. Who
ignored their notifications like that? I was itching to grab his wrist
and check it for him. "Did you want to get lunch?" he asked.

I concealed a smile. Unlike him, I didn't have a dimple to give
me away. "Thanks, but not today. I'm meeting one of my old co-
workers." It was a blatant lie—one I'd invented on the spot, but
I'd already told him about my summer lifeguarding here on the
island, so it was passable as a truth. I didn't want to push my luck
today. Making myself too available meant making things too easy,
and that was a surefire way to lose a guy's interest. I needed to
string him along for a bit. At least until I had some solid content
for Season Seven, and then I could spin things however I needed
to from there.

"Oh," he said, and there was that off-guard look again, like he
couldn't be bothered to try to conceal his expressions in the first
place. Which made no sense, because if he was that up-front and
honest about things, why did I have such a hard time figuring him
out? "Then I guess I'll see you later."

He made it a few steps and then rounded back to face me. I
plastered on a smile. Begging me to go to dinner already? Well,
in that case—

"Which way was the hotel?" he asked instead.

Now it was my turn to be caught off guard, but I was pretty
sure I did a better job of concealing my disappointment. "That

way." I might not have known about Catalina's bison, but I did still have a good sense of direction around Avalon, even after all these years.

He turned up the road toward our hotel and I continued past the mid-century houses into the heart of town. I spent the rest of the afternoon alone, enjoying all the little things I remembered from my childhood. I walked the sea-green pier, gulls crying as they swarmed fishermen with bucketsful of chum. I paid twenty-five cents for some feed pellets that I tossed to the garibaldi, and sat on a bench enjoying an ice cream cone by myself. Afterwards, I sat down at a burger place with a cheeseburger so sloppy it dribbled down my chin like one of those weirdly objectifying Carl's Jr. commercials.

Avalon was charming if you looked at it from the right angle, maybe slapped a filter over it. There was a time, maybe seventy or eighty years ago, when it was probably a classy place to vacation. Remnants of that time were scattered around the island—in the form of the Casino perched on an outcropping of rock, a Spanish-style bell tower, a hilltop mansion that belonged to William Wrigley Jr., of Wrigley's chewing gum fame. But the charm of its heyday was punctuated at every turn by different eras of attempted commercialization. A gift shop here. Longboard rentals there. Wine tasting. Electric bike tours. The corny, touristy elements were as much a part of Catalina's character as its most iconic buildings, stitched together like a quilt, telling the island's history. As with everything, you had to take the good with the bad to really get a clear picture.

So many of the places here were tinged with memories of my parents. I wasn't sure if I was saddened or relieved that they weren't here, together, to relive it all with me. There was a sort of comfort in being alone. It wasn't easy for me to just stop caring, the way Declan had made it sound. Being alone was the only time I didn't have to worry about what other people thought. There was always the small risk of someone recognizing me, and the constant worry in the back of my mind about what I was going to post next to keep our followers engaged. But at least I still had the little moments to myself. The good with the bad.

Sometimes, I found myself wondering when I'd let the bad start to outweigh the good.

From: Sun-N-Snorkels Ocean Sports Rentals (reservations@sun -n-snorkels.com)
To: Margo Anderson (go@sevenrulespodcast.com)
Date: Jul 17, 10:06 AM
Subject: Your upcoming reservation

Hi Margo,

This is an automated reminder that you have an upcoming reservation with Sun-N-Snorkels Ocean Sports. Please review the details of your booking below. Remember that all changes or cancellations require 24-hours' notice in order to receive a full refund. Otherwise, the prices listed below will be charged to your debit card on file, minus our current reservation fees.

Reservation date & time: July 18 at 1:00pm PST
2-person kayak rental—$17/hour (x4)
3-hour reservation (x4)
Taxes: $20.40
Total: $224.40

Feel free to reach out if you have any questions. We look forward to seeing you soon!
The Sun-N-Snorkels Team

CHAPTER

11

"But I booked for five individual kayaks," I said, holding up my fingers like a toddler who just learned to count. "One double and five individuals."

The cashier at the rental shack—a kid in a Hawaiian-print shirt, sunburned the color of a cooked lobster—shook his shaggy head. "Double kayaks are all we have left. The reservation says seven people. You didn't specify the type of kayak. You should have received an email yesterday morning to confirm."

"I didn't have reception yesterday morning." It was a half-truth. There was one point during the hike where I didn't have any bars, but I also hadn't bothered to check the email from the rental place afterwards. I was too busy scanning for emails related to the podcast. I glanced at Jo, waiting with Peter and the rest of the wedding party a few yards away while I tried to straighten things out. The plan had been for Jo and Peter to share a kayak but for the rest of us to have our own. That seemed easy enough to finagle. I turned back to the cashier. "Let me speak to your manager."

After a fruitless argument about their automated form and all the single kayaks being booked up for the day, the manager sent the cashier to the shed behind the shack. I marched over to Jo and the others and filled them in on the mix-up. No one seemed particularly bothered by the news that we'd have to share kayaks.

Liv mumbled something about going with the flow and Declan nodded, his expression unreadable behind his sunglasses.

"One of us will have to be alone," Autumn pointed out.

"I'll do it," Lucas offered, his face all scrunched up like he was angry at the sun. Autumn narrowed her eyes at him and he shrugged a shoulder. "Seems like the gentlemanly thing to do."

I stayed quiet. I wasn't a huge fan of sharing a kayak with other people. Dad had taught me how to kayak years ago, hauling a pair of single-person kayaks up to Lake Arrowhead or Silverwood in the back of the pickup every summer when I was growing up. And his number one rule for all things outdoorsy: only ever rely on yourself. With individual kayaks, if you tipped over or couldn't keep up, that was on you. But with doubles, you had to rely on the other person to have steady paddling arms, to pull their own weight, to have a decent sense of balance. And all that was ignoring the fact that I was used to kayaking in lakes, which were a bit more predictable than the ocean. The ocean had sharks, for one. Lakes did not.

I whipped out my phone and Googled *are there sharks near Catalina Island?* The first result was an article about a nineteen-foot-long great white that patrolled the local waters. Well, that answered that. The cashier was passing out the life vests and demonstrating how to put them on, much in the same way an airline stewardess would demonstrate the whole emergency exit plan: in great detail, covering their asses from getting sued. As though a life vest was going to save me from getting my legs nibbled off by a massive shark.

Jo was obviously kayaking with Peter, so my options were pretty limited. I stole a glance at Declan. He'd set his backpack on the counter at the rental shack and was tugging his T-shirt over his head, revealing broad shoulders and a toned chest with a dusting of coppery hair. I was fairly certain he could pull his own weight, but he also hadn't made any effort to talk to me after our hike yesterday, and I didn't really know what to do with that. I was used to leaving a few breadcrumbs, but it was mostly on the guy to actually make a move, and usually they were tripping over themselves to talk to me—at least up until we jumped into bed together, at which point I'd made a habit of ghosting them without a second thought. Still, I didn't exactly have infinite time to waste making this happen. If he wasn't going to initiate things, it was up to me. I crossed over to where he was standing by the lockers, tucking his shirt into his backpack and extracting a bottle of off-brand sunscreen.

"Declan. You're a—" I struggled to describe his build in a way that wouldn't sound completely objectifying, but the lack of a shirt was making that difficult. Biceps and shoulders and—look at his face, Margo. His face. "Capable-looking guy," I finished lamely. "You'd punch a shark for me, right?"

He gave me a bemused look, stepping out of the way to allow Liv and Autumn to pass with their own kayak. I didn't miss the way they cast curious glances in our direction. "What?"

"Speaking hypothetically, if the kayak were to tip over, and if a shark happened to be swimming by—"

"If this is your weird way of asking me to share a kayak with you, then I accept."

"Great." I watched him slather sunscreen over a muscled arm, my eyes drinking in the curve of his bicep a little too readily. I needed to focus. "Do you need me to get your back?" I offered, reaching for the bottle where he'd left it on the counter.

He slowed in the middle of smoothing sunscreen across his chest. His expression should have been unreadable behind his dark sunglasses, but the slight downward curve of his lips betrayed his hesitation. "Why?"

"I don't know if you've noticed, there's this thing called the sun," I said cheerfully. "And sometimes it can burn you, and we call that a—"

"Okay, I get it," he said, and—finishing up with his chest—he turned his back to me. Good. I kind of liked him being cooperative. Except now I was faced with a broad, masculine back. His shoulder blades were dotted with freckles, and I had to resist the urge to trace them like constellations, instead squirting some SPF 30 into my palm. It was surprisingly cool in the hot afternoon sun. I frowned, trying to decide where to start. I reached for a shoulder.

His skin was warm and he twitched away from my touch. "Shit, that's cold."

"Sorry." I probably should have rubbed my hands together to warm it up first, but it warmed up as I worked it over his back. A prickle at the back of my neck told me that Jo was watching us from where they were waiting down by the water, but I pretended not to notice. She'd be asking for updates on our little experiment pretty soon, and I wasn't sure what I was going to tell her—in part because I had no idea whether things were going well or not—so I focused on rubbing sunscreen on Declan instead.

I'd touched my fair share of guys before, but that had mostly been a lot of fumbling around in the dark, a few tequila shots deep, never making an effort to memorize their body. Not that I was making a conscious effort to memorize anything now, but there were details I noticed that I wouldn't normally have noticed. The indent of his spine. The dusting of freckles across his shoulders. The way his back rose and fell with his breathing, which was weirdly in time with my own, and I found myself holding my breath for a second to break the rhythm. "There," I said when I'd finished, acutely aware of the fact that this had been a lot less sexy than I'd imagined it in my head. "No sunburns in your near future." I didn't know what to do with the film of sunscreen left on my hands, so I wiped it on my own arms, feeling strangely self-conscious.

"Thanks." He turned around to face me again, shrugging on

his life vest and buckling it, which left only his arms and a sliver of flat, toned stomach visible. "Your turn."

"What?"

He arched a brow at my clothes. "I assume you're not leaving those on."

Obviously, I wasn't, but now I was conscious of every movement as I stripped off my tank top to reveal the crocheted bikini I'd worn for our partnership with the swimsuit boutique a couple years back. Declan's sunglasses left most of his expression to the imagination, but a muscle in his jaw feathered as I stepped out of my leggings and added my clothes to the pile of possessions that the rental shack was supposed to stow for safekeeping. I twisted my hair off my shoulders, pinning it to my head with a hand as I turned my back to him.

"Because I'm considerate, I'll actually warm it up for you," he said, stepping in closer as he squirted the lotion into his hand. His breath tickled the loose hairs at the nape of my neck. I reflected, briefly, that the sputtering sound of the lotion bottle was the antithesis of sexy, but then his hands found the small of my back, warm and slick against my skin.

He smoothed the sunscreen up my back and across my shoulders before working his way back down. He was plainly better at this than I was. His hands slid around to my sides, working over my hips. He was only doing it for the sake of coverage, I reminded myself, but I found myself imagining what it might feel like for his grip to tighten, drawing me backwards until I felt the fabric of his board shorts brush up against the back of me. Warmth pooled in my belly, seeping downward.

"You two almost ready?" Jo's voice called from somewhere down by the water, and my eyes shot open. We were still standing beside the rental shack. Beachgoers zipped past us on bicycles and roller skates. Somewhere nearby, a stereo blasted "Under the Boardwalk."

"Shit," I mumbled, snatching my life vest off the counter and brushing past Declan as I shrugged it on. I hoped he didn't pick up on how thoroughly his touch had disconcerted me, but for good measure, I explained, "We're supposed to be on a schedule." I'd only booked the rentals for three hours, and I had every reason to suspect that the manager had started the timer the moment she sent lobster-boy to fetch the kayaks out of the shed.

If Declan was fazed by the sudden interruption, he didn't say anything. Together, we lifted our neon orange kayak—plastic and surprisingly lightweight—and hauled it down to the water, where the rest of the group was waiting. Jo shot me a look that could only mean *we'll talk later* before helping Peter load their own kayak into the water at the direction of an employee. I wasn't sure I was looking forward to the conversation.

Declan and I were the last to glide our kayak into the shallow water, lapping over the pebbles that lined the shore.

"So, what's this about a shark?" he asked, perhaps only for the sake of breaking the silence after whatever had happened back by the rental shack. We sloshed in up to our knees, the cold water shocking me back to my senses.

I tried to chuckle, but it came out more of a nervous titter than anything. "Google has informed me there's a massive great white hanging out around here."

"Ah. I read something about that in the news a couple years ago. It bit someone's kayak." Our own kayak thumped hollowly against a stray rock as we dragged it into the water. "But it was an experimental bite, kind of like a dog, you know? They don't have hands, so they have to feel things with their mouths."

I noticed he had this habit of imparting random tidbits of information. Information that no one had asked for but he seemed all too happy to give, which might have been endearing, if the information in question didn't also terrify me. "Comforting," I grumbled.

I grabbed my paddle before hopping into the front seat. Declan climbed in the back and the kayak rocked with the newfound weight. It was long enough that his legs didn't need to wrap around me. I'd never sat in a two-person kayak—I'd been picturing Disneyland's Matterhorn Bobsleds pre-refurbishment; during a field trip with my band class in sixth grade, I'd been strapped to a lanky trombone player's lap in a bizarre form of public humiliation. I wasn't sure if I was relieved or disappointed to discover that double kayaks had their own seats.

The rest of the group were already out on the water, forming a neat little line like ducks in a row as they paddled out. I adjusted the straps on the blockish life vest, which I'd buckled in a sloppy dash to excuse myself from the sunscreen situation.

"I'm pretty sure the sharks won't be deterred by a bit of Styrofoam," Declan commented behind me.

"If I'm lucky, they'll be blinded by the sight of you." When this garnered no response, I turned to look at him. He was frowning at me with that stupid blank expression. "Get it, because you're so white, it's blinding—"

"I got it, it was just a terrible joke," he said. "I mean, resorting to ginger jokes? It's just lazy at this point."

Even in the hot sun, my cheeks grew warm. He had an incredible talent for making me feel ridiculous. "Not a ginger joke, a pale joke."

He shrugged. "It's the same thing." His exposed shoulders—although they *were* fair—weren't horrible to look at. My eyes couldn't resist tracing the curve of his bicep, the golden hair on his forearms, the light freckles that trailed down to his wrist. I huffed, inexplicably annoyed despite the fact that I couldn't seem to convince myself to look away.

He used his paddle to push us off from the shore, the muscles in his arms working, and the kayak bobbed precariously on the water. I snapped out of my arm-induced trance, my mind jumping right back to being shark food as I gripped the sides, paddle balanced across my lap. "Whoa, I wasn't—"

"Just paddle," he ordered.

Mostly because I didn't know what else I could do—and definitely not because his assertiveness kind of did a number on me—I faced forward again. I picked up my paddle and dipped it into the water in unison with his on the opposite side, and for a moment, the only sound was the *swish-swish* of our paddles mingling with the faint babble of voices and music on the shore. We paddled past the buoys that marked the end of the swimming zone and out into the open ocean. The muscles in my arms seared with exertion. I was out of practice. Jo and Peter were leagues ahead of us, paddling parallel to the craggy shore. Catalina was mostly uninhabited—aside from Avalon and Two Harbors, it was all cliffs and rolling, grassy hills.

"I thought you used to be a lifeguard," Declan said after a long moment.

I scrunched up my face against the bright sun, not sure where he was going with this, but I didn't turn to look at him. I kept paddling. *Swish-swish*. One paddle after the other. "I was."

"But you're scared of the ocean."

It was a statement, but there was a question buried beneath it. Like he was wondering if I lived in fear—of heights, of the ocean, of commitment—always too scared to take the leap. "I'm a little sketched out by it," I admitted. "More by what's in the ocean than the ocean itself. But pool lifeguards and ocean lifeguards are also pretty different. Ocean lifeguards have to do all this intense stuff like swim out past the pier and learn about riptides and stuff. Pool lifeguards practice pulling each other out of the pool at the local YMCA."

"You still saved people's lives though, either way."

I snorted. "Right. I think I pulled someone out of the water, like, two whole times, and both times they insisted they were fine and I'd interrupted their swimming session."

"Do you know CPR?"

"Of course, I—" I broke off when I glanced over my shoulder, and saw he was grinning at me. Rolling my eyes, I faced forward again. "You're shameless."

"What am I doing?" he asked innocently.

"It's the same line every guy tries on lifeguards." Not to mention I'd heard just about every pickup line in the book, lifeguarding aside. "And no, I'm not going to perform CPR on you. Unless you're, you know, actually dying." Flirting worked in my favor, but CPR wasn't exactly sexy. Not if you knew what you were doing.

"Bummer," he sighed. I'd come to expect he would try to push my patience to the very limit, so I was surprised when he changed the subject. "I wanted to talk to you about your plans for the bachelorette party tomorrow. I wasn't sure what you had in mind, but—"

"That's for the girls to know and you to wonder about," I interrupted.

"That sounds like something someone with no plans would say," Declan shot back. "Peter mentioned that he's not all that interested in spending time with the guys. Sounds like he'd honestly rather spend the evening with Jo."

I huffed. Of course he would, because apparently, Peter could do no wrong. My feelings toward Jo getting married would be a lot less complicated if the guy she was marrying was a total douche. "Don't you worry. I've got it taken care of."

"Big plans, huh?"

"At least five strippers," I invented wildly. "All of them dressed in maid outfits. Jo has a thing for it, but don't tell her I told you."

"As much as I appreciate the picture you're trying to paint here, I'm pretty sure there aren't any strippers on this island."

I pulled a face. "No male strippers? Are you sure about that?"

"I said *no strippers*. My research is nothing if not thorough."

"Right. You're a scientist or whatever. I forgot."

"Engineer," he corrected me. I rolled my eyes without turning to look at him, but I could practically hear the arched eyebrow. "And why do you say it like that?"

"Like what?"

"Like it's a bad thing. You say *scientist* the way normal people would say . . . I don't know, *asshole*, or something."

"It's just that STEM people always rag on everybody else. Like their field is the only field that matters." I remembered how hard my dad had pushed me to go into any field other than music. He wasn't even a STEM major himself—he'd majored in communications or journalism or something—but he always had this vision of a high-powered doctor or rocket scientist for a daughter, like it was somehow my responsibility to fill the shoes he hadn't bothered to fill himself. "I mean, obviously, I recognize how important scientists and engineers are to our everyday life. But how bland would the world be without artists and musicians and—"

"Podcasters?" Declan offered, but when I shot him a scathing look over my shoulder, his expression wasn't mocking. I didn't know what it was. He was frowning slightly behind his sunglasses, his mouth set in a hard line like he was focused on something—on paddling or on what I was saying, I didn't know.

I didn't know what to say to that, so I changed the subject as we paddled past Hamilton Cove, a mass of white Mediterranean-style vacation rentals and private villas, tiered like a wedding cake. "So much for this being a group bonding activity," I lamented. Jo and Peter were so far ahead, I doubted they would have heard me if I shouted at the top of my lungs. Jo had been asking me to take her kayaking for years, and I'd been avoiding it. My own kayak was rotting away in the outdoor storage at my mom's apartment complex, the plastic probably cracked and brittle from the heat.

"We're bonding," Declan pointed out.

"Ew," I said automatically.

In one swift motion, he pulled his paddle out of the water and thwacked me over the head with the wet end of it. "You didn't seem to mind back there on the beach."

My stomach flipped traitorously. "Asshole," I said, rubbing the spot on my head where the paddle had walloped me. I jabbed back at him with my own paddle. He parried the blow, and the whole kayak rocked threateningly. I gripped the side of the hollow plastic to steady myself, my heart shooting up into my throat.

"Watch it," he growled. We were still drifting in the same general direction as the rest of the wedding party, but with our boat veering sideways and neither of us paddling, it would soon be up to the tide which direction we were headed.

"I'm not watching it, you watch it, you hit me first—"

It was more like a slap fight than a sword fight, the way we smacked at each other with the ends of the paddles like wet, rubbery pummel sticks. I landed a particularly solid slap across Declan's face, and even I flinched at the loud *thwack* it made against his skin. He reached to touch his cheek, eyes wide with shock. Then he gave a wide, vengeful swing of his paddle, overestimated, and the kayak lurched sideways, and—

And I was submerged in cold water.

My life vest kept me from going under completely, but I had managed to land headfirst, which meant I got a nose- and mouthful of briny seawater that burned in my sinuses. I surfaced, buoyed by the vest and coughing as I peeled a lock of greenish hair out of my eyes. The water was choppy from our little accident. My legs felt like a couple of dangling Slim Jims, taunting the hungry sharks I imagined were circling not far below. Our kayak was flipped upside down but still buoyant. Declan clung to the side of it, looking as soaked as I felt, his red hair dark and soppy against his forehead. His sunglasses were gone. Lost somewhere in the water below, and who knew how deep that was? My stomach lurched at the thought and I splashed over and flung my arms over the keel for support.

In the distance, the other kayaks were rounding another bend, hugging the cliff-line. No one seemed to notice that the best man and the maid of honor had managed to capsize their rental. I turned back to Declan. He'd also been looking over at the others, but he turned and met my eye over the keel. We came to a silent, mortified agreement. We flipped the kayak and—after a few failed, flailing attempts to climb back aboard—we swam to the nearest shore, dragging it along with us.

The wet plastic thumped as we hauled it onto the rocky beach. Jagged rocks gnawed at my bare feet. Now that we were out of the water, we were both shivering, our breathing uneven. The sun was out, but there was a light breeze, and there wasn't a dry towel or change of clothes in sight. We'd landed on a small private beach beneath Hamilton Cove. I was pretty sure we weren't allowed to be here. Giving up on catching the others, we hoisted the kayak under our arms and started up the endless set of stairs that led through the private villas and back toward town.

I mulled over what to say, but I was at a loss. This whole adventure summed up our dynamic quite well. Despite our weird on-again, off-again chemistry, this served as a reminder that our personalities did not mesh. But maybe they didn't need to; I was looking for someone to break a few rules with, not someone to commit to.

"Don't say it," Declan said. He hadn't even looked at me since we got out of the water; he was carrying the front end of the kayak, which meant my only view was the back I'd been slathering sunscreen all over not half an hour ago.

For some reason, I was offended. "I wasn't going to say anything."

"You were going to say something. You always have something to say."

I gawked at the back of his head. It was hard to believe this was the same guy I'd almost let feel me up in the middle of a public beach. "And you don't?" I shot back. My already aching arms were screaming at the weight of the kayak, and my calves were sore from climbing up the infinite stairs, and I was sopping wet and shivering in the shade of the cliffs. I was not in the mood for this.

"No, I don't, but you're so insistent on arguing about everything—"

"Oh, so it's my fault we don't get along now?" I demanded.

He fell silent. All I could see was the backside of him, so I couldn't get a read on his expression. Not that I ever really got a read on him, even under normal circumstances. The inner machinations of Declan Walsh's mind were a mystery, and not one I was eager to sort out at the moment.

Finally, he said, "Maybe it's better if we don't talk right now."

That, at least, I could agree with.

By the time we made it back to the hotel, I was drier, but still annoyed and also deeply uncomfortable, eager to change back into my cozy pj's and order room service and then sulk for the rest of the evening. Declan and I trudged to our neighboring rooms, not bothering to exchange a parting word.

As soon as the door was locked behind me, I stripped off my damp swimsuit and drew myself a hot bath. I plugged my phone into the charger by the nightstand—thankfully, it was saved from being submerged because I had left it at the rental shack with my clothes. I checked my notifications, but there were no messages. Everyone else was still out kayaking, which wasn't a cell phone-friendly activity, so I didn't know who I was expecting to hear from. But I flicked through Twitter, debated Tweeting something, decided against it. I had nothing to announce and nothing particularly relevant to say. Forcing it felt sort of like getting up in front of the lecture hall to give a presentation, faltering when you saw all the judgmental faces staring back at you, forgetting what you wanted to say, and just saying *um, uh, so.* Do something. Anything. Picture them naked. Except there was no one to picture. Just a number. *96.2k Followers.* And I was the one standing naked in the middle of my hotel room.

Giving up, I set my phone down. The bathtub was full, steam

fogging the mirrors, so I turned off the faucet and lowered myself into the scalding water for a nice long soak. It was one of those big, roomy hotel tubs, and I cranked the jets on high and let the water pressure massage my back, working my aching muscles until I turned to jelly.

Growing up, our house didn't have a bathtub, only a shower. And then my mom moved into a similar situation in the apartment, and a few years later I was living out of a dorm, showering in a communal bathroom. It wasn't uncommon to find empty bottles of booze clattering around the tiled shower floors or used condoms stuck in the drains. One time I found a cactus in the toilet. Not a tiny potted succulent, mind you. Like an actual full-sized cactus. It was longer than my arm, and someone had tried to flush it down a regular old toilet in what I can only assume was some kind of drug-fueled paranoia.

Anyway, after the podcast proved a success, I moved into the apartment with Jo, where we did indeed have a tub, but it was small and cramped and neither of us ever used it. A Jacuzzi tub— with jets!—was something I'd only ever dreamt about.

Which was why I was deeply displeased when, about half an hour into my relaxation, someone knocked at the door. I had soaked until the water had turned lukewarm, and the mirrors had mostly cleared up, lingering condensation clinging to the corners. I debated just staying in the tub. It couldn't be anyone who mattered. The rest of the wedding party were still out kayaking, and probably wouldn't be back for at least another half hour, by my estimate. But curiosity got the better of me, so I dragged myself out of the water with a groan.

I grabbed the hotel robe off the hanger and bundled up to go answer the door. The plush fabric was soft and warm against my skin. I kind of understood why Declan was wearing nothing but a robe and his boxers the other morning.

I opened the door to an empty hall. I'd halfway shut it again by the time I noticed a six-pack of bottled sangria sitting on the worn hall carpet, a hotel room notepad propped up by the cardboard packaging. *Sorry for losing my cool today*, the hasty handwriting read, and beneath that, *text me if you want to talk about tomorrow*. In lieu of a signature, a phone number was scrawled at the bottom, complete with the 909 area code we'd grown up with. I'd changed mine to a 747 number not long after Jo and I had moved to NoHo, eager to put the past behind me. But now, for reasons I couldn't quite decipher, seeing my old area code sent a flicker of warm familiarity through me.

I stowed the sangria in the fridge, my eyes scanning the notepad a couple more times as I collapsed on the bed still dressed in the robe. Since when had I cared about things that reminded me of my hometown? I'd worked hard to get away from it. With a huff, I tossed the notepad aside and grabbed one of the bottles, popping the top on the corner of the mini fridge. It would take more than a few bottles of sangria for me to cave and text Declan first, but I grabbed my phone off the charger and programmed his number into my contacts anyway.

Curious, I opened Twitter again. A quick search for *Declan Walsh* brought up the same array of profiles it had brought up before, but this time I scrolled until I saw one that looked familiar. I would never have recognized it as him before, but apparently, that was less because he had changed and more because I really didn't remember what he had looked like back in high school. The profile didn't appear to have been accessed since senior year, when he'd so helpfully Tweeted a single Tweet: *what's even up with twitter, I don't get the hype*. Thank you for your input, seventeen-year-old Declan. I checked the top of the profile, but of course, there was no helpful *follows you* tag beside his username. He probably hadn't been online in ages, and even if he had, I doubted he would have had any reason to think about me prior to this vacation, let alone follow me.

Another knock at the door. "You didn't even give me a chance to text you," I called out.

But it wasn't Declan on the other side. "What? It's Jo. Let me in."

I rolled off the bed and unlocked the door.

"What happened?" she asked, as soon as she was inside. "One minute you guys were right behind us, and the next you were gone."

At least she had noticed. "We flipped the kayak and couldn't get it to turn over. By the time we got to the shore, it just felt like it was better to call it a day." I stooped to grab one of the bottles out of the mini fridge. "Sangria?"

She waved away the offer. "No, thanks."

"How was the rest of the kayaking trip?" I settled back on the bed. Jo hovered, which usually meant she didn't plan to stay long. If she planned to stay, she would have sat down and had a drink.

"Fine. Great," she said, unconvincingly. She picked up the notepad from where it was lying on top of the mini fridge, narrowed her eyes at Declan's note. "So," she said, setting it back down again.

"So," I echoed, pretty sure I knew exactly where this was headed.

"I take it everything is going according to plan."

"There is no *plan*. But I'm still living like there aren't any rules, if that's what you're asking."

"So is Declan going to be your guinea pig for all this?" she asked, a sharp note to her voice that I didn't care for. "No second thoughts?"

"I wouldn't call him a guinea pig," I protested. "He's . . ." But whatever word I was looking for, I couldn't seem to dig deep enough to find it. What was he? A lot of things I didn't particularly feel like summarizing at the moment. "You know, he's around a lot. We've spent some time together."

"Liv seems to be under the impression that you guys are already hooking up."

I snorted. I was sure Liv was under plenty of impressions, after the elevator encounter two nights ago. Not that it was any of her business, but at the same time, it felt like nothing was ever just *my* business these days, so I was resigned to it. I'd forfeited my right to privacy the moment I chose to put my personal life on blast. "We're not. Not yet, anyway."

Jo gave me a long, measured look. "But you're planning on it."

If I was being entirely honest, my plans weren't all that tangible. I hadn't thought that far ahead. Yes, the possibility of sex was something I'd vaguely acknowledged—mostly in the sense that it would mean an end to my ten-month dry spell—but I hadn't allowed myself to delve into the specifics. I did now, though. I thought about those well-muscled arms, the assertive tone he'd taken with me earlier, and I swallowed. "It's part of the experiment. You said it yourself. It wouldn't make for very exciting content if I just keep doing what I always do."

Jo folded her arms. A small smile formed on her lips. "This could be good for you."

I narrowed my eyes. I'd expected her to scold me, but this was . . . well, it wasn't scolding, but I wasn't sure I liked her cryptic statement any better. "What could be good for me?"

"This. Catching feelings."

"I am *not* catching feelings."

"It's part of the rules, and you're supposed to be breaking them."

"Okay, yeah, but I can't exactly force myself to catch feelings," I pointed out, more than a little defensive. "Either it happens or it doesn't." And it wasn't going to happen. Even with my aversions to commitment, I was willing to be open-minded for the sake of these two weeks, and the experiment. If I caught feelings for . . . *someone*, then I'd just have to figure out a way to deal with it. But the chances of that happening were miniscule. Practically nonexistent. I was certified heartless, and I had a whole track record to prove it.

Jo sighed and settled at the foot of the bed, the cushy comforter sinking beneath her weight. "Sorry. I guess I just get a little excited. Thinking about you stepping out of your comfort zone. Maybe getting a little taste of happiness."

I hunched my shoulders against the pillows. "I'm happy." And if I wasn't, my relationship status had nothing to do with it. It was strange how love had transformed Jo—how suddenly, the girl who I'd always known to be staunchly single didn't believe that being single could be fulfilling anymore. Being single wasn't my issue. It was everything else that was the problem.

"I'm not saying you need to find someone," Jo said, as though she had read my thoughts. She seemed to be choosing her words with care. "All I'm saying is that it wouldn't be *bad* if you found someone." A smile tugged at the corner of her lips. "And it's Peter's best friend. You have to admit, it would be kind of perfect."

My irritation flared. This wasn't supposed to be about her proving that she was right and I was wrong, but that's what it was starting to sound like, and I didn't like it. "If you're implying that Declan and I are going to live happily ever after," I said hotly, "you're mistaken. All I'm trying to do is find a way to save the podcast from totally tanking after—" I cut myself off before I said something I would regret, taking an angry swig of my sangria.

Jo's eyes flashed with something that might've been reproach, the amusement evaporating in an instant. "No, please, don't stop there. After what?"

I clenched my jaw, pretended to stare out the sliding glass door that led to my balcony, though I couldn't see much of anything from this angle. There was a hefty pause, during which we were probably both wondering if the other was going to push the issue any further. "It doesn't matter," I said after a long moment. "I'll do my share to make sure we have content for next season.

You just focus on the wedding." I sounded like a broken record at this point, but it was all I could think to say.

"Look," she said, softening again, "I get that none of this was ever part of our 'plan.'" She threw air quotes around the word, like living a commitment-free life was something we'd loosely discussed, and not something we had structured the entire podcast around. "But things change. You meet the right person and suddenly committing to someone doesn't sound so bad."

I fake gagged, sticking a finger in my mouth, and she grabbed one of the plush hotel pillows and chucked it at my head. "Ow, you made me spill my sangria—"

She pointed a bossy finger at me. "No one's making you catch the bouquet, but that doesn't mean it won't smack you in the face anyway."

"Is that a threat?" I asked, shoving the pillow aside.

"All I'm saying is, you can't plan for it. Sometimes things just fall into your lap."

"The bouquet can't smack me in the face if I'm not standing around waiting for it. I'll be at the open bar, making a solid effort to completely black out."

"So long as you're not blacked out during the maid of honor speech, you can do whatever you want."

Shit. The maid of honor speech. Kept forgetting I was supposed to make one of those. I hadn't even started drafting it.

Jo rose to her feet to leave. "Oh, and about tomorrow," she said. "You guys don't have anything *too* wild planned, do you?" She made it sound like an afterthought, but I had a feeling this was her reason for showing up to my room in the first place. Jo had a love-hate relationship with surprises. She Googled all the spoilers before we binged *Succession* and she always made me tell her what her Christmas gift was a few weeks ahead of time so that she knew how to react when she opened it. But she also got way too excited when Taylor Swift dropped *Folklore*, and improv theater is her favorite thing ever.

Basically, her relationship with surprises is a bit complicated.

"I have penis straws," I admitted. "I'm not exactly sure what the others are planning."

"Strippers?" she asked warily.

I almost told her what Declan had told me about there being no strippers here on the island, but thought better of it. I had zero desire to bring him back into this conversation, even peripherally. "Not that I'm aware of."

She ran her fingers up and down the column of her neck, a nervous tick that I had come to recognize over the years. "I sort of wish that Peter and I had just agreed to have a joint party. It seems like celebrating together would make more sense. But Autumn mentioned booking this thing on Groupon, and I know Liv has something planned . . ." She shook her head and smiled, but it came out looking sad. "Ah, well. It's just one night, right?"

"Right," I agreed, but my heart ached for her anyway. I didn't entirely understand how she could want to spend even more time with Peter when they already seemed to spend every waking moment together, but if that's how she wanted to spend her bachelorette party, who were the other bridesmaids to stop her?

An idea started to take shape in my head.

"All right," she sighed, apparently resigned to her fate. "See you in the morning."

"Good night," I called after her. As soon as I was alone again, I polished off the rest of my drink and set the empty bottle on the nightstand before returning to my phone. I opened a new message to Declan.

> **Margo:** So about tomorrow

> **Margo:** I might have a small favor to ask.

Seven Rules for Breaking Hearts ✅ *@7R4BHpodcast ·*
Jul 19
@JoHo_in_NoHo's bachelorette party today. Shoutout
to @LivHolistic and @Autumns_Closet for helping
coordinate!
💬 *27* ⇄ *1.3k* 🖤 *5.2k*

Liv, Laugh, Love ✅ *@LivHolistic · Jul 19*
Replying to @7R4BHpodcast
Ooooohhh we've been coordinating all right 😶

Autumn Figueroa ✅ *@Autumns_Closet · Jul 19*
Replying to @7R4BHpodcast
Can't wait! 🙌

John Smith *@wouldntuliketoknow · Jul 19*
Replying to @margoanderson
sexy. check ur dms

CHAPTER

13

The bachelorette was my one real, big responsibility as maid of honor. I needed to get it right. Which meant my contribution needed to be memorable. More memorable than a bunch of dick paraphernalia, though I had that in spades and would definitely be putting it to use regardless.

"'A small favor,'" Declan echoed, brandishing a dry-cleaning bag in my face. It was t-minus two hours until the parties were due to start, and we were standing in the hall outside our rooms. "I've been up since six a.m. Do you have any idea how hard it was to get my hands on this thing? They don't exactly sell them at Vons. And that's ignoring sizing issues."

"How much did you end up paying?" I asked.

"Two hundred for the night." It looked like it physically pained him. "And she wants it dry-cleaned again in the morning."

I whipped out my phone. "What's your Venmo?"

"I have no idea what that means," he said flatly.

"NASA really just hires anyone these days, huh?"

"Correct me if I'm wrong, but I'm pretty sure there's no Venmo on Mars."

"Not with that attitude, there's not."

Down the hall, the doors to the elevator rattled open, and Jo stepped onto our floor. She started toward us at a brisk pace, arms laden with a makeup bag, a can of hair spray, and a vaguely phallic object that might've been a fancy curling iron. "I hope you haven't planned anything that's going to ruin my makeup." Her gaze swept over the scene in front of her as she arrived at my shoulder. "Hey, Declan."

"What are you doing out here?" I demanded. "It's not time yet."

Her dark eyes narrowed as they came to rest on the garment bag folded over Declan's arm, but then they cut back to me. "I could ask you the same question."

Declan glanced at the bag on his arm like he was just remembering it was there. "My suit for the wedding," he explained. "I spilled sangria on it."

"His own sangria," I hurried to add. "That he was drinking by himself. In his own room." Actually, he had come over to my room last night after I'd sent him that text, but nothing had happened beyond us sitting on opposite sides of the bed and downing a couple bottles while we plotted together. Which was maybe a first. I could count on one hand the number of times I'd had a hot guy alone in my bedroom and *not* done something about it. But last night's conversation with Jo had lingered over me like a seaside haze, muddling the line where this experiment ended and the real Margo began. My irritation with him yesterday was real, but maybe that meant the rest of what I felt was real, too—the giddy feeling that overcame me whenever he flirted back, or the way my body responded to even a fleeting touch—and that made it harder to compartmentalize.

So no, nothing had happened last night. And I woke feeling pretty good about things this morning, even if the worry lingered.

"As long as it didn't stain," Jo said slowly. Apparently deciding that the garment in question—covered in sangria or otherwise—wasn't a pressing concern at the moment, she turned back to me. "I thought maybe it would be fun if I did your hair and makeup for tonight. You know, for old time's sake."

"Sounds fun." I steered her toward my room. "Make sure Peter behaves tonight," I called over my shoulder to Declan.

"Don't worry," he said with a wink. "I've got everything under control."

While Jo deposited her armfuls of beauty products on my bathroom counter, I shot Declan a quick text to finish off our interrupted conversation.

> **Margo:** I'll text you when it's almost time.

We'd agreed to keep our respective parties on opposite ends of the city. For now. Which wasn't easy, considering Avalon was a town of only five thousand or so people, and almost all the businesses were within a mile of each other, but so long as both parties adhered to the schedule, it would work.

"So, I understand that I'm probably not supposed to know what you're planning, but I'm going to need a hint," Jo said as she arranged her arsenal of makeup in chronological order across the marble countertop, starting with primer and leading up to setting spray. "What are we talking here? Glitter? Smoky eye? Does it need to be waterproof?"

"What?" I glanced at my phone, distracted by all the buzzing.

> **Declan:** sounds good

> **Declan:** have fun

> **Declan:** 🍆

I stared at the eggplant emoji. Unsettling and vaguely sexual. Jo was still waiting for my answer. "Oh. I mean, whatever you want," I said, smiling to myself as I tapped out a reply.

> **Margo:** ew, don't use that emoji with me

I locked my phone and hoisted myself up onto the bathroom counter. Jo had always done my makeup for special occasions. I liked to think it was my tenth-grade brown lip liner and over-plucked eyebrows that really set this arrangement in stone. She dabbed some silky-smooth primer on her fingers and started rubbing a coat of it over my face. I stared up at the ceiling so that she could get the area under my eyes.

My phone buzzed. Another text.

"Who's that?" she asked, screwing the cap back on to the primer.

"Probably nothing important." I snuck one last peek at the screen.

Declan:

I withheld a laugh. I was kind of surprised he knew what all those emojis meant, since all signs pointed toward him being technologically illiterate. "In fact," I said, swiping down on the screen, "I'm going to silence notifications. Don't need any distractions on your big day." More important, it would be easier to keep my collusion with Declan quiet this way.

"My bachelorette party is not my 'big day,'" Jo reminded me. "The actual wedding is."

"I like to think that the 'big day' is in the eye of the beholder."

"Ha, ha." As punishment for my bad joke, she bombarded me with a brush full of powder, and I scrunched up my face. When I was able to open my eyes again, she was debating between two different blushes. I turned to inspect my face in the mirror. It was impeccably smooth, but dusted in so much powder that I looked like I'd stepped fresh out of eighteenth-century France. "Hot and bothered, or in the mood?" Jo asked, meeting my reflection's eye.

My brain jumped right back to thoughts of Declan. "What?"

"The blush colors," she said, holding them up.

"Oh." I turned to look at them directly. "In the Mood, I guess."

Jo applied the blush, then stepped back and eyed me critically, frowning. Before I could ask what was wrong, there was a knock at the door. "I told Autumn and Liv to meet us here," she explained, clicking the blush compact shut. I hopped down from the counter and followed her to the door, hovering at her shoulder with my makeup half-finished as it swung open to reveal the person standing on the other side.

Liv only rarely wore makeup—usually, she opted for generously applied ChapStick and flakey, three-day-old mascara—but today she'd applied a dramatic winged eyeliner that emphasized her dark eyes, and she was wearing a blue sequin dress that contrasted nicely with her olive skin. She held up a baking pan covered in foil. "I baked brownies."

* * *

"I didn't know people still made pot brownies," I said, hands on my hips as I frowned down at the pan. "I thought they just went to the dispensary and bought those gummies in the fancy boxes." Mind you, it had been a few years since I'd gone looking to buy pot-anything. I'd gotten high a total of two times in college, the latter of which had ended in me shutting myself in the closet because I was convinced that my roommate was looking at me funny, and the only solution was to hide in the dark where she couldn't see my face.

We set the pan on the table on my balcony, foil peeled back to reveal an innocuous-looking layer of shiny, chocolatey crust. There were no knives in my room—a minor oversight that might've been solved with a quick call to room service—but Liv was already cutting the brownie into jagged squares using a ballpoint pen. "Call me old fashioned, but I like to have some control over the dosage," she explained.

"So, they won't be too strong?" Jo asked. She accepted the first cutting that Liv offered, a large corner piece with crispy edges. "Where'd you even bake these, by the way? They look pretty fresh."

"I convinced some older lady to let me use her kitchen." Liv passed me the next square. "Though I might've forgotten to tell her I was making special brownies." She tried to hand a piece to Autumn, who'd arrived outside my room about thirty seconds after the brownies dressed in a slinky satin dress that caught the light, but Autumn made no motion to take it. "What's the matter?" Liv asked her. "Not enough Michelin stars for your liking?"

"Hey, we don't do peer pressure around here," I interjected. "You don't need to eat any if you don't feel comfortable."

Autumn gave me a strained smile. "Are you kidding? This is Jo's bachelorette party. Just . . . try to cut me a smaller corner."

Liv obliged by breaking the square in half and shoveling the extra into her own mouth.

"Here goes nothing," I said, holding my square in a sort of mock toast. "To Jo and Peter."

* * *

Two hours later, I was high as hell sitting at the bar in one of the most expensive restaurants in Avalon, decked in a rainbow of Mardi Gras necklaces and sipping wine through a schlong-shaped straw that made the server do a double take. Autumn had booked a tasting tour on Groupon, which included an appetizer to share as well as a glass of wine at seven different restaurants. Glass number three: a pinot grigio that did not pair well with the Parmesan truffle fries Jo had selected as her appetizer for this stop, but I found myself shoveling handfuls of them into my mouth between gulps of wine nevertheless.

Autumn kept sipping from her glass and then setting it back down only to pick it up and sip from it again. "How do you know when it's kicking in?"

"You'll know," Liv said. I wasn't even sure she was high, though she'd eaten twice as much brownie as the rest of us. Four times as much as Autumn. Meanwhile, the edges of my vision blurred like static on an old TV as I glanced at my phone beneath the table. The cracked screen was so bright in the dimly lit restaurant that I was certain everyone would notice and pester me about who I was texting, but they seemed more concerned with the drinks and truffle fries.

Declan: How's it going?

Margo: Wrapping things up at stop number three. I'll keep you posted

"Margo." I glanced up. Jo was looking at me. "I'm asking you a question."

"What?" I locked my phone as the rest of the room came back into focus. Silverware clattering against plates. Chairs scraping against the shiplap floor.

I was certain she was going to ask me who I was texting—and a paranoid part of me thought maybe she already knew—but instead, she leaned forward on the table and gripped my arm like she was about to impart some deep, dark secret. "Be honest," she said, her tone very grave. "Does my hair look stupid?"

I hesitated. The hair itself wasn't really a problem, but there *was* the truly obscene inflatable crown perched among her curls, which I'd placed there earlier and then forgotten about. "It looks . . ."

"It looks like you have dicks in your hair," Liv helpfully provided.

"Yes, but does it look stupid?" Jo asked, to which there was no right answer, because yes, it did, but that was also kind of the point.

"These chairs." Autumn was rubbing the curved arms of the captain's chair she was seated in, oblivious to the conversation happening around her. "They have this sort of rustic chic to them. They're homey. It's like they're giving you a hug, you know?"

"No," I said, because the chairs were hard and wooden and I couldn't imagine anything that felt less like a hug.

Liv polished off her wine and stamped the glass on the table. "Where to next?"

"The world is our oyster," Autumn said, still stroking the arms of her chair.

Jo looked back and forth between the two of them. "We're getting oysters?"

"No, the itinerary," Liv said, in a slow and careful voice that suggested she was explaining the alphabet to a bunch of preschoolers. "Autumn booked a tasting tour, remember?"

"Oh." Jo released a *pfft* of air that suggested she couldn't be bothered with petty things like itineraries, which meant she was definitely high. "That."

"Give me that." Liv snatched Autumn's phone off the table. After a moment of searching, she passed the phone back and tossed a few dollar bills on the table as she rose to her feet. "Come on. Romano's is next and I could kill for some breadsticks right about now."

* * *

It was dusk by the time we made it to the last stop on the tasting tour: the outdoor bar by the cabanas, and the setting of choice for my own contribution to Jo's bachelorette party. The private beach had transformed from swanky resort to nightclub for the weekend, complete with a live DJ and string lights strung between the willowy palms. The sand was crowded with bodies, but I grabbed a seat at the bar where I accepted my seventh and final glass of free wine—an oaky merlot—before shooting a quick text over to Declan.

> **Margo:** We're here. Text me when you're on your way

> **Declan:** Just stopped back at the hotel real quick. Peter's changing now.

> **Margo:** How was dinner?

"Are your friends okay?" someone asked. I looked up from my phone. It was one of the bartenders—the same one who had served us the other day with the orange poppy tattoo, and she was once again eyeing me with obvious distaste. But this time, she was also pointing, so I followed her finger.

On the other side of the wraparound bar, Jo was waving the banana from the banana split she'd ordered in the air, her hands sticky with whipped cream. Autumn was craning her neck trying to bite the end of it, cheered on by a creepy older dude in a Speedo who was still wearing sunglasses at sundown. They were way too drunk and probably still reeling from Liv's brownies. "Shit," I mumbled, polishing off my glass and leaving my phone lying on the bar as I rushed to break up the fun. "Let's put that down." I gently extracted the banana from Jo's grasp and set it back in the sundae dish before steering the pair of them toward the dance floor, where Liv beckoned to the tune of "Rules" by Doja Cat. Considering she was the most sober of our group—or the one least affected by the pot brownies, at any rate—I'd enlisted her help in coordinating things, which meant keeping Jo nice and distracted until the moment was right.

When I returned to the bar, I scanned it for where I'd left the empty glass, but my phone was nowhere in sight. "Excuse me," I said, forcing myself to sound as polite as possible. The surly bartender looked up in the middle of filling a beer from the tap. "Did you happen to see where my phone went?"

There was a pause, and for the briefest of moments, I didn't think she was going to answer. She slid the frothy beer to a customer on the opposite side of the bar and then ducked beneath the counter, procuring my phone. "You shouldn't leave it lying around like that. People around here target drunk tourists. They'd pocket it without a second thought."

"Thanks," I said, distracted as I typed in my passcode to view my messages. The bartender watched me, a frown marring her features.

> **Declan:** Our waiter looked like Joe Pesci and they only had Coors Light on tap. So I'd say it was a solid ten out of ten.

> **Margo:** Of course it was. All the hot babes drink Coors.

> **Declan:** Unless you're drinking Coors right now, I refuse to believe that.

My stomach fluttered. It wasn't the first corny line he'd dropped on me, but the more he flirted, the more I thought he might actually mean it. But that wasn't the part that worried me. What worried me was that flirting with Declan didn't feel like I was going through the motions, reciting from a script. I was actually enjoying myself. I *liked* the little hints of interest. Who was I and what had I done with Margo Anderson?

My phone buzzed again. A double text.

> **Declan:** Also, who says 'hot babes' anymore?

> **Margo:** I don't know how dudes talk

> **Declan:** Really? I thought you were some kind of expert. Like a man-whisperer.

> **Margo:** Expert at avoiding commitment. Not so much the whole man thing.

"Boyfriend?" the bartender asked, and I looked up from my last text. She shrugged. "You keep smiling at your phone. Usually means you're talking to a guy."

Since when was I so easy to read? Maybe it was my face. The weed brownies hadn't worn off yet, but their effects had been less noticeable ever since I polished off my fifth glass of wine. I slid the phone into the pocket of my romper, more than a little wary of the bartender's sudden interest. "That's assuming I actually enjoy talking to men."

"You're right, I shouldn't have assumed. Though to be fair, you are completely covered in . . ." She made a vague gesture at my general person as she struggled to find the words. "Male genitalia."

I glanced down at my Mardi Gras necklaces. The beads were shaped like tiny penises. "It's my best friend's bachelorette party," I explained. "I should be out there dancing, but—"

"But instead you're sitting here, texting . . ."

"A guy," I admitted, slumping against the bar in defeat. I might have put my head down, hid my face in shame, but the whole countertop was alarmingly sticky. Even resting my elbows on it was a questionable decision.

The bartender gave me a knowing look. At least she was making a conscious effort to be . . . not friendly, exactly, but less standoffish. And my tongue was feeling looser than normal, thanks to all the alcohol tonight. "It's not what it looks like." I hesitated, but I supposed it wouldn't hurt to talk about it. Bartenders were probably used to playing therapist to random strangers. I glanced at her name tag. *Shelley.* Shelley seemed like someone who would give harsh advice, if needed. "I'm supposed to be conducting this sort of experiment."

She set about her work while she listened, ducking to grab a bottle of tequila from beneath the bar and measuring out a shot before adding it to the shaker. "Go on."

"So I run this podcast with my best friend."

She waved a hand to cut me off. "If this is your way of trying to get another free drink, we don't comp on Saturday nights."

My defensiveness flared, but it was just as soon smoothed over by the heady mixture of alcohol and pot brownies coursing through my system. "No, nothing like that. Our whole podcast was centered around these rules. For dating," I clarified. I was being vague, but I hoped it would get the idea across. "But then my best friend broke some of the rules. Publicly. And now everyone's questioning why we have the rules in the first place, so I'm supposed to be breaking them on purpose, to prove that we follow the rules for a reason. The guy I'm texting is sort of . . ." I wobbled my head back and forth, unsure of how to describe him. "Caught in the cross fire, I guess."

"Sounds like you're making things harder than they need to be. Life is complicated enough without imposing a bunch of made-up rules on yourself." Shelley double-fisted a bottle of Tito's and a bottle of Bacardi, adding a dash of each to the shaker before she popped the cap on and started shaking. "But don't take my advice. I'm a thirty-something still stuck working the same summer job I've had since I turned twenty-one."

I smiled, remembering the summer I spent lifeguarding in Two Harbors. Life was easier when I wasn't worrying about social media analytics every waking hour. "Spending your summers on an island doesn't sound so bad."

"It's not all it's cracked up to be. Only reason I still come work this gig every year is because there's nothing keeping me back home." She poured the mysterious concoction into a glass and topped it off with a slice of pineapple and a dash of Cactus Cooler before sliding it across the counter.

"For me?" I asked, eyeing it warily. "I thought you said no free drinks."

"I said we don't comp. That one's on me." She nodded at the drink in question. "Figured it might help you sort through your problems."

I probably should've been wary of this newfound generosity, but I was on the verge of admitting I was maybe more than a little confused about whatever was going on with Declan, and that deserved a drink. "Doesn't drinking create more problems?" I joked before taking an experimental sip. It was similar to a Long Island iced tea, except the Cactus Cooler completely and utterly failed to mask the burn of alcohol.

"You're asking a bartender for life advice," Shelley pointed out. "Alcohol's the only solution I can really provide."

"Touché." I stirred my drink with the straw—a regular straw, this time, because I'd misplaced the phallic one somewhere between drinks four and six. "Thank you. For the drink, and for listening."

"No problem." She braced herself against the counter, watching me with narrowed eyes. "Out of curiosity, though, why are you talking to me and not your best friend?"

"It's complicated," I said, because that was easier than explaining.

My phone vibrated against my thigh, and I extracted it from my pocket.

Declan: Here.

My head snapped up and I searched the crowd, but I didn't spot any sign of his familiar red hair. *Here?* He was supposed to text me when they were headed this way. Not when they had already arrived. I sent him a quick text back—*Where?!*—just as Jo materialized at my side, breathless and glowy from all the dancing. I locked my phone and stowed it back in my pocket. She flung a sweaty arm around my shoulder. With me sitting and her standing, we were close enough in height that she could shout directly in my ear. "Aren't you going to dance?"

"Just finishing my drink," I said, indicating the glass, which was nowhere near empty. I lifted off my stool to get a better look at the crowd, but it was almost dark now, and the DJ had a strobe light throbbing to the bass of a song that might've been "Sandstorm" by Darude—I was way too close to the speakers to make it out clearly, and also, did people actually play that song unironically? I reached back into my pocket and stole a glance at my phone. Declan hadn't responded to my last text. *Here.* What was that supposed to mean? Maybe he led them to the wrong bar. I would've noticed if they had arrived here at this bar. *Everyone* would have noticed if they were at this bar.

Jo was eyeballing my drink. "Can I try a sip?" Without waiting for an answer, she snatched the drink and took a few gulps, the straw forgotten entirely. "Not bad," she said, setting the now half-empty glass back on the counter. "Is that tequila?"

Shelley nodded. "Among other things. It's one of my own creations. Tentatively called a Channel Islands Iced Tea." She lifted a shoulder. "I'm still workshopping on the name."

Without warning, Autumn was there, too, looking about as sweaty as Jo's arm felt. "Let's give it a go," she said, smacking a twenty on the counter with all the bravado of a businessman buying a round of Gold Label Reserve for his colleagues.

Shelley opened her mouth to reply—probably to inform her that a twenty wouldn't even cover the one Channel Islands Iced Tea, not with how many shots she'd dumped into that shaker—but before she managed to say anything, our conversation was drowned out by a series of loud whoops and hollers from the end of the bar. Heads turned and necks craned to catch a glimpse at whatever was causing the commotion. A pair of women seated across from us covered their mouths to stifle giggles, one of them whispering behind her hands. The old guy in the sunglasses and Speedo pinched his fingers between his lips and wolf-whistled.

"Can't say I see that every Saturday," Shelley mumbled, turning her back on us to wipe down the opposite side of the bar.

My eyes fell on Lucas first, standing far enough off to the side that it was easy to spot him, even with the San Francisco Giants cap tugged over his curls. He was nursing a flask of God only knew what and kept his distance, probably trying to disassociate himself from the scene that was unfolding. I searched where Lucas was looking and was able to pick out Declan's red hair next—he was more in the thick of it, tugging on someone's arm and shaking his head as he mumbled something to someone just out of my line of sight. As though he sensed me watching him, he turned and caught my eye. He smiled sheepishly and held up a finger that plainly said *just a moment*, but he didn't have a moment to orchestrate a better entrance because Jo was already standing on tiptoe, trying to figure out what was going on. Autumn's twenty-dollar bill lay forgotten next to my half-finished drink.

Someone got up from the bar to get away from all the noise just as Declan gave the arm another forceful tug, and the person the arm was attached to stumbled into view.

"Peter," Jo said, her face lighting up like the Fourth of July at the sight of him, but her smile was replaced by a look of utter horror as the pair of them approached and she was able to see what, exactly, had caused all the commotion. "What the *fuck* are you wearing?"

CHAPTER

14

"The feather duster was a nice touch," I said, tilting my head toward Declan so that he could hear me over the music. I was close enough that I could've kissed him on the cheek. He breathed a laugh as Peter did a little twirl for Jo, who was looking marginally less disturbed now, though still a bit bemused. The brownies probably weren't helping matters, but all things considered, she had managed to stay pretty composed when her fiancé showed up to a very public bar dressed in a starched and ironed maid uniform. I would've preferred one of those lacy Halloween costumes with the generous cleavage and too-short skirt, but beggars couldn't be choosers on an island of a few thousand people. And besides, this kind of made for a better story.

"Believe it or not, they actually sold the feather duster at Vons," Declan said. He was leaning against the bar and sipping at a Maker's Mark neat he'd ordered from Shelley, who'd once again been all too happy to serve him on a moment's notice. I tried not to be too annoyed, considering it was her job, but I couldn't help feeling she treated him just a *little* different from the way she treated me.

"Have any trouble convincing him?" I asked.

"None. He said, and I quote, 'If it makes Jo happy.'"

On that, it seemed Peter and I were in agreement. I studied

the groom-to-be with a critical eye. The sleeves of the dress were strained by his broad shoulders, but otherwise, it looked like it was custom-tailored to him, complete with a little white apron and everything. I had to give credit where it was due—Declan worked quick. "I'm surprised the uniform actually fit."

He pulled a face. "Don't get me started. I had to ask fifty hotel employees before I found a housekeeper who was about Pete's size. His proportions are inhuman." He tore his eyes from the happy couple, and I realized that we were sitting even closer than I'd thought, but neither of us made any effort to move. "The housekeeper said she's going to check with a black light to make sure we actually clean it, by the way, so . . ."

"Can't say I blame her." Despite the fact that I was fairly certain Jo didn't *actually* have a maid kink—at least not so far as she'd ever told me—it looked like she was sort of getting into it. Peter was bent over in front of her stool, hands on his hairy knees as she spanked him with the feather duster, laughing maniacally. I'd created a monster. "I'll take it to the cleaners first thing tomorrow."

"Hey." Declan nudged my knee with his own. "We make a pretty good team."

I grinned, reaching for the glass in front of him. "Don't get too excited. This was a special occasion. I have no interest in helping you with your day-to-day pranks." I stole a sip of his bourbon and he made no effort to stop me, that familiar dimple shadowing his cheek as he watched my lips meet the glass. I used to hate that dimple. When had I stopped hating his dimple?

"Please, enlighten me," he said. "What exactly are my day-to-day pranks?"

"I don't know." I shrugged, aware of my own cheesy grin but making no effort to rein it in as I set his drink back on the counter, a faint lipstick print now staining the rim. "Saran-wrapping toilets and replacing shampoo with Nair, probably."

"I would never replace shampoo with Nair." He reached to

twist a lock of my hair between his thumb and forefinger, and my heart beat faster. "That's just cruel. And I like your hair too much."

I combed my own hand through my hair, sliding the lock from between his fingers in the process. It wasn't that I didn't want him to touch me. It was just that my hair was completely fried and I couldn't imagine that was very attractive. "So, you'll let me eat mayonnaise in place of pudding, but you draw the line at making me go bald."

He lowered his hand, still smiling. "Everyone has to draw the line somewhere."

Another chorus of cheers erupted and I tore my eyes from Declan's to see the source of the excitement. The DJ had switched over to a Megan Thee Stallion track and Peter was attempting to twerk while Jo swung the feather duster overhead like a lasso. Our work here was done. "Thank you for your help, by the way," I said, realizing I hadn't thanked him earlier.

Declan followed my gaze for only a second before turning back to face me. "Happy?" he asked in a low voice.

"So long as I've succeeded in making my best friend happy?" I said. "Yes." I was certain pictures of tonight would find their way to Twitter by tomorrow morning, and there was no telling what people would have to say. But right now, I didn't particularly care.

He watched me with an unreadable expression, hazel eyes searching my face. "How about we do something to make you happy?"

I gave him a quizzical look. "But I just said I was—"

"I mean something specifically for you," he interrupted. "No worrying about what Jo thinks, or whatever your social media people think, or even what I think. What would you do right now, if you could do anything in the world?"

I swallowed. There were a lot of things I'd be more than happy to do with Declan, and he was giving me an easy opening. My eyes trailed to his lips. Scattered freckles traced the curve of his cupid's bow, more on one side than the other, which gave his mouth a permanently crooked look like he was always holding back a smile. It would be so easy to answer his question with a kiss. Break a few rules. Actually do something worth talking about for Season Seven, instead of dancing around it and making excuses.

But for some reason, I found myself saying, "I'd go to the arcade."

* * *

"I'm gonna be honest," Declan said as soon as we stepped through the door. "I don't know what I was expecting, but it wasn't this."

"We can do something else, if you want," I offered, feeling more than a little self-conscious about my choice. The arcade was smaller than I remembered—island-sized, I thought—but that didn't make the flashing rainbow lights and the overlapping eight-bit noises any less jarring. It was empty at this hour, save for a worker at the deli counter, guarding paper soda cups, giant pretzels, and monstrous slices of lukewarm pizza. The whole place smelled faintly of ranch and garlic bread.

"No, it's not that." He walked over to the token machine and swiped his debit card. The old machine had been replaced with a fancy touch screen that spat out a preloaded card with credits instead of actual tokens. "Just . . . what made you pick the arcade?"

It was another of those questions that would've been easier to answer with *it's complicated* rather than try to explain myself, but I'd been doing that a little too often lately. It felt like I was overdue to be straight-up about something. "I used to come here when I was a kid. I guess I've just . . ." I shrugged, not quite sure how to put it into words. "Missed the more nostalgic side of the island, if that makes sense." Missed the days when my biggest problems were learning long division and choosing whether I wanted mint chocolate chip or cookie dough for my ice cream cone. Before the podcast, before my parents' divorce, before I'd learned to worry about the future, and the uncertainty of it all.

"Yeah, I get that." He watched me for a moment, his expression thoughtful before clearing his throat and sizing up the arcade. "Okay, here are the rules. We each pick a game we think we're good at. If I win both, then you have to buy me a slice of pizza. But if you win both, I buy you a slice of pizza."

I'd been stuffing my face with nachos and crab dip all night, but miraculously, I was still hungry. And pizza sounded pretty amazing right about now. Free pizza? Even better. "What if we both win one?"

"Then we each buy our own pizza."

I narrowed my eyes at him. He was wearing this silly flamingo-print shirt with the top button undone, a small bit of coppery chest hair visible. He should have looked ridiculous, but instead, I was having thoughts of grabbing him by the collar and pulling him close. "Why?"

He frowned, oblivious to the images racing through my mind. "Why what?"

"Why are you doing this?"

"Maybe because it seems like you've been doing a lot of things for other people lately, and I get the feeling it's been a while since you've let someone do something for you." For a moment, the look he gave me was so earnest and intense that I thought my legs might give out. It was like a curtain had been drawn back, all the banter and lighthearted jokes stripped away, leaving only the man beneath them. But then, he winked, and the universe righted itself. "Or maybe I just want you to buy me pizza."

"Fine," I said, tearing my eyes from him and scanning the arcade for my game of choice. I was sobering up a little, or at least I felt like I was, jolted awake by the noise and lights and the strange jittery feeling in my chest. "I choose Skee-Ball."

"What's Skee-Ball?"

I pointed at the Skee-Ball machine. "You know, where you roll the balls and try to make them jump into the rings—"

"Oh," he said. "I didn't know that had a name."

"What about you?"

His face split into an annoyingly confident smile. "Zombie Invasion."

We decided to tackle Skee-Ball first. It became immediately apparent that Declan had no clue how to play Skee-Ball—or at least he wasn't very good at playing it. He kept missing the rings entirely.

"I get the feeling you didn't play many sports growing up," I commented, just as he rolled one of the heavy plastic balls. It careened sideways and ricocheted off the hollow plastic siding of Down the Clown before clattering to the floor.

"You knew me in high school." He stooped to collect the ball before it got away. "Did I seem like the type to play sports?"

"You seemed like the type to get kicked off the team." I made two fifty-pointers in a row, easily outstripping his score.

"I got kicked off of my Little League team when I was eleven," he said when he'd straightened back up, ball in hand.

"Stop. You did not." I laughed, but when he only responded with a sheepish smile, I realized he was serious. "What happened?"

"I was making a run for second base and one of the other kids came up behind me to tag me out. I panicked and elbowed him in the face. It was an accident," he said quickly, because my face was probably horrified. "No one believed me, though. He had this massive black eye afterwards. My mom was super mad because she'd paid for the whole season in advance. They refused to give us a refund. Said it was all in the contract."

"That doesn't seem very fair. And it doesn't seem like enough of a reason to kick you off the team."

"There might've been another time playing shortstop." He

bent to line up his next shot. "And also, the one and only time they made me the catcher. I guess I'm not very good at thinking on my feet, in physical situations."

I raised my eyebrows. "Good to know."

He shot me a confused look, brow furrowed for the briefest of moments before realization dawned. "Athletic situations," he amended, a blush creeping up his neck. "I should have said *athletic situations*. I'm fine in bed." I resisted the urge to laugh as he cleared his throat and lined up his last shot. There was also no way he could beat my score at this point, so finishing was more a matter of principle. "Not that you were asking. Just, you know. Public service announcement."

"I'm sure the public will appreciate that," I said in a mock-serious voice, still fighting off the giggles. "So what I'm hearing is that under no circumstances are you allowed to participate in the garter toss, unless we want someone to end up with a black eye." He rolled the ball so hard that it bounced off the backboard and I flinched. "Or, alternative solution: we make all the single guys at the wedding wear umpire masks, just to be safe."

"That would make it easy for the single girls to figure out who's available," he said, straightening up. I ignored the prickling irritation at the thought of anyone eyeballing *him* like he was available, despite the fact that I had no intentions beyond these two weeks. His final score flashed on the red LED screen above the game: a measly 110. "Looks like you win this round."

It wasn't until Zombie Invasion that I had the sneaking suspicion he was letting me win.

We huddled on the bench, which was obviously made for children, because it was far too small for two slightly-taller-than-average adults. The bare skin of my legs brushed up against his, and when I bent to grab the blue laser gun, I purposely let my hand graze his thigh. Every touch was charged, hypersensitive, but I didn't dare try anything more blatant. I was hovering in this weird place, unsure of how to move forward. I was fairly certain I was overthinking this.

It wasn't that I was still questioning his interest; he'd made it clear he was attracted to me, and it was especially clear tonight, both of us giddy, our guards down. The problem was, I was starting to second-guess how far that interest extended. What he was expecting from this. Because he'd made it clear he didn't want to be an anecdote for the podcast, and I'd let him believe he wouldn't be, and now I wasn't sure where that left us. Despite the catchy podcast title, I was pretty sure I hadn't broken any hearts in the past. I'd never let things get far enough for that. And now, faced with the prospect of taking things far on purpose, I wasn't sure I could go through with it. I was standing at the precipice. I could step off the ledge or chicken out, but instead I was rooted in place, paralyzed by indecision.

The inside of the game booth was hidden behind a dark curtain, the only light emanating from the bluish, pixelated screen. Declan swiped the card and fired his gun at the two-player button. "Ready to get owned?"

"'Owned'?" I repeated. "Is that still a thing people say, or are you just so out of touch that you're still using slang from the *Call of Duty* lobby when you were twelve?"

The game had already started, and I'd lost valuable time with my little dig. But after a couple well-placed headshots, I took the lead. I glanced sideways at Declan as we struggled to hold off a torrent of badly animated zombies. He was focused on the game. There was no reason I should have been outshooting him. I liked my fair share of video games—usually party games like Mario Kart or Rock Band, and a short-lived but embarrassingly passionate stint of FarmVille back in middle school—but zombie shooters were not my forte.

"Oh, shit," Declan said, just as his character's health bar ran empty. I held out for a couple seconds longer, and then my character died, too.

"That's it?" I asked.

"We'd have to add more credits if we wanted to keep playing," he said. "But you won fair and square. I owe you a slice of pizza."

I wanted to point out that I didn't actually win fair and square because I was certain he'd gone easy on me, but free pizza sounded nice and sobering right about now. Nothing like a slice of greasy, cheesy pizza to settle the stomach. I set my laser gun back in the holster and struggled to my feet on wobbly sandal heels. "Yeah, let's—"

My right heel gave out from under me and I fell back, landing squarely on his lap.

The split second that I sat there, shocked, seemed to last a lifetime. Through the light, summery material of my romper, I could feel him pressed up against me, and I jolted to my feet like I'd been electrocuted, planting my hands on the screen to steady myself. I didn't even want to imagine what sort of view Declan was getting right now, the way I was bent over. Without looking at him, I stumbled past the curtain and back out into the arcade.

Okay, I was officially chickening out.

The air in the arcade felt strangely cool, my face was so hot with embarrassment and the stuffy air in the Zombie Invasion booth. Declan stepped out behind me. He had the grace not to say anything, but when I hazarded a glance at him, there was a rosy tint to his cheeks, and I thought I saw him reach to subtly adjust something in his shorts. He cleared his throat, louder than was necessary. "So, pepperoni or cheese?"

"Pepperoni all day," I said quickly, hoping that if I responded in a normal, non-robotic way, it might make the situation feel less awkward. It didn't.

Declan avoided looking at me. "I'll, uh . . . be right back."

"Okay."

I sat down on the stool in front of Wheel of Fortune as he made his way over to the counter to pay for the pizza. What was wrong with me? It wasn't my attraction I was second-guessing. It was more the point of all this, of putting in all this work to build a connection with someone, if I didn't plan on it extending past this vacation. It felt disingenuous; I'd sort of started to like Declan as a person, and I didn't want to play games with people I actually liked.

He stole a glance over his shoulder and gave me a small, sheepish smile. I looked away, willing my face not to betray my thoughts.

He rejoined me a moment later with the slices of pizza and two paper cups balanced in his arms. "I got you a soda," he explained as he handed one of the cups to me. "I remembered you got Sprite on the ferry, so . . ."

"Thank you." I followed him through the doors to an outdoor table. The night air was damp, thick with salt water. "You know, I didn't even recognize you on the ferry."

Settling on the opposite side of the table, he arched an eyebrow. "I kind of figured when you tried to introduce yourself to me later." He took a sip of his drink. "So I've been meaning to ask. How's the podcast going?"

I studied him as I chewed my pizza, already on edge. "What makes you ask?"

He shrugged. "I figured you guys are probably working on it some in the middle of all this. With the whole sponsorship thing or whatever."

"We're not recording until September." My heart stuttered in my chest, like I was already being caught in a lie. But I hadn't done anything. There was nothing to lie about. And there was no reason he would know about the rule-breaking thing—that, at least, I felt confident about. He didn't use social media and I'd been pretty vague about everything outside of my conversations with Jo. But I had a feeling he was maybe testing the waters, poking around for some sign that I intended to use him for the podcast.

"I finally listened to it, you know," he said. "Season Two, Episode Six, I think it was. You were telling that story about the guy from Portland who wanted to pee on you?"

I resisted the urge to hide my face in my hands. "Oh, God." That episode was all about Rule Number Two: if you were too embarrassed to talk to your girlfriends about it, think twice. Of course, we never made any rules about being too embarrassed to talk to high school acquaintances. And for some reason, it was humiliating to think that Declan had listened to me telling *that* story, of all stories. "I promise it's not always like that. And I totally didn't let him pee on me, by the way, if you listen until the end."

He chuckled, shaking his head. "I'll take your word for it."

"Why'd you pick that one? What did you do, close your eyes and pick an episode at random?"

"It was the first one that came up when I Googled the podcast." He looked torn between amusement and some other emotion I couldn't quite put my finger on. "I mean, it was pretty entertaining, I'll give you that. I can see how you guys got your following." There was an uncomfortable pause, and I sensed there was something else coming. "But I don't get it, though. The whole thing seems . . ." He trailed off. "I don't want to sound insulting."

"No, go ahead and say it." I'd heard it all before. The internet didn't pull any punches. Which didn't mean I was totally comfortable with all the venomous comments, but I was used to them. Numb to it all, in a way, so long as it didn't affect our partnerships or numbers.

Still, he hesitated, seeming to chew on the word as much as his pizza, biding his time. Finally, after another sip of his drink, he got it out. "Depressing."

I gaped at him. That was a new one. "Of all the impressions you could have got, depressing?"

He shook his head, looking thoughtful. "I mean, not the sex stories and all that. But all the rules, all the reinforcement of the 'no commitment' thing, it just seems . . . I don't know." He lifted a shoulder. "Lonely."

I narrowed my eyes. "There are other relationships that can be just as fulfilling as romantic relationships, you know."

"Of course, I know that," he said. "I guess I'm just curious where you see yourself. Long-term." He held up a greasy pizza hand in deference, a balled-up napkin in the other. "By all means, if you plan to be running the podcast at fifty, I fully support that. But is that what you want? Would it make you happy?"

I exhaled through my nose. "I don't know." I could just leave it at that. Twenty-somethings the world over were forgiven every day for not knowing what they wanted to do with their future. But the truth was, I knew enough to know I wasn't totally content. And that was enough to make me keep talking. "I sort of feel like it's all I have going, right now. I keep hoping I can use my experience with the podcast to transition into something bigger. Maybe get a job promoting art or music or something like that." I'd juggled several ideas—anything more meaningful than promoting lingerie brands and travel companies. As nice as all the free stuff was, I hadn't found the podcast to be very fulfilling for a while now. It was just that all of my own ideas came up short without Jo to back me up. Jo had come up with the initial idea for *Seven Rules*, and it had been Jo who marketed it, Jo who planned out our episodes, Jo who arranged for guest speakers and managed our partnerships.

Without Jo, I wasn't sure I was much of a podcaster. I was just Margo, a girl with trust issues and the occasional funny Tweet, who'd managed to hide how mediocre she was behind the smoke and mirrors of Photoshop, green hair dye, and a pasted-on sort of confidence that just barely held it all together at the seams. And who cared to listen to her?

Declan nodded, his brow creased in thought.

"I'll admit, sometimes it all feels kind of meaningless." Was I still going? Apparently, I was, but it felt sort of good to get it all out in the open. To talk to someone who didn't give two shits about the character I'd spent the past four years method-acting; Go's tricks hadn't worked on him, but he seemed perfectly content to just *talk* with Margo, and that bolstered my confidence. "Especially ever since this whole wedding thing. We make up all these rules for being independent and avoiding commitment, and then Jo runs off and gets married, and what do I have to show for it? A bunch of followers on Twitter and a string of hookups with people who don't matter." It was as close as I decided I was willing to get toward telling him the truth. It wasn't my place to spill the beans about what we were planning for next season, but my feelings were still my own, and I was allowed to talk about them. "Does that make any sense?"

"Yes," Declan said. "Like I said, most people would call that feeling *lonely*."

"I'm not lonely," I protested.

He rose to his feet, collecting our trash and tossing it in the nearest trash can before offering me a hand. I hesitated a split second before accepting it, feeling ridiculous as he helped me to my feet. I wasn't the sort of girl people carried over puddles or pulled out a chair for. And I didn't deserve it from Declan, of all people. Up until tonight, I'd treated him less like a person and more like one of these paper cups: convenient in the moment, but easy to dispose of when the time came. Which said less about him and more about me.

"It's okay to be lonely, you know," he said as we started up the road toward our hotel, the bachelor and bachelorette parties forgotten. "It doesn't make you weak or anything. It makes you human."

I huffed, the rush of air stirring a stray lock of hair from my face. "You're just full of insight tonight, aren't you?"

He smiled and shrugged. "I'm just saying. Everybody gets lonely."

I didn't say anything. A part of me could concede that yes, maybe, I was lonely. I was lonely because I felt like everything was going to change after the wedding, and I was lonely because I didn't believe in any of it. I didn't believe in love, or soul mates, or marriage. But deep down, a part of me mourned the optimism I'd lost along the way. Maybe the future would've looked a little brighter if I believed in those things.

CHAPTER

15

We entered the quiet hotel lobby and Declan pressed the button to call the elevator. "Sorry," he said as we waited, interpreting my silence as something other than discontented self-reflection. "I didn't mean to force my opinion on you."

"You're fine," I sighed. But I felt he deserved more of an explanation than that, as ridiculous as it felt to admit it to myself. Tonight was a night for honesty, it seemed, whether I meant for it to be or not. I'd been honest about wanting to visit the arcade, and I'd been honest about the podcast. Maybe I could be honest about this. "You're probably right. I am lonely, sometimes. It's just I can't let the loneliness take over. That's not me."

When the elevator arrived, we stepped inside and he pressed the button for the fourth floor. He leaned up against the railing, right next to me, far closer than he needed to be in the confined space. The doors closed, sealing us off from the world, and then everything was quiet. Wasn't elevator music supposed to be a thing? There were no speakers overhead, so I could practically hear the strain of the cables as they began to hoist us up.

"You really are jaded, aren't you?" he asked without looking at me. I could see his face reflected in the mirrored panels across from us; he was staring at the floor, unseeing, his arms folded over his chest.

"How could you not be? Just look around."

"I believe there are good relationships out there."

I blew out a breath. Hoped my skepticism didn't translate into bitterness. "I haven't seen much proof of that."

He shifted so that he could look down at the real me, and not my reflection. His gaze roved over my face, searching for something. "So, just hookups, then?"

"Just hookups," I confirmed, wobbling in my heels. They'd be the first thing to go, when I got back to my room. We were standing very close, and the way he was looking down at me had my heart pounding against my ribs, a drumbeat in the quiet elevator. I'd never quite understood the whole elevator cliché, but I sort of understood it now: there was nowhere to hide from what you were feeling. "One night, and one night only."

It was meant as just another one of my rules, an unspoken one that for some reason bubbled to the surface, but it came out sounding a hell of a lot more like a proposition. He shifted again, this time to angle his entire body toward me. "Sounds like you're scared of something," he said, voice dangerously low.

What was happening right now? I'd just resolved to let go of whatever this was. To back out before someone got hurt—before I took things too far. But I lifted my chin. Met his gaze with my own defiant one. "I'm not scared."

It came a fraction of a second before I was expecting it. His hand found my neck and pulled me toward him, mouth catching mine. His lips were warm, the hand on my neck strong and purposeful as it slid upward and tangled in my hair, angling my mouth toward his. A surprised moan escaped me. Remembering that I was in possession of a pair of hands and knew how to use them, I raked my fingers over his shirt, the muscular contours of his body evident through the thin material.

And then one of my stupid heels gave out from under me.

I stumbled, breaking the kiss with a gasp like I was surfacing from underwater. My fingers found the firm muscle of his biceps and his hand slid down the small of my back, catching me just shy of falling flat on my ass. My eyes flicked up to his. He looked as surprised as I felt.

Shit. Declan just kissed me.

Despite my earlier determination, I couldn't bring myself to pull away. I had no interest in leading him on—not when I knew how disastrous that sort of thing could end. My heart beat a staccato in my chest, so rhythmic and strong that I wondered whether he could feel it in my fingers still clinging to his arms. But he didn't pull back, either. His breath came in soft puffs of air, inches from my lips. He smelled like bourbon and seaside air and just a hint of sweat from a night of partying, masculine and almost intoxicating. We were close enough that I could count his freckles. His mouth parted slightly, a question. Maybe it was because I was lonely. Or maybe it was because this was what I knew—a surefire way of wrecking whatever he saw in me, showing him firsthand that I was good for a good time and nothing more than that. Whatever it was, I answered by kissing him back.

It started simple, experimental, but that didn't last. His lips were warm and soft, and I parted them with my tongue, craving more. He let out a muffled sound like a groan and responded by pushing me up against the mirrored paneling. If we were going to do this, we were going to do this right. Tonight was the perfect storm and I was magnetized, an electric current running through my body. My hand skated downward, fingers grazing against flat, muscular stomach through the cottony fabric of his shirt, until I found the waistband of his shorts.

"Slow down," he muttered against my mouth. I pulled back, mystified by anyone telling me to slow anything down—I knew what I was doing and I did it well. But before I could ask what he meant, he was kissing down my neck, stealing my breath as his hand reached beneath the shorts of my romper to grip my bare ass. Pressed against the beveled paneling, he ground his hips against mine, and I hooked a leg around him almost instinctively. He pressed kisses into the column of my throat, teeth grazing the sensitive skin where my ear met my jaw.

"Declan—" I whispered, not entirely sure what I was going to say, but then his mouth found mine again. He kissed me hungrily, like every second spent away from my lips had deprived him somehow. My head was spinning. I couldn't think straight. I latched onto a single thought, the only one that was coherent, running like a steady undercurrent beneath the alarm bells and evacuation plans.

I didn't want to share this.

I didn't want to talk about it on the podcast, and I didn't want to talk about it with Jo. Maybe it was greedy of me. Hypocritical, even. For months, I had silently judged my best friend as she sneaked around on dates and only told me about the guy she was seeing in bits and pieces. And yet here I was, wanting to keep even the bits and pieces to myself.

Declan fumbled with the top button on my romper before his hand slid beneath the fabric, cupping my breast over my bra. His thumb traced the line where the lace met my skin, raising goose bumps. I could feel his arousal through his shorts, pressed against me. "Fuck, Margo," he said against my lips, his voice rough and barely more than a whisper. "I want—"

We were interrupted by a grinding, mechanical sound, and the elevator jolted to a stop.

The lights flickered and then we were plunged into darkness. Declan's hands left my body, leaving cold in their wake as he dug his phone out of his pocket and shined the flashlight at the door. Polished steel bounced the light back at us. The light from his phone shifted to the panel of buttons. The little screen denoting the floor had gone blank. "Shit," he mumbled. "People have got to stay on top of inspections with these things."

I breathed a surprised laugh, though there was nothing funny about whatever was happening. He pressed the button to open the doors, but the elevator didn't respond. I shivered in the distance between us, my body screaming at him to *touch me again!* But instead, he ran a hand through his hair, mussing it as he stepped back from the panel and stared at the blank screen, as though he could will the floor number to appear. "We might be here awhile."

My heart battered against my rib cage like it was desperate to find his. I took a deep breath and exhaled, hoping to calm it. "I can think of a few ways we could put the time to good use."

He flashed the light at me, and I winced against the blinding white before he pointed it back at the door. His expression was distant, like he hadn't quite heard what I said. He pressed a series of buttons on the panel to no avail and then, giving up, he wedged his fingers into the crack between the doors and tugged. Somewhere in the elevator, metal creaked.

My heart shot up into my throat, images of dark and bottomless elevator shafts replacing the far more pleasant thoughts I'd been having only minutes ago. "Maybe we should call someone."

Ignoring me, he gave the door another solid tug and inched it open. I backed myself into the arm rail on the far side, hoping to put as much distance between myself and the elevator shaft as possible, but when he yanked it again and the door finally gave, there was no dark and bottomless pit. There was concrete and—about four feet higher than it should have been—a well-lit hall.

Declan sank onto a knee and rested his hands on it, palms up. "Come on. I'll give you a boost."

I hesitated. "Shouldn't we wait for someone?"

"They're probably going to do the same thing. It looks like the elevator lost power." When I didn't look totally reassured, he added, "We can call the front desk to notify them once we're in our rooms."

Somewhere, in the part of my mind that wasn't panicking, I registered that he said *rooms*. Not *my room*, or *your room*, or *whichever room we're going to share tonight*. But I was too busy worrying about getting out of the elevator safely to worry about what he meant. I used the arm rail for balance as I kicked off my heels, one at a time. "If you're sure," I said, taking a tentative step up into his waiting hands. I tossed my shoes out of the elevator ahead of me. As soon as my hands were free and firmly planted in the hallway, he boosted me up, and I landed on my stomach on the threadbare hotel carpet. I had to army crawl my lower half out of the elevator.

Behind me, Declan used his hands to push himself out of the elevator like it was a pool, his ropey forearm muscles straining against the carpet. Once we were on solid ground again, we sat for a moment, him catching his breath and me trying to still my thundering heart. The sign just outside the elevator informed us that we were on the third floor. After what felt like an eternity, he wiped his forehead with the back of his hand and stumbled to his feet. He offered a hand to help me up. This time, I accepted it more readily, tugging at the hem of my romper to straighten it— and to subtly relieve a pretty severe front-wedgie that had somehow happened when I pulled myself out of the elevator. The top of the romper was still unbuttoned. Declan's eyes skittered past my cleavage as he looked up and down the hall.

"So," I said in my best sultry voice. "Should we pick up where we left off?"

He turned back to me like he'd only just remembered I was standing there, hazel eyes flitting over my face. His mouth opened like he was about to say something, then snapped shut. A muscle feathered in his jaw. "We should go to bed," he said after what felt like an eternity. "I think the stairs are this way."

I gawked at him. No one had ever turned me down like that before. Not after a kiss like that. "What's the matter?"

"Nothing. It's nothing," he said, but he was walking toward the stairs without looking at me.

I stumbled after him, carrying my heels in my hand. I had to jog barefoot up the stairs to match his pace, my footsteps slapping in the empty stairwell, probably waking half the hotel. "Do I not do it for you, or something?" I was pretty sure I did it for him just fine, if what I'd felt through his shorts was any evidence. We emerged onto the fourth floor and turned down our hall.

"No, it's not that, it—" He broke off as we reached the door to my room, turning to face me. "You're amazing." He swallowed, Adam's apple dipping as his eyes raked over me—over my bare legs and the hint of lace bra peeking out the front of my romper before coming to rest on my face. "But I'm not really a one-night-stand type of guy."

I barked a laugh, but his expression didn't falter. Oh my God. He wasn't joking. "Seriously?"

"Yes."

"Then why did you just kiss me?" I demanded, a surge of adrenaline and embarrassment swirling somewhere in my gut. Churning. Boiling over in the form of hot, bubbling anger. "I mean, what did you think was going to happen?"

He reeled back like I'd slapped him. "Okay, first of all, a kiss doesn't have to lead to sex, and it's kind of sad that you think that."

"Oh, come on, you don't just kiss someone like that and expect it not to lead to sex," I snapped. "I mean, what the hell else is it supposed to be? Romantic? Was I supposed to find some deeper meaning in a drunken elevator kiss?" When he didn't say anything, I kept on going. Anything to fill the silence. "What, did you think I'd magically catch feelings for you or something?" I twinkled my fingers mockingly, like magic-love-jazz hands. "Learn to love again? With you, of all people?"

The second I said it, I knew I'd gone too far. His jaw clenched. "Obviously, I should have known better."

It was too late to take it back. "Yeah, maybe you should have," I said, tone laced with ridicule. Because if he was going to make me feel this ridiculous, I sure as hell wasn't letting him off the hook. "Maybe you should have known that you are the last man who could ever make me feel anything."

He stepped toward me, quirked his head in a way that was probably supposed to be derisive, but I could tell he was angry. "Is that so?"

I raised my chin. "You were an asshole in high school and you're an asshole now. You think I'd want to sleep with you?"

"It sure seemed like it, back there." His breathing was heavy, chest heaving like he'd run a marathon. Almost as heavy as it had been in the elevator, but this was a very different sort of rise I was getting out of him. When he spoke, it was in a low, gravelly tone that made me feel things no matter how much I couldn't stand looking at him right now. "It's not my fault that you're not comfortable accepting that maybe, just maybe, there are men who like you for more than your body."

"Fuck you, Declan," I spat.

We were standing inches from each other. I couldn't even tell what the emotion behind his eyes was anymore—anger, lust, embarrassment. Maybe it was all of them at once. Whatever magnetic pull we'd generated in the elevator hadn't dissipated, but it was mingling with a stronger emotion. One that was much more familiar: loathing.

I couldn't stand Declan Walsh. That I'd almost managed to convince myself I wanted him was downright laughable.

Which was why it was with only the faintest pang of regret that I tore my eyes from his, breaking the spell. I unlocked my room with the keycard and slipped inside, alone, before slamming the door in his face.

Season Four, Episode Six—Avoiding the Boy Next Door
27 min 13 sec

Jo: *Hello, hello, and welcome back to the fourth season of* Seven Rules for Breaking Hearts. *Today, we're going to be talking about the long-coveted idea of the girl and boy next door. Right, Go?*

Go: *That's right. The girl next door has become almost synonymous with "relationship material."*

Jo: *The girl next door is sweet.*

Go: *Approachable. Dependable.*

Jo: *But the boy next door is a bad idea.*

Go: *That's the whole point of Rule Number Six. You want to pick guys who are easily avoidable. The sort you're not going to bump into the next time you're buying condoms at the grocery store.*

Jo: *The problem with the boy next door is that he's always around. He's a hard guy to avoid.*

Go: *Which usually results in one of two things—either you have to stop going to all those places you'd normally go, or you get used to having him around, and next thing you know, you're sharing a house in the suburbs with a golden retriever and two-point-five kids.*

Jo: *The stuff of horror movies.*

Go: *It really is. Which is why today's episode is going to be centered around the sort of guys you don't want to hook up with—unless, that is, you're looking for something serious. You probably don't want to hook up with the resident advisor in your dorm, for example.*

Jo: *Or the guy who sits next to you every Monday and Wednesday during history lecture.*

Go: *The cute cashier at your local Trader Joe's.*

Jo: *Your best friend's brother.*

Go: *Thank God neither of us has any brothers.*

Jo: [laughs] *We're basically talking anybody and everybody who runs the risk of getting a bit too tangled up in your life. It's better to keep a safe distance.*

Go: *That's right. Because the harder they are to avoid—*

Jo: *—the harder it is to avoid your feelings getting all scrambled up along the way.*

I woke to my alarm with a splitting headache. Whatever success I'd had in keeping my drinking to a minimum was effectively shot to hell last night, but somehow I found myself wishing I'd drank more so that I wouldn't have to remember it. I was still dressed in my romper, penis-shaped Mardi Gras beads threatening to strangle me in my sleep. If that wasn't some sort of big, fat metaphor dangling right between my boobs, I didn't know what was. I yanked it from around my neck—stopping midway to untangle it from my hair—and threw it in the trash.

I reached for my phone to shut off the alarm and checked my notifications. Two missed calls from Mom last night; I forgot to tell her yesterday was the bachelorette party. I made a mental note to call her back later and switched over to my messages, groaning with relief that I hadn't sent Declan any angry texts after we parted ways. But at the bottom of our texting thread was a fresh message, sent at 6:03 this morning.

> **Declan:** can we please talk about last night

My memory of last night was foggy up until the arcade, and everything that happened after. Those parts were Technicolor, surreal, like an exceptionally vivid dream. I had kissed Declan. Not just kissed him back, but actually wanted him. I had broken Rule Number Six, and I'd broken it bad. There was no way I could dodge him for the rest of the trip. He was the best man, and I was the maid of honor, and they'd planted us in rooms that were right next door. We were going to keep bumping into each other, whether I liked it or not.

But what bothered me more than any rule-breaking was that he was the one to reject me. Not just reject me, but actually get mad that I wanted to have sex with him. Every inch of me burned with humiliation. I didn't know what sort of weird, puritan background he sprang out of, but where I came from, it was a little old-fashioned to judge a girl for enjoying sex. Archaic, actually. The burning welled in the pit of my stomach, embarrassment brewing with anger. Loathing.

Declan Walsh was a fucking asshole.

In conclusion, no, I didn't want to talk to him about last night. Instead, I opened a new message to Jo.

> **Margo:** Sorry I disappeared last night. I think the brownies caught up with me.

I had already showered and was sorting through all the clothes I'd brought—I was running low on underwear and would have to figure out where the laundry facilities were, and soon—when my phone went off.

> **Jo:** You're good! Too hungover for cake tasting?

> **Margo:** No such thing

> **Margo:** Hey, so, hypothetical question

Jo: Shoot.

I'd already typed out the first half of a message—*say a guy refuses to have a one-night stand*—but my thumb hovered over the send button before highlighting the message and deleting it instead. Jo would see right through it, and she would want to know more, and I wasn't in the mood to be interrogated about the elevator kiss, or my feelings, or anything else.

Margo: Would it be totally bummy if I wore jeans instead of a dress?

Jo: It's the cake tasting, not the actual wedding. Just make sure you're photo ready

Shit. I almost forgot we were supposed to be taking pictures for Castaway Catalina's website today. I checked the time and did some quick math in my head. If I started now, I probably had enough time to make myself somewhat presentable before leaving the hotel. I dug my makeup bag out of my luggage and set to work.

* * *

Half an hour later, I bumped into Jo in the stairwell—there had been an OUT OF ORDER sign slapped on the elevator, which meant either Declan had called the front desk last night or someone had found it parked on the third floor early this morning, because I definitely hadn't remembered to call.

Jo frowned at my outfit. "Are those my jeans?"

"No," I said. Yes, but she had bagged them up for donation the last time the Salvation Army was in the neighborhood, and they were perfectly good jeans. A comfortable boyfriend style that she'd complained were too long for her legs, but on me, they were a perfect ankle cut. Technically, they were mine now.

"Huh." She didn't look entirely convinced, but she kept walking. "Weird. I guess all jeans sort of look alike, don't they?"

"Leather jackets, too, when you think about it." I may or may not have dug a brown leather moto jacket out of the bag as well. Studded, artfully distressed. Not really Jo's style, but it would've been a shame to let it go to waste.

She gave me a funny look and I whipped out my phone to Google whether taking items out of someone else's donation bag qualified as stealing. We emerged into the bright and airy hotel lobby. Morning sun streamed through the wide windows, gleaming off the polished tile floors. "Oh, good," Jo said. "At least one of the boys made it down here in a timely manner."

At the mention of boys, plural, my head whipped up. Sure enough, Declan was standing in the lobby on his phone, dressed in a hooded NASA sweatshirt and a pair of joggers and looking like he hadn't gotten much sleep. And to think I was worried about jeans looking bummy. I grabbed the sleeve of Jo's blouse to stop her walking ahead of me. "What's he doing here?" I hissed.

"What, Declan?" she asked innocently, with a glance over her shoulder at where he was standing by the sliding glass entrance, still glued to his phone and blissfully unaware of our presence. "I invited him."

"Well, uninvite him."

Her brow creased. "Why? I thought he was, you know, part of the plan."

"Yes, but—" I had no interest in delving into the specifics of everything that had happened last night. I didn't need unsolicited advice and I didn't want to tell her that I was bailing on the plans for Season Seven. It wasn't that I cared whether she'd approve or not; as far as I was concerned, I was only giving her a say out of courtesy. "I don't want to be seen with him in public too often. You know, to keep things under wraps."

"Oh, that's not going to be a problem." She dismissed my concerns with a wave of her well-manicured hand. "I thought it might generate a bit of interest if we leak a few pictures of you guys together before Season Seven. You know, get people talking." She held her hands up like she was envisioning the trending topics on Twitter. "'Hot mystery guy spotted on Margo's arm prior to the wedding. Who is he? A boyfriend? A wedding date? A summer fling?'" She winked. "They'll have to tune in to Season Seven to find out."

I closed my eyes, trying to shut out the image. It didn't matter that I had planned to use pictures with Declan to do exactly that. It sounded ten times worse, somehow, coming out of someone else's mouth. Speaking it into existence. I exhaled through my nostrils. "But I don't want him in the pictures," I said firmly. "Please tell him to go back to his room."

When I opened my eyes, Jo had taken a step back. She looked me up and down with a frown, as though really seeing me for the first time. "Dude, are you sure you're feeling okay?"

"I'm fine," I lied. "It's just that he doesn't know about the plans for the podcast, you know? I don't want to risk him finding out."

"Chill out. I've got it covered. Remember how Renee told him he has a good face for advertising or whatever? Well, *he's* under the impression that she asked for him to be there, and *Renee's* under the impression that she's supposed to shut up and not ask questions about what's going on between the two of you. It's all part of the new social media calendar I'm working on."

"Aren't you busy planning a wedding?" I asked, but she was already marching toward Declan, full steam ahead.

"It's called time management," she said over her shoulder. "Maybe you'd know about it, if you spent less time going through my Goodwill bags."

I pressed my lips together and hurried along behind her. "It was the Salvation Army bag."

"Morning," Declan said when he finally looked up from his phone. I pretended not to hear him. "Peter's waiting in the golf cart."

"He's awake?" Jo asked. "He didn't answer my text, that little—"

In the blink of an eye, she was out the door, leaving me and Declan alone in the lobby. For a long, painful moment, we stood there—him looking at me, me looking anywhere but him. I wasn't sure what I was waiting for. An apology, maybe, but then again, I wasn't sure what I was expecting him to apologize for that I wasn't equally guilty of. Rejecting me, though that didn't exactly warrant an apology. People were allowed to reject other people. I was admittedly a little confused about how we'd gone from making out in an elevator to shouting at each other outside our rooms, but I had no idea how to address that. I'd never done this before. The morning after . . . after a whole lot of nothing, really. Under any other circumstances, I would have up and disappeared.

I stared at an abstract black-and-white painting of what I thought was maybe a horse. Or maybe it was a seahorse. The walls of the hotel lobby were vaguely ocean-themed and not very interesting. I could only get away with looking at them for so long before I'd have to face the music.

"Look," Declan said after what might've been the longest moment of my life, "about last—"

"Bye," I said, darting out the door.

I fought the urge to hide my face as I hopped into the backseat of the golf cart. Jo had already hopped in the front next to Peter, which meant I was stuck beside Declan. I gripped one of the side rails so that I could lean as far away as possible without falling out of the cart. The last thing I wanted to deal with was an accidental thigh graze or stray elbow right now, so the natural solution was to treat him like the kid with chicken pox. He gave me a bemused look as he climbed up next to me, but before he was able to resume the attempted conversation, the golf cart puttered to life.

Jo had discovered Peter's reason for not texting her back this morning—he'd dropped his phone in the toilet after returning to his room last night and had left it "sitting out to dry" on his balcony overnight. "I didn't mean for it to happen," Peter was explaining as we buzzed down the main road into town. As though anyone had ever *meant* to drop their phone in the toilet. "But Lucas puked, and it was this really nasty bluish-green color, so I was trying to take a picture to send to my dad—"

"Why would you send a picture of your friend's puke to your dad?" I asked.

"His dad is a gastroenterologist," Declan interjected. I immediately regretted asking. He could've just let Peter answer. Or Jo.

"Like I was saying." Peter shot a scathing look in the rearview, apparently as annoyed by our interruptions as I was. "I was *trying* to send a picture to my dad, but then Lucas stood up, so now we don't even know what's wrong with him. He could be sick or something."

I wondered how a doctor had managed to produce . . . well, Peter. Jo had mentioned something about his mom running some high-powered PR firm, too. Maybe two smart parents canceled each other out. Holding back a laugh, I asked, "Out of curiosity, was Lucas drinking something blue?"

"Pretty sure he was drinking Hpnotiq at one point," Declan provided.

I pretended not to notice that he was talking. "What I'm not understanding is what Lucas standing up has to do with anything."

"I was standing over him, sort of like—" Peter let go of the steering wheel to mime holding a phone directly over someone's head. Jo grabbed the wheel to keep the cart from veering onto the sidewalk. "His head knocked it right out of my hand."

"Wait. You were sending your dad a picture while your friend was *actively* puking? You couldn't wait until he was done?" I shook my head, laughing, both entertained and a little concerned. To be fair, it was his bachelor party, so he was probably pretty drunk. And possibly still wearing a maid uniform. Oh my God, this story got ten times better as soon as I pictured the maid uniform. "So did you get the shot, or what?"

Peter pouted in the rearview. "Well, now we'll never know, because Jo says setting the phone out to dry isn't going to help."

She patted him on the shoulder. "You're supposed to put it in rice."

"I already called room service, and they said they don't have any—"

"Wait," I interrupted, realization and panic setting in all at once. "What did you do with the maid uniform? Is it still in your room?" I sincerely hoped it wasn't lying somewhere covered in Hpnotiq-colored vomit. I had no clue what it would cost to buy a replacement uniform, but considering I already owed Declan two hundred dollars just for borrowing it from the housekeeper, I wasn't eager to find out.

"I took it to the dry cleaners this morning," Declan said. For the first time today, I met his eye, and my resolve weakened. "That's part of why I was up so early."

I would probably regret asking. I didn't need to give him another opening; it would be smarter to call it quits now before I allowed things to get any messier than they already were. But curiosity got the better of me. "What was the other part?"

Up front, Jo quirked her head, listening in.

"Couldn't sleep. Kept thinking about how badly I wanted to talk to you."

I wanted to ask more, but I didn't like the idea of someone eavesdropping on us. Not even if that someone was my best friend. I'd only gotten myself into this situation because of my brilliant idea to break the rules, but it felt like we were past that—

past the point where it was any of Jo's business. I'd have to tell her soon that I was changing my mind so that we'd have enough time to figure out something else for Season Seven, but I had more pressing issues at hand. Declan was searching my face, expectant, waiting for some hint of how I felt. "Later," was all I said, and he seemed to take the hint.

We pulled up to the sprawling green lawn outside of the venue, which butted up to an airy white building overlooking a secluded beach. Renee met us at the door and ushered us past the dining room and through the kitchens, into a small back room with a table and a wall blanketed in fake foliage, where she plied us with stemless glasses of red wine.

The last thing I wanted to do was drink right now, but I accepted it anyway because I didn't know what else to do with my hands.

Renee clapped her hands together. She looked different today than she had at the ziplining course. Her hair was twisted in a sleek braid and she'd swapped the khaki shorts for a chic blue dress with princess sleeves. Like a chameleon, I thought, blending in for whatever activity was planned for the day. "So the purpose of today's cake tasting is going to be twofold. First and foremost, we want to help Jo and Peter make a final decision on their wedding cake, so we've got a few different options laid out here for you all to try." She indicated the stainless-steel table, where an array of cake slices waited on gold-trimmed plates. "And then we're also going to snap some fun little pictures for the website, which will also be available to share on your own personal social media, if you like."

The photo wall was covered from floor to ceiling in fake greenery, with looping neon letters that read *life's batter with cake* nestled in the foliage. It was cheesy and not at all on-brand for us, but it was also contracted, so we'd be posting something later whether we liked it or not.

"You'll remember Rory, of course. He's going to be snapping pictures throughout the whole process, so just pretend he's not here." Rory did his little wave thing. His hair was in a man-bun today and his camera looked lighter than last time, the sports lens swapped out for a portrait one.

Renee launched into an explanation of the various cake options. "So, in terms of the base, we have our regular chocolate and our dark chocolate. And then of course we have classic white cake—can't go wrong there—and then the premium options, which are red velvet and carrot cake."

Jo was nodding along thoughtfully. Peter looked like it was all cake to him. I was busy wondering what sort of experimental drugs you'd have to be on to order a carrot-flavored wedding cake when I realized that Rory had inched closer to me. "How about we get some pictures of you while they're busy with the tasting?"

"Sure," I said, glad to have something to do. I set my wineglass on the corner of the table. Rory asked permission to pose me, placing his hands on either side of my shoulders and moving me into position in front of the foliage wall, just to the right of the neon sign.

I felt like my arms were stiff and awkward at my sides, so I placed one on my hip, but then it felt like I was posing for the Miss America pageant, so I removed it again. "What should I be doing with my hands?"

Rory stepped back and gave me a long, assessing look. "You." He snapped his fingers to get Declan's attention. "Let's get you in on this."

Declan set down his wine and cake and hurried over, so obedient you'd think *he* was the one under contract with these people. Maybe we all were, in a way, considering they were paying for his vacation as much as mine. Rory ordered him to place a hand around the small of my back, and Declan obliged, though I didn't miss the faint blush tinging his cheeks as he did so. My mind snapped back to last night, how natural everything had felt in the elevator, how readily he'd touched more than just my waist. I still didn't understand what had gone wrong, but that fact that he had *wanted* to touch me had to count for something. That level of want couldn't evaporate into thin air.

Or could it? I'd thought it myself—*the perfect storm*. Last night, it had felt like everything was falling into place, like we were meant to end up alone together in that elevator. That kiss had stolen my breath away; it was totally different from the other kisses I'd had in the past. And that seemed dangerous. Maybe it had only worked in that moment. Maybe it was the alcohol, and the arcade, and that wistful feeling I'd had as we walked back to the hotel, like maybe, just maybe, if I could learn to think about relationships like everyone else, I'd find that part of me that was missing.

But no. I'd said it myself, just a couple nights ago in the room with Jo. I didn't need to fill some kind of void in my life, no matter how empty everyone else seemed to think it was. A single word pinged around inside my tired and aching skull: *lonely*. Because that's what it came down to. More labels. As though social media hadn't slapped me with enough of them.

Rory stepped back and peered through the viewfinder on his camera. "Okay, now talk," he ordered.

I frowned at him. "What?"

"Talk about something. Laugh. I don't know, tickle each other. Whatever you have to do to look more natural. We're going for fun. Candid. Try to look like you're enjoying yourselves."

I gave Declan a threatening look, because there was no chance in hell I was letting him tickle me. He breathed an uncertain laugh. "You look, um—" He seemed fearful of saying the wrong thing. "Nice. Pretty, I mean."

"I look hungover," I said flatly. I indicated his NASA sweatshirt. "I see you're repping your brand."

He withheld a smile. "NASA isn't a brand, it's a government agency. My sister gave me this for Christmas after I told my family I'd gotten the job." With the hand that wasn't at my waist, he tugged at the collar of the sweatshirt, self-conscious. Rory was snapping away in the background. "Jo said it was a casual shoot."

"Casual doesn't have to mean *just crawled out of bed*," I joked, before remembering with a twinge of guilt that he'd actually crawled out of bed hours ago, despite the long night of drinking and getting trapped in elevators, just to do me a favor. I couldn't fault him for dressing a bit bummy. "Thank you for taking the maid uniform to the dry cleaners, by the way."

"No problem." He shifted and cleared his throat. "Look, about last night—"

Rory heaved a sigh. "All right, this isn't working. You two." He got Jo and Peter's attention and waved them over. "Let's get you over here for a bit. You"—he pointed an accusing finger at me and Declan in turn—"go drink some wine or something. Try to loosen up."

I was all too happy to obey. Declan followed me with a glance over his shoulder at Jo and Peter. Already they looked far more natural than we did; Jo had smeared frosting across Peter's nose and he was laughing and trying to dodge her as she tried to lick it back off. Despite my initial concerns, they really did look happy together.

"This is exhausting," Declan said in a low voice. "I don't know how you deal with it."

My chest tightened. *Exhausting.* He would be exhausted by my lifestyle—by anything beyond these two weeks. I'd known that for a while now. Should've known it from the moment I tried to search his name on Instagram while standing outside that club in Studio City, though there was no reason at the time for me to connect his lack of social media presence to my own complicated relationship with the internet. There was no reason I would've connected me to him.

Why was I even thinking about this?

"You didn't have to come," I reminded him.

He shrugged. "Jo said Renee wanted to get me in a couple pictures. Though she didn't mention that they'd be couple-y pictures."

I didn't know what he meant by that—maybe that he wouldn't have shown up, if he'd known he was going to be posing with me. He certainly wouldn't have shown up if he'd known Jo's true intentions for the pictures. "Yes, but you're not under contract," I pointed out instead.

"Did you guys want to try some of the cake?" Renee had materialized between us, showing absolutely zero interest in why we were standing so close or what we were talking about. I wondered how Jo had managed to convince her to mind her business without compromising the partnership; that was always a fine line to tread. "We've got a couple extra pieces here."

I accepted the plate. "Which flavor is it?"

Renee waved a hand, mumbling something about cream cheese and Funfetti before she scurried off again.

Declan had also taken a plate, and we ate in silence as we watched our best friends pose for photos. Peter had scooped Jo into his arms and she was giggling like a kid while Rory went mad snapping pictures. The cake was actually pretty amazing. It was moist and fluffy, and there was this subtle, homemade taste to it.

"I almost told Jo I wasn't going to come," Declan said quietly, reverting to our earlier conversation. "But I wanted to talk to you."

"You realize you could have just texted me, right? You had already texted to say you wanted to talk."

The corner of his mouth twisted in a smile. "It didn't seem like the sort of conversation that should happen over text."

I didn't know what to say to that, so I shoveled cake into my mouth instead. Watched as Jo and Peter wrapped up their shoot, until Rory beckoned us back over. I wasn't eager to pose for more pictures, but instead of saying no, I cast a glance at Declan, ready to follow his lead. "You have some frosting—" I pointed at the corner of my mouth. Declan nodded through a mouthful of cake, setting his empty cake plate on the table as he bent to grab a few napkins from the holder, and—

And wine spilled over the front of my jeans.

My empty wineglass shattered on the floor, knocked over by Declan's ill-placed cake plate. "Oh, shit," he said, voice muffled by the cake. Frazzled, he grabbed a whole stack of napkins and wadded them up to dab at the crotch of my jeans. "I'm so sorry, Margo, I didn't mean to—"

"Give me those." I snatched the napkins out of his hands and patted myself down a couple times before deeming it a lost cause. The stolen jeans were a light-wash denim. Or at least they had been, up until a few seconds ago. Now the front of them was more of a dark reddish-purple.

"I'm such an idiot." Declan dragged his hands down the sides of his face, tugging his skin so that he looked like he was melting from sheer stress as he watched me toss the napkin wad in the trash.

"Dude, that sucks," Peter lamented, though whether it sucked that my jeans were ruined or it sucked that Declan was an idiot, I couldn't have guessed.

"Do you need a ride back to the hotel to change?" Jo offered.

Renee was snapping her fingers and ordering someone to grab a dustpan and a mop while the shutter on Rory's camera clicked in the background. If #winecrotch turned up in the trending section on Twitter tomorrow, I'd know who to point the finger at.

I tried to play it off, waving an airy hand. "No, it's fine. I can just wear them like this." But even as I said it, I could feel the wine seeping into my underwear—a comfy pair of boy shorts that Strawberries & Cream Intimate Apparel would likely not be replacing anytime in the near future, considering they'd terminated our partnership without warning.

"I'll take her," Declan offered. He turned to Jo and Peter. "You guys finish the cake tasting, and I can take her to get new jeans." His gaze cut back to me, eyes searching my face for some sign of an argument. "It's the least I could do."

I *wanted* to argue. Not because I was opposed to buying a new pair of jeans, but because I was still on the defensive. Still reeling after last night. But instead, I found myself saying, "All right. As long as we're not interrupting things here."

"Please, don't worry about us," Jo said earnestly. "Take the golf cart. Peter and I can get back on our own. We'll see you guys at dinner." Dinner. I had completely forgotten that Jo booked a reservation at the Crab Shack for the wedding party tonight. "Right, Pete?"

Peter relinquished the keys, looking more than a little put out that he wouldn't get to hop any more curbs on their way back to the hotel. "Right."

CHAPTER

17

An uncomfortable silence hovered between us, filled by the rumble of the golf cart as we drove back through the main square of town. Declan stopped at an intersection to let a gaggle of teen girls cross the road to the beach. "I'm sorry about your jeans," he said after a long moment.

"You're good. It's not like I paid for them." He turned to look at me, his eyebrows scrunched together. "I stole them out of Jo's Salvation Army bag," I rushed to explain. "Not one that was already donated or anything. It was sitting in our living room for like, a month."

"Calm down, Swiper," he laughed as he turned his attention back to the road. "I'm not worried about where you got your jeans from. I was just thinking about some of the stuff you said last night."

I pretended to be interested in the hem of my tank top, which had managed to get a little wine on it, but not enough to really matter. I could've gone a little longer before having this conversation, but there was no avoiding it now. "Which part?"

"The part about the future?"

Considering a lot of last night was a blur for me, I had no idea what he was referring to. "What about it?"

We rounded a corner and the cart putted to a stop in front

of a boutique store with a garish window display of secondhand jeans with bedazzled back pockets. He threw it into park. "You mentioned something about wanting to get more involved with music. Or art."

Had I talked to him about that? Silly as it might have been, I still didn't want to listen to him ragging on me for my useless major. "Oh, that. That's just an idea for a side project. Not like it really matters."

"It sounded like it mattered to you last night."

"That was the alcohol talking," I invented. In fact, just go ahead and chalk up the whole night to drunk talk, drunk thoughts, drunk actions. Easier than thinking through the specifics of my motivations.

He turned off the cart, but didn't hop out just yet. I didn't like the way he was looking at me: like he was remembering everything from last night, right down to the mortifying rejection at my hotel room door. "Maybe you don't know this about me, but I'm not into dancing around things," he said. "I like to talk. Be real with one another. Honest."

I snorted, and avoided his eyes by watching a family of vacationers exiting the pharmacy. "Believe me when I say that I have never once doubted your capacity for raw honesty."

"I'm being serious."

"So am I." When he didn't say anything, I glanced over at him. His forehead was creased with worry, and I sighed, wishing it didn't make me feel guilty for dancing around things, but it did. "Look, I'm not saying we can't talk it out, but can we please find me some jeans first? This is getting kinda uncomfortable."

"Oh, yeah," he said, realization lighting up his face as his gaze fell upon the wine stain. "Sorry." He pulled the key from the ignition and we headed inside.

The boutique was filled, as I had anticipated, with the sort of clothing usually reserved for rhinestone cowgirls. Which was bizarre, considering we were nowhere near a rodeo. "There's a changing room in the back if you need to try anything on," the shopkeeper said, indicating something that was not an actual room, more just a wall of curtains. "No need to ask."

I thanked her and began searching the racks for anything that wouldn't make me look like I'd recently discovered the info-mercial for a BeDazzler. Declan followed right behind me, like a freckly, redheaded shadow. "So, about last night," he continued. "I know how it must have come across and I'm sorry. I didn't mean to insult you or give you the wrong idea. I mean"—he lowered his voice to a husky whisper, and the way it dropped half an oc-tave did things to me, no matter how much I tried to pretend I didn't care—"of course I wanted to fuck you. Badly. I'm pretty sure you know that. It's just . . ." He trailed off, and my stomach somersaulted, waiting for him to finish. "I've had a few one-night stands and they just don't end well for me. I have a tendency to get attached. To want more."

And just like that, my heart sank. *To get attached.* The exact opposite of my own inclinations. I knew exactly where he was going with this, and it was probably best to head things off at the pass. Save at least a shred of my dignity.

I put on a show of checking the price tag on a truly hideous pair of Daisy Dukes. "I get it. You don't have to explain. We're on the same page."

He gave me an odd look. "Are we?"

"Yeah," I said with a shrug. "It's probably good nothing else happened. We are two people that never should have kissed in the first place." I'd said enough, but I just kept going, because it was easier than getting rejected all over again. "I mean, it was prob-ably just circumstance. You were available. I was available. And you never really noticed that I existed, prior to the whole wedding thing."

Declan frowned. "What?"

"You know." I shrugged as I dug another pair of jeans out of the rack. "Single people always look for a hookup at weddings."

"Not that. Though I'm not sure that's true, by the way." It was definitely true, on a conscious level or otherwise, but I wasn't about to argue. "I meant the part about me not noticing you existed."

"Well, yeah." The jeans were my size and miraculously un-bedazzled. Like finding the needle in a haystack. I searched for a price tag. "You said it yourself. You didn't even know I played tuba—"

"It was my first week!"

"But even if it wasn't," I insisted. "You never really gave me the time of day, and then you were too popular to even notice, and I get that, it's just—"

"Margo," he said, deadpan. "I was practically in love with you for all of high school."

It took a few seconds for what he had said to click into place. I looked up from the price tag. He shook his head, faintly, like he was at a loss for words. Like it should have been obvious. "No, you weren't. You never even talked to me."

"Because you hated me after the tuba thing."

"I wouldn't say I hated you," I hedged.

He sketched a brow. "Well, it certainly didn't seem like you liked me very much. You avoided my table like the plague during lunch. You never laughed at any of my jokes. And you practically begged the Spanish teacher to put you in a different practice group just so that you wouldn't have to say, '*Buenos días*, Declan,' every time we sat down."

I gaped at him. I might've been ignorant about romance, but I did know that here, standing in the middle of this ridiculously tacky shop, wearing stained jeans—it wasn't exactly the way you picture these sorts of confessions, the way they show them in the movies.

"Does Peter know?" I asked. If he knew, then there was a chance that Jo knew, and I couldn't help wondering if that had been the source of her hesitation at the start of all this. Why she'd said she wasn't comfortable hiding it from Peter. But if she'd known and hadn't told me . . .

"Yes. He knew about it back then, anyway. We haven't talked about it recently, with the wedding . . ." Declan trailed off. "Jo?"

I wasn't sure what he was asking. "I haven't talked to her about last night, if that's what you mean."

"Why not?"

"What would I even say?"

I meant it genuinely, but now that it was out in the open, it sounded more like a challenge. Go ahead, Declan. Explain to me exactly what happened between us last night. His bright hazel eyes studied my face. They were very nice eyes, I thought. Mossy greens and warm earthen browns. Even his eyes had freckles—little flecks of dark brown that I only noticed standing close like this, in the well-lit shop.

"So," I said finally, because neither of us seemed likely to put much else into words at the moment. "You liked me."

"Yes. I mean, I still do, obviously."

"Why?" I asked, even as my stomach was doing a backflip. I wasn't even sure what I wanted to hear. "We barely even talked in high school."

His courage was bolstered by the question. He moved closer to me, close enough that I could feel that magnetic pull, the temptation to run my hands up his stomach again, to feel his hands on me. But he didn't close the gap. "You were feisty and funny and talented and probably way too beautiful for me. You still are," he rushed to add. "But you're not all those things because you're worried about what other people think; you're just you. You're just so sure of yourself, all the time. It's magnetic. It always has been."

My heart did something funny in my chest as I realized he'd

voiced exactly what I was thinking. *Magnetic.* Which meant he felt that pull, too. "I'm not sure of myself," I said, a last-ditch effort to convince him—and maybe to convince myself—that this was a bad idea. "And you're wrong. I'm always worried about what other people think. Just look at my social media." I breathed a humorless laugh. He had never so much as glanced at my Instagram, and probably never would. "I'm always second-guessing everything. I archive, like, half my Instagram pictures after posting them."

He exhaled, the corner of his mouth lifting in a half-hearted smile. "Last night?" he ventured, uncertainly. "Did you second-guess that?"

"Parts of it," I admitted.

"That was probably my fault," he mumbled as his fingers found the belt loop of my jeans, and pulled slowly, experimentally. I didn't fight it, letting him tug me closer until we were almost pressed against each other. "But for what it's worth, I vote that you stop second-guessing things. Stop second-guessing this, anyway." His other hand came to my hip, slipping just beneath my shirt, his thumb teasing skin-on-skin as he pulled me against him, sending a shudder through me.

I closed my eyes. "Seems like that's how people get themselves into trouble."

"What kinds of trouble?"

Trouble like commitment. Trouble like a guy who doesn't do one-night stands kissing a girl who doesn't want a boyfriend. Like leaked images of a summer fling that probably deserved to be more than just another anecdote, but that was all it was ever going to be, once the truth came out. But I didn't say any of that, because I was scared it would ruin this, that he'd pull away and this time, we wouldn't be able to talk it through. "Trouble like two slightly tipsy people getting stuck in an elevator," I said instead.

Now he did laugh, deep and quiet, a soft rumble in his chest as I ran my hands up to his neck to pull him closer. His nose brushed against mine, skated down it, but he didn't close the gap. His breath was warm and shallow, but then it hitched, and for a moment I worried he would pull away again. My fingers curled against his neck, against the rough stubble that traced his jaw, my eyes still shut. His thumb traced slow, teasing circles on my hip that set my skin on fire.

"Please," I muttered against him, though I wasn't entirely sure what I was begging for.

With a frustrated exhale, he pressed his lips to mine.

I was kissing Declan, and this time, I had no excuse. No *perfect storm* to write it off like it was nothing. There was nothing perfect about this, kissing him in broad daylight, in wine-soaked jeans, in the middle of a tacky clothing store. But at the same time, everything was perfect about it. He was gentle but purposeful, his hands leaving my waist to capture my face and angle it toward his. His tongue slipped into my mouth, tasting like the samples of Funfetti cake. All the fire of last night came rushing back, stronger than ever. It wasn't enough. I pressed my body against his, wanting to feel him, closer—

He broke the kiss, and I could have shouted at him for all the mixed signals, but then I realized he was looking down at my jeans. "Almost forgot," he said, his voice thick. "Should we—"

"Yes," I said, almost as eager to change into clean clothes as I was to rip them off entirely. I glanced over at the shopkeeper. She was clacking away on an old plastic register with her long acrylic nails, paying us no mind.

Struck by a sudden bold idea, I took Declan by the hand.

"Come with me," I said quietly. I dragged him to the back, to the curtain-enclosed changing area, and pulled him through the curtains with me.

"I don't think I'm allowed—" he started to say, but I kissed him before he could finish the thought. It was all the persuasion he needed. He let out a groan of surrender that sent a fresh wave of desire trickling through me as he pressed my back against the mirror, his hands working their way beneath my tank top and skidding up my bare skin. I reached to shrug one of my bra straps off my shoulder to allow easier access.

I broke the kiss to whisper in his ear. "I want you to touch me."

He was all too happy to oblige.

His hand slid beneath the underwire to cup my breast, finger drawing those familiar circles around my nipple, and I arched into him. He bent to kiss my collarbone. "You feel so good," he whispered against my skin, and it sent a shiver through me, my arms erupting into goose bumps.

But as much as I wanted this, I remembered what he'd said last night about one-night stands. What he'd reiterated today. "We don't have to do anything if you don't want to," I said.

He didn't say anything, kissing up my neck until his lips found mine again and caught them in a rough kiss. His fingers fumbled with the button of my jeans. Then, to my surprise, he dropped down to the floor, onto his knees, tugging my jeans down with him.

"What are you doing?" I hissed. My bold idea had been a make-out session and a bit of groping, but nothing more until we got back to the hotel. I tried to peer around the curtains, half-expecting there to be some slit the shopkeeper could spy through, but they were closed.

He shot me a roguish look as he pulled down my underwear as well. There was that damned dimple again. "Making up for last night."

Any protest died on my lips the second his mouth was between my thighs. I moaned, then clapped a hand over my mouth when I remembered we were about fifteen feet from the cash register. My legs felt like they might give out from under me. As though he read my mind, he scooped one of them up and pulled it over his shoulder, steadying me. His fingers dug into my hips, angling me toward him. I buried my hands in his hair.

"You taste like wine," he mumbled, and his breath was pleasantly warm against me.

I wasn't sure how I strung two coherent words together, but somehow, I managed to say, "Shut up."

If I'd thought I was breaking Rule Number Six last night, I was sure as hell breaking it now.

18

"I've never done that sort of thing before," Declan said.

"What, gone down on a girl?" I teased. The answer to that was obvious: he knew what he was doing.

"No, I mean in public like that."

"Actually, neither have I," I admitted.

He shot me an incredulous look from the driver's seat of the golf cart as he turned over the engine. His hair was messy from the way my fingers had tangled in it only moments ago, before we'd paid for my new jeans and a fresh pack of underwear without making eye contact with the shop owner. I'd changed before leaving the shop, eager to toss the wine-stained jeans in the nearest trash can. "You're just saying that."

"No, I'm not. Didn't you see the way I sort of panicked?"

"Out of all your various escapades—"

"Is that what we're calling them?"

"—you're telling me you've never done anything in public."

"Never," I confirmed.

It was bizarre how readily the conversation flowed. Like this was the most natural thing in the world. I didn't often do much talking with my hookups after the hookup part was done—usually, it was more collecting my clothes in the dark and tiptoeing out of a strange apartment, trying not to wake their roommate—but now here I was, my legs still jelly, admitting to Declan that we'd just done something I'd never done before.

The breeze in the golf cart tousled my hair, and I ran a self-conscious hand through it to try to keep it in order, my fingers catching on a couple knots. I still needed to figure out what I was doing with it for the wedding. The color was looking worse by the day, brown roots peering through the faded greenish-gray.

"Peter said the cake-tasting appointment was from eleven to noon," Declan said, consulting his smartwatch. "Should we see whether they want a ride back?"

"Jo said they're fine walking," I said. "And besides, don't you want to get back to the hotel? Pick up where we left off?" I slid a hand up his thigh just as he was steering the golf cart away from the curb. He'd already paid more than enough attention to my needs, and I was happy to return the favor.

He glanced at my hand and braked harder than necessary as we came to a stop sign. The tires squeaked. "Watch where you're going, asshole, there are kids around," snapped a woman who was crossing the road, without a child in sight.

"Sorry." Declan gave her a sheepish smile and an apologetic wave, which only earned a scowl. Fixing his eyes back on the road, he swallowed and said to me, "As much as I would like to, I think it would be better to wait."

I withdrew my hand from his leg. "Wait until what?" I was willing to respect his aversion to one-night stands. Fair enough. Everyone had their boundaries. But in that case, there really wasn't anything to wait around *for*. He didn't do one-night stands, and I didn't do relationships.

Which meant we were at a stalemate, of sorts.

"Until I can take you on an actual date," he said.

I withheld a scoff, mostly because I didn't want this to go downhill like our conversation last night. "I don't do dates," I reminded him. There was something about dates that just struck me as . . . corny. Holding hands across the dining table or licking from the same ice cream cone while walking the pier or standing on your parents' porch after being dropped off from prom, waiting to see whether your date was going to give you a kiss. I had a hard time believing that there were grown adults going on dates, in this day and age. People these days met on Tinder. Texted for a week. Met up at a bar and went home together and had mediocre sex and then never spoke again.

Declan was watching me as we pulled into the hotel parking lot. "What do you mean, *don't do dates*? I get that you don't want a relationship, or whatever."

I snorted. I couldn't help wondering whether he would even want a relationship with me, given the opportunity. I wasn't exactly prime girlfriend material. Especially not for someone with his apparent aversion to social media.

He gave me a look that was in between stern and amused, the corner of his mouth hitching in a half-smile that didn't quite meet his eyes. "It's just dinner. Or it could be lunch, even." He paused like he was waiting for me to protest, but I didn't. "One date. That's all I'm asking."

He wasn't wrong. It wasn't a lot to ask for. But I couldn't shake the claustrophobia settling around me, boxing me in. Like the careful walls I'd built were shrinking ever closer, until there was no room to stretch or grow, to do anything that didn't fit into the neat little confines of my own making. Until there was barely room to breathe.

I released my breath in a huff. "I don't know how to respond to that."

"You don't have to give me an answer now," he said, shutting off the engine. We were parked outside the hotel. "Just think on it." He pinned me under one of those rare earnest looks, the curtain pulled back. "Please."

"All right," I agreed, because for whatever reason, I didn't want to give him an outright no. Not when he was looking at me like that. "I'll think on it."

Climbing the stairs to our rooms left both of us winded, so by the time we arrived outside our respective rooms, neither of us had the energy to discuss it further. Declan excused himself to shower and I swiped my keycard, flopping onto my bed face-first and heaving a sigh into the comforter. If this was how I was going to go, smothered to death by an Egyptian cotton duvet cover because I couldn't find the willpower to get back up, then so be it.

Sometimes, I wished I had other friends I could talk to— friends whose entire lives didn't revolve around whatever was best for the algorithm. I needed to confide in someone, a neutral party, if only to get my head on straight. It was starting to feel like I had a couple screws loose. This thing with Declan had veered out of podcast territory and into uncharted waters. One week into my two weeks without rules and already I'd decided that I didn't want to do this, but I also didn't know what that meant moving forward.

It wasn't that living without the rules was terrible or life-changing or anything. It felt, for the most part, like I was just living my life. And that was the issue. I'd always put details of my life out there for everyone else's consumption, but I'd been able to compartmentalize it. The bits and pieces I put out were Go, and everything else was Margo Anderson. But this . . . somehow, this experiment had started to feel too personal. That was Margo last night in the elevator, and Margo in the changing room, and Margo right now in the hall. It wasn't an act for the sake of telling another story. It was real, and it was my life.

From somewhere deep in the sheets, my phone blasted a muffled version of "Cherry Bomb" by the Runaways—a custom ringtone I'd set years ago, and had forgotten to change because I usually left it on silent. I groaned and felt around for the phone before rolling onto my back. My heart sank when I saw the incoming call.

Mom, her beautiful contact photo split in half by the crack running down the middle of my screen. Not the ideal person to confide in. But I slid to answer anyway.

"Sorry for not calling you back," I said as soon as I picked up. "The past few days have been hectic."

I should have done my best to say more before Mom launched into one of her usual monologues, because once she started, it was hard to get a word in edgewise. "Margo," she said, as though she couldn't believe her ears. You'd think it had been years since we last spoke, not a handful of days. "How are you feeling? You sound tired. Your voice is all crackly. Maybe you need to drink some water. I know weddings can be exhausting, but you have to remember to take time for yourself, otherwise the stress can take a toll on your—"

"I'm literally fine, Mom," I interrupted. She'd always worried about me, but it had gotten worse ever since I'd helped her get by after the divorce. Every day, I'd come home from work and it would be *dinner's on the table* and *remember to take your vitamins* and *are you sure you're getting enough sleep*. My well-being became the one thing she thought she could control, but the truth was, nobody could control that but me. I could stress myself half to death and no amount of homemade mashed potatoes or gummy vitamins was going to fix it. "I just got back to my room two seconds ago."

"Is the wedding keeping you on your toes?" she asked, sympathetic. "I can't imagine what they have you guys doing out there for two whole weeks. It's kind of weird for the bridal party to be that involved. When I was in Diane Feldman's wedding—"

"I told you, it's a vacation. I've barely had to do anything wedding-related at all. Really, it's not bad," I insisted, because I knew she would beat that particular dead horse to a pulp if I didn't put a stop to it now. And it was easier to downplay how much side work I did for the podcast. She'd only worry I was working too hard, if she knew. "Actually, I meant to tell you, that's why I didn't answer last night. We were doing the bachelorette party."

"Oh! How fun. Did you play—what's the game?—Pin the Peter?"

"Peter wasn't at the bachelorette party, Mom, he was off with the guys." I extracted a throw pillow from its awkward place beneath my back, and added it to the hoard propped up against the headboard. "For most of the night, anyway."

"No, peter is slang for, you know," she said slyly, but I did not, in fact, know. When she elaborated, it was a near whisper, as though this were top-secret information and the government might be listening in on our mother-daughter phone call. "A guy's *business*."

It was a solid few seconds before my brain registered the euphemism. Dicks. She was talking about dicks. "Okay, ew, I did not need to know that."

"There's a game, it's like Pin the Tail on the Donkey, I've seen it in movies—"

"Mom—"

"Where they make a little cutout that looks, excuse the clinical language, but, well, it looks like a penis—"

"Mom!"

She made a *tsk* sound. "I thought you guys were all cool with this kind of talk. That's what the whole podcast is about, isn't it?"

One of the first ground rules I'd laid out for my mom was that she was never allowed to listen to the podcast. She knew what it was about, but so far as I knew, she'd never gone and listened behind my back. I was pretty sure she didn't want to. "Yeah, my podcast with my best friend, not with my mom."

"You know, it's the twenty-first century. Girls can talk about sex with their mothers. It's natural."

"I would sincerely rather we didn't," I said. But then my smart ass got the better of me. "Anyway, what do you know about any of that, it's not like you've been getting any."

"Margo!"

"You said you want to talk about it," I promptly reminded her.

There was a stern silence on the other end, but if I knew my mom, she was suppressing a laugh. Finally, she said, "I'm divorced, not dead."

I jolted upright in bed. "Wait, does that mean you've been seeing someone?" I wasn't sure how I'd feel about it, if she was. On one hand, good for her. About time she let go of all the tainted memories with Dad and moved on to someone new. On the other hand, this was Mom. The idea of her dating around was kind of freaky. Like watching a dog walk on its hind legs.

"No, of course not," she sighed. "What I meant is that I remember those days just fine."

"Do you think you ever would? Date again, I mean." It wasn't a subject we'd ever really broached. And while it was difficult—and more than a little strange—to imagine, maybe I wouldn't mind seeing my mom get back out there. Maybe it would instill some semblance of hope back into my generally bleak outlook on love.

As though she had read my thoughts, she said, "You're one to talk. You know, most parents of twenty-somethings hope they live long enough to meet their grandkids, but here I am hoping I live long enough to see my daughter have an actual boyfriend."

I knew where I got my dry humor from, at least. "Thanks for that."

"I'm serious. I swear, you were more put off by the whole situation with your father than I was. So what if one man turned out to be a bad egg. That doesn't mean marriage is a waste of time." She heaved another sigh into the phone, and abruptly, I felt a little guilty. Like my pessimism had somehow been burdening my mom all this time, and I was too caught up in my own feelings to see it. "If I could take it all back, I would," she continued. "Not the marriage, I don't mean. But all the lies. Keeping it a secret.

Everything you were exposed to afterwards. A kid shouldn't have to see their parents like that."

A fist-sized lump had formed in my throat and I swallowed, picking at the sheets. "I don't actually hate marriage, Mom," I tried to reassure her, but it came out sounding pretty unconvincing, given my long history of cynical comments. "I'm just . . . not sure it's for me."

"All I'm saying is, don't count your chickens before they hatch. You never know. You could meet the right person and change your mind." She didn't sound particularly hopeful. A part of me wanted to cheer her up, to offer some tiny glimmer of hope. I thought about mentioning Declan. He did just ask me on a date, after all. But it would be false hope, at the end of the day. Fool's gold.

I shook my head, an unsuccessful attempt at rattling the thought loose. "Now you sound like Jo," I joked, hoping instead to lighten the mood.

"Then Jo is a good friend. I wish I had a friendship half as strong as you two. When your dad and I split, I swear it felt like I didn't have a friend in the world. Not Diane Feldman, that's for sure. You shouldn't take real friendships for granted. They're harder to come by than you think."

Okay, mood *not* lightened, despite my half-hearted effort. "I know," I mumbled.

She must have caught on to the fact that I wasn't exactly enjoying the conversation anymore, because she said breezily, "Well, I'm sure you've had enough of me for one day. But try to call me again before the actual wedding?"

"Will do. Love you."

I hung up and stared at the crack running down the home screen. My wallpaper was one I'd pulled off Google ages ago: a picture of the Palais Garnier in Paris, which I'd wanted to visit since I was fourteen and saw it in one of my mom's coffee-table books. But for all our sponsorships, nothing had earned me an invitation to any concert halls. Opera houses didn't need my flimsy social media posts and name-dropping. I thought briefly about changing my wallpaper, then thought better of it. What would I even change it to?

I remembered the day Jo had come home from the gym, about five months into seeing Peter, and set her phone on the kitchen counter while she poured a glass of water. I hadn't meant to look. It was only a passing glance at the lit-up screen, but it made me do a double take to look at her new wallpaper: Jo and Peter at a Halloween party, her dressed as Morticia Addams and him as Gomez complete with a penciled-on mustache, their smiling faces squished together so that they could both fit into the frame.

That was when I'd known. If not known, then started to suspect. Something was different. Everything was *going* to be different.

And I was right. It had been different ever since.

Tossing my phone aside, I dragged myself out of bed and stripped off my tank top to change into my outfit for dinner.

Season Two, Episode Nine—Defining "Dating"
24 min 51 sec

Jo: *We've got an anonymous question here, submitted through our website form—this listener asks, "What are your thoughts on casual dating?"*

Go: *Personally, not my thing. But, you know, there's a reason we didn't include it in the rules. Lots of people, you meet someone on a dating app, the first thing they're gonna want to do is meet up somewhere to get to know each other.*

Jo: *But you don't like doing that.*

Go: *I'm not trying to get to know anyone.*

Jo: *For me, I think it really depends on how we're defining "dating." You're grabbing coffee together, not signing a marriage certificate.*

Go: *But I mean, what's the point, then? The whole purpose of going on dates is talking, asking each other questions. It's one thing to go out for drinks first, just to make sure they're who they say they are, but it's another to actually spend that quality time. Like, everything you're doing has to have an end goal. What's the end goal of getting to know someone? Usually, it's a relationship. So if you're committed to staying single, I just don't see the point.*

CHAPTER

19

The Crab Shack was one of those small, hole-in-the-wall places where the lighting was always dim no matter the time of day and the walls were cluttered with black-and-white photos of local history. Oceanic accoutrements—nets and life rings and rusted lobster traps—dangled from the exposed beam ceiling. But it had a decent menu and prices that didn't make my eyes bug out of my head, which made it a reasonable choice for a group dinner.

"These are a lot bigger than the one that got me," Peter said when the food arrived, comparing his injured finger to the disembodied claws on the platter in the middle of the table. He'd gone on a guided scuba-diving tour after the cake tasting earlier today; according to Jo, he had level three amateur scuba certification, which—if I was being honest—was higher than I would've expected from him.

"That's because these are imported from Alaska," Jo explained, reaching across the table to take his hand in hers and press the injured finger to her lips. "It's a whole different kind of crab."

Peter turned adoring eyes on her. "You know so much." He patted her hair, which was currently twisted up in a pair of fun buns on either side of her head. "I swear there's a dictionary in there somewhere."

"Encyclopedia," I corrected him, but no one seemed to hear

me, because the compliments had devolved into some serious PDA, turning the rest of the wedding party into third-through-seventh wheels. I was sitting next to Autumn. Declan had stolen the seat on the other side of me, but otherwise, we hadn't spoken since my promise in the hotel parking lot. I meant it when I told him I would think things through, but how long did he plan to wait?

"But I thought JPL was a campus, though," Autumn was saying. "That's what my physics teacher told us in high school."

Declan had an arm leaned on the table, his free hand digging a chip into the spinach and artichoke dip. "They call it a campus, but no one actually holds classes there. It's more referring to the layout. Lots of separate buildings."

"So, you're staying in Pasadena, then?" Liv asked from the other side of the table.

Declan wobbled his head back and forth as he finished chewing. "More like Glendale."

"NoHo to Glendale isn't a far drive," I said. If I hopped on the 5, I could make it from my place to his in maybe fifteen minutes.

Liv snickered. "That's practically a road trip."

She wasn't wrong. The drive might've been fifteen minutes on a good day, but your average day in L.A. was *not* usually a good day as far as traffic was concerned. Most people didn't set their dating apps to a radius wider than five miles, because five miles could take an hour if the universe decided to screw you.

Beneath the table, Declan nudged me with his knee. "Driving to come see me?"

I grinned despite myself. "No promises."

His eyes searched my face. "I'd like that." There was a pause, during which all the possibilities flashed through my mind. "Though if you're hoping to stay the night—"

"Could somebody pass me the crab legs?" Lucas interrupted. He was seated at the very end of the table like a kid in a high chair, looking woefully hungover after the Hpnotiq incident. Liv went for the bowl. "No, not the snow crab, the king crab."

Before we were able to resume our conversation, Peter dragged Declan into a conversation about the FIFA World Cup, the nuances of which were lost on me because I'd never given soccer a second thought. Declan nodded as he listened, apparently absorbed in whatever Peter was saying, but beneath the table, his hand settled on my thigh. Not making a move, really. Just . . . there. Warm and familiar. Like we'd done this a million times before.

Without knowing what else to do, I slipped my hand palm-up beneath his and interlaced our fingers. No one could see that we were holding hands beneath the table, but my heart was doing something funny anyway. The last time I'd held hands with someone was probably when my dad helped me cross the street when I was five—and oh my God, now that I was thinking about it, how ridiculous was that? I'd prided myself on dishing out dating advice but I'd never once taken the time to hold someone's hand.

Declan's thumb traced light circles over mine. He hadn't looked at me when I slipped my hand into his—hadn't acted like I'd done anything remotely out of the ordinary. Which I was grateful for, because I think I would've melted of sheer embarrassment if he'd called attention to it. Almost involuntarily, my fingers squeezed, seeking reassurance. Reassurance for what, I didn't know. Maybe that this was okay, that we weren't blurring an already muddled line between wedding hookup and something more. But he turned to look at me. I gave him a small smile, lifted a shoulder. *I don't know.* I didn't know what was happening, and I didn't know what any of this meant. But despite my dismissal, he held my gaze. Peter was still droning away on the other side of the table.

"Are you two having a staring contest or something?" Jo's voice interrupted.

I jerked my hand away, coming back to earth. "Yes," I said stupidly.

Declan's gaze lingered on me for a split second before he withdrew his hand and went back to picking over his food. "She blinked first, so I win."

Jo's eyes darted back and forth between us, narrowing as they went.

"So, I never asked," I said, hoping to change the subject as I cracked into another crab leg. They were the thick, spiky kind I normally would have used a nutcracker for, but none was provided, so I had to get creative with my fork. "What cake did you guys decide on?"

Jo pinned me under a suspicious glare. "The regular chocolate, with a buttercream frosting." Somehow, she managed to make it sound like an accusation.

Peter must have picked up on her tone, but not on her reason for it, because he pulled a frown. "Do you think it's a bad choice?"

"No, I think it's great," Jo said. Then, a little too cheerily: "How did you like the cake, Declan?"

I tried my best to send Jo a telepathic message that I was going to kill her later, apparently to no avail. Autumn sipped at her lemonade, eyes jumping back and forth between us like she was watching a tennis match.

"I liked the one I had later. After we left." Declan tried to hold back a grin as I redirected my murder-glare at him, but his dimple gave him away. I poised my tennis shoe over his foot, a threat.

"You guys got more cake after you left?" Peter asked, sounding about as put out as a kid who wasn't invited to his friend's birthday party. I expected it was a foreign feeling for him. Peter Figueroa was never left out of anything.

"Oh, yeah." Declan nodded, a little too enthusiastic. "Great cake, too. Possibly the best I've ever had."

A fluttering sensation shot through me, though it was mingling with paranoia that everyone was about two seconds away from figuring out what we were talking about. Liv was hunched over a plate of massacred crab legs, a napkin tucked into her shirt and hands slick with butter, but her chewing had slowed. Even Lucas had sat up a little straighter in his chair.

But Declan had started this little game, and I was going to finish it. "Declan enjoyed it," I said coolly, "but I've had better."

His eyebrows shot up, but he didn't look particularly offended. "Really? Because it seemed to me like you're the one who wanted more cake. Which you could have, by the way, if you weren't so stubborn."

"I could always find cake somewhere else." I pressed the toe of my tennis shoe into his foot, hard. He responded with a sharp intake of breath, but it wasn't enough to shut him up.

"Yes, but would you like it as much as this particular cake?" he inquired politely. "I mean, from everything you've said, it kind of sounds like you're bored with other cake. And you *did* just mention something about coming over to my place for some more cake."

Realization was dawning on Jo's face as she looked back and forth between the two of us. There were only so many things Declan and I could have done to warrant the awkwardness of this whole exchange. And more important, there were only so many things cake could be a euphemism for. I imagined the crab, dropped in a pot of seemingly harmless water, only to be slowly boiled alive before it even realized what was happening. That's what was happening to me. I was the crab, and this cake euphemism was the boiling water.

"I didn't realize you'd tried this particular cake already," Jo said slowly.

I shot her a look, doing my best to silently beg her to put a pin in it. I could explain everything later, preferably in private, and preferably after I'd had the chance to gather my thoughts.

"Why are we still talking about cake?" Peter demanded.

"Yes," I agreed, "why *are* we still talking about cake?"

Declan cracked one of the crab legs and extracted a succulent bit of meat, dipping it in butter. "I would think, logically, if you wanted a slice of cake, you would be willing to let me at least take you out for dinner first. Dinner before dessert and all that." He popped the meat into his mouth and chewed, looking horribly self-satisfied.

"Okay, what the hell is *cake,* because I *know* you're not talking about wedding cake," Liv interjected. "Is this like Netflix and Chill? Hulu and Cake?"

"Oh, come on," Declan said. "We're at *least* HBO Max."

This wasn't fair. The water was officially boiling. Say goodbye, crab-Margo.

"Now I want cake," Peter said, snatching the dessert menu from where it was tucked behind the napkin holder. "Do they have any here?"

"I'm officially sworn off cake," I said, looking daggers at Declan. "I think I'll go on a diet."

"Won't you at least have some at the wedding?" Peter asked.

Declan pretended to pout. "Yes, won't you?"

Giving up on crushing his toes, I swung my foot backward into his shin. With a sharp intake of breath, he finally buckled, reaching beneath the table to rub his leg. "Ow, shit, Margo, that hurt."

"Good. About time I pay you back somehow."

I could tell by the enthusiastic look on his face that I just gave him an opening for another dirty joke. But Jo spoke first. "Do I need to remind you that you promised me you wouldn't ruin this vacation by bickering?"

"Bickering?" Declan repeated, looking back and forth between us.

I huffed. "I never promised that."

"I believe your exact words were, 'I'm not going to go all Red Wedding on the best man.'"

A grin had taken over Declan's whole face. "Red Wedding!"

"Okay, but it's not my fault he always knows how to get a rise out of me," I sputtered. Declan opened his mouth, and I tried to shut him up with a threatening finger. "Don't you fucking say it. Don't you dare."

"You're pretty good at getting a rise out of me, as well."

He said it. He fucking said it.

Liv leaned toward Autumn, both watching our exchange unfold with all the interest of a pair of scientists working on their PhD thesis. "I can't even tell if these are euphemisms anymore."

"Oh, they're *definitely* euphemisms," Autumn assured her.

"Euphemisms?" Peter lowered the dessert menu with a thoughtful frown, having finally acquired basic deduction skills. He looked around at all of us. "We're not actually talking about cake, are we?"

Lucas shook his head as he stirred the celery around in his Bloody Mary. "For God's sake, just fuck or whatever. Eat your cake. Just let the rest of us enjoy our dinner in peace."

"Thank you, Marie Antoinette," I grumbled, about two seconds from hiding my face in the drink menu.

Peter's eyes were like round, shiny marbles, ready to pop out of his head. "You and Margo," he said, looking at Declan, and then at me, and then at Declan again. "Dude. You and *Margo.*" The legs of his chair scraped against the floor as he stood to reach across the table and give Declan a congratulatory clap on the shoulder, like we'd just announced our engagement. "This is awesome. Bartender! Let's get some shots of Cazadores over here."

"Oh, no, thank you," I called to the bartender, as Jo yanked Peter back into his seat. My face was on fire, everyone was in on the joke, and Declan was smiling like he'd just won gold in the Olympic sprint. And here I was, unable to keep up.

Dinner was obviously a bad idea.

"Who's up for some dessert?" Declan asked, as soon as we all stepped out of the Crab Shack and onto a busy side street in Avalon. It was quieter now than yesterday, but the weekend crowds still lingered, people with towels slung over their shoulders as they hiked back to mid-century hotels and island locals drinking and heckling passersby outside a cantina.

"I swear, if you say anything about cake—" I began.

He held up his hands in surrender. "Chill. I was going to suggest ice cream."

"Actually," Jo interrupted, "I was thinking of stealing Margo for a bit so that we can go pick out my shoes for the big day."

The girls took the hint without hesitation and Lucas didn't seem to care either way, but Peter exchanged an uncertain look with Declan. "Oh," Peter said. "Well, we could come with you."

"It's bad luck to see the bride's shoes before the wedding," Liv said as she tugged at my arm.

"It's—what?"

Autumn grabbed her brother by the arm and steered him away, up the street toward our hotel on the hill, and Lucas followed suit. For the briefest of moments, Declan locked eyes with me, uncertainty lingering there. As playful as our exchange during dinner had seemed, it had probably raised a few questions.

"We'll catch you guys later," Jo said, herding me like a willing but confused lamb toward the main street where most of the shops were.

"You already bought your shoes," I said, because there was no way she'd trust an island this small to have anything halfway decent. "So what's up?" I had a feeling she wanted to confront me about my evasiveness with the whole Declan thing. And all the crazy mixed signals. Because as much as I'd been frustrated by his mixed signals in the beginning, I was giving off plenty of my own, in just about every possible direction. But I didn't know how to stop it. "If this is about everything with Declan, I've been meaning to talk—"

"Are you kidding?" She steered me into a touristy shop, complete with island-shaped magnets and lifeguard beach towels in the window. Inside was muggy and smelled like cheap tropical-breeze-scented air freshener, but the only people in sight were the cashier and some lady in skinny jeans, so it was a safe place to talk without worrying about who overheard. "About time. You're, what, a decade overdue?"

I stared at her. "What?"

"You *like* him."

"No, I don't."

"Yes, you do. I've seen you with guys, Margo. Our whole lives, I've watched how you are about things," she reminded me. "Whatever this is, it's different. I can feel it."

"And you're . . ." I frowned, sizing her up. "What, happy about that?"

She shrugged as she picked up a palm tree snow globe and shook it, pretending to be an interested customer. "I'm just excited to see you finally let yourself go a little."

I wrestled with the compulsion to deny, deny, deny. As much as what she was saying was true—maybe I did like Declan, a little—I didn't want to admit it. It was as close as I'd come to breaking

Rule Number Two, only it wasn't Declan that I was embarrassed by. It was me. I was embarrassed to show any sign of weakness, to finally throw in the towel and admit that maybe Jo was right. Maybe I *was* overdue to let go, a little.

Maybe this experiment was good for me.

"I can't wait to start outlining Season Seven," Jo said excitedly. "We're going to have so much to talk about."

And there it was—the other wrench in the gears, the thing that was holding me back from wanting to talk about it. I was no longer keen on turning this all into some funny anecdote designed to get a cheap laugh out of our listeners, but it felt impossible to say that out loud when I had signed my life away to sponsorships and Spotify exclusives. I'd initialed every page of the contract with Castaway Catalina, which meant the entirety of these two weeks was commodified. I had to have some sort of content.

"Did you know?" I asked, after a long moment.

She knit her brow. "Know what?"

"That Declan had a crush on me in high school." When she only gave me a dumbfounded look, I was pretty sure I had my answer. "He said he told Peter about it way back when," I explained. "I didn't know if Peter had told you."

She shook her head. "He never mentioned it." There was a thoughtful pause before she added, "But that honestly doesn't surprise me."

"It doesn't?" I asked, taken aback. It had sure as hell surprised me.

"He literally went to every single one of the school concerts," she reminded me. "What other guys do you know who willingly sat through the same renditions of Tchaikovsky and 'Ride of the Valkyries' semester after semester?"

I didn't know how to answer that, so I fell silent, feigning interest in the impressive collection of beach bum T-shirts on display, all featuring small animals of some sort—cats, dogs, bunnies, turtles.

It was true that Declan had shown up to a few of our end-of-semester performances, but I'd always assumed he was scoping things out for his next stunt.

"So," Jo said, finally getting around to what she really wanted to ask, "what exactly happened between you two?"

"Last night at the bachelorette party," I started, hesitant.

"I thought you went to bed."

I winced. "I might've gone and made out with Declan in an elevator instead."

"That's it? You just kissed?" She sounded disappointed.

I sighed. I was going to have to explain things sooner or later. Might as well get it over with. "He has this thing about one-night stands. He wants to go on an actual date before screwing my brains out, or whatever."

"I gathered that during the whole cake conversation," she said dryly. "So you guys haven't actually done anything, then? No wonder there was this weird"—she made a funny gesture with her hand, wiggling her fingers at me—"tension between you two, back at the table."

"I didn't say that. We sort of . . . fooled around in a dressing room earlier today, when he took me to buy new jeans."

She picked up a hideous men's XL T-shirt of a worm wearing sunglasses. "I've heard you describe just about every sex act humanly possible, sometimes in graphic detail, so there's no way you're getting away with a lame description like *fooled around.*"

"Fine." I cast a nervous look around the shop to make sure no one was eavesdropping, and then I muttered, "He went down on me."

"He ate you out in a dressing room?" she blurted, way louder than was necessary, because the lady in skinny jeans—in the middle of checking out at the register—turned to shoot us a disgusted look. Seeming to realize how tactless this was, Jo lowered her voice. "How did that go?"

"Best orgasm of my life, I'm pretty sure."

"Wow." There was a long pause, during which Jo seemed to be processing this new information. I could practically see the wheels turning in her head. "Well, what are you going to do?"

"What do you mean?"

"You can't just let that sort of thing go." She took the worm shirt to the register and I followed her. The skinny jeans lady dodged us like sluttiness was contagious. "If you don't go on that date, I promise you, you'll regret it for the rest of your life."

I pressed my lips together as Jo handed her card to the clerk and he bagged up the T-shirt. *I know.* That was the only reply I could conjure up, but I couldn't bring myself to say it out loud. I knew I would regret not going on the date with Declan, and I couldn't help being a little annoyed at myself for it. That I'd finally given in to *wanting* something from someone else. And it was more than just the sex, though I wanted that, too.

Actually, now that I thought about it, I was also kind of annoyed at myself for feeling annoyed. Like I'd let the podcast—this whole lifestyle we invented—sink its claws into me and make me feel guilty for something that was perfectly normal. We'd conceived *Seven Rules* as a response to all the pressures and shame society put on single women, but what was the point if all we'd done was invent new ways to shame ourselves along the way? This wasn't what it was supposed to be about. This guilt I was feeling—it wasn't empowering. And now that I was really thinking about it, that kind of defeated the whole purpose.

Jo finished checking out and we exited the shop back onto the street. It was dark now, the old stucco buildings and golf carts along the curb illuminated by yellowish streetlights. We walked along the sidewalk, past the locals drinking on the patio of a cantina, mariachi music spilling out into the street. "How's your mom been?" she asked. Maybe she was changing the subject because she'd picked up on my surly silence. "She's still planning on coming to the wedding, right?"

"Of course. She wouldn't miss it." I tried to shake the confusion swirling in my brain, focus on something else, because dwelling on it wasn't making matters any simpler. "She's good, I think, but I get the feeling she's bored ever since I moved out. We actually talked about dating last night, believe it or not."

"Her dating, or you dating?" Jo waggled a brow.

Okay, so maybe she hadn't changed the subject entirely. "Her dating."

"Oh, God. I can already picture it. Your mom could be a total cougar."

I snorted. "I'd prefer not to have a twenty-year-old stepdad. But really, I just want her to do what makes her happy. Though if she had her way, that'd probably be me moving home. Easier to make your kid keep you company than figure out how to use Bumble."

"Do parents even use Bumble? I thought they just met people in the fruit section of the grocery store, picking out cantaloupes or something."

We reached the hotel and crossed the lobby to the stairs. The elevator still looked to be out of order—not that I was eager to take it, after what happened last night. We hiked the stairs to the third floor, where Jo should have broken away to head to her room. Instead, she stopped in the stairwell, clutching the black plastic bag from her recent purchase to her chest. "Speaking of moving home," she said offhandedly, "I've been meaning to talk to you about the apartment."

Oh. That. Just another conversation I'd strategically avoided for the past several weeks. But it seemed tonight was a night for getting things out into the open. If she wanted to have this conversation here, in this echoey industrial stairwell, then so be it. "I figure you're going to get a place with Peter, aren't you?"

"Yeah, but what about you? The rent's kind of high by your-self."

I shrugged a shoulder, leaned my back against the steel arm rail. "I can find a roommate or something."

"I was thinking I could help you buy out of the lease early. If you want."

"Oh." I hadn't expected that. The lease wasn't due to end until November, and I hadn't really thought through what I would do afterward. If I broke it early, then I could probably stay with my mom for a while to save money. Which maybe wasn't a bad thing—I'd get to spend time with Cat Benatar, try to figure out what I wanted to do with my life without the pressure of paying a three-thousand-dollar rent by myself each month. "Usually, when you get married, I'm supposed to be the one giving you a gift, not the other way around."

"You already got me the kayaking trip," she reminded me. "We signed the lease together, we break it together. I'd be a pretty shitty friend if I left you hanging."

"I'll think about it."

"All right." She shoved the plastic bag into my arms. "This is for you."

I pinched the plastic between two fingers and held it at arm's length, like it was full of toxic sludge. "Why?"

"Because I bought it for you."

"You bought me a T-shirt with a worm in sunglasses," I said flatly. I dug the T-shirt out of the bag and held it up to inspect it more closely. *Fishing for fun on Catalina Island*, read the ugly Comic Sans letters across the top. Great. So the worm was fish food. An omen for when I was going to inevitably throw myself overboard on the ferry ride home rather than deal with the consequences of my actions.

She shrugged. "It reminds me of you. You think you're playing it cool, but really you're all . . ." I could tell she was racking her brain for something to make this gift make sense.

"Slimy?" I volunteered. "Covered in dirt?"

"According to Liv, earthworms actually symbolize a fresh start. New beginnings."

I shook my head, laughing. "I can't believe you just tried to draw a comparison between me and a cartoon worm."

"You're welcome."

We stood there, neither of us sure whether we should stay or go. I could've jogged up the stairs to my floor, Jo could've disappeared down the hall to her room, but instead the pair of us were hanging around an empty stairwell, like there was something more that still needed to be said. Maybe there was. I chewed my lip. "I've been meaning to ask you something."

She nodded, like she'd been expecting that.

"How would you feel about coming up with some other content for Season Seven? I don't really . . . I mean, I'm not sure I'm comfortable with what we have planned anymore." I'd known it for a while now, but admitting it out loud made me feel restless. Fidgety. Like I was opening myself up to judgment and prying questions about what all this was supposed to mean when the truth was, I was still struggling to figure it out. I crossed my arms, but it felt awkward with the plastic bag in my hand, so I uncrossed them again. "You know, now that the situation has changed," I finished lamely.

Jo nodded. "That's fine by me." When I frowned, she squeezed my arm and added, "No, seriously, I get it."

I blew out a breath. "Do you ever miss the way things were? Before *Seven Rules*. I mean, I know the podcast has made our lives a million times better, and don't get me wrong, I'm grateful for that, but sometimes I miss when we were simpler. When we were just us."

"Margo and Jocelyn." She smiled faintly. "Not Go and Jo."

My heart ached with the realization that my best friend had been feeling the same way I was feeling. That maybe I wasn't alone. For years, I'd thought that Jo modified my name to match with hers. But now, looking at her, it was plain as day that we'd both been drowning in shallow water, in this superficial image we'd built for ourselves. We were both playing a character, hiding the real us behind a microphone, behind a nickname, behind a screen. How hadn't I realized it sooner?

"I'm thinking I need to make a conscious effort to be myself more often," I admitted, and I had a feeling I knew exactly where I wanted to start. "Hold me accountable?"

"Oh, believe me," Jo said, and now her face split into a real smile. Her signature red lipstick was mostly gone, faded throughout the day to nothing more than a faint stain, but somehow, she looked more herself than ever. "I will."

CHAPTER

21

The Vons in Avalon didn't carry any Arctic Fox in the shade Phantom Green. There were four boxes of hair dye in total, three of which were L'Oréal Paris in varying shades of blond. I grabbed the last box of Clairol—and one of those single-use deep conditioning masks, for good measure—and then I went up to the checkout.

The cashier eyed the box dye as he rang me up. "Light Cool Brown," he read off, his eyes flicking to me. "Tired of—" He squinted at my split ends. "What color is that, anyway?"

"It used to be green, among other colors," I said. "And no. Not tired of it. I just decided that I like the idea of changing things up for a bit." Maybe I'd go back to dyeing my hair random colors in a month. But if I did, it would be because I wanted to. Not because it was how my followers recognized me or because my green hair was *iconic* according to some random BuzzFeed article.

I stepped out of Vons to a bright and cloudless morning, gulls crooning overhead. Some of the foot traffic had died down with the end of the weekend, though there were still plenty of ferries bussing people back and forth from the mainland at all hours of the day. Monday—we were now eight days into the vacation, with less than a week until the wedding. As bizarre as it sounded, I was actually excited about that. There was still plenty of uncertainty about the future, but last night had brought on something of an epiphany for me. I was happy for my best friend. Ecstatic, really, that she hadn't let the podcast or our listeners' opinions hold her back from doing what she wanted to do with her own life.

I could learn a thing or two from that. I pulled my phone out of my pocket and sent her a quick text, the plastic bag full of hair dye and conditioner slung in the nook of my arm.

> **Margo:** Hey. Did you need me for anything today? Because if not, I was thinking of maybe going out on that date thing

Jo texted back almost immediately. And then texted again. And again.

> **Jo:** AAAAAAAAHH

> **Jo:** I can't believe it

> **Jo:** This is amazing

> **Jo:** No I don't need help with anything today

> **Jo:** TELL ME EVERYTHING

> **Jo:** Text updates

I laughed despite myself, a giddy feeling welling up inside me. My phone was going haywire—it couldn't keep up. I'd needed a new phone long before dropping it outside that club in Studio City, but I was putting it off because I'd probably just turn around and break the new one anyway. Part of maintaining all my social media was keeping my phone with me at all times, so it had always been easier to let it be a little broken in. That way, the next time I dropped it outside a club, or spilled wine on it, or left it lying in the sun while I was tanning by the pool in the apartment complex, it wouldn't make much of a difference.

But now, I was starting to think that I was overdue for a new one. A clean slate. Maybe I'd find a new way to compartmentalize my work—I could get an iPad for managing my social media and leave all that junk off my personal phone. That way, it would be easier to step out of the influencer headspace and learn to just live my life. Form better habits. Maybe cut back on screentime.

I shot Jo another quick text before locking my phone.

> **Margo:** I'll tell you all about it later. In person.

* * *

A box of hair dye, a shower, and a little over an hour later, I knocked on the door to room 403. Declan answered looking freshly showered himself, his hair still damp and a clean but threadbare gray T-shirt pulled taut over his broad chest.

"Hey." He leaned a muscled arm against the doorframe as he took in my appearance, gaze flicking over me. I'd pulled my freshly dyed hair into a high ponytail and thrown on a casual combination of jean shorts, Rainbow-brand flip-flops, and the earthworm T-shirt that Jo bought me, all in preparation for the day ahead. He appeared to be at a loss for words. "Your hair," he said finally. "It looks—"

Before he was able to finish telling me whatever it looked like, I grabbed him by the front of his shirt and pulled him into a rough kiss. For the briefest of seconds, it was clear that he was caught off guard, because he tensed. But then his arm left the doorframe and found my waist, pulling me in close as he deepened the kiss.

I was breathless by the time I pulled away. "Go on a date with me?" It was breaking Rule Number Four. He had said he wanted to take me on a date, but here I was, taking matters into my own hands and planning one for him. But I didn't particularly care.

"What, now?" he laughed. He ran a hand through his damp hair, mussing it. "I kind of expected you to hold out a little longer."

"This vacation's too short to waste time playing stupid mind games." He was only slightly taller than me, but I stood on my tiptoes anyway to plant another quick peck on his cheek. "And besides. I've got it all planned out."

His eyebrows shot up. "Oh, you're taking *me* on a date?" He shook his head, grinning like a kid on Christmas. It was kind of adorable. "I'm not sure that's what we agreed to."

Since when did I even think words like *adorable*? Yet here I was, cheesing just as hard as he was. "Shut up. You have fifteen minutes to get ready."

"Where are we going?"

"It's a surprise." I stepped back and gave him a quick appraising look to make sure his clothes would work for what I had planned. Everything looked to be in order. "Just make sure you put on some sunscreen."

He winked. "Only if you'll help."

* * *

"Surprise," I announced, more than a little nervous as I spread my arms wide and posed in front of one of the Hummers like they'd offered me a sponsorship. When Declan only stared, I turned to look at the Hummer, in part to hide my insecurity. I'd never done anything like this for a man. I needed a little reassurance that I'd done an okay job, and him just staring at me wasn't helping matters. "You wanted to see the bison, so I thought I'd take you to see the bison."

We were at the start of the same dusty road we had hiked before, only this time we wouldn't have to break a sweat hiking it. The tour guide had told us it was a day's hike to see the buffalo on foot, but that translated to only a couple hours on one of the open-air Hummer tours.

"Wow. This is so . . ." He broke off, and I wondered what word might fill in the blank. Ridiculous. Stupid. Sweaty, dusty, not really a date-worthy activity. But then his arms came to my waist from behind, and he kissed the back of my head—a much more public display of affection than I was used to. Warmth rushed to my cheeks, but I didn't totally hate it. "Thoughtful."

"You remember a lot about me," I said. Including little things, like me drinking Sprite on the ferry, or eating my ham sandwiches with mayo in high school. "I figured the least I could do was remember something you mentioned less than a week ago."

"This isn't exactly cheap," he mumbled against my hair.

I pulled away, leading him by the hand. "Well, you did pay for my dinner last night." When he resisted my attempts at dragging him into the Hummer, I turned and looked him in the face. "Seriously, it's no biggie. I want you to see the buffalo."

The shadow of a dimple appeared in his cheek, and he shook his head as he climbed up into the Hummer beside me. "You do know that they're technically bison."

"The tour calls them buffalo, smart guy."

He slung an arm around my shoulder as we waited for everyone else on the tour. The driver—the same gruff-looking woman as before—was already seated up front, waiting to scan the QR codes on people's phones. "I like the hair, by the way," Declan said. "Didn't really give me a chance to say it earlier." His fingers toyed with a loose tendril near my face, and a fresh wave of goose bumps erupted on my skin. "I mean, I liked your old hair, too. But this is nice. What made you decide to dye it?"

I fought a blush. He must really like me, if he thought my washed-out green hair had looked anywhere near good. "Felt like I needed a change. And I wanted to make sure it looked okay for the wedding."

"It looks more than okay."

Now I did blush. Next to my face, his smartwatch lit up. *Text from Erin*. I didn't mean to glance at it, but I did anyway. Force of habit—a screen lit up, and there I was, checking it.

"My sister," he explained. "I'll text her later."

"What's up with the smartwatch?" It had been eating away at me for the past week. For someone who hated technology, he sure was confusing about it. He worked as a mechanical engineer, probably dealing with all sorts of complicated crap like satellites and space shuttles, but he apparently didn't know how Venmo worked. He had a smartwatch, but zero social media presence. I didn't get it, but I wanted to get it, and this time it wasn't just because I was hungry to stalk his nonexistent Instagram.

"Erin gave it to me as a joke. I hate smartphones. She thought a smartwatch would be funny." Another text came through and he reached around me to dismiss it with his other hand, so that I was completely encircled in his arms. "It is kind of useful, though."

"What's your issue with technology, anyway?"

"It's not technology. Just social media. And that's Erin, too, actually." He seemed to hesitate before elaborating. "She got cyberbullied pretty bad by these girls after posting a couple videos of herself singing, back in the early days of YouTube. My parents took the case to the school board and everything. It was a whole mess. There are still news articles floating around somewhere. Pretty much scared me off the whole social media thing long before Instagram even existed."

"Wow. That sounds terrible." I couldn't imagine being in her shoes—putting myself out there like that only to have my dreams completely and utterly wrecked by the internet. I had a hard enough time dealing with the Twitter comments. "So, she's older than you, I take it."

"Significantly older." I raised a quizzical brow, and he elaborated. "She's eleven years older than I am. Not a half-sister. My mom got pregnant with her when they were still in school. Dad married her right away, but they decided to wait awhile before having another."

"Are your parents still together?"

"Yeah, they are. Stupidly in love, too. It's kind of gross," he added with an embarrassed smile, because he probably thought I couldn't imagine anything worse than two people happy and in love. He was wrong, though. I didn't hate the idea of love. It was just that I'd seen so few examples of it growing up that I'd always had a hard time believing it existed. But this week—talking to my mom about the possibility of putting herself out there again, and watching Jo and Peter—a part of me had started to rethink that. Maybe it was rare. Maybe for every couple that found love, you had a hundred false starts. But even if it was a one-in-a-million chance, it existed.

And that gave me a tiny glimmer of hope. Small. Almost in-consequential.

The Hummer's engine turned over, a last call for any dawdling passengers before we roared off into the hills. Declan narrowed his eyes at me, and I realized that I'd been staring at him a little too hard, trying to imagine his parents and whatever *stupidly in love* looked like. "What are you thinking about?"

"Are they redheads, too?" I asked, hoping to really round out the image I was painting in my head.

There was a slight pause. "My sister and my mom, yes," he admitted, as much as I could tell he didn't *want* to admit it. "My dad's bald, but when he was younger his hair was more of a . . . blondish color."

"Strawberry blond?" I teased. When he only pressed his lips together, I threw my head back and cackled. "Oh my God, I knew it. You're like the Weasleys. A whole family of redheads."

"There's only four of us. And strawberry blond does *not* count as a redhead."

"Whatever you say, Ronald."

He shook his head, dimple indenting his cheek as he tried to hold back a smile. "I'm going to kill you."

The Hummer was packed with passengers now, and with a lurch, it started up the hillside. The whole thing rocked on the unpaved road as our driver shouted over the engine to point out the Wrigley Memorial and Botanic Garden on our left, the Trans Catalina Trailhead on our right. Declan kept his arm around me, holding me close. The smell of fresh, woodsy soap mingled with his sunscreen.

"My parents divorced, right before graduation," I admitted.

"I'm sorry to hear that," he said, maybe because he didn't know what else to say.

But now that I'd brought it up, I felt the need to get it all out in the open. To explain why I saw things the way I did, why I'd spent my whole adult life dodging even the idea of commitment. "Apparently my dad was having an affair for years, but they stuck together and played pretend because they didn't want me to deal with a move and a divorce before I'd finished school. I don't know how she did it, honestly. When I was little, before the affair started, we used to come here to the island once every summer, just for a couple days. We stopped visiting after Mom found out about the affair, but I never even noticed. There was always some explanation. *No vacation this year because Dad can't get the time off work* or *we're sleeping in separate rooms because your father snores and it's keeping me up at night.*" I shook my head, my eyes stinging not because I was sad when they finally split, but because to this day, I was embarrassed that I'd been so oblivious. "I don't know how I didn't see it. I should've noticed, should've told them they didn't need to stay together just for me."

"It wasn't your job to tell them," Declan pointed out. "If they chose to stay together, that's on them. You can't blame yourself because they chose to keep a secret."

I stared out the other side of the Hummer and pretended to

be interested in the sloping hills of Hermit Gulch as I dabbed my eyes on the back of my hand and sniffed. Wow, real solid start to a date, Margo. Dump all your baggage on him and cry.

He leaned over and pressed a kiss into my hair without saying a word, and somehow, it made me feel ten times more vulnerable than everything we'd done in the dressing room yesterday.

Within half an hour, the Hummer rumbled past the spot where Declan and I had given up on our hike. Another driver radioed in to provide updates on where the bison herd was grazing. Our own driver narrated the landscape for us, gesturing at this cactus or that leafless bush or somewhere out at the wide blue Pacific. At one point, there was a flurry of excitement as she tried to point out a pod of bottlenose dolphins on the horizon, but despite craning my neck and trying to follow Declan's well-intentioned but confusing attempts at describing it to me ("Look, you can see where the water looks a bit different, over to the east"), I couldn't make it out.

"Oh well," I said as I gave up and stopped straining against my seat belt. "I've seen dolphins plenty of times on the ferry ride over. It's not the end of the—"

POP.

The Hummer careened sideways. Dead trees and brush battered the side door as the driver came to a jerking stop, the whole vehicle enveloped in a cloud of dust.

"What happened?" Declan called up to the driver, as I wondered wildly whether someone had placed a curse on us. First the elevator and now this.

Without answering, the driver hopped out and marched around to the other side of the vehicle. The dust was beginning to settle, and I watched as she knelt, inspected something, then straightened up, shaking her head. She ushered for us all to hop out of the vehicle. We were near the crest of a small hill. The ocean was crystalline in the midday sun, but every other direction was dirt roads and grassy hills.

"Flat." Our driver nudged a particularly jagged-looking rock with the toe of her boot. The passenger-side tire was mangled on its rim. "We'll have to call the office. Have another driver come up to take you all back down."

Declan bent to inspect it. "It looks like the rim got bent, too." He turned to look at her, squinting in the bright sun. "Did you have a spare? I can swap it out."

"For legal reasons, I really can't—" she tried to protest.

But he was already walking to grab the spare and the toolkit from the back. "It's fine, I'm not going to sue or anything. And besides." He jerked his head in the direction of the other passengers, where a woman was shielding the top of her head with a magazine she'd grabbed from the door compartment, and another guy had impressive armpit stains. "I doubt the rest of your passengers want to wait around in this heat until whoever you call gets here.

The driver didn't protest, but she looked on worriedly as Declan knelt by the front of the vehicle and positioned the jack. I stooped down beside him, ready to help. "What can I do?"

He was busy cranking the jack, but he still took the time to glance over at me with a skeptical eyebrow. "Oh, you're going to help? With those . . ." His eyes darted to my hands, where I was making grabby motions for him to give me something to do. "Dainty fingers?"

"I'm sorry, what did you just call them?" I asked, stopping the grabby hands and inspecting my own fingers. My hands weren't exactly small.

"They're all girly. You have nail polish on them. It looks like you've never changed a tire in your life."

They did indeed have polish—a coral pink gel manicure that was about a week-and-a-half's worth of grown out. "For your information, I've changed two whole tires before," I said, watching his muscular arms work the jack. "And you're one to talk. It's not like your hands are all calloused or anything."

With a sigh, he stopped in the middle of his work to point out one of his own fingers. "Look, that's a callous, right there."

"A pencil callous," I teased. "You probably do math all day at work."

"For *your* information, my job is pretty hands-on. I help build stuff and everything."

"Stuff?"

"It's top secret."

"Somehow, I don't believe you."

"I literally work for NASA."

"Yeah. You're their math boy."

"Oh, that's an official job title, is it? Math boy?"

"It is now."

He extended a hand. "Lug wrench." I searched the toolbox and passed it to him. I knelt beside him until he finished swapping the blown-out tire for the spare, smacking the thick black rubber as though to test it. "Should be good to go now," he said to the others as he got back to his feet. He accepted the toolbox from me and went to stow it in the back.

"That'll get us down the hill, maybe," said the man with the armpit stains, eyeing the fresh tire with a generous dose of skepticism. "But there's no way we can make it out to the buffalo on a spare like that."

"On behalf of the company, let me just apologize," said the driver hurriedly. "I can provide you all with vouchers to take one of tomorrow's tours."

While the driver did her best to sweet-talk the irritated passengers back into the vehicle, Declan walked back over to me. He folded his arms and leaned his back against the hood. Already the back of his neck and his forearms were looking a little sunburned, and the rest of him was soon to follow.

"Well, this isn't exactly the date I had in mind," I said apologetically, as though I could somehow have prevented this from happening. Maybe I really *was* cursed—it felt like the universe was conspiring against me, determined that any attempts at getting to know Declan should run aground. Which would probably be a fitting punishment for all the years I'd spent bashing commitment and doling out questionable advice.

He turned to our driver, who had successfully herded all but one of the women back into the vehicle. The last woman—the one shielding the top of her head with a magazine—was demanding compensation for heat exhaustion. "How much farther to the bison?" Declan called.

"Last we checked, they were maybe a mile, two miles that way," the driver said, with a vague wave over the grassy hills. She looked happy for the momentary diversion, though the magazine woman was tapping an impatient foot. "But he's right. There's no way we'll make it on a spare. We have to turn around, to ensure we can get all the passengers safely back into town."

Now Declan turned back to me. "What's that in hiking terms?" he asked in a low voice.

"Two-mile hike is maybe . . ." I shrugged. "An hour or so, if you're making decent time."

"Cool. We'll hike it, then," he said, loud enough for the driver to hear. "Thanks."

With that, he started marching off in the direction of the bison.

"I'm sorry, but I can't wait here to give you a ride back," the driver shouted. "I have to get the other passengers back."

"It's fine," I called over my shoulder as I hurried to catch up. "Don't worry about us." The Hummer hadn't made it all that far, and it sounded like the herd was a little closer to Avalon today. As soon as we were out of earshot, I bumped arms with Declan. "You do realize we're not even a little bit prepared for a hike, right? I mean, look at our shoes."

We both glanced down. I was wearing sandals—my feet were

already covered in dust and dirt, just from helping change the tire—and he was wearing a very run-down-looking pair of Vans. They might've been the same pair he'd worn in high school. I made a mental note to buy him a new pair of shoes, ASAP.

"Ah, we'll live," he said dismissively. "What are you worried about? A few callouses on your perfectly manicured feet?"

"It's called a pedicure when it's your feet, you absolute caveman. And getting a pedicure is very relaxing, by the way. You should try it sometime."

He shook his head, laughing. "So, are we doing this, or what?"

I knew he was referring to the hike, but I couldn't help my thoughts drifting, wondering what *this* was between us. I'd signed on for two weeks without the rules, but it was starting to look like things might extend beyond that. We'd talked last night at dinner about me visiting him at his apartment. Of all the realizations I'd come to this week, perhaps the most liberating was that I *liked* not worrying about the rules, or our listeners, or how this fit into our brand. And I liked spending time with Declan.

I just worried that there was a chance it would blow up in my face the moment I stepped off the ferry next week and went back to life on the mainland—back to reality.

He was still waiting for me to answer about the hike, his gait slowing. "There's a very good chance I'm going to regret this," I said, already imagining the long walk back. "But yeah. Let's do it."

We were sweaty and sunburned by the time we crested the final hill, where the herd of bison came into view. They were little more than fat brownish dots in the distance, grazing lazily in the late afternoon sun, but we didn't dare move any closer. The sea of grass rippled in a light breeze, creating the illusion of greenish-gold waves separating us from the herd. Beyond, the cliffs of Catalina zigzagged against blue water.

"Wow," Declan said, slightly winded from the climb. "Quite the view."

I whipped my phone out of my pocket. "Here, get in a picture with me."

He tilted his head toward mine to get in the frame. We wore matching cheesy grins, both looking sweaty and dirty and a little too proud of ourselves for finishing the hike. "Ew, that one is bad," I said.

"You look fine." He leaned in to press a kiss to my sweaty temple, and I snapped another. He pulled away to frown at the new picture of him kissing the side of my head, me still grinning like an idiot. "You're not going to post that, are you?"

A week ago, I might have. But if I was ever going to post a picture of a man, I realized now that I wanted it to be for real. Not just for the sake of stirring up conversation. "Why?" I nudged him with an elbow. "Not ready to make things Instagram official?"

"We're covered in dirt. And I'm like five shades redder than normal." He shook his head. "Your followers would rip me to shreds."

"Don't worry," I said, tucking my phone back in my pocket with a small smile. "It's not for Instagram. It's for me."

At that, he seemed to relax a little. A strange, guilty feeling swirled in my gut as we tore our eyes from each other to watch the bison, but I couldn't discern the source of it. I'd decided not to use any of this for the podcast. I'd successfully brought it up with Jo, and we'd agreed to think about other possible content for Season Seven. So what was left to feel guilty about?

Declan folded his arms and frowned. "I wish I'd brought binoculars."

I shook off the inexplicable guilt, tried to focus on the conversation at hand. "Don't tell me you actually own binoculars."

"What?" He shrugged, arms still crossed as he watched the bison in the distance. "They're useful."

"You're the definition of a nerd. Remind me how you managed to be popular in high school?"

"If I had to take a guess," he said, inclining his head thoughtfully, "probably the same way I managed to finally win you over. With my ineffable charm."

I withheld a laugh. "Okay, now you're going to have to elaborate on where you learned the word *ineffable*, because I have no idea what that means."

"Sometimes I read the dictionary for fun." He was so serious when he said it, I wasn't sure whether or not to believe him. I just stared. "I'm joking," he said, catching my expression. "Obviously." But judging by the guilty laugh that followed, it maybe wasn't obvious.

We both settled into the grass so that we could watch the herd and appreciate the view for a little while before we'd have to face the long trek back to Avalon.

"You know, I'm not a complete lost cause when it comes to school," I said after a moment. "I might've kinda tanked that last semester in high school, but that was mostly because of all the stuff with my parents." They'd held out for so long on telling me about the divorce, but I wished they had held out just a little longer. The announcement came a month before the end of the school year—according to them, because they wanted to give me time to pack and decide who I'd rather live with before the lease on our apartment expired in June. But I ended up so distracted sorting through eighteen years of my life and searching for a job to help my mom afford her new apartment that I bombed a couple of my finals. My application to Thornton was rejected and I found myself back at the YMCA that summer, watching a bunch of retirees do water aerobics. "I did a lot better in college."

He seemed more focused on me than the bison. "What was your favorite subject?"

"Music." I hesitated only a fraction of a second before adding, "I majored in it, actually."

A part of me still half-expected the verbal beatdown—*why would you waste the money, that's a dumb major, how's that job at McDonald's working out for you*—but instead, he asked, "Really?" He actually sounded excited by this revelation. "Do you still play the tuba?"

"Not really," I admitted. "But that's because I was more on the industry track. Don't get me wrong, I liked being in band and everything, but I always preferred being on the other side of things. Getting to enjoy the music rather than making an idiot of myself up on stage, playing probably the dorkiest instrument ever invented." I'd chosen the tuba when I was in fourth grade because I thought it would be funny. The goofiest-looking, goofiest-sounding instrument. It was funny all right, but I found as I got older that most people were laughing at me, not with me.

Declan held back a smile. "I always thought it was kind of hot. Your lips on the mouthpiece—"

I shoved him playfully. "God, you're the worst." When the laughter died down, I said, "Jo reminded me that you used to come to all of the concerts."

"I like music." When I shot him a skeptical look, he confessed to the rest. "And it was an excuse to see you. I even brought flowers the first time. Waited by the stage and everything. I was planning to apologize for the shaving cream thing and tell you how I felt. But then I saw you—you were wearing this long green dress and your hair was up in this sort of—" He drew a circle around his head like a halo.

"Braid crown," I provided, because I remembered the performance he was talking about. It was the winter recital during sophomore year. The music teacher had stuck a few plastic sprigs of holly in all the girls' hair and we'd performed a sloppy orchestral version of "Jingle Bell Rock."

"I chickened out last minute and shoved the flowers at Jordan Gardner before booking it out of the theater."

I threw my head back and laughed. "You didn't!"

Declan nodded gravely. "I did."

"I remember that! They were carnations. We all thought Jordan had a secret admirer or something."

"He never told you who gave them to him?"

"To be honest, I don't think he saw your face. He never would've shut up if he'd known it was you," I said, still laughing. I leaned over and bumped my shoulder into his. "*I* never would've shut up if I'd known the flowers were meant for me. I probably would have teased you relentlessly as payback for the shaving cream incident."

Declan smiled at me faintly. "No chance you would have re-ciprocated, then?"

"Oh, I might have come around. Eventually." It was strange to imagine all the what ifs in my past. Maybe I wouldn't have had such an aversion to commitment, if I'd had some positive roman-tic experiences of my own. If someone had stepped in before the pessimism had taken root and shown me that there were still healthy relationships out there. "Better late than never, right?"

Without warning, his hand found the back of my neck and pulled me over to him for a kiss. It was a tender kiss, not all noisy passion but the kind that made the world around me go quiet, like I'd hit pause. I was used to drunk kisses that made my head spin, but this—this was serious and sober, grounding me and bringing me back to earth.

When we finally broke the kiss, neither of us pulled away. His fingers trailed the curve of my jaw. "What was that for?" I asked against his lips.

"Better late than never," he echoed.

I shook my head, smiling. "You're shameless."

"Speaking of music," he said, leaning back, "I'd actually been meaning to bring up that thing you mentioned the other night. About wanting to get involved in promoting the arts or some-thing along those lines?"

"Oh, that." I remembered now that he had tried to bring it up yesterday in the golf cart, but I'd brushed it aside. Now, I shrugged. "I don't know. It was just an idea. I'd like to get back into doing something with music, but it feels like the industry is sort of im-penetrable. And then on the flip side you have the internet, all these artists getting big on YouTube and TikTok. So I'm not even sure how much the industry even *needs* someone like me at this point, you know? People are figuring it out on their own. It feels like I got my degree at the least relevant point in history, ever. And then I feel hypocritical for even thinking that way because look, I've built a whole career around the internet, so who am I to complain?"

"I don't think that's true," he said, looking thoughtful. "The internet has made things more accessible, but you still have a whole skill set you took four years to develop. There's a lot of different ways you can use that. And lots of jobs require degrees, if that's the route you choose to go. Take my job, for example. I don't think they would've let me just waltz in and start building a rover—"

I held up a hand to stop him from going any further. "Pause, rewind. You actually build rovers? Like the little robot guys that send pictures from Mars?"

"I've helped on one of the teams that built a rover, yes. And they're not technically robots, by the way," he said, as casually as if he were talking about spreadsheets or end-of-year reports. I opened my mouth to ask more but he waved away any potential questions. "Anyway, you're sidetracking me here. What I'm getting at is that my sister works for Allegro Records. Not sure if you've heard of them."

Heard of them? They were one of the most interesting up-and-coming record labels in L.A. A nonprofit record label, opening their doors to a wide array of musicians with the help of some generous donations. They'd already succeeded in introducing a lot of fresh, unique talent to the industry. I had a music production course during my junior year and it was safe to say my professor was obsessed with Allegro. He brought up the way they were—and I quote—*revolutionizing the industry* at least once a week. "Are they taking on interns?" I asked.

"I was thinking more along the lines of putting you in touch with artists you could interview for a podcast." He frowned. "But if you'd prefer an internship, I'll have to ask Erin. She could probably make that happen. Especially since you have the degree for it."

"Either of those things would be amazing. Seriously, whatever she can wrangle for me, I'm there."

Declan clambered back to his feet and offered a hand to help me up. "Well, seeing as we're not getting any closer to these bison, we might as well head back."

I placed my hand in his, letting him drag me to my feet. "This hike is going to suck. Hard."

"I don't know," he said, watching as I dusted off the back of my shorts. "It could be worse."

I narrowed my eyes at him. This was the same guy who almost passed out hiking up the hill earlier this week. "How so?"

A smile dimpled his cheek, and he shrugged as we started back down toward the trail, and toward Avalon. "At least I'm in good company."

* * *

It was a six-mile hike back down to Avalon. As soon as we arrived at the hotel, we stumbled into the elevator—which was apparently up and running again, and despite my earlier reservations, I was too exhausted to take the stairs. My feet were blistered and dirty, and my calves were aching from carrying me up and down hills all day without proper footwear. Declan looked as beat-up by the elements as I felt. His nose and cheeks were sunburned to a blushy color that Jo probably would have paid good money to find at Sephora, and there was a streak of dirt across his forehead from wiping sweat on the back of his hand. He collapsed against the handrail in the elevator, rubbing a hand over the spot where his shoulders connected with his neck. "I don't think I've ever been this sore."

"Tell me about it," I laughed, bending to massage my legs. But despite our mutual exhaustion, I couldn't help wondering where things were about to go from here. Minor hiccups aside, the date had gone surprisingly well—at least I thought it had, given my minimal experience with dates in general. So, now what? I wasn't sure there was a smooth way to transition from tired and sore to *hey, want to share a bed tonight?*

Once we were outside our respective rooms, Declan hovered with his keycard in hand, but made no motion to invite me inside. Instead, he ran a nervous hand through his hair. "So, I know you might have agreed to this whole date thing on the promise of sex," he started awkwardly. "But I regret to inform you that I'm currently kind of sweaty. No, incredibly sweaty."

I nodded. "Jo calls it *swamp ass*."

He let out an uncomfortable laugh. "What?"

"Swamp ass. You know, when it gets all sweaty up in the crack—"

"You do not need to elaborate, I've got the gist of it," he insisted, but his amusement was beginning to slip through the cracks—ass pun not intended—because his laugh was more genuine now. He shook his head and, in an attempt to get the conversation back on track, said, "Point being, it's the polar opposite of sexy."

"I didn't take you on a date just to get you in bed," I said. But neither of us could deny that there was a sort of pent-up tension lingering out in the hall, keeping us from retiring to our separate rooms. I chewed my lip, and our eyes locked, and in an instant, I knew we had both come to the same obvious conclusion. The only possible way we were going to turn the sweaty, dirt-covered aftermath of a six-mile hike into anything resembling a turn-on. "Swamp ass might not be sexy—"

He closed his eyes like the phrase physically pained him. "I am begging you to stop calling it that."

"—but I have a solution in mind."

* * *

Why did I never think things through?

Spontaneity was not a strong suit of mine. In theory, spontaneity was great, because it meant I didn't have to commit to anything beforehand. But in practice, I found that it often resulted in me deciding to do things without taking the time to fully consider the consequences of my actions. Jumping the gun and suggesting that

Declan and I shower together, when we hadn't had sex yet—that might have been a little reckless, on my part. I definitely didn't think this through.

We stood on opposite ends of his hotel bathroom as the shower warmed up, fogging the mirrors. There was a small travel bag un-zipped by the sink, a bottle of toner sticking out that I could only assume was part of his five-step skincare routine—which I might have teased him about, if my thoughts weren't elsewhere. With his back to me, he tugged his T-shirt over his head, the muscles in his back rippling. I tore my eyes away as I shimmied out of my shorts. My heart was thrumming in my chest. Why was it doing that? I'd been naked in front of plenty of guys before, and Declan had already gone down on me. But for whatever reason, I felt exposed. Vulnerable. This wasn't a drunken hookup, but it also wasn't some perfectly staged evening like I imagined it should have been, complete with candles and perfume and a lacy thong. There were no smoke and mirrors. There was only me, covered in dirt and my makeup smudged with sweat. I couldn't help worrying that it wouldn't be enough.

Behind me, the glass door opened and closed again; Declan had stepped into the shower. I kicked my dirty clothes into a corner, realizing as I did so that I hadn't bothered to grab any clean ones from my hotel room. I worked up the courage to face the shower. The glass was fogged, so I couldn't see anything except vague move-ments. I took a deep breath—last chance to bail—and then I opened the shower door, crossed one of my arms over my chest for some semblance of dignity, and stepped inside.

The noise I let out the second I was beneath the steaming water was not even a little bit sexy. But my concerns about being attractive were momentarily forgotten, because the rush of the hot water against my aching muscles felt so good that I was ready to sink into a puddle by the drain. I was standing facing Dec-lan, with my back to the showerhead, but I kept my eyes closed, letting the water beat against me until my hair was sopping and falling in my face.

A hand grazed my cheek as he swept a stray lock of hair behind my ear. My eyes fluttered open. Declan was drinking me in, his gaze inching patiently over the curve of my hips, up my waist, to where I still had a protective arm across my chest. He lingered for a moment on my lips before his eyes finally met mine. Water clung to my eyelashes, and I reached with my free hand to wipe beneath my eyes, hoping I didn't look like a raccoon thanks to whatever was left of my mascara.

"Hi," he said, his voice low.

"Hi," I whispered back, the sound nearly swallowed up by the rush of the water.

He stepped closer. A hand came to my waist, slick as he traced the lines of my body, like he was trying to memorize them. I let my eyes break away from his long enough to venture over his body, over the freckles that dotted his shoulders, down to the faint trail of hair beneath his belly button, before darting back to his face.

"We should probably wash up first," I breathed.

"We should," he agreed, and I was almost disappointed when he tore his eyes from mine and grabbed the pine-scented body wash from the shelf. But then his hands found my waist again, slipperier than before, and he started to work the soap into a lather over my skin with hungry attention. I let my arm fall from my chest so that he could run soapy hands over my breasts, and I failed to hold back a moan. He took the opportunity to pull me closer to him and trailed kisses over my jaw, down my neck, across my collarbone.

"You're so fucking perfect," he whispered against my skin, his hands slipping down my back so that he could cup my ass, easing me against him. He was hard. Heat pooled between my legs. "Even better than I imagined." His fingers slipped between my thighs, teasing slow circles.

"Imagined me, did you?" I breathed.

His breathing was as heavy as mine was. "I've had plenty of time for imagining over the years."

"Tell me about it."

He bent to kiss my neck. Our bodies were slick and warm beneath the shower. He held me against him as his mouth moved over the sensitive spot where my jaw met my ear, where he whispered, "I thought about doing this. Touching you. Getting you off."

He slipped two fingers inside, the heel of his palm still rubbing against me. I moaned, my fingers digging into his shoulders. "Keep going."

"Our first night here, when we went out to dinner and you were wearing that sexy little sundress. I could barely focus on dinner. All I kept thinking was how badly I'd like to get you out of it." His hand wound me tighter and tighter until it became difficult to stand. "And the other night, in the arcade. When you sat on my lap."

"Tripped," I managed to correct him, though I was barely coherent.

He breathed a laugh. "I thought about taking you right there and then. I got hard just feeling your ass against me."

His fingers pushed me over the edge, until all I could manage was a small *oh* and the pleasure crashed over me in waves. It was impossible to stand, but that didn't matter because he held me in his arms and kissed me. It was a slow kiss, like he was savoring the way I moaned into his mouth. When he pulled away, he asked in a husky voice, "Meet you in the bedroom?"

"Meet me?" I repeated, dazed.

"I haven't exactly washed myself off yet," he pointed out.

As though I needed visual confirmation, I looked him up and down. His chest and abs were slick with water and some of the soap from my own body. "I could help with that."

He laughed hoarsely. "I wouldn't complain."

I wasn't much help. While he lathered his chest with body wash, I let my fingers slide down his stomach, tracing the faint trail of hair beneath his belly button before I took him into my hand. He replied with a groan, hips bucking, and then the shower was forgotten entirely as his mouth covered mine. He reached over my shoulder without looking to shut off the water. A fog lingered. He scooped me into his arms—my thighs tightening around him—and he kicked open the shower door, glass still slick with condensation.

He carried me out to the bedroom and we flopped onto the unmade bed, not caring if we got the sheets wet. He kissed down my neck and over the curve of one of my shoulders as he positioned himself between my legs. "Do you have any condoms?" I asked, breathless as his hands roved down my body until they came to settle on my hips, pulling me toward him. I could feel him pressed against me, but it wasn't enough.

If there was such a thing as a record scratch in real life, this was it. Declan blinked, and I almost wondered if he'd heard me, but then the hunger in his eyes gave way to a sort of horrified comprehension. He pushed himself up onto his knees between my legs and ran a frustrated hand through his damp hair. "Shit. No."

"Seriously?" I asked, propping up on my elbows. It came out sounding way more demanding than I meant for it to, because the last thing I wanted to have to do was wait another night.

"I don't do one-night stands, so I'm not sure this should come as a surprise. And I didn't exactly set out on this trip with the expectation that you'd give me the time of day—let alone want to have sex with me," he added dryly, when I only stared at him with my mouth half-open.

Instead of a condom, he extracted a pair of clean boxer briefs from his gym bag. "Okay," he said, looking frazzled as he pulled on the underwear and turned in place, searching for something else. "Okay, give me a minute."

"Where are you going?"

"I'll be back in a few." He buttoned his jeans and pulled a T-shirt over his head before stooping to catch my mouth in a deep, longing kiss. "God, you look good in my bed," he mumbled against my lips before pulling away and heading for the door.

"What am I supposed to do while you're gone?" I asked, dragging a sheet to cover myself.

He shrugged with his hand on the door handle, the shadow of a smile creeping across his face. "Keep yourself entertained?"

"Declan—"

But he had already slipped out the door.

I flopped back against the pillows with a frustrated groan. Was this the universe's way of punishing me for all my wrongdoings? It sure felt like it. Jo would probably call it karma and Liv would do a tarot reading. *The upside-down Ace of Wands means trouble in your sex life*, the cards would probably say, though I was pretty sure they'd fail to tell me what I was supposed to do about that. I snorted at the thought, then felt weird for laughing by myself while laying naked in the middle of Declan's hotel room.

Sooner than expected, the door opened, and Declan slipped back inside, out of breath.

"That was fast," I said, sitting up. "Where did you go?"

"I got a condom from Peter." He pulled it from his jean pocket, flashing the foil wrapper. "Easier than going all the way to the store."

I raised an eyebrow as I watched him strip back out of his clothes. "You stole a condom from the soon-to-be newlyweds?"

"I'll buy them a whole box as a thank-you." He stepped out of his boxer briefs, tossing them aside. Then he was back on top of me, pressing warm kisses against all the places that had grown cold in his absence. First my lips, then down my neck to the space between my breasts. His tongue flicked over each nipple as he reached between us to roll on the condom.

"Oh, of course," I mumbled in reply. "You can leave it on the gift table at the wedding."

"No gift wrap," he shot back, as his kisses ventured farther south. "Just a box of condoms, sitting out with all the other gifts."

"Obviously."

He kissed between my legs, his tongue parting me, but this time he didn't linger there. Instead, he straightened up and knelt between my thighs. My breath caught in my throat as he positioned himself over me, grabbing me by the hips and tugging me closer. A thrill shot through me as I waited for a familiar pressure, that first mind-numbing thrust. Instead, he bent to kiss my neck again.

I released the breath in a frustrated exhale. "Stop being such a tease," I whispered into his ear.

He straightened up just enough to look at my face. "I've waited years to do this." He kissed me and I caught his bottom lip with my teeth. "I think you can handle a few minutes."

"I can't. I want you now."

"Yeah?" He was as breathless as I was, his entire body pressed up against me, as close as it was possible to be without actual sex. I imagined it was taking every last bit of willpower he had to drag this little game out. "Tell me how badly."

"You managed to get your way with the whole date thing, but there is no way you're making me beg for you to fuck me." But the way I squirmed against him meant my body was begging him anyway, even as I was insisting otherwise. "Let's just say *badly* and leave it at that."

He let out a husky laugh. "Good enough for me." Then he kissed me again, tender and slow, as slow as the way he sank into me. I let out a ridiculous, desperate noise at the feel of him inside me, but he seemed to like it, because he groaned and deepened the kiss, his tongue dipping into my mouth. His hips moved against mine, both of us finding a shared rhythm. After a moment, he broke the kiss, and I tried to protest, but then he shifted onto his knees, changing the angle so that he could reach between us and draw slow circles over me again, and I forgot what I was going to say entirely.

"Is this good?" he asked, his voice thick.

It was better than good, but I wasn't sure how I was going to let him know that, because my capacity for speech had abandoned me. My eyes fluttered and I arched into him, reaching over my head to brace my hands against the headboard. "Oh, God."

He managed a breathless laugh, which was—somehow—indescribably sexy. "I'll take that as a yes."

His brow knit in concentration as he focused on thrusting while bringing me to orgasm. Pressure built up again until I couldn't breathe, couldn't think about anything but the feel of him and the way he was touching me. I came undone, my legs tightening around his hips as fresh waves of pleasure shot through me. It seemed that was what he was holding out for, because he caught my mouth in a kiss and then his body was shuddering against mine. He moaned into my mouth, a deep and masculine sound that I wanted to swallow whole.

"Fuck," I breathed as he collapsed on top of me. After taking a few seconds to catch his breath, he rolled over and tossed the condom in the trash. "I think we might have to shower again."

I admired the muscles in his arm as he swiped a hand across his brow, which was damp with sweat. Still catching his breath, he turned onto his side and drew me to him. He kissed me and reached around to give my ass a squeeze. "I think we should buy more condoms."

I laughed. "You're shameless."

The hand on my ass delivered a quick smack. "So you keep telling me."

"I like it." I searched his face for some sign that I shouldn't say what I wanted to say next—that maybe I had read him wrong and this would end the moment the wedding was over and we went back to our separate lives. But I wasn't even sure what that sign would be, so screw it. I went ahead and confessed. "I like *you*."

Rather than respond, he studied me with a hint of a smile on his face, like I was a puzzle he was enjoying trying to solve. I started to feel a little self-conscious. "What?" I asked.

"Nothing." He adjusted, rolling onto his back and tucking me into his shoulder. It felt so natural, being in bed together like this. Easy. Like I didn't have to overthink it. "I don't want to scare you off."

I snorted. "I think that would have happened a long time ago, if it was going to happen."

He hesitated a few seconds before speaking again, his voice a deep rumble where my cheek was pressed against his chest. "You said something the other day about weddings. How people always look for a hookup." He angled his head so that he could look at me and I nodded because yes, I remembered saying that. "Is that what this is? A wedding hookup, and then next week it's back to business as usual?"

"No," I admitted. "This isn't just a hookup."

His arm drew me closer to him, and he kissed the top of my head. "I know it's soon to be having the *what are we* conversation and I'm not saying I need a definitive answer," he mumbled against my hair. "And I know dating is probably complicated with the podcast and everything. But I really like you, Margo. I've always liked you, but I think I like you even more than I thought I would."

I smiled to myself. "I know the feeling."

"Enough to consider moving forward with this? After we get back home?"

"Okay." I pulled away from him and sat up cross-legged in bed, dragging the sheets with me. "Let's talk logistics."

"Sexy." He gave me a roguish wink as he folded an arm behind his head, which only emphasized his bicep.

"Shut up," I said, grinning despite myself. But if we were going to do this, I needed to make sure I laid it all on the table. "I'm thinking about moving back home with my mom." When he stared at me, nonplussed, I elaborated. "I know I said that we're only a fifteen-minute drive from each other, but I'm going to be living in Fontana again. That's like an hour drive from Glendale."

"The apartment in Glendale isn't my apartment."

"What?"

"It's Erin's. I've been splitting my time between her place and my parents' place to cut down on the commute while I look for somewhere closer to work. I could find somewhere in the middle. Claremont, or La Verne, maybe."

I hesitated, chewing the inside of my cheek. "It's a bit early to be making a decision like that because of me."

"I'd be closer to my parents, too. And my friends. Peter mentioned that he and Jo are looking at places in Rancho." When I didn't look entirely reassured, he added, "Trust me, it would be beneficial all around."

"Okay, so the podcast," I brought up instead. I wanted to make sure I covered all the bases. "Even if I figure out something outside of *Seven Rules*, social media is a big part of my résumé. I think I'm always going to be putting out content, one way or another. Are you sure you're okay with that?"

He shrugged. "As long as we can keep our personal lives and our public lives separate, I don't have a problem with it."

Guilt clawed at my insides, and I realized the source of my earlier unease—this had started with plans to use him for the podcast, and while my intentions had changed, I wondered whether he'd instill so much confidence in us, if he knew the truth. Perhaps it was one of those things I was better off not confessing.

What would be the point? To alleviate my own guilt, yes, but if that meant hurting him in the process . . .

"So, that's it, then," I said after a pause. "You want to keep this thing going, after we go back to real life?"

"I want *you*, Margo." Declan pulled me over him so that my legs were straddling his waist. Heat erupted low in my belly, but he only dragged my mouth down to his and caught it in a soft kiss. "I want to give this a fair shot."

"Okay," I agreed, my heart stuttering in my chest. "So we give it a fair shot."

The rules had served a purpose. They helped me keep a wall up, and that had stopped me from getting hurt because I never put my heart out there in the first place. Without the rules, I was defenseless. I was wearing my heart on my sleeve for the first time in my life, and all I could do was hope it was for the right person. Someone I could trust not to turn around and shatter it into a million pieces.

From: Renee Dunkirk (renee@castawaycatalina.com)
To: Jo Hernandez (jo@sevenrulespodcast.com)
CC: Margo Anderson (go@sevenrulespodcast.com)
Date: Jul 25, 9:03 AM
Subject: Pictures

Hi ladies,

I shared some of your recent Twitter and Instagram posts with my superiors and they are loving everything you've shared so far. Just a friendly reminder as we approach the big day: our contract stipulates at least five plugs on the next season of your podcast. While I'm aware you haven't begun recording yet, we want to ensure we get a jump on discussing the sort of language you'll be using to describe the nature of our sponsorship. I've attached a document that offers some potential phrasing, but of course, everything is up for discussion.

Feel free to reach out to me with any questions.

Cheers,
Renee

CHAPTER

23

"We could reframe it." I paced, my heels clacking on the wooden deck of the restaurant where the rehearsal dinner was being held. "Focus on how you broke the rules instead of me. We could close out by talking about the wedding, use it as a sort of grand finale to end the podcast."

Jo frowned as she adjusted the brightness on the projector. Afternoon sun beat down on the outdoor restaurant, washing out the white projector screen, but she insisted on fiddling with it all the same. Probably just needed something to distract her from the mounting nerves. "But I didn't break the rules."

I stopped pacing to gawk at her. "Hello? Rule Number Seven. I'm pretty sure you caught feelings long before planning to walk down the aisle. At least I hope you did."

"That's not what I meant," she said. "It's more that I didn't keep track of when and where I was breaking them. I couldn't tell you if I texted him first. I wasn't planning on turning it into a story."

There was something in her tone that felt almost accusatory, but given it was the afternoon before her rehearsal dinner, it was probably best not to open that particular can of worms. "So we make something up," I suggested, tossing up my hands. "We have to come up with something. The contract with Castaway Catalina is calling for five plugs, so we need to generate enough content for five episodes, at minimum." I chewed the inside of my cheek, mulling over our options. We'd talked things through the last few days and come to the same conclusion: *Seven Rules* didn't make sense for either of us, moving forward. Unfortunately, there were various legal roadblocks to up and quitting. "Maybe we could renegotiate. She did say it was up for discussion."

Renee was nowhere to be seen at the moment, probably barking orders in the kitchens or on the phone with the florist. She might've been Castaway Catalina's marketing director, but today she'd transformed into an event coordinator, determined to oversee everything and make sure it all looked flawless in pictures. Employees in cream-yellow tiki shirts bustled back and forth, their shoes thumping against the hollow deck. Tomorrow's reception was going to be held in the wide, opulent ballroom of the Catalina Casino, but there was another event booked for that location today, so the rehearsal dinner was being hosted by the beach club at the outdoor restaurant that abutted the bar.

"Can we talk about this later?" Jo asked. "It's kind of hard to focus right now."

"Yeah, sorry."

She quadruple-checked the HDMI cable like it was going to disconnect itself at any moment. "Do me a favor and double-check that Declan brought the USB."

"He did." She'd already had me check with him three separate times, but she gave me a look that had me holding up my hands in surrender. "Okay, double-checking."

Declan was at one of the tables arranging name cards for the seating plan. A smile crept over his face as I approached him. I was wearing a slinky champagne-colored dress, and his eyes raked over my body before returning to my face. "What's up?"

"Jo's asking about the USB again."

His eyebrows shot up, and he reached into the breast pocket of his dress shirt. "Should I just give it to her?"

"No, she's already got enough on her plate," I said, placing a hand over the pocket to stop him removing the USB stick. "Better that you hold on to it."

"I'll take your word for it."

He resumed setting name cards around one of the circular tables. I watched as he placed *Mr. Tony Montpelier* on the plate in front of me and I was struck by a sudden idea. "Where's my mom's card?"

He glanced around at the names already on the table, and then shuffled through the remaining cards in his hand. "I haven't seen any Andersons."

"That's because her last name is McCarthy. Blanche McCarthy."

Any effort at searching for her name card was immediately abandoned, his face lighting up with alarming glee. "Your mother's name is Blanche?"

"It's a tradition in our family to give everyone old lady names. I was thinking 'Millicent' if we have a daughter. Thoughts?" His mouth opened, then closed. He looked like he didn't know whether he should take me seriously and was scared of saying the wrong thing. I laughed and shook my head. "I'm kidding. Seriously, where's her card?"

"Over there," he said, pointing to the next table over. He watched as I grabbed the name card from the seat beside Tony's— sorry, Mrs. Amanda Sutherland—and swapped it out for my mom's. "What are you doing?"

"Mom's had a crush on Tony since he first started reporting for channel two."

"Playing matchmaker now, are you?" Declan observed with a hint of a smile. "I thought you didn't believe in that sort of thing."

"I'm a reformed woman," I said coyly.

I turned as though to leave, but he caught me by the waist and pulled me in. "Is that so?"

"It might be."

His hands bunched the slinky fabric of my dress as he pressed his body against mine and caught my mouth in a kiss. It would be hours before we got back to the hotel, but maybe there was a chance we could slip off somewhere, once the rehearsal dinner was all set up and ready to go.

"*So* weird." We broke apart. Jo was standing a couple feet away, her binder splayed open in her arms and her eyes darting back and forth between the two of us. "Like watching my parents kiss."

"Oh, I'm sorry, was that too chaste for you?" I shot back. "Hoping to see some tongue?"

"Yeah, and then I can go bleach my eyeballs."

I nodded at her binder. "What's that?"

"A copy of tonight's schedule." She extracted it from the rings of the binder and handed it over to me. "I'm hoping everything goes according to plan, but I figure if anything goes wrong, you could help—"

"Make sure it gets back on track," I said, accepting the schedule from her outstretched hand. I glanced at the paper. *4PM— meeting w/ the wedding party to discuss the procession*, read the first line. "Got it." Trust Jo to have a plan for everything.

* * *

Almost as soon as the rehearsal had wrapped up, the guests started arriving. It was a balmy night, the stars overhead drowned in fairy lights strung across the restaurant. My mom beamed at me from a few tables over, dressed in a mint-green pantsuit and wearing lipstick for possibly the first time ever. She kept waggling her eyebrows at me and jerking her head in Tony's direction as if to say *look who I'm sitting next to*—the exact opposite of playing it cool, but he didn't seem to notice.

I was seated at a table with the rest of the wedding party. Jo was wearing an ivory cape dress with her black hair swept into a sleek French twist—she looked like she'd stepped out of a fashion magazine, and of course, Rory the Photographer was here to make sure he got it all on camera, snapping candids while we tried to enjoy our dinner. Beneath the table, Declan's hand rested on my thigh while he got into a heated conversation with Lucas about whatever the hell the Space Force did. He'd relinquished the USB stick to Peter, who was currently setting up the projector ahead of his parents' speech. I scooped shrimp-and-crab ceviche onto a tortilla chip as I listened to Liv explaining the pitfalls of living with three roommates she met on Craigslist.

"There's like, a drool stain on the couch from where the one chick keeps falling asleep. And we're telling her, *Mari, it's a pull-out bed, you don't have to sleep on the couch,* but she just passes out watching *Schitt's Creek* every night." She rolled her eyes. "But I mean, on the flip side, we're only a few blocks from the beach. So it's a trade-off, you know?"

"I can't even imagine," Autumn said. "My roommate at FIDM is bad enough, and there's only one of him."

"To be fair, dorms are their own nightmare," I chimed in through a mouthful of tortilla chip. I swallowed and went for another. "One time I found a cactus in the toilet."

Autumn looked like she was about to ask some follow-up questions about the cactus, but Liv cut her off. "Where are you planning to go now, with Jo moving out?"

"We're thinking about buying out of the lease," I said. "After that, I might stay with my mom for a bit, and then—" I cast a sideways glance at Declan, who was still absorbed in his conversation with Lucas. It had devolved from Space Force to an impassioned debate about government spending, and so far as I could tell, they were yet to find any common ground. "I guess I'm just going to see where life takes me."

For the first time in what felt like a long time, that wasn't a scary prospect. For all I'd dreaded this wedding, it was starting to look like I would come out the other side unscathed. Things would be different. Jo and I were working on plans to retire the podcast, and then I'd have plenty of time to figure out what my future was going to look like. There was still a hint of the unknown, but there was something exciting in that. No longer constrained by rules or a brand, I'd be free to make my own choices. Do what worked for me, rather than what worked for everyone else.

Beneath the table, I slid my hand over Declan's thigh—he was wearing dress slacks today in place of his usual jeans or board shorts. He broke off in the middle of whatever he was saying to arch an eyebrow at me. I gave him an innocent smile.

"I don't understand how you guys afforded that apartment in the first place," Autumn was saying. "I mean, I get decent ad revenue from my videos and everything, but L.A. rent is ridiculous. If it weren't for student housing, I'd be living with my parents for sure."

Liv pulled a face. "No offense, but I could never."

"That's because your parents are on the opposite side of the country."

"No, but like, even if they lived here, there's no way—"

I stopped listening when Declan leaned in close, warm breath tickling my ear and his voice dropping low. "Any interest in—"

"Hey, man." Peter materialized beside us, tossing a thumb over his shoulder at the projector. "I can't get this thing to work."

Declan exhaled and shot me an apologetic look. "Hold that thought," he muttered, and with a swift kiss, he left me at the table to go teach his best friend the basics of using a thumb drive.

One of the servers stopped by the table to refill my champagne flute, her gaze trailing after Declan. She turned back to me, mouth twisting in a wry smile. "Cute."

It took me a moment to recognize her. Her California poppy tattoo was covered by the long-sleeve shirt beneath her uniform and her choppy hair was slicked back in a bun. "They have you serving champagne?" I asked.

"All hands on deck tonight," Shelley said in a bored voice. She nodded at the projector, where Declan was busy helping Peter figure out the slideshow. "So what happened with your boy problems? Get everything worked out?"

Shit. I'd forgotten that I had talked to her about that. I'd been vague, I was pretty sure, but I'd also been high that night, and a little tipsy. "More or less," I said, not sure I wanted to talk about Declan to a virtual stranger. Especially not when that stranger had been less than friendly on at least one occasion.

"That's the guy you were texting?" When I didn't confirm or deny, she smiled faintly. "Figured as much. He was with you that day at the bar. And at your friend's bachelorette party, too."

"He's not—" I started to say, not entirely sure where the sentence was heading, but I was distracted when Declan came up behind me. He jerked his head toward the dark beach, away from the rehearsal dinner. "Excuse me," I said to Shelley as I tossed my napkin on the table and rose to my feet, all too happy to dodge any more prying questions. I followed Declan away from the chatter. The stairs from the deck spilled right onto the beach, where the smell of the ocean clung to the evening air. My heels were unsteady in the sand, but he steadied me as he pulled me into the shadows beside the stairs and kissed me.

I'd waited all afternoon for a moment alone with him, so I wanted to enjoy this, but the conversation with Shelley was still whirling in my head. Why had she decided to bring that up? Maybe she was just being friendly—making conversation, and my socalled boy problems were the one thing she knew about me. But I couldn't shake the feeling that something was . . . off.

"Okay, what's going through your head?" Declan asked against my lips, pressing his forehead against mine. "You're distracted. I can tell."

I hesitated. "You know that server I was talking to? The one who's bartended for us a couple times."

"I've probably seen her in passing, but I wasn't really paying attention, if I'm honest." Declan's hand was on my waist, holding me against him, but he drew back just far enough to look me in the eye. His brow knit in concern. "Why? What's up?"

I searched his face, trying to find the words to explain. I wasn't sure where to begin. With the no-rules experiment, maybe, but I really didn't want to drag all that to the surface. I could tell him about my first encounter with Shelley. About how it was another in a long line of uncomfortable exchanges with people who seemed determined to be rude to me simply because I was an influencer—but how vapid and ridiculous did that sound? Poor little podcaster, getting bullied by the same people who were doling out free shit. Declan was pretty understanding, but I wasn't sure he'd understand that. My relationship with social media was the antithesis of his own.

"Is everything okay?" he asked when I still hadn't said anything.

Before I could answer, the steps leading to the deck creaked beside us. A female shadow loomed over us, silhouetted by the lights of the restaurant. "Oop! Sorry. Didn't mean to—" I recognized the voice a split second before she recognized my face. She squinted in the dark. "Margo?"

"Mom." I wriggled out of Declan's grasp with all the embarrassed urgency of a teenager caught making out in the backseat of her parents' car. "Hi."

Declan shot me a quizzical look and warmth crept up my neck. I was a grown woman. I was allowed to be alone with a guy, but somehow, getting caught creeping around in the dark made my brain short-circuit. And it seemed like short-circuiting maybe ran in the family, because Mom was hovering over us, her mouth half-open. Come on, it wasn't *that* shocking to find me with a guy. But when Tony Montpelier materialized at her shoulder, it started to make sense. They were the ones trying to sneak off to the dark beach. And Mom was the one feeling like she'd been caught red-handed.

A smile lit up my face. Mom placed a hand on Tony's chest to stop him coming any closer. "Actually, I just remembered that I need another drink," she told him. "Preferably wine. Anything with bubbles gives me a headache."

Tony looked back and forth between my mom and where Declan and I were standing in the sand next to the stairs. He was plainly confused, but he didn't argue, disappearing into the crowd to find her a glass of wine. I intertwined my fingers with Declan's and dragged him around to the bottom of the stairs. "You've got him fetching drinks for you already?" I asked, amused.

"I've still got it." Mom's wedge heels thumped as she came down the stairs and planted her hands on her hips. "So," she said, her eyes flicking to Declan and back again, "you're catching the bouquet, right?"

"Mom," I said warningly.

Declan reached around me to shake her hand. "Ms. McCarthy. I'm—"

"Declan Walsh," she interrupted. "I saw your name on the program for tomorrow. And I remember Margo talking about you in high school." She shot me a look that told me *that* particular conversation wasn't over. I'd eventually have to explain how I'd gone from hating his guts to holding his hand in the span of two weeks. Not that I was entirely sure how to explain. Maybe mention something about his *ineffable charm*.

Declan grinned. I could already feel this train going off the rails. Separately, my mom and Declan were good at embarrassing me. Together—that just wasn't fair. "Margo's talked about me?" he asked.

"Complained is probably more accurate. And she drew a mustache on your yearbook photo."

"It wasn't a mustache," I grumbled, though it was true I'd taken a fine-tipped Sharpie to several of my classmates' pictures one day when I was bored. Declan's senior photo sported a top hat and some pretty impressive muttonchops.

"First the Red Wedding comment and now this?" Declan looked positively tickled by this revelation. "Didn't realize you spent so much time thinking about me."

Mom took a step back and gave him a quick once-over. "You're taller than I expected," she said, sounding pleased. "Margo always made you sound sort of small. Great hair color, too. You know, I had a boyfriend in high school with red hair—"

"Mom," I said through gritted teeth, because I could only imagine a handful of things worse than her assessing all of Declan's physical qualities like a rich person assessing a racehorse at the Kentucky Derby. "Please."

She narrowed her eyes at me. "Did you do something to your hair?"

I reached a self-conscious hand to my hair, which I'd curled this morning. "I dyed it brown."

"It looks good. Healthy."

"Thanks."

She seemed to realize that she was overstaying her welcome. "I'll have to chat some more with you two lovebirds tomorrow," she said with a small smile, and I shut my eyes in an attempt to block out the cringe. Beside me, Declan shook with laughter. "I need to go find Tony. What time is it? I imagine they're going to kick us out of here pretty soon."

I patted around for my phone before remembering I didn't have any pockets, and I'd left my bag hanging off my chair. Declan's smartwatch illuminated as he lifted it to check the time. "Almost seven."

"I think I left my phone back at the table," I said.

We exchanged a quick *see you tomorrow* with my mom and

hiked back up to the deck. "She seems cool," Declan observed, once again failing to conceal his smile.

I rolled my eyes. "You just like that she shares your knack for embarrassing me."

"Which part embarrassed you? The part where she ratted you out for talking about me in high school, or the part where she called us lovebirds?"

I shot him an exasperated look as we arrived back at the table. The rest of the wedding party was off mingling with guests. Bussers were spiriting the dirty dishes and used silverware away. I lifted my napkin from where I'd tossed it on the table, but the only thing beneath it was a stray salad fork.

I stopped a passing food runner, her arms laden with used dinner plates. "Did you happen to see a phone lying around here?"

"I don't remember seeing one," she said with a shrug. "But you could check tomorrow with the lost and found, after we're finished cleaning up. There's a chance it'll turn up there."

As soon as she turned her back, I stooped down to rifle through my bag, but my search only turned up a hairbrush, my wallet, and a six-month-old pack of Wrigley's Spearmint. I straightened up and braced myself against the table, watching the bubbles rise in the champagne flute as I racked my brain for what I could have done with my phone. I knew I hadn't carried it down to the beach with me, but I was certain I'd brought it tonight, because I remembered checking the time earlier while we were still waiting for dinner.

Declan was hovering at my shoulder. "Did someone take it?"

"Why would they take it?" I asked. "It's worthless. It's like three years outdated with a crack right down the middle of the screen."

"I'm not talking about the resale value," he said with a grave look.

I swallowed. There was plenty on my phone that was better left there—conversations with Jo, old screenshots of people's Tinder profiles that I was roasting, Google searches that would probably look weird out of context. But nothing worth stealing. Nothing that was going to make or break me. "They'd have to have my passcode. And there's nothing on there of interest." But even as I was saying it, uncertainty welled in my gut. My social media profiles. I'd heard from other influencers about hackers holding their accounts hostage. But this wasn't a hacker, and I wasn't some major celebrity. I didn't have enough money to be worth the time or the effort. They'd have better luck just hocking the crappy phone.

"I'll ask around," Declan said. "Find Lucas or Autumn. See if anyone saw anything."

I nodded, coming to the only conclusion that made sense. Someone had pocketed my phone once before this vacation, under the guise of helping me. The same person I'd been talking to before Declan dragged me away from the table. Had I really been that gullible? I'd spent years expecting the worst of people, but there was still a small part of me that hoped they'd prove me wrong. I should have known better.

Trying to shake the embarrassment stinging my cheeks, I said, "I'm going to talk to Renee."

Renee was running through tomorrow's drink list with a couple of the bartenders, but Shelley was not among them. "Go," Renee greeted with a surface-level smile as I approached. "Enjoying your evening?"

I took a deep breath. I'd never liked having these conversations— the sort where people tiptoed around what they actually wanted to say, all in the name of professionalism. It hadn't been my intention to pawn the business side of things off on Jo, but it came so naturally to her. Reading the emails, reviewing the contracts. "I prefer being called Margo," I said to start with. "And no, actually. I'm not."

Renee must have realized that I hadn't come over here to catch up, because she dismissed the bartenders with a quick nod. They busied themselves on the opposite side of the wraparound bar, uncorking bottles of champagne and pouring drinks for guests. "What can I do to change that?"

"I think one of your employees might have taken my phone."

Renee's smile turned strained. "That's not possible. Castaway Catalina holds their employees to the highest standard. We conduct annual background—"

"Regardless of whatever precautions you've taken, my phone is missing," I interrupted.

Renee nodded at the restaurant behind me. "Perhaps one of the guests took it."

I faltered, turning to look at the crowd mingling between the tables. Friends, some of them. I recognized Jo's parents. But mostly strangers. As far as I knew, Jo and Peter came from good families filled with honest people, but everyone was related to someone. It was just as likely that my phone got picked up by a cousin with sticky fingers as it was that a server slipped it in her apron.

I chewed the inside of my cheek, thinking through my options. Shelley was nowhere to be seen, and I didn't have any proof that she was the culprit aside from a couple awkward exchanges and a gut feeling. It was all circumstantial, at best, and at worst, I might cost someone their job with a baseless accusation. "We keep a lost and found at our main office," Renee said. "I'll check first thing tomorrow."

I tore my eyes from the party. "I'd like it if you could check now, please." Maybe I'd get lucky and someone had grabbed it for safekeeping.

"The main office is closed for the evening. Even if one of our employees did find it, they'd have to wait until tomorrow to turn it in."

"Shit." I ran a hand through my hair. My one saving grace was that my phone was locked when I left it on the table. There were probably a few tricks for getting past that, but with any luck, whoever took my phone wouldn't know them. More important, there was a chance the phone thief wouldn't know whose phone they'd stolen. They probably snatched it off the table without paying any attention to who was sitting there, and now they'd wipe it and sell it for a quick buck without ever realizing what they had.

"I'll see about compensating you for the phone," Renee said. "The last thing we'd want is for your vacation to end on a sour note."

"Thanks," I mumbled, though the money wasn't really my concern.

I broke away and searched for Declan to see whether he'd had any better luck with the wedding party. I found him standing near our table, looking like he wasn't sure what to do with himself. "Liv said she saw your phone on the table when she was getting up to go talk to Peter's cousin who owns a dispensary, but she hasn't been back over here since. And by all accounts, Lucas has been stuck in the bathroom since before the slideshow even started. Says the ceviche messed with his stomach. I haven't had a chance to talk to Autumn."

I exhaled through my nose, trying to calm down, but it was difficult when my life was quite literally in someone else's hands. "Autumn wouldn't take my phone."

"She might've seen something," he pointed out.

I marched over to where Jo was laughing at something her dad said, the back of her ivory cape dress to me. I tapped her on the shoulder. "Jo." She turned, a flute of champagne in her hand and her face still fixed in a smile, but it faltered when she caught my expression. "Where's Autumn?"

Her brow creased. "Why? What's wrong?"

"Someone stole my phone."

"What, seriously?" She grabbed my arm as though to steady me—or steady herself. Because if my life was in someone else's hands, hers might as well have been, too. Every snarky text, every social media login. "Who would do that?"

"That's what we're trying to figure out," Declan said.

Jo blinked at him like she was just remembering he was there. "She's with Peter. They're taking their parents back to the hotel," she said after a slight delay. When I grabbed Declan's hand and turned to leave, Jo made as though to follow along, setting her champagne on a nearby table. "I'll come with you."

"No, you're fine," I said as I backed away. "Stay. Enjoy the party. Don't let my problems ruin your night."

She didn't look entirely reassured, but she nodded anyway. "I'll ask around here. See if anyone saw anything."

Declan and I ran through a series of possible scenarios as we made our way back to the hotel. Maybe we could monitor places like Craigslist and Facebook Marketplace to see if anyone listed it. Maybe someone had pocketed it on accident. Maybe I could wipe my iCloud from the nearest computer, but that wouldn't solve the problem of everything that was already saved to my phone. We caught up with Autumn and Peter as they were crossing the lobby to head back to the rehearsal dinner. The keys to the golf cart dangled in Peter's hand.

"What's going on?" Autumn asked. "Calling it a night already?"

"Did you guys see anybody hanging around the table, after I left?" I asked, looking back and forth between the two of them. "Anything suspicious?"

Peter looked a little dumbfounded, but he shook his head. "Just a couple of the servers," his sister informed us. "But they were all doing other things. Picking up plates or filling drinks. Nothing out of the ordinary."

"Did you see a blond server? She was talking to me right before I got up, wearing a long-sleeved black shirt beneath one of those yellow—"

But Autumn was already shaking her head. "I don't think so."

We said our goodbyes and they headed back to the party while Declan and I lingered in the lobby, trying to figure out what to do. I was running out of possible leads. I thought about texting Jo to ask whether she'd discovered anything back at the rehearsal dinner, but oh, yeah. I didn't have a phone.

Giving up, I boarded the elevator and asked Declan to text her for me.

"I don't have her number," he reminded me. I recited it from memory—she'd had the same one since our junior year of high school—and he tapped out a quick message to check in. "I'm gonna go back to the restaurant and keep searching, after we get you to your room."

I shook my head. "Don't waste your time. Whoever took it obviously took it on purpose. They're not going to just give it back."

"Do you have your location turned on? Find My iPhone? Something like that?"

I huffed, but it came out sounding pretty feeble. "I never set it up." I folded my arms and leaned my back against the handrail, frustrated tears stinging at my eyes. How could I have been so stupid? People had been telling me for years that I was too careless with my phone, yet I'd never bothered to do anything about it. Made excuses for it, even.

"Hey. We're going to figure this out, all right?" Declan wrapped me in his arms, strong and reassuring, and I stiffened. I didn't deserve this right now. I'd brought this on myself. I'd grown careless, and look where that had landed me. "You said there's nothing super important on it." It wasn't phrased quite like a question, but I heard the question buried beneath it. He was worried, based on my reaction, that there might be some horrible secret that was going to come to light.

"There's nothing bad." As much as I blamed myself for falling into the same old trap—being too gullible—I couldn't help trusting Declan anyway. I sniffled against his chest. "Just lots of pictures." My voice came out all pitchy and pathetic. I hated the way I sounded right now. Like a stupid little girl, lost without her security blanket. "Probably a few screenshots. I don't know. My whole life is—"

"Margo. Listen," he interrupted, his tone stern. He pulled back far enough to look me in the eye and cupped my face with his hand, swiping a tear away with his thumb. "So long as you're not sending people death threats or running some money-laundering

ring I haven't heard about, you'll get through this. Right? You're a good person. It sucks, but it's not going to be the end of the world."

I nodded, shutting my eyes tight. He was right. It was just a phone. Just a stupid little handheld computer that I'd thrown my whole life at for the past three years, but none of that really mattered, because all the things on my phone weren't *me*. Not really. They were more of a rough sketch—something that captured a vague likeness of the greater whole but missed all the finer details. A handful of text messages wasn't my friendship with Jo. And my phone wasn't my entire life.

I'd be fine.

My eyes were still closed when Declan kissed me. It was a repeat of our first kiss in this same elevator, only it wasn't fire that threatened to swallow me whole, but that feeling of a wave rushing over me—shocking my senses and calling me out of my stupor. I responded without letting myself stop to overthink it. Parting his lips with my tongue, seeking distraction. The elevator arrived on the fourth floor without a hitch this time, and he walked me over to my room and kissed me again. His hands tangled in my hair as he backed me against the door beneath the brass 402.

"Don't go back to the restaurant," I whispered against his lips. "Come to bed with me."

I didn't remember finding my keycard or unlocking the door, but in a flash, we were stumbling into the dark room and he was tugging my dress over my head. Moonlight spilled in through the sliding glass door to the balcony. We didn't bother catching the lights. The back of my knees hit the mattress and I sank into it, my hands fumbling with his belt.

He licked his lips as he watched me ease down his zipper, seeming to wrestle with himself. "You don't have to do this right now, if you don't want to."

Except right now, this was all I wanted—to lose myself in this moment, and to forget all the rest of it. I answered by tugging down the elastic of his boxers and taking him into my mouth. Above me, there was a sharp, surprised inhale, and then his fingers worked their way back into my hair. His breath caught as he watched me.

"You're so fucking beautiful," he said, so low that I wasn't sure he meant me to hear it. He stopped me before he finished, easing me back onto the bed and unhooking my bra so that he could take my nipples into his mouth and suck on them in turns. His fingers hooked my underwear and tugged them off, and then I was pulling him over me.

"Condom," I whispered.

He reached for the box of condoms I'd bought and tucked into the drawer of my bedside table a few days ago. He eased one on before flipping onto his back and drawing me over him, and then he was inside me again. There was nothing but this—me and him and a dark hotel room, and everything outside of this didn't matter.

But as I drifted to sleep that night, an uneasy feeling churned in my gut. I couldn't shake the feeling that something bad was going to come from this. I just didn't know what.

Seven Rules for Breaking Hearts ✅ @7R4BHpodcast ·
Jul 26
https://bit.ly/6akb3o2
💬 1374 ⇆ 12.8k 🖤 36.3k

Raquel O'Brien @raqyoursaqsoff · Jul 26
Replying to @7R4BHpodcast
I don't understand what happened to you guys. I really liked your message in the beginning but now it's starting to feel like it's all been a lie . . . ☹️

Jessica @messy_jessy8273 · Jul 26
Replying to @7R4BHpodcast
ok but ive BEEN saying its all an act. these types of girls

*will do anything for attention and this is proof. its one
thing to live your life however you want. its another to use
someone like this just for the clicks. #Cancel7Rules*

andycakes *@miranda_lovee · Jul 26*
Replying to @7R4BHpodcast
*Not even surprised. @margoanderson you disappoint but
it's whatever. Should have unfollowed a long time ago.*

"I'm not sure it's my color," I said, turning in front of the floor-length mirror in my room for a final inspection of my bridesmaid dress. Jo had let us choose our own style so long as the color met her requirements, and I'd gone with a strappy dress with a plunging neckline and flowy, knee-length skirt. Perfect for a beach wedding. But it was the color that was bothering me: a pale robin's-egg blue that made me look completely washed out.

"Blue is literally everyone's color," Liv called from out on the balcony. She'd insisted on applying her makeup in natural lighting, so now she was squinting at the tiny mirror in her eyeshadow palette, balancing it in one hand while she applied mascara with the other. "Blue is the color of calmness. Serenity. No one looks bad in blue."

Calmness and serenity were two emotions I was having a pretty hard time feeling right about now. My eyes were burning from lack of sleep. As much as I was trying to focus on the day ahead, I couldn't help feeling like I was sitting around waiting for the other shoe to drop. Declan had tried to reassure me before we were forced to go our separate ways this morning, but as soon as I was alone, it was like I got stuck in my head all over again.

"If they do anything to your social media, we could always—what's it called—track their IT address," he'd told me.

"IP address," I'd corrected him with a fond look. "And are you sure they let you graduate with an *actual* degree, or did you frame up a piece of paper you printed off Google Images?"

"Mechanical engineers don't need the internet. That's what computer engineers are for."

It had made me laugh at the time. Now I was feeling sick to my stomach. I was ninety-nine percent sure that tracking an IP would be completely useless in this instance. There was every chance they'd just use my cell service rather than connecting to any Wi-Fi, for one, and I didn't know how that worked. But I was also feeling a bit desperate. I should have asked him if he worked with any computer engineers who could give us a more definitive answer.

To distract myself, I was trying to fixate on the one thing I could control. The dress. Which I actually couldn't control at all, because this was the color Jo wanted and there was also no way I was finding another dress on this short notice. But maybe I could do something to spruce myself up. Add some blush. Put my hair up. Let my hair down. I didn't know, something.

"You don't think I look sort of washed out?" I asked Liv as I leaned in the doorframe that led out to the balcony. It was hazy this morning, a thin gray mist hanging over Avalon.

She paused in the middle of applying her mascara to give me an appraising look. "You're just pale, babe. Not as pale as your man, but . . ." I frowned at my own arms, turning them over to check the undersides. I thought I was pretty tan, by my own standards, but maybe that was because I'd been comparing my skin to Declan's all week. "Anyway, be thankful the dress isn't worse," she said. "I was in my older sister's second wedding. Two words: baby poop yellow."

"That's three words," I pointed out.

Autumn emerged from where she'd been changing in the bathroom, looking distressed. She planted her hands on the hips of her bridesmaid dress—a chic, one-shouldered number with structured pleats. "I cannot be seen like this."

I frowned at her. The blue was a little different from her usual dark-and-earthy palette, but it didn't look bad. "What's wrong with it? It looks fine to me."

"Of course it doesn't look bad, I got one of the girls in the design program to tailor it for me." She pointed a coffin-shaped nail at her smooth, tan calf. "The problem is that I'm bruised like a fucking banana. I bumped it on the corner of my chair last night."

"So what?" Liv said, blotting her lipstick with a tissue. "Margo has blowjob knees, and you don't see her trying to hide it."

"They're not blowjob knees," I said, exasperated. "I fell and scraped them at a restaurant, the first night here." I ushered Autumn back inside and searched my makeup bag. "I'll cover it for you."

Normally Jo was the makeup expert, but she was off somewhere having first-look photos taken with Peter. I squatted in front of Autumn with a concealer palette in hand as she pointed out the bruise, barely noticeable against her bronzy skin. "Look, it's all green and nasty-looking."

"Hey, Margo," Liv called from out on the balcony, while I was in the middle of debating whether orange or pink would better conceal the bruise. "Did you post on Twitter this morning?"

"I don't have my phone, remember?" I shouted back, distracted. Orange, I decided, dabbing my brush in the concealer. Only as soon as I started applying it, it became woefully apparent that orange was not the right color.

I grabbed a few tissues off the nightstand. Before I could finish wiping it back off—with Autumn wincing and sucking air through her teeth like I was *trying* to hurt her—Liv shoved her phone into my hand. "You might want to check this out."

"What—" I stared at the screen. Wow, no cracks or anything; some people really took care of their phones. It was open to a Tweet from the *Seven Rules* official Twitter account, posted today from mobile at 10:37 a.m.:

https://bit.ly/6akb3o2

That was all it was. Just a URL. My heartbeat thudded in my ears as I pressed my thumb to the link. It loaded to a random website called GossipHub, and for a split second, I was almost relieved—maybe whoever had stolen my phone had decided to use our social media following to increase their own traffic, and this whole nightmare would end there. But then I scrolled and saw the picture at the top of the article.

It was a picture of me and Declan. The selfie we'd taken on the hike to see the bison—both sweaty and a little sunburned, him pressing a kiss into the side of my head. Okay, so whoever had stolen my phone decided to leak the picture. It wasn't the most flattering picture, and it wasn't how I would've chosen to announce to the world that I was seeing someone, but I could live with it. Except then there was the title above the article: SEVEN RULES CO-HOST MARGO ANDERSON DIDN'T JUST LIE TO FANS. SHE LIED TO HER BOYFRIEND TOO.

My mouth ran dry.

Between screenshots of my private conversations and flashing ads for magic weight loss pills, someone had laid it all out there. The Patreon post. The plan to ditch the rules for two weeks. They'd even posted a screenshot of my search history on Instagram from that night at the club in Studio City, when I'd clicked on a couple different *Declan Walsh* profiles to no avail. It was clear that someone had at least a rough idea of what was happening in our lives, and then they had used my phone to piece the rest of the story together. Except it wasn't the real story—they were painting me as the villain. Like I'd been planning this for weeks.

I closed out of the article and opened Instagram without asking Liv whether it was okay, typing my own username into the search bar in a panic. The URL in my bio was changed so that it now linked to the same article, and the podcast's official Instagram was the same. I switched over to the browser and pulled up our website. Even LinkedIn. Everywhere I went, the link followed.

I looked up at Liv and Autumn in a daze. "What do I do?" I asked stupidly, because right now I couldn't think straight.

Liv held up her hands when I tried to give her the phone back—like she wanted to wipe her hands clean of it. "This is above my pay grade."

"I think maybe you should talk to Jo," Autumn suggested.

I swallowed. Nodded. She was right. If anyone would know how to solve this, it was Jo. She'd always been better at this sort of thing than I was.

The landline phone on the nightstand rang—a jarring, metallic sound that should have jolted me out of my stupor, but it didn't. I grabbed it off the cradle. "Margo Anderson," I answered wildly, because how were you supposed to answer a hotel phone, anyway?

It was one of the employees down at the front desk. "There's a golf cart here to take you to the Casino."

Right. I couldn't talk to Jo right now because she was currently smack-dab in the middle of the biggest day of her life. I hung up and turned back to Liv and Autumn. "It's time to go to the wedding."

* * *

By the time we were standing in front of the guests, the haze over the island had scattered, making way for another beautiful day. A salty breeze stirred the palms that lined the walkway. Peter waited beneath an arch of wisteria in front of the old Art Deco mosaic that adorned the Casino, shaded by the round arches that guarded the entrance. Rows of white chairs were arranged before us, almost all of them filled. A golf cart approached in the distance.

It felt like today was happening on fast-forward. I hadn't even seen Jo since last night. On the other side of Peter, Declan caught my eye and smiled, his hands clasped in front of him as we waited for the golf cart buzzing down the boardwalk toward the Casino. We hadn't had a moment alone in all this, either. I needed to figure out how I was going to explain the article—I doubted he would have seen it yet, but it would have to be addressed sooner or later. Guilt ripped through me. I should have told him last night. Should have come clean about the podcast and the plan to take a couple weeks off from the rules the moment I felt uneasy after that conversation with Shelley. Now, every explanation I tried to conjure up felt like I was doing damage control. This wasn't me being honest—I was caught red-handed, and now I had to scramble to explain.

The golf cart rolled to a stop. It was decked in flowers and layers of white tulle, and someone had prematurely scrawled *just married* across the back in white chalk paint—fun and cheesy and very on-brand with everything this island was about. Necks in the audience craned to catch a glimpse of the bride. Jo's dad was driving, and he honked the horn twice before jumping out to help her with her dress.

The music changed as Jo stepped out of the golf cart and accepted her father's proffered arm. She fussed for a couple of seconds with the sleeves of her dress—they were loose and off-the-shoulder in a way that looked elegant, but also effortless—before she took her first step down the aisle.

The ceremony was short and sweet, which I was grateful for, given the way the sun was beating down on the wedding party. They got through the vows without any objections, Peter swept Jo in a kiss, and then it was done. They were married. The guests were ushered inside the Casino Ballroom while the wedding party hung back to take pictures before we were excused so that the photographer could get some pictures of just the newlyweds. Stepping into the air-conditioned Ballroom, I wiped my forehead on the back of my arm and broke away from the rest of the wedding party to throw back a shot of tequila at one of the bar carts. Afterwards, I grabbed a seat next to Declan at the table.

"You look amazing," he said in my ear.

And there was the guilt again, clawing at my throat like it was desperate to find a way out. I swallowed. "Thanks. You clean up pretty nice yourself." Jo had selected a rich shade of blue for the groomsmen, though Declan had already shed his suit jacket, revealing a white dress shirt and loosened tie underneath.

"Is everything all right?" he asked, setting a hand on the knee I hadn't realized I was jiggling. I forced it still. "You seem . . . I don't know, tense."

"Just weddings, you know?" I said with what I hoped was an airy wave of my hand.

His forehead creased in a frown. "I'm not sure I do."

But thankfully, he didn't press me any further. Dinner was served as soon as Jo and Peter returned with the photographer, and afterwards they rose for the first dance. One of the live musicians sawed out a rendition of "Thinking Out Loud" on the cello. Under normal circumstances, I probably would have turned to Declan and cracked an Ed Sheeran joke, just to get under his skin—*wow, I can't believe your cousin wrote this*—but it didn't feel right, at the moment. Nothing felt quite right, but I was going to have to work past that, because I needed to come up with a solution. Damage control.

On a chalkboard propped up by an easel, beneath *Jocelyn & Peter* in elegant white calligraphy, someone had written out the schedule. But they might as well have wiped it clean because the longer the reception progressed, the more things seemed to be happening out of order. It was impossible to catch Jo to pull her to the side and tell her what was happening because there were at least two hundred people packed into the ballroom and every last one of them seemed to be vying for the couple's attention, eager to offer congratulations and well wishes and to compliment her dress. I was pretty sure I was supposed to make the maid of honor toast half an hour ago, but tapping my fork against the champagne glass had zero effect on the crowd, so I'd just downed it and gone back to the bar cart for something a bit stronger. Around the same time, Jo decided to toss the bouquet. It plopped right into my mom's waiting arms, and she beamed like a kid on Christmas as she approached me at the bar cart.

"Look," she said, winded and a bit sweaty from dancing with Tony and then squabbling with a bunch of twenty-somethings over the bouquet, but she looked radiant nonetheless. "I don't think Jo threw it at me on purpose, but maybe she did. It should be yours though." She started to hand the bundle of lilies to me, but when I made no effort to accept it, she seemed to think better of the idea. "Why are you over here by yourself? Where's your boyfriend?"

"He's not my boyfriend," I said glumly. "And I'm kind of doubting he ever will be, after today."

"Hey." Her hand found my shoulder and squeezed. "What's wrong? Talk to me. Let me help."

"I appreciate the offer, Mom. Really," I added, when she didn't look reassured. "But it's not the sort of thing you'd be able to help with."

"Can I get you anything?" the bartender interrupted. "Because you're holding up the line."

A handful of guests in crisp button-downs and summery floral prints had racked up behind us. "Something that doesn't taste like alcohol," Mom said.

The bartender pulled a face that suggested alcohol was always going to taste like alcohol, but under Renee's watchful eye, she was obliged to recommend something anyway. "We have Buffalo Milk."

"Okay, can someone actually explain to me what Buffalo Milk

is?" I interjected. "Because I'm pretty sure no one's driving out there each morning to milk the bison."

"It's sort of our local version of a White Russian, I guess. Kahlúa with vodka and a couple cream liqueurs."

But despite having asked, I barely heard the bartender's explanation; Jo had broken away from dancing with a few of her cousins to approach the band. Now was my chance to talk to her. I didn't expect her to help me solve anything here and now, but I needed to tell her what had happened.

"Ooohhh, I'll take one of those," Mom said, turning to me. "What about you, do you want one?"

But I was already excusing myself and hurrying across the dance floor, my heels clicking on the polished wood as I wove between couples. I caught Jo by the arm just as the guitarist was starting up an acoustic version of "Suavemente," his fingers caressing the neck of the guitar. "I need to talk to you," I said over the amplifier.

She'd kicked off her heels and there was a sheen of sweat across her forehead from dancing. "Can it wait?"

"Not really. It's kind of an emergency."

She cast a wistful gaze at Peter, who was loosening his tie and rolling up his sleeves to come join her on the dance floor.

"You know I wouldn't ask if it wasn't important," I added. There was a beat, and then she nodded.

We pushed through a pair of French doors onto the open-air promenade that wrapped around the upper level of the Casino. Ivory pillars framed the sapphire bay dotted with sailboats and private yachts, and beyond that, the houses and hotels of Avalon clung to the hillside. A breeze rolled in off the water, stirring the wispy sleeves of Jo's wedding dress. Curled tendrils framed her face, and she tucked them behind her ears before folding her arms. "What's up?"

"Whoever stole my phone used it to post a link to all of our social media." No sense in beating around the bush. I leaned my back against one of the pillars—something to stabilize me, to keep me from tumbling right over the railing and washing out to sea. Washing out to sea might've been simpler, at the moment. "It's an article. About me."

Her eyebrows shot up. "About you?"

I felt a pang of irritation at her surprise—as if Jo and her wedding were the only ones worth writing an article about—but that wasn't fair. Today was her wedding day. She had every right to be surprised that someone had picked today to write about me, and I needed to be empathetic. "I mean, you're involved in it. There are screenshots and stuff," I said, racking my brain to remember if there was anything incriminating on her part, but I was fairly certain there wasn't. "But it's more about me and Declan. They're framing it like I'm some sort of mastermind, dating him just to . . . I don't know, stir up drama for the podcast, or something."

She blew out a long breath. "Shit."

"I know."

"I told you this was a bad idea from the start."

And just like that, my empathy was shot to hell. I gave her a murderous look. "Oh, you told me?" I repeated scathingly. "None of this would have happened if you hadn't decided to go off and get married—"

"Oh, is *that* what we're making this about." Jo sputtered a laugh, but it was devoid of any humor. She turned like she was going to walk away, hands going to her hair in a frustrated motion, but she seemed to remember that it was styled, a beaded veil trailing from the half-knot at the back of her head. She rounded on me again, dark eyes narrowing. "So all your support, your encouragement through all this—standing up there with me today—all that was just for show?"

This conversation was going off the rails. I should have known better than to bring it up with her today, of all days, but I didn't know who else to turn to. "I support you. Of course I do."

"Then you can't get mad at me for wanting to live my life!"

"I'm not mad," I said, but I was so frustrated that it came out sounding angry anyway. "It just sucks that it had to come at my expense. At the expense of the podcast. I mean, we lost sponsors—"

"The podcast?" Jo tossed up her hands. "What does that even matter? We agreed we're going to quit, and now suddenly you want to act like I'm taking something away from you."

"Because *you* backed us into a corner!"

"Yeah, and it looked like that corner was working out fine for you all week," Jo snapped. "You're only doubling back now because it's blowing up in your face."

My mouth snapped shut. She was right. I was fine with quitting the podcast. In many ways, I'd been looking for a way out for a while, even if I wasn't wholly conscious of it. And now here I was, all my frustrations—frustrations that didn't even matter anymore—bubbling to the surface, rather than owning up to my mistakes. It wasn't fair to me, and it wasn't fair to Jo. I swallowed. "I'm asking you to help me figure out what I'm supposed to do about it."

"On my wedding day," Jo pointed out, and I winced. "You're asking me to stop in the middle of my wedding to help you solve your problem. You're my best friend, and I love you, but the codependency thing—it's fucking bullshit."

I was on the cusp of an apology, but at her words, a sarcastic laugh ripped from my throat. "Codependency thing?"

Her eyes flashed dangerously and she pointed a perfect, shell-pink fingernail at me. "Don't act like you don't know what I'm talking about. We've done everything together, ever since we were kids. Your problem isn't with weddings, or Peter, or whatever else you've invented in your head. You're scared of people abandoning you." I opened my mouth to argue, but she just kept going. "You're so scared of it that you do this . . . this thing where you self-sabotage and push everyone away, just so they never get the chance to hurt you."

It was like the air had been knocked from my lungs. All I could do was gape at her.

Jo pressed her lips together, like she was holding back from saying more. She exhaled through her nose, long and slow. "I'm sorry. That was uncalled for."

The silence dragged on for a moment and I absorbed what she was saying. The worst part was that she wasn't wrong—it was hard for people to abandon me when I never let them get close in the first place, but somewhere along the way, I *had* become dependent on my friendship with Jo. "No," I mumbled, my voice cracking, like it was fighting me saying the words out loud. "You're right." Not telling Declan about the plans for the podcast . . . maybe it had been a simple mistake, or maybe that was self-sabotage, too. But it didn't matter now. The damage was done. I shook my head faintly. "We can talk about it later. You should enjoy your wedding."

Jo nodded slowly. I could tell her brain was already shifting into problem-solving mode, the cogs turning. "I'll send Peter to grab my phone from the hotel. That way you can delete all the posts. Change our logins. Assuming someone didn't change them already."

I bit down on the inside of my cheek. I didn't know what I'd expected. Even Jo wasn't capable of snapping her fingers and making it all go away. But a small part of me wished there was something more definitive. "Don't worry about it. It's already out there. Might as well own up to it, right?" I tried to pull a self-deprecating smile, but I had a feeling it came out as more of a grimace. "What am I going to tell Declan?"

Jo's eyebrows slanted uncertainly. Her makeup was fresh and light today, the feathery brows and soft blush a stark contrast to her usual sharp contour and wine-stain lips. "The truth?"

"I'm not sure the truth is going to paint me in the best light, at the moment," I pointed out.

"Okay, then make something up."

"I can't do that either. I don't know what to do."

She studied me for a long and quiet moment, the music from the live band spilling out onto the promenade through the crack between the French doors. "I know you're new to the whole relationship thing, but you're going to have to talk to him one way or another. You can't ignore him all night."

I blew out a breath, rapidly coming to the same realization. I needed to come clean, whether I felt ready or not.

* * *

Back in the ballroom, Renee had a microphone in her hand and was barking some order at the bartender, who was trying to manage the twenty-person pileup happening in front of the bar cart. The band had switched to a Latin song I didn't recognize. Declan was sitting alone at our table with a glass of water, cheek resting on his fist as he watched Jo's parents dance a merengue.

He glanced over at my approach, looking surprised when I sat down. "Hey."

"Hey," I echoed, unease roiling in my gut. I wasn't ready to do this. I had to do this.

"Are you avoiding me or something?"

"Yes," I admitted. "But not because of anything you've done."

I hated myself for the wounded look that crossed his expression, but in a blink, it was gone, carefully concealed behind a mask of concern. "Do you want to talk about it?" he asked.

Even when I was pushing him away, here he was, worrying about me. God, I'd make a shitty girlfriend. Maybe that was the real reason I'd avoided relationships for so long. Because as scared as I was of getting hurt, I was equally scared of hurting someone else. The *Breaking Hearts* part of the podcast was a marketing gimmick; in reality, no one had ever asked me for more than I was able to give, and that suited me fine. But more than anything, I was terrified of putting someone through what my dad had put my mom through. What too many selfish people put the people who loved them through every day: heartache and betrayal. I just never envisioned that betrayal would look like this.

I took a deep breath before I worked up the courage. As soon as the words left my mouth, there'd be no turning back. "Where's your phone? I need to show you something."

Over by the stage, feedback wailed from a microphone near the speaker.

Declan extracted the phone from his pocket with a frown. He entered the passcode before passing it over to me. "I don't—"

"I promise I can explain everything." There were no social media apps on his phone, so I pulled up the browser and searched for GossipHub. It wasn't big enough news to make one of the headline articles for the day, but there it was in the sidebar, the little thumbnail of me and Declan together. I waited for the page to load before I passed it across the table. My heart crawled up into my throat, so high that it felt like I was going to vomit it right up. "Just . . . before you hate me, please hear me out."

He shot me a quizzical look before his attention turned to the screen.

Up on the stage, Renee had the microphone in her hand and the band was winding down. "First and foremost, on behalf of Jo and Peter, allow me to thank you all for being here to share in this momentous occasion. Tonight's festivities are provided by Castaway Catalina Events. Please consider us for the next important event in your lives, whether it's a birthday party or a work retreat."

One table over, a teenaged Hernandez cousin coughed into his hand, and it sounded suspiciously like *tacky*. Beside me, Declan's lips parted slightly, his brow knit as he flicked a thumb over the screen to scroll down the article.

"And now, I think we're a touch overdue to hear from our maid of honor. So, Margo, if you don't mind coming up here to give your toast—"

Whatever else she'd said was drowned out by my heartbeat hammering in my ears. Declan looked up from his phone, slowly, like he'd just registered that someone had said my name. His hazel eyes found mine, but there was none of the warmth in his expression that I'd grown so used to, none of the quiet amusement or the bright, uninhibited curiosity. There was just . . . nothing. Like a curtain had drawn shut, and the lights on the stage had dimmed.

"Margo," Renee said again, her voice echoing in the wide ballroom.

"Please," I whispered, searching his face for some sign that he wasn't going to shut me out completely—that this was just an intermission, and we'd be back for a second movement. "Just give me a few minutes. I can explain."

Before I knew what was happening, someone was ushering me out of my seat and shoving a microphone in my hand.

CHAPTER

26

Champagne sloshed over my trembling fingers as I climbed the steps to the stage and turned to face the audience. I didn't remember grabbing my champagne flute off the table. The lights had always disarmed me, standing on this side of a stage—it took my eyes a few seconds to adjust so that I could pick out individual faces in the crowd. Bile burned at the back of my throat, and I was tempted to wash it down with the champagne, but I had to make a speech first. I could do this. I hadn't prepared what I wanted to say, but I was always better at improvising. I'd put on an act for the podcast a hundred times. I just needed to say a few words and smile for the camera.

"Hi," I said, and my own quivering voice echoed back at me, magnified times ten. Okay, so maybe this was a little different from improvising behind a computer screen. "For those of you who don't know me, I'm the maid of honor. Some of you might know me as Go from the podcast that Jo and I run together, but in real life, my name is Margo." My gaze met with Jo's where she sat beside Peter at the sweethearts' table, and she nodded her encouragement. I directed all my attention toward her because I was scared that if I looked over at Declan, I'd fall apart.

"I met Jo the first day of kindergarten. She wasn't ready to spend a whole day at school away from her parents, so I tried to cheer her up by smearing Crayola paint all over my face." A few people laughed. "We might've gotten put on time-out, but it worked. By the end of that first day, Jo was fine. And that was the last time she was scared to take the next step. Since then, she's always been the first one to do everything. The first to volunteer to speak up in class. The first to go to college. And now, the first to get married."

Peter leaned over to whisper something in her ear. Jo frowned, tearing her eyes from the stage to search the ballroom.

I took a deep breath, the rush of air picked up by the microphone, but it felt like I couldn't breathe deep enough. I didn't want to be up here. I needed to wrap things up. "I've always looked up to Jo, because all those firsts have inspired me to do better in my own life. When I look at Jo and Peter, I see something to strive toward."

Jo mumbled something. Peter was rising from his seat. Somewhere, a door slammed—one of the French doors, I realized, as heads in the audience whipped around for the source of the sound. Unable to restrain myself any longer, my gaze cut to Declan.

Or rather, to his chair, because it was empty.

I turned back to Jo, my mouth half-open. *Go*, she was mouthing. Why was she mouthing my name? It wasn't until she stood up and flung a finger at the French doors where Peter was slipping outside that I realized what she meant. "Go!" she ordered, and this time she shouted it.

"So, here's to Mr. and Mrs. Figueroa," I said, my voice cracking as I raised my champagne flute in a sloppy toast. "May you have many happy years."

Half of the guests were too busy craning their necks and muttering their confusion to bother raising their glasses in a toast, but I didn't wait around for them to catch up. I chugged my champagne and shoved the microphone into Renee's arms. "What—" she sputtered, but I didn't wait around to hear the rest of the sentence, because I was flying down the stairs and across the dance floor. Behind me, the band struck up a jazzy version of "Crazy in Love" to fill the lingering silence, but the click of my heels seemed to echo off the domed ceiling anyway.

I burst through the French doors onto the promenade, but there was nobody standing there. The sun was setting behind Avalon, the sky a grayish-purple and the mountains charred black against the yellow glow of the city, the promenade lit by yellow overhead lights. I followed the pillars as they wrapped around the cylindrical building, to the east-facing side that looked back toward the mainland.

I saw Peter first—standing with his back to me, his arms folded as he said something in a low voice that I couldn't quite make out. Declan appeared as I rounded the building. He had a shoulder leaned against the pillar as he stared out at dark water, which seemed to stretch on forever before it was swallowed up by the night. They both looked over at the sound of my footsteps.

Peter glanced back and forth between the two of us, and seemed to conclude it was best if he saw himself out. "All right, man. I'll see you next weekend." He caught my eye as he turned to leave and raised his eyebrows. It was a brief expression, there and then gone again, but his meaning was clear: *good luck*.

Declan had straightened up so that he wasn't leaning against the pillar, but he made no effort to initiate conversation. I wanted nothing more than to bury my face in his chest, to have him draw me into his arms and whisper into my hair that it would be all right. But the chances of that happening looked pretty slim, at the moment. I took a deep breath and took a tentative step toward him. "What's next weekend?"

He made a show of buttoning his suit jacket before stuffing his hands in the pocket of his dress pants. "Going over to Pete's house to help pack."

In the midst of everything, I'd almost forgotten that Jo was moving out of our apartment. I'd be packing myself, soon. "You're leaving."

He pressed his lips together. I got the impression he didn't want to meet my eye—he kept looking back at the water, even though it was dark. "The wedding's over. I figured I'd catch the last ferry tonight. Have some time to relax before going back to work on Monday."

He wasn't giving me much of an opening, but he also wasn't walking away yet, and I thought maybe that was a good sign. I searched for the right words. Reggae drifted from one of the yachts parked down on the water, followed by a splash and raucous cheers. It felt like it was worlds away. "I know I probably don't have the right to ask anything of you," I said, my voice unsteady, "but please. All I'm asking is that you hear me out."

"What are you planning to say? That it's all made up? You sent those texts, Margo." He looked like he wanted to say more but his mouth clamped shut. A muscle feathered in his jaw. The unspoken accusations hung in the air between us: I sent those texts. I made that Patreon post. And I searched up his name on Instagram before this vacation ever happened, but not for the reasons he was thinking.

"I know I did," I said. "But it's not the way the article made it look. I didn't plan for any of this."

"Didn't plan to catch feelings, you mean?" he shot back.

Tears stung at my eyes. I wanted to rip my heart out of my chest if it meant I could stop feeling like this, because yes, of all the rules I'd broken, I'd broken Rule Number Seven the worst. And I didn't want to regret that, but I was having a hard time being okay with it right now, because this fucking hurt. Even worse, I wasn't sure I deserved to feel sorry for myself.

"I didn't plan for things to go this way." My voice was barely audible, more a whimper than anything. "I called everything off.

Ask Jo. I'd decided I was going to, that night in the arcade, before anything had even happened between us. The search history, me taking that picture the day of the hike—I promise that was all a coincidence. I didn't do this on purpose. I wouldn't."

"But if things had gone differently—"

I shook my head. "That's not what I'm saying."

He tossed his hands up, the calm exterior shattering. "That's exactly what you're saying, Margo!" His voice cracked with barely contained emotion. "You planned to use me for the podcast from the beginning, you just didn't count on actually liking me. What, was I supposed to be the safe option? You said it yourself the night of the bachelorette party. That I should have known I was the last man who—" He broke off in a humorless laugh, running a hand over his face. "Oh my God. Everything your mom said last night . . . even the fucking Red Wedding comment. It was practically staring me in the face."

"It wasn't . . ." I started to deny, but that was the thing: it *was*. Everything he was saying about me was true, no matter how desperately I wished it wasn't.

He shook his head, staring at me in disbelief. "I told you. That first day at the bar, I was straight up with you. I told you I didn't want to be another story for your podcast and then I walked away. When you kept flirting with me, I thought maybe—" He ran a hand over his face again, cutting himself off. "Fuck."

"I know," I whispered, shuttering my eyes against the tears. God, how many times today were my glaring shortcomings going to smack me in the face? "I wanted to tell you."

"You wanted to tell me," he echoed with a scoff. "Right. And what about all the days since changing your mind? If you can't be honest with me, then be honest with yourself for a second. Did you ever plan to tell me the truth?"

"I'm telling you the truth tonight."

"Like it counts when it's all over the fucking internet." He took a step toward me, until we were almost pressed up against each other, and for one wild moment, I wished he would kiss me again. But instead, his voice was deadly calm. "Here's what the truth looks like from my perspective. You walked into this with every intention of using me. And then you were either still planning to use me for the podcast or you were too chicken to come clean. But either way, you were more than happy to let me keep fucking you in the meantime."

I was so surprised that I choked on a laugh. "You're being an asshole."

"I'm being the asshole?" He laughed too, but it came out hollow. "You know what the worst part is? If you had just talked to me, you would have known that I don't have a problem with your podcast. Hell, I wouldn't have cared if you talked about me, even. My problem is with you using this"—he gestured between us— "for a cheap story. Reducing it down to another anecdote about why it's better to follow the rules. Because the rules are all bullshit, Margo. You know they are."

"I'm sorry." There was no blinking back the tears that spilled down my cheeks now. "I don't know what else you want me to say. I've never felt like this. About anyone," I emphasized, but he only scoffed and turned away. "Tell me what I'm supposed to say to make it better. Because I have no clue. This is all a guessing game for me."

Declan closed his eyes like he couldn't stand looking at me. The lights of the Casino danced on the lapping waves below. It should have been romantic, under any other circumstance. "Never mind," he said after what felt like an eternity. His voice was low now; it wasn't shaky or desperate to make me understand. It was empty. Flat. The curtain was closed. And somehow, that was worse than if he'd yelled at me. "If you don't already know, then what's the point?"

Before I could conjure up a response, he brushed past me, walking away.

"Declan, wait—" I called after him, but he was already rounding the bend without so much as a glance over his shoulder.

I hugged my arms around myself as I stood there alone on the promenade, wounded and angry with no one to blame but myself. The night air turned cool as I stared out at the bay, people drinking on the aft decks of their private yachts or strolling the sea-green pier, tossing bits of fish and chips into the water and watching the garibaldi swarm by the soft glow of the pier lights. Eventually I worked up the motivation to head back inside, if only for the sake of showing face as the maid of honor, even though the best man had dipped out.

The party was winding down. There were still a handful of couples slow-dancing to a classical cover of what might've been an *NSYNC song and I'd apparently missed the cake cutting because the dessert table was decimated and Jo had frosting in her hair. But there was still a line trailing from the ill-prepared bar cart, and a second bartender had jumped in to help keep up with demand: Shelley, her hair in a messy topknot and a grouchy look on her face like she'd been dragged here in the middle of her day off.

And suddenly, I'd found an outlet for my frustration.

I stormed over to the bar cart, ignoring the muttered protests of other guests who thought I was cutting the line. "How did you get in?" I demanded.

Shelley gave me a bemused look in the middle of shaking a cocktail. "Renee called me to bring supplies and help out. Said they underestimated the number of bottles." She poured the drink into a plastic cup, garnished it with a slice of pineapple, and passed it to the person standing behind me.

"I meant into my phone. Did you jailbreak it? Hack it somehow?" I blew out a breath. "I guess it doesn't really matter. The damage is done either way."

She made a sound that was somewhere between a laugh and a

scoff, and looked to her coworker for help, but the other girl was too busy whipping up another Buffalo Milk to care. "I don't know what you're talking about."

"Yes, you do," I said firmly. "I get that you don't like people like me. You think we're rude and entitled and that we expect everything for free, and maybe you're right. If I'm honest, I don't always like people like me these days, either. But I need you to get the article taken down. If not for me, then for Declan. Hate me all you want, but he didn't do anything to you."

Her brow knit. For a moment, I thought maybe she would keep denying it. But then she mumbled some excuse to the other bartender and pulled me aside. "Look," she said, and then she paused for a long moment. I got the impression she was trying to work out what she could say without implicating herself. "I'm not saying I took your phone. But whoever did take your phone, it doesn't matter. It's out of their hands now."

"Do you know the person who runs GossipHub?"

She shook her head, almost imperceptible, like to shake it any more would be admitting to something.

"This could cost you your job, you know," I said slowly. "If I told Renee." In truth, getting Shelley fired wouldn't make a difference, so I wasn't sure I cared enough to tattle. It wouldn't make me feel any better about myself. But if there was any chance the threat would scare her into fixing this, then I was more than happy to hold it over her head.

"I don't work for Renee. My company is contracted through hers." She glanced over at the bar cart. This conversation was already boring her. "And anyway, you can't prove anything."

"So it's my word against yours."

She huffed a laugh. "You're not as important as you think you are. Just some girl with a microphone and too much time on her hands."

The realization washed over me all at once. I wasn't gullible.

And it wasn't trusting people that was the problem. I wasn't to blame for shitty people who turned around and used that trust as an excuse to take advantage, and I wasn't about to let Shelley ruin this for me, when I was barely learning to trust again. The damage was done, but that didn't mean I had to go back to my old ways. It felt *better* to give people the benefit of the doubt, and if they chose to go and screw that up, at least they only had themselves to blame. "I'm a person," I snapped. "Isn't that enough?"

Shelley just shrugged, either because she didn't know how to answer or simply didn't care. Someone's hand found my arm, warm and reassuring. "What's going on?" Jo asked as she came up beside me and gave Shelley a quick once-over.

"Nothing worth mentioning." I turned to leave. Renee had hurried over to see what all the commotion was about, standing a few yards away and wearing a confused expression. "Might want to screen your contractors a little better," I said as I pushed past her. "I think one of your bartenders has sticky fingers."

CHAPTER

27

I'd only been back on the mainland for seven days when I finished boxing my things and wrote the check to break the lease, but it felt a lot longer. For seven whole days, the only notifications that lit up my new iPhone were Bath & Body Works sales and my YouTube subscriptions, and the occasional text from Jo or Mom. I hadn't bothered downloading Twitter or Instagram yet. Jo had wiped the URL from all our profiles the morning after the wedding and consulted Peter's mom to see if there was anything we could do about the GossipHub article. But in the meantime, I figured it was best that I steered clear of social media, at least for a while.

I slammed the tailgate on my dad's old pickup and climbed up into the driver's seat. Everything that mattered, I'd fit into the bed of the truck, and I'd sold everything else on Facebook Marketplace. The couch? Seventy dollars. The TV? Traded it for a hundred-dollar gift card to Klatch Coffee. I even gave the shower curtain to some lady who made splatter art and claimed that she *went through these things like toilet paper.*

The IKEA desk had been moved to Jo and Peter's new one-bedroom apartment in Rancho, along with the rest of her stuff this past weekend. I thought maybe there was a chance I would bump into Declan while carrying boxes up the stairs, but it seemed he'd coordinated with Peter to schedule around my appearances.

"Just give it time," Jo said while we were unpacking dishes on the floor of her new kitchen, surrounded by an ocean of cardboard and bubble wrap. "He'll come around."

That was what she kept telling me, but I was starting to wonder where people in relationships got all their patience from. Or maybe it was precisely *because* they were in a relationship that they were so patient—it wasn't like they were the ones waiting around for a text or a phone call that would probably never come.

Jo had offered to help me with my own move, but I'd talked her out of it. I'd made up some excuse about how she should take the time to settle into her new home with her husband, but really, it was because I thought maybe it would be easier without any distractions. Now, as I reached the interchange to hop onto the 210 East and passed beneath a sign indicating the turnoff for La Cañada Flintridge, I was regretting that decision. To distract myself from turning west for the Jet Propulsion Laboratory, I grabbed my phone out of the cup holder and asked Siri to call Jo.

"Are you busy tonight?" I asked as soon as she answered.

"We're over at Tío Oscar's house for the Dodgers game." I had to keep my phone on speaker because there was no Bluetooth built into the truck, but it sounded like maybe she had me on speaker as well—a TV chattered in the background, and forks scraped against plates. "Why, what's up?"

I winced, already anticipating the verbal lashing, but this was why I was calling her. "How bad would it be if I texted him again?"

I'd sent Declan a couple texts this week, the same day that I activated my new phone.

> **Margo:** Hey, it's Margo. Got a new number. Figured I'd let you know, just in case you ever wanted to talk.

Margo: And again . . . I'm really
sorry. For everything.

He didn't text back.

"I know you're really committed to the whole *fuck the rules* thing these days, but maybe you don't need to break that one," Jo was saying. "If he wants to talk, he knows how to get ahold of you. Right? Like I said. Just give it some time."

"But what if I don't have time?" I asked wildly as I flicked my blinker to merge with traffic. "What if he turns around and meets someone else, and they start dating, and things get serious, and I'm over here—shit." The lifted truck behind me sped up to stop me getting over, forcing me to swerve into the shoulder. I slammed my hand on the horn.

"Everything okay?"

"Fine, just drivers being assholes."

There was a pause, and then she asked, "Are you on the 210?"

"I'm heading east, I promise."

"Margo," she sighed, "I don't—"

She broke off when Peter mumbled something in the background. I couldn't understand him between the chatter of their TV and the rattling of my clunky truck. "What was that?" I asked, holding the phone closer. "What's he saying?"

More muttering. "Hold on," Jo said. "I'm giving the phone to Peter."

There was a series of rustles, and then the line went quiet. For a split second, I thought maybe they'd hung up, but then I realized that Peter had taken the phone off speaker. "Listen," he said, more authoritative than I'd ever heard him sound—Jo definitely wore the pants in that relationship. "Declan is my best friend and I know you're madly in love with him or whatever, but first of all, my dude has no game. Notice how he spent ten freaking years not knowing how to talk to you until you gave him an opening. So

I don't think you need to worry about him picking up girls at the nearest bar or anything."

I sputtered a laugh despite myself, remembering the story about Declan waiting after my concert and shoving the carnations at Jordan Gardner.

"But second of all, I don't think a text is going to win him over. Don't take this the wrong way, but you hurt his feelings pretty bad. And a text is easy to ignore."

"So you're saying I need to do something he can't ignore?" I asked, perking up. It felt like both Peter and Jo were making a solid effort to be impartial in all this—not that I really blamed them—so that was as close to real advice as I was likely to get.

"Margo, do *not* take that as a sign to show up at his work," Jo shouted in the background. "There's like a ninety-nine percent chance they'll arrest you for trespassing on government property."

"Hey," Peter said. "That's not true, they do campus tours for students and stuff all the time—"

"Oh my God, shut *up*—"

They bickered back and forth for a few minutes before Jo wrestled the phone from her husband and made me promise I wasn't about to hop off the freeway and turn around. She didn't need to worry—I was already about five exits past the interchange, and anyway, I wasn't going to stoop that low.

We chatted for a while about other things before the conversation drifted to the podcast. Neither of us had any ideas for Season Seven, but Renee had already sent several follow-up emails since we got back to the mainland, reminding us that we were contractually obligated to shout them out—or else Jo would be responsible for the cost of both the wedding and the two-week vacation, which we agreed was out of the question. We'd planned for the podcast to be back on air by September, but already it was the first week of August.

After rehashing a few lackluster ideas and failing to come to any sort of decision, we hung up. I pulled into the carport out-side my mom's apartment. I was able to haul my stuff into my old room in a couple trips. It still felt like a sauna because Mom never ran the air below eighty-five and my black tuba bag was still propped up against the side of my dresser, exactly where I'd left it when I moved out. My old fuzzy pink blanket was folded at the foot of the bed with a little welcome basket full of soap and candy bars and a handwritten note—*happy to have my girl home*, it said, signed with a heart-shaped smiley face.

In the middle of unpacking, there was a knock on my bedroom door, and Mom opened it without waiting for an answer. We'd have to work on that. She was dressed in a ruffly black dress, beaded clutch in hand, and she smiled when she saw me sitting on the bed in my old university sweats. "It's so nice to see you in here again." Cat Benatar took advantage of the open door to weave between her legs and hop up on the bed next to me, purring. I scratched beneath her chin. Nothing as flattering as a cat actually wanting to spend time with you. "There's leftover pizza in the fridge and ice cream in the freezer, so help yourself while I'm gone."

Ah, yes. Not even my mom would be wallowing on the couch with me tonight and watching reruns of reality TV, because tonight she was going out to dinner with Tony. "Have fun on your date." I hoped it sounded like I actually meant it. I wanted my mom to be happy, but it was hard not to feel a bit disheartened when she had a date on a Monday night and I had . . . well, nothing except a tub of Tillamook Mudslide and a bottle of three-dollar wine I picked up at Sprouts. And Cat Benatar. Who I now realized did not want my company, but rather had snuck into my room to knead my fuzzy blanket.

"Oh, I will," Mom said, with a naughty wink as she turned in the doorway to leave.

"Tell him to have you home before midnight," I called after her. "Otherwise you're grounded."

"No promises."

The smile stayed plastered on my face until I heard the jangle of her keys being lifted from the hook of the entryway, and then the front door closing behind her. I looked around at all the half-emptied moving boxes and lost all motivation. I could finish unpacking tomorrow. For now, I flopped back on my bed and grabbed my phone off the pillow.

I wasn't sure what to do without all my usual apps, but on the bright side, I'd clocked a lot less screentime this week. I pulled up the conversation with Declan—empty save for my unanswered text—and drafted a new message: *I miss talking to you.*

I hesitated before clicking send. Why did I always hesitate? Like I wasn't entitled to express myself honestly, like I always needed to be filtered, every word picked apart before it was approved for sending. I'd had enough of censoring myself. If nothing else, the fiasco with the GossipHub article had taught me a thing or two about honesty. I needed to learn to say what was on my mind. No filters, no editing.

I closed my eyes, pressed send, and chucked my phone across the bed like it had bit me. The message would probably go unanswered. If I was honest with myself, it deserved to go unanswered. But over the course of the last three weeks, a tiny bubble had blossomed in my chest. Some small part of me that dared to hope, to believe in happy endings, and I was terrified of popping it. Scared of going back to the way things were. So I just had to keep hoping, and I hoped against hope I'd get an answer.

* * *

The following Thursday marked a new low.

I told my mom that I needed to run back to the apartment in NoHo to finish tidying up, but instead my truck was idling next to the curb on a shady street in La Cañada Flintridge as I stared at the gleaming black sign that marked the entrance. It had the blue-and-red NASA logo and everything, because of course it did. JET PROPULSION LABORATORY, it said, and beneath that, CALIFORNIA INSTITUTE OF TECHNOLOGY. The campus itself was massive, if Google Maps was any indication. Building after concrete building tucked into the arid foothills of the San Gabriel Mountains.

I thumbed the corner of the envelope resting on my lap and chewed the inside of my cheek. This was stupid. I didn't even know which building he worked in. How many people actually worked here, anyway? I had imagined myself walking into an air-conditioned government building and asking the receptionist to point me in the direction of Declan Walsh in the Mechanical Engineering Department, but I was coming to the fast realization that there was no front desk and there was a very good chance that no one would know who the hell I was talking about.

I shifted the truck back into drive and flipped a U-turn, snatching the envelope off my lap and reaching across the center console to shove it into the glove box. He hadn't texted me back. Twice now, which meant he didn't want to talk to me, let alone find me wandering around his work with an envelope full of cash, blurting his name and job title at random passersby. He'd probably call security and have me chucked back out into the street.

I drove aimlessly for about ten minutes before I spotted a telltale red roof and crisscrossed palm trees. I wasn't particularly hungry, but it felt like I needed to do something to kill a little time before showing up back at my mom's again, so I swung into the parking lot. It was packed to overflowing and the drive-thru line spilled out into the road, but that was normal for In-N-Out. I grabbed a parking space right as an old dinged-up Explorer was backing out, and then locked the truck and headed into the dining room, where I ordered Animal-style fries and a chocolate shake before snatching up the booth that had just opened. The tabletop was still littered with used napkins and wadded-up wrappers from straws, but I plunked down onto the bench as I waited, double-checking my receipt for the order number.

When, exactly, had I turned into the sort of girl who showed up outside a guy's work? That was definitely a new low. I'd always known I wouldn't be very good at dealing with rejection—I'd just been lucky enough not to deal with it up until this point. My phone buzzed while I was waiting for my fries and I fished it out of my pocket.

> **Jo:** Is there a REASON your location is off??

> **Jo:** 🤔

I'd learned my lesson with the stolen phone and set up Find My iPhone this time around, as well as sharing my location with Jo and my mom. But the flip side of that, of course, was that Jo kept checking to make sure I wasn't doing anything stupid. While I appreciated the concern, I was able to recognize stupid all by myself. And this had definitely been a dumb idea.

> **Margo:** Don't worry. I'm at In-N-Out

> **Jo:** Which In-N-Out?

> **Margo:** That's not important

> **Jo:** Omg I'm actually going to kill you

> **Jo:** WHICH In-N-Out, Margo???

I stared out the window. The In-N-Out lot was full, so now people were parking in the sporting goods lot next door. I watched from a distance as some bearded dude in a sky-blue polo shirt and a baseball cap tried to cross the driveway in the middle of traffic. A car slammed on their brakes and honked, and he waved them off with a hand. A short, curvy woman scurried along behind him, her ponytail swinging. I turned my attention back to my phone.

> **Margo:** I think I'm in Tujunga, maybe? Not sure

> **Jo:** You tried to show up at his work, didn't you

> **Jo:** Should I be relieved you're not in government custody atm?

> **Margo:** I just drove by. Didn't even try to go inside

> **Jo:** You're aware that's stalker behavior, right?

> **Margo:** I'm not stalking anybody. I didn't even see him.

> **Margo:** And I decided it's best that I drop it, anyway

> **Margo:** If he wants to talk to me, he knows my number.

One of the workers called order eighty-seven over the intercom, and I rose from my seat, leaving my milkshake on the table in hopes of marking my territory. When I approached the counter to grab my fries, the guy in the hat was waiting in line with the woman. I probably wouldn't have given them a second glance, were it not for the woman's hair: deep red, pulled back in a high ponytail so that it bobbed back and forth like a metronome as she approached the counter to place her own order. I stared at the back of her head, only half-listening to the employee asking if I needed any extra spread. There was something familiar about her, but I couldn't place it. She was too old to have gone to school with me. Maybe I'd seen her somewhere before? Granted, L.A. County was pretty massive and it wasn't often I had any excuse for hanging around Glendale, but still.

It wasn't until I heard the soft rumble of the man's voice beside her, ordering a three-by-three with extra cheese, that I actually glanced at his face. It was like I'd stepped into a cold shower. My whole body tensed, and I searched for the nearest exit, which was—obviously—the front door. But it was too late, because I was frozen in place beside the pickup counter with a tray of Animal fries in my hand, and now he was turning to go find a seat.

"Margo?" Declan recognized me a lot quicker than I had recognized him, though he looked equally uncertain about how we should handle this unexpected run-in. He was holding the receipt in his hand, but he glanced at the door like he, too, was debating making a run for it. But that would mean sacrificing the triple cheeseburger he'd just paid for, so instead he settled on saying, "Hi."

Whether I liked it or not, my mind jumped immediately to that night in the shower together, to the steam and the water running over our bodies, to the way he'd muttered *hi* then, his voice thick with want. This wasn't the same voice, now. There was no desire in it, except maybe the desire to evaporate into thin air so that we didn't have to have this conversation.

"Hey," I said, doing my best to act natural, even with my fight-or-flight response screaming for me to bolt and never look back. "Long time no see."

He'd swapped his green Caltech hat for a brandless black one and he'd grown a short beard over the past three weeks. It was the beard that had thrown me off—a shade more golden than the hair on his head, but I should have recognized him anyway. I'd lulled my brain into a false sense of security by driving a few measly blocks from his work.

"Do you need a table?" I jerked a thumb over my shoulder. "Because I have one, but it's a little dirty, if you don't—"

"We ordered to go." He cast an uncertain look at the red-haired woman, seeking her approval. She nodded. "But I guess it wouldn't hurt to sit down for a minute."

As I led them over to the dirty booth where my half-melted milkshake was waiting, I struggled to remember everything I'd planned to say earlier. But now, faced with the reality of actually saying it, the words felt hollow. Scripts didn't work for me, and I certainly hadn't planned for this—running into him on his lunch break after I chickened out outside his work. Exactly how stupid did you have to be to think that JPL employees didn't swing by the nearest In-N-Out for lunch? Because I was that stupid, apparently.

"This is my sister, Erin," he said as they settled into the opposite side of the booth. "Erin, you remember I mentioned Margo—"

"Of course." Erin cast her brother a quick, knowing look that suggested he'd been talking about me pretty recently. Whether that was a good thing or a bad thing, I couldn't tell. "Nice to meet you."

I couldn't imagine there was much nice about any of this, given how awkward it was, but I appreciated her saying that nonetheless. I smiled and shoveled Animal fries into my mouth to avoid having to say anything else.

Declan fiddled with a straw wrapper that someone had left on the table, looking more uncomfortable than I'd ever seen him. He was the guy who could always crack a joke, always do something to break the ice, but currently, there was a glacier between us. "Erin's the one that I mentioned works, at, uh—"

"At Allegro Records," I said, now regretting the fries, because my mouth was stuffed full. I chewed frantically before swallowing and wiping my mouth on a napkin. "I remember."

"I've been meaning to message you, actually." He seemed to relax a little now that we'd landed on a safe topic of conversation, but I got the impression the walls were still up. He didn't quite look at me as he spoke, his eyes fixed on the straw wrapper. "To see whether you still wanted to set up those client interviews, or an internship, or whatever."

"Allegro is always looking for ways to get our artists more exposure," Erin chimed in, much warmer than her brother. She resembled him more in hair color and mannerisms than anything else—where he was tall and lean, she was short and soft. But when she smiled, I noticed they shared the same asymmetrical dimple. "I'm not sure about our internship opportunities at the moment, but I could always look into it."

I was pretty sure Declan had only suggested it to diffuse some of the awkwardness—if he'd wanted to message me, he would have done it already—but I pounced on the opportunity anyway. "An interview would be great. I'm looking into starting a new podcast."

Declan's eyebrows shot up, his eyes rising to meet mine. "Really?"

"Really," I confirmed, with a hesitant smile. "It's still in the early stages, but with *Seven Rules* coming to an end, I figured I might as well bank on the following we've built."

For a moment, I thought I caught a flicker of something familiar in his eyes. The corner of his mouth hitched in a half-smile. "That's great. I'm happy for you."

"Don't get too excited," I said. "I'm not sure our old listeners will care much about a music podcast, but I guess it doesn't hurt to try."

Erin's brown eyes flicked back and forth between us, and

Declan—catching his sister's eye—cleared his throat. "I'll text you the contact details," he said.

"Thanks."

An uncomfortable silence descended over our booth. I wondered if I'd made a mistake by inviting them to sit with me. If maybe the better option had been to duck out of the restaurant and pretend I hadn't seen him, because now there were probably questions racing through his head about what I was doing here, in Glendale, alone at an In-N-Out. And really, there was only one logical explanation. An explanation that happened to make me look like a clingy ex-girlfriend at best, and an outright stalker at worst.

"I'm glad to see you're doing good," he told me after a long moment.

"You, too." But I knew I needed to say something more. The words just tumbled out. "I mean, you look great. I like the beard."

"Ah." He ran a hand over his jaw, self-conscious. "Erin keeps telling me to shave it."

"I told him he looks like a caveman," Erin said, gesturing at the scruff. "No girl's ever gonna want to kiss him with all that."

At the mention of kissing, Declan's gaze held mine for one long, fleeting moment. I swallowed and tore my eyes from his, popping the bubbles on the lid of my milkshake that marked it as *cola, diet, other*. "He makes a pretty handsome caveman, so he gets a pass."

He gave a husky laugh, turning toward the window with a light blush tinging his cheeks. Erin frowned, her gaze cutting to me. I searched for something more to say—something to at least end things on a friendly note, if nothing else. One of the employees called an order number over the loudspeaker.

Declan released a breath like he'd been about to say something, too. "That's us." With that, he was sliding out of the booth after his sister. My mouth was still hanging open, but no sound was coming out. He stole a glance back at the table. "Nice seeing you."

"You, too," I said in a small voice, and then I watched him walk away.

I wrestled with myself for maybe ten, fifteen seconds. I could let him go. Do exactly what I'd promised Jo and drop it, accept that he would text me if he ever decided he wanted to talk. But it felt like if I let him walk away a second time, I'd never see him again. And while I didn't get the impression that he was open to hearing another half-baked apology, I still wanted closure. Even if that closure was as trivial as an envelope sitting in my glove box.

I flung myself out of the booth. "Wait up!" He was already cradling the brown paper bag in his arms, but turned, his brow creased in a question. "Come with me to my truck," I said, breathless. "I need to give you something."

Erin shot her brother a quizzical look when he handed her the In-N-Out bag, but she didn't try to follow as I led him out into the parking lot and over to my run-down Chevy. He waited as I unlocked the passenger's side door and grabbed the envelope out of the glove box before handing it to him.

He stared at it. *Declan*, I'd scrawled on the front of it, and nothing else. It felt a bit underwhelming, in retrospect. I should have done more. There was no letter inside, no explanation, because I'd planned to say everything I needed to say to his face. He looked up from the envelope, his expression unreadable. "What's this?"

"It's two hundred dollars and some change. For the maid uniform and the dry cleaners," I explained when he only frowned at the envelope. "I promised I would pay you back."

When he looked up again, there was that familiar flicker again—something bright and curious, a laugh condensed down to a single look. But then he blinked, and it was gone. "You've been driving around with this in your glove box?"

I winced. "Come on. You don't really believe I'm hanging around by myself at an In-N-Out in Glendale because I felt like it, do you?"

He exhaled slowly. "Margo—"

I waved my hands to stop him going any further. "Don't say anything." I couldn't handle getting rejected all over again. "And before you tell me something dumb about how you can't accept this, it's not up for discussion."

He pressed his lips together. It looked like maybe he wanted to say something more, but he held back. "Thank you."

"I'll watch for that text. About working with Erin, I mean." I pushed past him because I couldn't stand to look at him without kissing him, but the narrow space between the cars forced us together. His hand caught my shoulder as I brushed into him. My pulse rocketed beneath my skin, but he only stepped out of the way, hand dropping back to his side. My skin tingled where he'd touched me, frayed nerves screaming for him to grab me, stop me, make me stay for just a minute longer.

But he didn't try to stop me. He just nodded faintly, Adam's apple bobbing in his throat. "See you around," he muttered, but he managed to make it sound more like a goodbye.

I tried my best to ignore the tears welling in my eyes as I climbed up into the cab of the truck and turned the key in the ignition.

CHAPTER

28

It was 8:36 at night and a full week later when Declan finally texted me his sister's contact details. My phone buzzed when I was curled up on the couch, Cat Benatar nestled between my legs as I watched *Friends* reruns with my mom. I texted him back to say thanks and watched as the notification switched to delivered, but he didn't text me again. Not that I really blamed him. A simple *thank-you* wasn't really conducive to conversation.

I was starting to be okay with the way things had turned out. I wasn't happy, per se, but I understood why things had happened the way they did. And despite my mistakes, I'd learned a thing or two over the past month-and-a-half. Most important, I'd learned to hope. So maybe it wasn't such a bad thing that I'd screwed up something good, if that was what it took for me to recognize that there *were* good things out there; maybe I could live with my screwups if I just focused on a brighter future.

I debated whether I should even reach out to Erin. Would spending time getting to know his sister only prolong my suffering? But after exchanging a few texts with her, I realized that this was strictly professional. And when she offered for us to use one of the sound booths at Allegro to record the first season of my new idea for a podcast, I was sold.

"How was traffic?" Erin asked as she led me into the studio. The whole setup was a far cry from the desktop computer and IKEA desk that Jo and I had managed for years. One of their volunteers worked the console as we stepped into the sound booth. A microphone dangled in front of my face where I settled onto a stool.

"Not terrible." I was disappointed—but not surprised—to realize that we were alone in the sound booth. A small part of me had been holding out hope that Declan would turn up, but I realized now that was silly, because of course he wouldn't. This was strictly professional. And I was okay with that. I had to be.

Erin was obviously waiting for me to say something else, so I said, "I was thinking we could kick things off with a one-on-one discussing Allegro's mission, what you're doing different, you know. Then maybe we could arrange a couple artist interviews from there?" The last part came out sounding uncertain. I'd grown comfortable with the same old song and dance in the years spent on *Seven Rules*; these were uncharted waters for me, and in a way, I was looking to Erin for guidance. Degrees aside, she knew the music industry firsthand, and I didn't.

She nodded slowly. Her hair was loose around her shoulders today, and with the way it caught the stark overhead lights, it reminded me of molten copper. "That sounds reasonable." Where her brother's eyes were a bright hazel, hers were a deep honey brown, but she studied me with the same curious intensity. "Did you have an idea of a title for the podcast itself?"

"I was thinking *Charting the Chorus*. My plan is to focus on personal conversations with artists. You know, give them a bit of exposure while also diving into the more technical side of the industry, their creative process, that sort of thing." When Erin only smiled faintly, warmth crept up my neck, and I added, "I'm still workshopping the name."

"No, I like it," she assured me. She nodded at the volunteer at the mixing board, and he flipped a switch. "All right. Should we get started?"

The entirety of the recording was finished within the hour. I stumbled over some of the initial questions, but once we got through the first five minutes, conversation flowed. I would probably need to clean up some portions where we veered off-topic and I still needed to create a decent intro and outro, but overall, I felt like the interview was a success.

"Thank you again," I said as I rose to my feet and slung my bag over my shoulder to leave. "I'll be sure to email you the final edit before posting anything. And if you're willing to share to Allegro's social media, that would be a massive help." I'd created a few tentative profiles for the new podcast, but I'd kept them confined to my Mac rather than managing them from my phone—I found that it helped me compartmentalize.

"I'll talk to the guy who's managing our content right now, but I don't think that'll be a problem," Erin said. She didn't rise from her seat to walk me out. Instead, she pinned me under another of those looks. Under any other circumstance, her warm brown eyes might have made her seem kind and approachable, but right now she was staring at me so intently that it made me feel restless. "Why did you quit the other podcast? If you don't mind me asking."

"No, I don't mind." More than anything, I was relieved she wasn't asking me something more accusatory. Like what I had done to hurt her brother. "And I didn't quit. Technically. We just haven't quite figured out how we're going to wrap things up." Assuming we ever actually got around to it. But even as I was learning that I didn't owe anything to my audience, I still wanted the chance to tell my side of the story after the whole GossipHub fiasco. "There are some . . . things that I want to explain to our listeners. And I'm not sure how I'm going to do that just yet."

"Declan mentioned something about an article," Erin said delicately.

"He told you about that?" I wasn't surprised, but the mere

mention of the article was like a punch to the gut. I had to come to terms with the fact that the story was out there. Even if we were able to convince GossipHub to take it down—and after consulting the PR firm and an attorney, I wasn't entirely sure I wanted to open up that legal can of worms—there was no stopping people from talking. But there was also nothing stopping me from defending myself. "I never meant to hurt him. And my feelings were genuine. Are," I amended, because even as I came to terms with the way things had turned out, my feelings hadn't changed. "I know it maybe doesn't look like it, with the way the article framed things. And I feel like I owe him more of an apology, but I get the impression maybe he doesn't care to hear it."

As soon as I was finished talking, I regretted opening my mouth. Erin didn't bring me here to be my therapist or even a friend. This meeting was meant to be professional, but instead here I was, spilling my guts to his sister. "Sorry," I mumbled, embarrassed. "I shouldn't dump that on you. That was unprofessional."

"You're fine." She seemed to hesitate before releasing a sigh. With a motion of her head, she confirmed with the volunteer that the microphones were off. "I don't know how well you actually know my brother, but he's not the biggest fan of texting."

I snorted, because yeah, that sounded like Declan. "Peter told me something similar. But I already tried talking in person. You were there at In-N-Out, you saw how that went."

Erin studied me for a moment. "I haven't read your article," she admitted. "But given what I already know, I'm not sure I should be taking your side." I swallowed, nodded, because I completely understood. "At the same time," she continued slowly, "it does seem like you care about him."

"I do care about him," I assured her. "I don't need him to take me back or anything. I just want him to know that I'm sorry." I ran a hand through my hair before letting it drop to my side, defeated.

"It just feels like no explanation is going to be good enough." Perhaps because what I'd done wasn't excusable. In failing to tell him the plans for the podcast, I had betrayed his trust, and there really was no excuse for that.

"He'll hear you out whenever he's ready," Erin said.

I ended up leaving the studio right around the time that rush hour traffic was clogging up the 10. I flicked on my blinker and squeezed in behind a Prius still sporting an *Obama '08* bumper sticker. Once I was safely on the freeway, I turned on the radio and pressed seek until I found a random station—the Chevy was too old for an auxiliary port and the only CD within arm's reach was my dad's scratched-up Brooks & Dunn that spent more than half its life lying faceup on the passenger side floor. As I listened to the DJ laughing with a caller about her dating app experience, an idea started to take shape.

It was a gamble. There was every chance it was a bad idea. Harebrained, even. But I also didn't have anything to lose. I needed to find some sort of closure in this whole mess, even if there was a chance that closure would push Declan even further away.

I reached across the center console to fish my phone out of my purse, and asked Siri to call Jo. It barely rang before she picked up. "I'm thinking it's time we record Season Seven," I said by way of greeting.

"With what content?" she asked, her voice a bit tinny, which was always a surefire sign that she had me on the Bluetooth in her Honda Civic. About that time—the clock in my dash read 4:36 p.m., which meant she was just leaving her job at the PR firm that Peter's mom owned. "I'm married and you're . . ."

She trailed off. There was a fun little fill-in-the-blank: *Single. Stupid. Pining after a guy who wants nothing to do with you.* But even as I recognized the implausibility of my current situation— less than a month ago, I would've never in a million years imagined myself here—that didn't change the reality of it. "Let me worry about the content," I said.

"The last time you said that, it ended in your phone getting stolen and your personal business leaked all over the internet," she pointed out. Which yes, that was true, but this time was different. "I think we should just tell Renee there's been a delay. Buy ourselves a couple more months. I'm super busy with work, anyway."

"I'll record by myself. Actually, it might work better that way." I realized that it sounded like I wasn't giving her much of a choice, so I added, "If you're okay with that."

There was a lengthy pause. I could practically hear the raised eyebrows when she asked, "What on earth are you going to talk about?"

"That part's tentative. Conditional, I guess, in a way."

"Whenever you'd like to start making sense, that would be great."

"I need permission first."

She sighed. "If you want to handle it, it's no skin off my back. I just want to make sure you know what you're doing."

"I know what I'm doing," I assured her before exchanging a quick goodbye and hanging up. Traffic was creeping at a snail's pace—the sort of stop-and-go that had a history of getting me into trouble. But it was also the exact sort of drive that made me antsy. If I was going to be sitting here for a couple hours, I might as well do something productive with my time. "Hey, Siri. Send a text to Declan Walsh."

"What do you want it to say?" she inquired.

I mulled over the best opener for a message like this. I wasn't used to asking people for permission to mention them on the podcast—before all this, I probably would've changed his name and maybe added a few unflattering details for the sake of plausible deniability. But in this case, that would be counterproductive.

I needed to talk to him first. Assuming he'd ever bother reading the message, let alone responding.

Distracted, I almost rear-ended the Prius in front of me and had to slam on my brakes. My bag went flying out of the passenger seat, Wrigley's gum and loose change scattering on the floor. In the rearview, the guy in the car behind me was flipping me the bird.

Okay, so maybe this wasn't my brightest idea. The message would have to wait. "Cancel," I said before mumbling something to myself about calling him later. I wasn't sure he'd answer, but Erin did mention that he hated texting, so maybe a phone call had a better chance.

"Calling Declan Walsh," Siri announced.

"What? No, you can't do that—"

But it was already ringing. I dug my phone back out of the cup holder, my thumb hovering over the button to cancel the call. On one hand, it was better to wait, but on the other, I was curious whether he'd pick up. It rang once.

Twice.

Three times.

He was going to let me go to voicemail.

I was in the middle of trying to decide whether I should leave a message when something clattered on the other line. Was that . . . the start of his voicemail? It sounded like him dropping his phone. But then I heard a muffled voice say, "Shit," followed by ragged breathing. "Hello?"

I froze. Was he . . . with someone? My heart was beating so hard that it made me nauseous. I was teetering on the verge of hanging up, but he would've already seen my name on the incoming call. There was no point in chickening out now. "Sorry," I said quickly. "I can call back if—if it's a bad time, or something."

"You're fine," he panted. "You just caught me in the middle of a run. What's up?"

Relief flooded me. I hadn't figured out how I was going to approach things just yet, but my brain kicked into overdrive, finding something to fill any awkward silences before they happened. "I just left my first meeting with your sister."

"How'd it go?" He was probably asking to be polite, but I could almost imagine that this was normal, that we talked like this all the time, like I hadn't just called him out of the blue.

"Good. I think." I wondered whether Erin would relay her own version of events, including everything I'd said, but I didn't have time to worry about that. "Listen, I wanted to get your permission before recording the final season for *Seven Rules*."

There was a long pause before he asked, "Why would you need my permission?"

"Because I want to talk about you. Everything that happened between us." The word *us* brought with it a familiar pang, because there was no us, but there could have been. "Not to use it as a story, but just to kind of explain to everyone how I fucked up. You know." I cleared my throat in an attempt to dislodge the lump that had wedged itself there. "Clear the air. I can leave your name out of everything, if you want."

Another pause. I thought maybe he would just hang up. I wouldn't have blamed him if he did. "Considering my name was already published in the article, I don't think that'll make a big difference," he said. "But as for the rest of it, yeah. Permission granted."

"Thank you." I should probably have ended the conversation there, but I couldn't help myself. I blinked back tears so that I could keep my eyes on the road. When had I become the girl who cries at everything? When I got my heart broken, apparently. "I really am sorry for the way things turned out. I miss spending time with you." I waited for him to say something, but I was only able to stand the silence for a few seconds. I sniffled. "Shit. I'm sorry. This wasn't supposed to be that kind of call."

"It's okay," he said, but his voice was strained. It didn't sound very okay. It sounded like he wanted to get as far away from his phone as possible.

"I know podcasts aren't really your thing, but I'll send you the file after I finish recording, if you want to listen to it ahead of time. You know, for your approval."

"Sure," he said. "I'll listen to it."

It was more of a confirmation than I'd dared to hope for.

Season Seven, Episode Ten—Signing Off
10 min 54 sec

Margo: *Which brings us to the present.*

While I don't feel I owe anyone an explanation, I wanted to give Seven Rules *a proper ending. One that has hopefully addressed some of your lingering questions and set the record straight. This wasn't the final season I'd envisioned; when we first talked about the possibility of breaking a few rules for the sake of generating new content, I believed I was immune to catching feelings. I had to learn the hard way that I had it all wrong.*

I'm not sure I know what being in love with someone feels like yet, but I think I've got a pretty good idea of the falling part. You stop caring what the outside world thinks. I would have fallen for Declan either way, because if there's one thing I've learned, it's that love doesn't play by the rules in the first place. It's taken me way too long to realize that, but better late than never, right?

To our listeners, I owe you all an apology. I'm sorry if you feel that we've misled you these past few years. I can't make up for that, but at least now I can set the record straight: I was wrong. It's possible to be perfectly happy being single, but you don't need to follow a bunch of rules to do it. So forget the rules and live your life however you like. It won't always work out. A lot of the time, it probably won't. But at least you'll know that you've been honest with yourself. And in my experience, that's a lot easier to live with than living a lie.

Declan, if there's any chance you've listened long enough to get to this point: I'm sorry. Maybe you're going to hate the way I've gone about this, and that's okay. If nothing else, I hope you're able to see that you were a lot more to me than just another anecdote. I should have been honest with you from the beginning, but somewhere along the way I became so scared of messing up what we had that I ended up making it all worse. I don't expect you to forgive me. I just want you to know that I recognize I was wrong. About basically everything. The one good decision I've made these past few months was getting to know you. You've changed my life for the better, even if you no longer want to be a part of it.

So, one final time, I'm your host, Go. Henceforth known only as Margo Anderson.

This is it.

The end.

Thank you for listening to *Seven Rules*.

ONE MONTH LATER

Margo: Where is the green room?

Concertgoers spilled out onto South Grand Avenue. I fought against the current, a salmon swimming upstream toward the gleaming steel building, lit by purple spotlights in the dark. A massive, curved installation like a flag frozen in the wind welcomed visitors to the Walt Disney Concert Hall. The underground parking beneath the building was packed to the brim, so I ended up paying thirty dollars for two hours at an open-air lot a few blocks away.

Trees lined the avenue, but all except the lanky palms were stripped of their leaves by the gusting Santa Ana winds—a good indicator that fall had touched down in Los Angeles. I typed out a quick follow-up message as I jogged up the steps and set foot in the cool, modern foyer, still buzzing with people after the show had ended.

Margo: I'm here. Not sure where I'm supposed to be going.

I tucked my phone back into the pocket of my moto jacket. In the short time we'd been working together, I'd learned that Erin would answer, eventually—she just had a habit of taking her dear sweet time doing it. I approached an attendant in a black vest, the concert hall's insignia machine-stitched over his breast in gleaming gold thread. "Excuse me. I'm supposed to be meeting Marcus Kowalczyk in the green room, but I'm not sure where I'm going."

His eyebrows lifted in a way that suggested he did not, under any circumstances, believe that I was there to meet with one of the most prominent up-and-coming conductors in the nation. I was suddenly feeling severely underdressed in my tattered jeans, a threadbare Guns N' Roses T-shirt peering out from beneath my jacket. "I'm Margo Anderson," I explained. "From the *Charting the Chorus* podcast. I'm a friend of Erin Walsh?"

"If someone is planning to meet with you, they'll have to meet you out front," he said in a bored voice.

There was no such thing as flashing a wristband for a free drink around here. I mumbled some excuse about finding a restroom and slipped down one of the halls, but I was no closer to locating the green room here than when I was standing outside. After a couple minutes of aimless wandering, my phone buzzed.

> **Erin:** Sorry

> **Erin:** Just come to the stage

> **Erin:** Things are a little hectic down here

Relief swept through me and I headed to the nearest set of doors leading into the concert hall, only to be halted by an usher. "Concert's over."

"I'm not here for the concert, I'm here with—" Beyond his

shoulder, I spotted a curtain of sleek red hair. Erin was talking to someone up on the stage. "There she is, that's her. Erin!"

The skirt of her asymmetrical dress whirled as she turned, shimmery green fabric catching the overhead lights. Crap. I was definitely underdressed. "Let her through," she called to the usher with a wave.

The usher stepped aside and I slipped into the colossal concert hall. The seating was constructed arena style, rising like cresting waves on all sides of the stage. I met Erin down in the Front Orchestra. On stage, a handful of men and women in formalwear—employees or members of the orchestra, I wasn't sure—were clearing away the chairs. "Where's Marcus?"

"He's around somewhere," she said, distracted. She whipped her phone out of her clutch without looking at me and shot off a quick text. "Just have a seat real quick. I'll see if I can find him." With that, she scurried off.

I knit my brow and sank into a chair in the front row, shrugging off my leather jacket. My dynamic with Erin was mostly professional, but even if we weren't friends, we were at least friendlier than this. To be fair, we were meeting well outside of our usual safe little sound booth at Allegro Records. But when she'd offered to introduce me to Marcus Kowalczyk—who wasn't even one of her clients, more like a friend of a friend—I figured I could step outside of my comfort zone for a bit. And besides, I'd always liked concert halls. Even when there wasn't a concert happening, there was something a bit awe-inspiring about the sheer size of them, the way music could bring so many people together under the same roof. Right now, though, the hall was looking a bit rough in the wake of the crowd. A half-finished cocktail in a plastic cup was balanced on the arm of a chair a few seats away, and stray popcorn littered the floor, trampled flat by the dress shoes of the workers coming and going.

This was supposed to be a casual meeting. No interview yet, just some basic introductions to see if we meshed well enough to record together for half an hour or more. Maybe casual didn't mean jeans and a T-shirt, though. I picked at loose threads around the hole in my jeans, wishing I would have thought ahead. Even during my high school performances, we'd dressed better than this, so I should have known everyone performing here would be in black tie. Maybe I'd gotten a little too comfortable recording podcasts in pajamas or old workout clothes with sweat stains under the arms.

I extracted my phone from my pocket. I had resisted the urge to search for articles about the final season of *Seven Rules*, despite the tenth and final episode going live a few days ago. It didn't really matter how it performed, so long as I'd dropped Castaway Catalina's name often enough to get Jo off the hook and gotten my own version of the GossipHub story out into the open. The people who cared enough to listen would listen, and the ones who wanted to believe the worst wouldn't have heard me even if I was standing right in front of them shouting. That was just how things were, and it was easier to accept that when I wasn't obsessing over our analytics or reading through comments. Instead, I opened a message with Jo and initiated a game of Cup Pong.

Out of the corner of my eye, I realized that someone was cutting through the front row of seats and I tucked my legs in out of habit. There was plenty of room to just go around me, but I felt like I should be making myself as small and inconsequential as possible before someone decided I didn't belong here and kicked me out into the street.

Jo: Trying to distract yourself from checking Twitter?

> **Margo:** Trying to look like I'm busy. It's only workers here right now. And Erin, but I don't know where she went.

> **Jo:** Best two out of three?

> **Margo:** You're on

I'd managed to clear three of Jo's cups on the first round and was watching the screen for her to finish her turn when a bouquet of red carnations filled my vision.

My first thought was that they smelled amazing. My second thought was that someone had the wrong girl, because I wasn't one of the performers. I looked up.

Declan was standing in front of me, wearing a pair of jeans and the same NASA hoodie that he'd worn on the island. I blinked. Okay, so I wasn't hallucinating. "Sorry," he said, withdrawing the bouquet when I didn't accept it. "I didn't mean to shove them in your face like that. Just nervous, I guess."

I gawked at him, my brain working overtime to catch up. "What are you doing here?" He'd sent an email last week giving me the stamp of approval to upload the audio files for Season Seven, but that was it. The message had been short and purposeful. No *how are you* or *seeing anybody lately* or even *hope your new podcast is going well.* "And why do you have flowers?"

"Better late than never?" He smiled guiltily, the dimple appearing in his cheek as he made another attempt to offer me the bouquet, and this time I accepted it. He sank into the seat next to mine. "Probably would have made more sense if you were up there performing, but since your tuba-playing days are apparently over . . ."

We were close enough that I could feel the warmth radiating from him. He smelled like I remembered, pine and seaside air and another smell that was distinctly him. I wanted nothing more than to hug him tight and refuse to let go, but I couldn't do that, so I hugged the carnations to my chest instead. "I've maybe dabbled in it once or twice since moving home," I admitted. "My mom still had my tuba lying around in my old bedroom. It's super out of tune, though."

"So, what I'm hearing is that I should have waited for your return to the stage for a redo on the whole flower thing."

I laughed. "You might have been waiting awhile." I remembered the story he had told me about shoving the flowers at Jordan Gardner, why he claimed he had showed up to the winter recital that year in the first place. *I was planning to apologize for the shaving cream thing and tell you how I felt.* But this time around, he didn't owe me an apology. And I wasn't sure he felt anything. I swallowed. "What sort of redo are we talking here?"

He adjusted himself in his seat, his brow knit as he seemed to search for the right place to start. A look I was all too familiar with these days, because I'd been doing a lot of searching myself. "I listened to the podcast. All of it."

"I figured as much."

He exhaled. "I should have stayed and talked it out at the reception. A part of me wanted to, but another part of me was so upset at seeing those screenshots, feeling like you'd lied to me about everything . . ." He drifted off, frowning at the empty stage. "I told you that I don't do one-night stands because I have a tendency to get attached. After I saw the article, I started questioning whether the feelings were one-sided. If I was the only one getting attached while you were playing me like a fiddle." He snorted. "Or a tuba, I guess."

I shook my head, fighting a smile. Even as he was pouring his heart out, he couldn't resist a bad joke. "I never lied about how I felt. I should have told you about the other stuff sooner, but everything that happened between us was genuine." Embarrassment crept over me, so I focused on my carnations, rubbing one of the soft petals between my thumb and forefinger. "I've spent my whole life getting cold feet before even getting to know people, but it all came so naturally with you. I don't think I could have faked that if I tried."

"I know," he said, voice low in the empty auditorium. The workers had mostly finished with clearing off the stage. "I mean, I realize that now, looking back on it. I'm sorry I didn't realize it sooner."

Someone dimmed the lighting, but it didn't go completely dark. A trail of recessed lights in the floor pointed the way to the nearest exit like an airport runway. "Why didn't you text back?" I asked quietly.

He winced. "I don't really like having those conversations over the phone. But I wasn't sure I was ready to meet up in person either, because I felt like the moment I saw you I would want to be okay with everything, and I was still trying to work out which parts I was actually okay with." He smiled a little sadly. "And then that day at In-N-Out, you caught me super off guard. And then you handed me the money, and it seemed like maybe you meant it to be a goodbye, like that was your way of tying up loose ends so that you could close that chapter of your life."

A surprised laugh escaped my lips; I couldn't help it. "It was an excuse to talk to you. I'd sat in my truck outside of your work for twenty minutes like a total weirdo, and then I gave up and drove to In-N-Out to collect my thoughts. I never expected you'd just walk in—"

His cheek dimpled in amusement. "You never expected to run into *me*, when you were the one hanging around my work?"

"Okay, so maybe I should have expected it," I conceded with a smile. "But still. It definitely wasn't meant to be a goodbye." My heart hummed in my chest, not a frantic rhythm but a long and sustained note, heartstrings threatening to snap. "I wanted so badly for you to kiss me again. Hug me. Something to show me that you still felt—"

He buried a hand in my hair and tugged my mouth to his in a rough kiss. It was fierce and purposeful, and that was all the reassurance I needed to kiss him back. He drew me toward him and I didn't hesitate to abandon the bouquet and shift onto his lap. There was still a lot we needed to talk about. What we were jumping into; what we were working to move past. But at least for the moment, I was happy not to talk. His hands dug into my hips and ground me against him, a small groan escaping his lips where they'd melded with mine. My heart sang.

There was a clanking, echoey sound, and the lights rose again. The visual equivalent of dousing us in a bucket of cold water. "Not on my watch," Erin's disembodied voice said, magnified throughout the concert hall like she was some kind of music god.

I sputtered a laugh as I looked around the bright auditorium. "Is she watching us?"

"Probably," Declan muttered. Despite his grin, his eyes were still hazy with desire. "She had to pull a few strings to convince them to let us in here. Can't have us breaking any rules, I guess."

Never mind the fact that rule-breaking had kind of become my new thing. But there'd be plenty of time for breaking the rules later—I hoped. I moved back to my own seat, hugging my arms around myself to warm all the places he was no longer touching me. "So I take it she's not actually introducing me to Marcus Kowalczyk."

For a moment, he stared at me with a flat expression. "Who?" Then realization dawned. "Oh, yeah, I'm pretty sure we're all going out for drinks. Or the three of you are going out for drinks, I mean. Don't mind me. I've just . . ." He ran a hand over the back of his neck, visibly nervous. "Inserted myself into your evening,

I guess." There was another pause, and then his expression shifted from awkward to stricken. "Please don't turn that into a dirty joke."

I shook with laughter. "Would I really be me, though, if I didn't turn it into a dirty joke?"

"Probably not," he conceded with a badly concealed smile. "And I do prefer you to be you."

"So, are you inserting yourself into this one evening, or are we talking about more than one night?" I waggled a brow, because there was definitely a dirty joke in there somewhere, but I was more than happy to let that one speak for itself.

He looked like he couldn't decide whether he should laugh or bury his face in his hands. "I think maybe I've mentioned my thoughts on one-night stands. So, yes. More than one night." His hazel eyes flitted over my face, and I thought that maybe his usual curiosity had settled into something else—something warmer, more familiar. "If you'll have me."

I feigned having to think about it, tapping a finger to my chin. "Hmmm."

"Take your time." He folded his arms and sank into the chair like he was settling in for a long concert. "I'll be right here, if you need me."

"Okay. I've decided."

He straightened up, planting his hands on the armrests. "Should I be seeing myself out?"

"No," I said slowly, "but I have one condition."

"What's that?"

"I'm pretty sure you still owe me a date." His eyebrows shot up. That was plainly not what he'd been expecting me to say. "I mean, you did ask me, and then I took you on a date, but we never got the chance to do things the other way around."

He smiled. "I'd be more than happy to take you on a date." He dragged himself out of his seat and offered me a hand to help me to my feet. "Though I'm compelled to point out that we *are* supposed to be meeting that Marcus guy tonight."

I collected my bouquet of carnations off of the chair beside me and placed my hand in his. I couldn't fight the smile when he tugged me into his arms. "I think I can settle for a rain check."

EPILOGUE

TEN MONTHS LATER

An August sun seared down on the open deck of the ferry as we entered the final stretch of the crossing from Long Beach to Avalon. On the horizon, the golden-green cliffs of Catalina jutted out of the dark water. As soon as we docked, Declan hauled our luggage down the ramp and scowled up at the sky. Whatever the sun had done to him, I suspected it was personal. "Next time, promise me we'll go somewhere that won't require me to pack three bottles of sunscreen."

I looped my arm through his—with some difficulty, because he insisted on carrying my suitcase as well as his and wouldn't take no for an answer this time. "Where did you have in mind?"

"Oh, I don't know, Ireland?" he suggested. "Wales? Literally anywhere that's not sunny. I'm begging you. I'll do anything."

"Ireland it is. I could show you around."

The narrow streets of Avalon were swarming with people as we made our way up the hill to the Santa Catalina Resort and Spa. The hotel had given us each one night's credit for the elevator fiasco, but it turned out that by downgrading to a slightly smaller room, one night's credit stretched pretty far. We had a whole week to ourselves on the island sans obligations, and I'd been looking forward to it for months.

The past year had kept us busy. Declan was sharing an apartment with a coworker in San Dimas, which was maybe a little farther than either of us would have liked, but we'd made do. Still, we were starting to discuss the possibility of finding a place together whenever his lease ended. The first two seasons of *Charting the Chorus* had done reasonably well. It was a very different sort of podcasting experience, meeting up with all these different creatives and just talking rather than chasing new ideas for content. And while the subject matter was vastly different, a surprising number of *Seven Rules'* old followers had been willing to give it a listen, which helped boost early numbers. Before I knew it, I had a pool of brand-new potential sponsors and a whole new following.

The best part was that these new followers didn't really care to stick their noses in my personal life.

After a smooth check-in, Declan unlocked our hotel room with a swipe of his keycard, and I stepped inside first as he jostled with the luggage. It was a modest room, with breezy white curtains framing a small window overlooking the street. Less gaudy than the rooms Castaway Catalina had set us up with, but the only time we'd be spending in the room would be sleeping or in each other's arms, so I wasn't too concerned with the view. I went to inspect the bathroom. An elegantly tiled shower stood in the far corner, and already I was daydreaming about pulling Declan in there with me, sun-kissed and exhausted after a long day out on the beach.

Back in the room, he'd abandoned our luggage by the door and seated himself on the bed. He beckoned me over by patting his leg. As soon as I was close enough, his hands found my waist and he pulled me on top of him, so that I was straddling him atop the plush comforter.

He kissed my collarbone and my neck but stopped short of my lips, staring up at me with a warm look that I'd come to recognize. "Happy early one year of dating." After the conversation in the

Walt Disney Concert Hall and a night of one too many celebratory drinks in a nameless pub with Erin and Marcus Kowalczyk,
we'd spent several weeks debating when we officially started dating. I argued that, miscommunications aside, I had technically
agreed to date him back when we were on Catalina in July. He
argued that that wasn't how that worked and that it wasn't official until he asked me to be official, which he ended up asking in
October, a couple weeks after we made up. We compromised and
agreed to plan the one-year vacation for late August.

"Hard to believe it's already been a year," I breathed. "I mean,
I've known you forever, but this year has flown by like it's nothing."

He gave me one of his usual mischievous looks. "They say
time flies when you're having fun."

"Is there a particular kind of fun you had in mind?"

"I can think of a few kinds." He flipped me around and pinned
me to the bed, so abruptly that I let out a little shriek of surprise
that he muffled with a kiss. He broke the kiss to stare into my eyes,
sweeping a strand of hair from my face with his thumb.

"What?" I asked.

"Nothing," he said, voice low and a bit gravelly. "I just love
you."

My heart positively soared. It wasn't his first time saying it,
and I knew it wouldn't be the last. But I hadn't quite gotten over
the thrill of hearing those words, words I used to swear up and
down I didn't believe in, words that had come to mean everything
to me over the course of the past year.

"I love you, too."

Even better? Knowing how much I meant it whenever I said
them back.

I didn't need a relationship to be happy. But life certainly looked
a little brighter, from my standpoint, ever since I'd found someone I
wanted to share it with. Sometimes I worried about silly things like
first loves being doomed to fail. I worried about statistics and about

whether or not I was in the right position to make serious choices for my future, working a part-time job and living out of my mom's apartment. I had a tendency to worry about a lot of things, but I'd also learned firsthand that imposing rules on myself just didn't work. And if anything, Declan and I had made a habit out of defying the rules. So any rules about first loves not working, or being in the right place at the right time? There was no point dwelling on those. We would make it work, one way or another.

No keeping secrets. No caring about what other people thought. And, most important: no rules, from here on out.

ACKNOWLEDGMENTS

My husband helped me brainstorm the idea for *Seven Rules for Breaking Hearts* while on a seven-hour road trip from California to Arizona and then again on the drive back—so, first and foremost, I have to thank George for tirelessly hashing out ideas with me and reading through half-drafted versions of everything I write. I'm not sure I'd be very good at finishing what I started without all your help and support.

Of course, this story wouldn't have gotten very far without my wonderful agent, Amy Stapp, who toughed out even the roughest of my rough drafts. Your feedback has never been anything short of amazing, and our calls always motivate me and help me see the potential in each story. And thank you to my brilliant editor, Eileen Rothschild, for helping transform this book into something I can be proud of. So many of my favorite scenes would not exist without your feedback!

I also have to thank Michelle Wolfson for stepping in and patiently answering my questions while Amy was out of the office; my foreign agent, Taryn Fagerness; the fantastic team at SMP, including Lisa Bonvissuto, Kejana Ayala, Alyssa Gammello, Marissa Sangiacomo, Lani Meyer, Layla Yuro, and everyone working behind the scenes; and Maja Tomljanovic and Olga Grlic for the gorgeous cover—it's exactly what I envisioned.

A huge thank-you to my two critique partners: A. R. Frederiksen for being one of the first to read this story and always providing feedback that's both honest and encouraging, and Lauren Liem for your invaluable thoughts on Margo's goals and sense of direction. And thank you to all of the awesome podcasters who've welcomed me onto their shows these past few years: Joe, Dan, Luke, Anne, and Robbie. I never would have had the idea to write a story about a podcast if I hadn't had such positive experiences as a guest speaker.

I don't have enough space to thank all of the friends and family who have supported me over the years, but I want to at least try to thank those who have been actively involved in my process: my mom, for encouraging me to write from an early age and giving me a book on how to get published for my sixteenth birthday; Aunt Jamie, for reading all my favorite books so that I always had someone to talk to about them and for attending midnight releases with me; and Ryan, for reading my early stories and roasting my description of the love interest that one time (it haunts me to this day).

Lastly, I want to talk briefly about the setting. Catalina Island has always been one of my favorite places in California; like Margo, I've spent countless summers there over the years, which really helped shape this story. So, thank you to all the locals and seasonal workers for sharing their island and tolerating us mainlanders—whether it's letting us hitch a ride on the back of your golf cart or serving us our fifth glass of Buffalo Milk, your patience and hospitality are much appreciated.

George H. Miller IV

KRISTYN J. MILLER is an author and freelance editor with a background in marketing and museum work. She grew up in Southern California, where she spent summers escaping to Catalina Island, but these days she lives in Maine. She has a B.A. in literature from the University of Redlands and is working on her M.A. in history and museum studies at the University of New Hampshire. *Seven Rules for Breaking Hearts* is her debut novel.